MW01697667

IN HARM'S WAY

OTHER BOOKS AND AUDIOBOOKS
BY TRACI HUNTER ABRAMSON

UNDERCURRENTS SERIES

Undercurrents

Ripple Effect

The Deep End

SAINT SQUAD SERIES

Freefall

Lockdown

Crossfire

Backlash

Smoke Screen

†Code Word

Lock and Key

‡Drop Zone

Spotlight

Tripwire

ROYAL SERIES

Royal Target

Royal Secrets

Royal Brides

Royal Heir

GUARDIAN SERIES

†Failsafe

**†Safe House*

**Sanctuary*

On the Run

In Harm's Way

STAND-ALONES

Obsession

†Deep Cover

Chances Are

Chance for Home

Kept Secrets

Twisted Fate

Proximity

Entangled

†Mistaken Reality

A Change of Fortune

*Whitney Novel of the Year

†Whitney Best Mystery/ Suspense Novel

‡RWA Hearts through History Award

IN HARM'S WAY

A GUARDIAN NOVEL

TRACI HUNTER ABRAMSON

Covenant

Covenant Communications, Inc.

Cover image: *Woman Taking Picture Outdoors* © erikreis; *Helicopter Rescue* © ozgurcankaya.

Cover design copyright © 2021 by Covenant Communications, Inc.

Published by Covenant Communications, Inc.
American Fork, Utah

Printed in the United States of America
First Printing: March 2021

10 9 8 7 6 5 4 3 2

ISBN 978-1-52441-467-2

PRAISE FOR TRACI HUNTER ABRAMSON

"*In Harm's Way* (a Guardian novel, book 5) by Traci Hunter Abramson is an exciting romance novel filled with suspense and drama. It is a well-written and engaging story with an intriguing and suspenseful plot and interesting characters who are likable and relatable. The fundamental ethics and beliefs of Christianity are woven into the plot, creating an entertaining and clean romance that will delight readers from the ages of sixteen all the way to a hundred and two!"

—Readers' Favorite Five Star Review

For Margaret Weber

Thank you for making everything beautiful

ACKNOWLEDGMENTS

In a world filled with chaos and uncertainty, thank you to those who have been my rock through the production of this book. Samantha Millburn, you continue to amaze me with your editing talents and your ability to juggle so many balls so successfully. Thanks to Margaret Weber and your team of amazing graphic artists and to Robby Nichols for your constant support. Thank you to Amy Parker for not only reinventing the wheel when it comes to publicity but also for always being willing to try new things.

Thank you to my critique partners, Paige Edwards, Ellie Whitney, and Kyla Beecroft, for helping me polish this novel into something worth sharing. Thank you to the CIA's Publication Review Board for ensuring my work can be brought out into the world, and as always, thank you to my family for your constant support and patience when I lose myself in my fictional world. A special thanks to Lara Abramson for keeping me on track during these crazy times.

Finally, thank you to everyone in the Covenant family for allowing me to do what I love and to the readers who continue to support me in doing what I love.

GUARDIANS CHARACTER MAP

Ace (A)—Senior guardian, currently based in Europe, married to Kristi
Kristi (S)—Financial manager, married to Ace

Kade (K)—Guardian based in Virginia Beach, married to Renee
Renee (R)—Computer programmer/analyst, married to Kade

Nolan (N)—Guardian, currently based in South America, engaged to Elle
Elle (J)—Journalist, engaged to Nolan

Troy (T)—Guardian, currently based in Maine
Cas (C)—Guardian, based in Paris
Donovan (D)—Guardian, based in Africa
Erik (E)—Guardian, based in Asia
Ghost—Unnamed guardian, based in Central America

Hannah (H)—Program manager

CHAPTER 1

Senator Walter Royce didn't pay attention to the posted menu outside the busy restaurant in Montmartre as he walked through the entrance. He had one purpose for being here, and it had nothing to do with the food.

"*Un*," he told the host, holding up one finger to make up for his complete lack of a French accent. On the surface, his trip to Paris was nothing more than a quick family getaway, but in reality, it was a much-needed excuse.

The host said something in French, and Walter shook his head apologetically. "I'm sorry. I don't understand. Do you have an English menu?"

The younger man nodded and showed him up a half flight of stairs to the dining area. Walter took his seat at a table in the center of the room, and the host handed him a menu.

"*Merci*." Once alone, he glanced around the establishment. Through the windows, he could see the tables filled with patrons lining the sidewalk and waiters breezing in and out of the kitchen. In contrast, the indoor dining area was nearly empty. Four locals chatted in French over the remnants of their lunch, and on the far side of the room, an older couple studied their menus.

Walter glanced furtively at each person. Everywhere he looked, he expected to see someone staring at him, someone noticing why he was really here. He had spent the morning with his wife and daughters at the Eiffel Tower, taking the appropriate photos to make sure everyone would see him as the tourist he claimed to be. He had bowed out of their shopping plans, but he doubted he would be able to sneak away again without raising suspicions.

His stomach jumped with nerves, and he struggled to focus on the menu before him. When the waiter arrived to take his order, Walter indicated his choice by pointing.

Out of the corner of his eye, he saw the party of four stand up to leave at the same time the host approached to seat another guest. Anticipation snaked through him. Was that him? The infamous Gavrie Morozov? A well-known Russian operative, the man was a chameleon. He also had the skills needed to solve Walter's problems and put him back on track to his destiny.

A moment after the host left, a heavily accented voice carried to him. "Why am I here?"

Walter started to turn around to see the man now seated behind him.

"Don't look at me," the man commanded. "Just answer the question."

Walter forced his gaze to stop at the window. Trying to focus on two women seated outside, he willed his heartbeat to slow. "I need help."

"What kind of help?"

"My former bank notified me that someone was looking into my old account information," Walter said. "Someone knows I'm working with your people."

"Who knows?"

"I'm not sure, but I think it's the guardians." Walter lowered his voice further. "And I think I know who's helping them."

"It sounds like you need someone eliminated."

Walter's stomach curled. He had killed a man himself only a few weeks before. The nightmares from that moment still haunted him, and now here he was, negotiating to take another life. When his alliance with the Russians started more than a decade ago, he never anticipated he would be in this position now.

Silence stretched for several seconds before Walter said, "I don't know if there's another choice."

"My associates need something in return."

"What?"

"Access to the detailed budget."

Walter sucked in a deep breath. The requests from the Russians in the past had been more subtle, but complete access? If they knew where the money was going, they would know everything, including military plans and intelligence objectives. Walter was supposed to be the key to balancing the volatile relationship between the two superpowers, not the gofer giving one a significant leg up on the other. What would the Russians do if he refused? Would they cut off his funding? Or eliminate him in the most final sense of the word?

"Even if I give you access, what good would that do?" Walter asked. "I can't make changes significant enough to make a difference."

"You're on the Senate Intelligence Committee. You have access to information we need."

The noose around his neck tightened. He didn't have any other option. "I'll make it happen."

"Good," the man said, his accent thickening. "While you're at it, I suggest you propose to trim expenditures in a few places, especially anything that might be providing funding to the guardians."

"I tried that before."

"Try again." The voice was low but firm. "Now, where do I find this problem of yours?"

"In Washington, DC," Walter said. "You'll find him on Capitol Hill." Walter pulled a folded envelope from his back pocket and dropped it to the floor. He looked down as though noticing its presence for the first time, then cleared his voice. "I think you dropped something."

The other man leaned down and picked it up. "So it seems."

* * *

Troy steered the cabin cruiser into the little cove beside the only two houses on the private island. No sign of intruders. No one nearby on the water. He'd been away from his new home for only an hour while he'd conducted a perimeter check of the island and familiarized himself with the surrounding waters, but his years of living in the city had heightened his suspicious nature.

His acute awareness of his surroundings wasn't necessary today. Ace was right. This was the perfect spot. No one passing by would ever suspect a top-secret government organization to be working off this little piece of land a half mile off the coast of Maine.

As members of the guardian program, Troy and seven other operatives, or guardians, had faked their deaths in order to save their lives. In so doing, they had stepped into the unique career of protecting the many undercover operatives who needed support when the government couldn't provide it through normal channels. In addition to the eight guardians, two computer programmers and their financial manager kept the information from all military and intelligence organizations flowing, even though few people knew of the program's existence.

For years, Troy had lived in northern Europe, protecting assets operating in Russia and many of the countries that had once comprised the Soviet Union. After only two weeks on this island, he could admit he rather liked the quiet, even though the solitude had taken some getting used to.

He breathed in the crisp autumn air. He loved this time of year: the vibrant colors, the morning frost, the crunch of leaves, and the proof that he wasn't anywhere near his childhood home in California. Shaking that image aside, he steered toward the wooden dock and cut the engine.

He still wasn't quite sure how he had been chosen to trade places with Ace, the senior guardian, but for whatever reason, he was here now while Ace and his wife, Kristi, were living in his apartment in Helsinki to hide Kristi's pregnancy from her family.

Troy couldn't begin to imagine what it would be like to be married, much less to have his wife pretend he didn't exist. That was the price Ace and Kristi had been willing to pay for love.

He leapt onto the dock to tie off the boat. In his current role, he wouldn't be meeting anyone any time soon. All Troy had to worry about for now was how to adapt to living in solitude.

* * *

Jocelyn could hardly believe how fast her life had changed. Last week, she had been running a multimillion-dollar graphic design company and living in the city. Now here she was standing on the dock of a tiny fishing village in Maine with suitcases in hand and her camera bag hanging from her shoulder. She must have lost her mind.

A sense of unease rose within her only to be overshadowed by a bubbling sense of adventure. She was ready for something new, she reminded herself. Even though building a successful business had earned her admiration and respect, she had reached the pinnacle of the life she had created. It was time to stop going through the motions and start *living*.

She couldn't remember what it was like to spend time doing something she wanted or having friends outside of work or even the last time she went out on a real date. Not that she was likely to have many prospects here.

Jocelyn approached a small office at the edge of the harbor. A man around sixty emerged from inside. "Can I help you?"

"I hope so. Can you tell me which of these boats belongs to Kristi Hartinger?"

He waved in the general direction of a strip of sailboats. "Her slip is over there, but she left her boat in dry dock while she's gone."

"Oh." Jocelyn hadn't considered that her sister wouldn't have left her boat at the harbor. "I don't suppose you know of anyone who can give me a lift out to Heritage Island, do you?"

"You a friend of Kristi's?"

"I'm her sister, actually." Jocelyn closed the distance between them and extended her hand. "Jocelyn Hartinger."

"Little Jocelyn Hartinger. Well, it has been a while since you've been home." He shook her hand. "Wally Brown. I'm an old friend of your grandfather's."

"Oh, yes." Jocelyn fished through her memory but couldn't recall meeting him before. "It's good to see you again."

"Kristi didn't tell me you were going to be staying out there."

"She didn't know. I'm between jobs and decided to spend some time off the beaten path."

"Heritage Island is certainly that." Wally waved at her suitcases. "Tell you what. You leave those here in my office. You'll want to pick up some groceries and supplies before you head out there. I'll make a few calls and find someone to give you a ride."

"Thanks so much." Jocelyn glanced at her suitcases, debating whether she should leave them with someone she'd just met. When he set them inside the office and closed the door, she reevaluated. After all, the town had only a few thousand people in it, and the most important thing she brought with her was still hanging from her shoulder.

"Be back in an hour or so," Wally said. "I'll have a ride lined up for you."

"Perfect. Thanks." Jocelyn found the grocery store first. Since calling for takeout wouldn't be an option while she was at her sister's house, she walked through every aisle of the store. By the time she reached the checkout counter, the cart looked like she was buying for a family of six rather than one person.

After a quick stop at the diner and the bakery, she finally returned to the harbor. A boat was docked by the harbor master's office, and a man in his early thirties stood beside Wally.

"Gil here is going to take you out to the island." Wally motioned to the lanky man beside him. "You're on his way home."

"An island is on your way home?"

"I live on an island a ways up the coast from you." Gil stared at Jocelyn for a minute as though not sure what to do next.

"Maybe you should help the lady load her stuff," Wally prompted.

"Yeah, right. Sorry." Gil picked up a few grocery bags. "Your suitcases are already on board."

"Great. Thanks." She gathered several of the shopping bags and helped carry them onto the boat. Following Gil's example, she placed them in the locker on deck.

As soon as they finished, Gil asked, "Ready?"

"Yes." Jocelyn climbed aboard. "Thanks again, Wally."

He waved.

Gil cast off and placed his wide-palmed hands on the helm. Jocelyn sat and took a moment to size up the man beside her. The cap on his head and fishing equipment on the boat left little doubt as to what he did for a living.

He started the engine and glanced at her. Jocelyn caught the flash of interest on his face, and a ripple of unease flowed through her. She was going to a deserted island with a man she didn't know. What was she thinking?

She patted her pocket and confirmed her phone was close by. Wally knew where she was, and Gil seemed harmless enough. Fighting back her unease, she gripped the camera bag in her lap. A few more minutes and she would be on her sister's island, alone, with nothing to do but relax, take photographs, and listen to the waves crash against rock.

They cleared the harbor, and another thought popped into Jocelyn's mind. If Kristi was out of the country for the next year, where was her dog?

CHAPTER 2

"Samson, stay." Troy held his hand up, pleased when the dog obeyed. Troy didn't know how Kristi's black lab had gone from growling at him two weeks ago to being his best friend, but rarely did Samson let him out of his sight.

Whether he was in the orchard harvesting apples or sitting at his desk searching for connections between Walter Royce and the Russians, he always knew Samson was nearby. If only the dog could help him prove his suspicions that the senator was actually the traitor who had orchestrated a recent assassination attempt.

Troy and Kade, the other guardian headquartered in the United States, had been working nonstop looking for clues, but so far, all they had were suspicions. Today, instead of continuing his research, Troy had to make an unexpected trip to Bangor.

When he'd returned home from his earlier excursion on the water, he'd discovered the internet was no longer working. Until he picked up some new wiring to fix the satellite and make the needed repairs, the motion sensors and security cameras on the island weren't going to do him any good. While he was on base, he would also make a stop at the commissary. Even though Ace and Kristi had left him a fully stocked pantry and freezer, the refrigerator was empty.

While he knew he could use Ace's boat to go into the village and buy most of his supplies, he suspected he would do best to avoid the locals and their innate curiosity. Nothing worse than trying to be invisible in a town where everyone expected to know your name. Instead, he opted for trying to stay invisible in the air.

Troy stepped up to the cliffs overlooking the windward side of the island where a Coast Guard helicopter was parked. The helicopter had been a recent addition to the guardians' resources, thanks to their benefactor in the Senate, Senator James Whitmore. Troy had yet to meet the man who was responsible for the guardians' funding, but he suspected they would speak soon enough now that Troy was standing in for Ace and monitoring the guardians' resources.

Troy lifted his binoculars. The evening sun glistened off the water, the darkening sky providing him with the perfect takeoff conditions. It was light enough that he wouldn't have to use his running lights when he took off, but it was dark enough that he should be able to go unnoticed while he made his way inland.

He scanned the area again. Once he was satisfied that there weren't any fishing vessels on the water nearby, he moved to the helicopter.

Samson took a step forward.

"Oh, no you don't. You're staying here." Troy climbed into the aircraft and waved at Samson. "Go on home."

Samson whimpered.

"Go on." Troy waved again. "I'll be back in a few hours."

Samson circled and backed away from the helicopter pad. Apparently he understood well enough to know he wouldn't want to be too close when the engines started.

Troy pulled on his helmet, checked the local air traffic, and started the engines. A moment later, he lifted off, the dog waiting at the edge of the trees with a mournful look on his face.

"Dumb dog," Troy muttered. If Samson were smart, he'd make use of his doggie door and go wait for him back at the house. He didn't want to think about how cold it would be when he returned in a few hours. He increased his speed. The sooner he took care of his errands, the better.

* * *

Jocelyn set the last of her groceries on the dock beside her suitcases. "Thanks for the ride."

"No problem." Gil motioned to the string of grocery bags. "Are you sure you don't want help carrying everything up to the house?"

"I'll be fine, but thanks," Jocelyn said.

"You have my number. Give me a holler if you have any trouble."

"I will. Thanks again." Jocelyn lifted a hand for a last wave and glanced at the cabin cruiser tethered on the other side of the dock. Where had that come from?

With a shake of her head, she picked up the jug of milk and three of the grocery bags, her camera case still hanging from her shoulder. Leaving everything else, she made her way down the path to the main house.

A dog barked, and a moment later, Samson emerged from the nearby woods.

"Samson." Jocelyn shifted the milk jug into the crook of her arm so she would have a free hand and held it out to let the dog reacquaint himself with her. "Hey, boy. Remember me?"

Samson sniffed her hand and licked it. Pleased the dog still recognized her as a friend, Jocelyn ran her hand over the dog's head.

"What are you doing here?" Jocelyn glanced at the bungalow. Maybe Kristi had renters watching after him. Her eyes narrowed. The bungalow didn't have any smoke coming from the chimney, and this time of year, she didn't know if the heater alone would be able to keep it livable. Strange.

Noting the birds in the nearby trees that appeared to be eying her groceries, Jocelyn continued forward. "Come on, boy. Let's get this stuff inside."

She pulled her keys from her pocket and selected the key her sister had given her shortly after their grandfather's death, unlocking the door and walking straight into the kitchen to set the groceries and her camera bag on the kitchen table. Three trips later, with Samson trotting behind her, she hauled her suitcases inside.

She opened the refrigerator; her sister must have cleaned it out before she left. Except for a couple bottles of salad dressing and some condiments, only a box of baking soda and a jar of maple syrup remained.

Starting with the milk, Jocelyn unpacked her groceries. When she finished, she moved into the living room and started a fire. It took her two tries, but she was pleased that she managed to handle the task on her own. She'd even remembered to open the flue. Samson must have approved of her efforts because he circled once and lay down on the rug in front of the hearth.

"I guess you aren't going to help me put the rest of the groceries away."

Samson whimpered but didn't move.

"Okay, fine." Jocelyn finished putting the food away and walked back outside.

The familiar roar of water against land washed over her. She'd missed this.

She looked out over the little cove where the pier stretched out into the water. Her gaze wandered past the cabin cruiser docked there and landed on the lobster pot bobbing at the end of the dock. She rubbed her lips together. It had been too long since she had enjoyed a lobster dinner that she had prepared herself.

She made her way down the stairs leading from the deck to the yard and pulled up the lobster pot to find it empty. Pity.

Raindrops splattered on her, and she quickly headed back inside and locked the door behind her.

Deciding she should at least pretend to settle in, she gripped the handles of both of her suitcases. She debated briefly which bedroom to take, opting for the one she had always claimed when she stayed here as a kid. She hauled her luggage behind her and stepped through the open doorway of the room she thought of as hers.

The furniture was the same as she remembered: a queen bed with a thick blanket on top, a rocking chair in one corner, and a wide dresser with a mirror dominating the longest wall.

Too tired to deal with unpacking tonight, she pushed her suitcases against the wall. Time for some food and a good night's sleep.

* * *

Troy shut down the helicopter engines and stored his helmet. Exhausted and wanting nothing more than his bed, he climbed out into the frigid air and grabbed the box closest to the door. Once he locked the helicopter to make sure no critters tried to go after anything inside, he headed into the darkness.

He stumbled on the edge of the path leading to the house, barely reclaiming his balance to keep from tumbling. He set the box he carried on the ground and fished his cell phone from his pocket. After he activated the flashlight feature, he picked the box up again and positioned his hand so the light would guide him down the trail.

By the time he reached the stairs to the deck, he decided to leave the rest of his purchases in the helicopter until morning. The temperature would protect his refrigerator stuff, and the canned goods certainly wouldn't suffer from a night left out in the cold.

He set down the groceries, turned off the flashlight on his cell, and fished out his keys. After he unlocked the door, he collected his purchases again and carried them inside, nudging the door closed with his hip.

Too tired to deal with putting everything away, he passed through the kitchen and set the box on the washing machine. He returned to the kitchen and glanced at the time. Past midnight.

Exhausted, he headed for his room. Samson let out a bark and met him at the edge of the hall.

"It's just me, boy."

Samson's alert posture relaxed at the sound of Troy's voice. Troy ran a hand over the dog's head, and Samson's tail wagged.

"Come on. Let's get to bed."

Samson darted into Troy's room and jumped onto the bed.

"Oh, no. You're not sleeping with me." Troy pointed at the dog bed on the floor. "Go on. Go lie down."

Samson jumped back onto the floor.

"You know better than that."

Not looking the least bit guilty, Samson made his customary circle and settled into his dog bed.

Troy stripped out of his flight suit and pulled on a pair of flannel pajamas. A minute later, he climbed into bed and let the roar of the Atlantic lull him to sleep.

CHAPTER 3

The sun was up by the time Troy finally rolled out of bed. He took a quick shower, dressed for the day, and slid his waistband holster into place. The idea that he would need to be armed while on an island by himself bordered on ridiculous, but he wasn't sure he believed Ace's claim that they didn't have any significant predators here.

After he put on his shoes and grabbed his jacket, he walked into the living room, where Samson lay by the fire. Warm embers lay in the grate. Odd. He hadn't expected the fire to last all night. Then again, he hadn't gotten home until nearly one in the morning.

Still groggy from the lack of sleep, he crossed to the kitchen and retrieved a yogurt. His first bite reminded him that he wasn't in Europe anymore. Man, what he wouldn't give for a good cup of lingonberry yogurt. He finished his snack and headed for the door.

Time to retrieve the rest of his supplies from the helicopter. He hauled the box of canned goods to the house first and was halfway back to the helicopter to get the cooler when reality caught up with him. He had eaten yogurt for breakfast. Where had that come from if the cooler was still in the helicopter?

He reached the clearing and pulled the cooler to the edge of the helicopter door. He opened the lid. Sure enough, the case of yogurt he had purchased was nestled inside, unopened. He could have sworn he had run out of yogurt two days ago.

"Must have been one hiding in the fridge," Troy mumbled. He grabbed the cooler, locked the helicopter, and headed back down the hill to the house. When he entered the kitchen, he set the cooler in the middle of the floor and pulled out the milk to put in the refrigerator. But there in the door where the milk went was a full, unopened gallon jug. Where had that come from?

Troy slid the gallon he had purchased beside the one already in the refrigerator and crossed to the window. Only the cabin cruiser bobbed in the water beside the dock. The extra groceries had come from somewhere. Who had been on the island? What did they want? And were they still here?

Troy took a step toward the door and stopped. Was that water running?

He followed the sound until he reached the master bedroom. The bathroom door was closed.

He let out a relieved breath. Apparently, Ace and Kristi had decided to come back for a visit. They could have at least given him some warning.

Though he was tempted to simply knock on the master bathroom door, the last thing he wanted was to startle a pregnant woman while she was in the shower. Knowing Ace, he would be checking the grounds to ensure they were alone on the island. He went out onto the deck and called, "Ace?"

When no one responded, he pulled out his phone and dialed Ace's number. Still no answer.

"Where is he, Samson?" The dog wagged his tail but didn't give any indication of where his owner was hiding out.

Troy peeked through the french doors to see if Ace was on the deck, but it, too, was empty.

He tried calling Ace again. This time, the phone rang twice, and Ace's voice came over the line.

"Hey, Troy. What's up? Is everything okay?"

"Yeah, but you and Kristi about gave me a heart attack. You should have told me you changed your travel plans."

"How did you know we changed our plans?" Ace asked. "We didn't tell anyone we changed our itinerary."

"I'm standing in your house listening to the shower." The water shut off. "At least, I was."

"What?" Ace asked. "What are you talking about?"

A sense of unease crept up Troy's spine. "Aren't you back on the island?"

"No. We had a potential security issue in Paris and had to take a flight from Amsterdam to Helsinki instead of going to Tallinn to catch the ferry."

"Any idea who's in your house?"

"Not a clue."

Troy's free hand went to his gun. "I'll call you back."

He pocketed the phone and moved to the hall, his mind racing for some logical explanation of someone making themselves at home in Ace and Kristi's house. The fact that Samson had let someone in nagged at him, but he proceeded to the bedroom cautiously. Samson followed.

Light spilled beneath the bathroom door. How did one approach a stranger in a bathroom?

Troy's hand flexed on the grip of his pistol. He was still contemplating his next move when the door swung open. Troy acted on instinct, and his gun came up. "Hold it right there."

A woman squeaked in alarm. Her body jolted. Wide green eyes darted to the gun, and she stumbled back a step. Troy couldn't miss the absolute shock and terror evident in the woman's expression or the way her face had paled. A thread of guilt needled through him at causing her such distress. If he didn't know better, he would have thought he was the intruder instead of the other way around. He pushed that thought aside. He was supposed to be alone.

He took a moment to assess the woman in front of him: bare feet, damp hair, face free of makeup. She took another step back.

"Who are you?" Troy demanded. "And what are you doing here?"

Slowly, her eyes lifted to meet his. She swallowed hard but didn't speak. Troy opened his mouth to repeat his question, but she finally managed to find her voice. Rather than answering his question, though, she asked one of her own. "Who are you?"

Troy debated how to answer. Though his clients knew him by the nickname Ghost, he wasn't sure he wanted to open that can of worms. Instead, he offered the alias he planned to use in town, the same one he used at the Coast Guard station.

"I'm Ty Dodson. I'm staying here while the owner is away."

"And the owner's name is . . . ?"

"Kristi Hartinger." Troy steadied his gun and repeated his earlier questions. "Who are you, and why are you here?"

"I'm Jocelyn Hartinger. I'm Kristi's sister."

"Kristi's sister?" Troy lowered his gun slightly. "Did she know you were coming?"

"No. I tried calling her this morning to let her know I was here and to see who was supposed to be watching the dog, but she didn't answer." Jocelyn nodded at his gun. "Would you mind putting that thing away? You're making me nervous."

Troy lowered his weapon but didn't holster it. Samson nudged past him and nuzzled against Jocelyn's leg. She patted his head.

"You're the one who's taking care of Samson, then," she said.

"Yeah." He glanced at the dog, debating whether to let Samson's reaction serve as a character witness. Still skeptical, Troy pulled his phone from his pocket. One-handed, he pulled up Kristi's number and pushed the button to FaceTime her.

Kristi's face filled the screen a moment later. "Is everything okay? You said someone is at the house?"

"A woman is here. She says she's your sister."

"Jocelyn?" Kristi asked. "What would she be doing there?"

"You can ask her. Can you tell me if this is her?" Troy hit the button on his phone to flip the screen toward Jocelyn.

"Yes. That's her."

Troy flipped the screen back to himself once more.

"I'm sorry. I had no idea . . ." Apology lit Kristi's face. "Let me talk to her."

Gun still in hand, Troy handed over the phone.

"Hey, sis." Jocelyn lifted a trembling hand and waved at the screen. "When I said you should have someone check on the house for you, I didn't realize you brought in an armed guard."

"What are you doing there?" Kristi asked. "Why aren't you in Boston?"

"It's a long story." Her eyes lowered to the gun again. "Can you tell this guy he can put away his gun?"

Troy holstered his pistol and took the phone from Jocelyn.

"I am so sorry about this," Kristi began.

"It's okay. I'll call you later."

Troy ended the call and studied Jocelyn. "Now that I know who you are, can you tell me why you're here?"

"Like I told Kristi, it's a long story."

"I've got time."

She rubbed her hands over her bare arms. "Let me grab a sweater, and we can talk by the fire. I'm freezing."

"Fine." Troy headed toward the living room and let out a sigh. What was he supposed to do with Kristi's sister here? And how long was she planning to stay?

* * *

Her hands still shaking, Jocelyn took her time selecting a sweater. She'd never had a gun pointed at her before, and she was quite certain she never wanted to repeat the experience.

Who was this guy, and why had her sister chosen him to watch after the island while she was gone? Kristi could have told her she had a house sitter.

She debated briefly calling her sister back before dealing with the intruder, but a phone call wasn't going to take care of the problem at hand, nor would it calm her racing heart.

She donned a pair of socks and pulled her sweater over her head. Gathering her courage, she went into the living room.

Samson had curled up by the fire. Ty stood beside him looking like a combination of the all-American boy next door and a model for the cover of a sports magazine. His athletic build appeared to stem from genetics and regular activity rather than carefully planned workouts in a gym, and his facial features as well as his light hair and the hint of a European accent made her think the man had some roots in Scandinavia. Sweden maybe?

He turned, his blue eyes landing on her.

Jocelyn lowered her eyes to his hands to make sure they were still empty before she met his gaze. "My sister never mentioned you to me. How do you know Kristi?"

"We work together sometimes."

"And you're living in this house?" Jocelyn asked.

"That's right. Kristi asked me to look after the place while she's overseas."

"What do you do for work, then?" Jocelyn didn't notice any brand names on his clothing, but the jeans and sweater appeared to be expensive, and both fit him perfectly. "I can't imagine most jobs allow their employees to take off for a year to hang out on an island."

"I work from home."

"Doing?" Jocelyn prompted.

"Security mostly," Ty said.

"Security for what?"

"Sorry. I'm not at liberty to discuss my work." He motioned to the couch and waited for Jocelyn to sit before he sat beside her. "What about you? You knew your sister wasn't here. Why did you come to Heritage Island?"

"I needed to get away from the city for a while. I figured Kristi would love having someone here to watch after things while she was gone."

"You didn't think to call her first?" Ty asked.

"I didn't think I'd have to. She mentioned she'd have a renter for some of the time she was gone, but I figured her renter would be in the bungalow," Jocelyn said. "Kristi's never let anyone besides family stay in the main house before."

"She thought it would be easier on Samson if he could follow his usual routine."

"I guess that makes sense." She glanced toward the kitchen.

"How did you get here anyway?" Ty asked. "I didn't see another boat."

"Someone from town dropped me off."

"And how long were you planning to stay?"

"I haven't decided." Jocelyn noted the wariness in his voice. Even though she could afford to rent someplace along the coast to stay, the joy of being on the land of her heritage tugged at her. "I can move into the bungalow so we both have our own space."

"I don't know . . ."

"You won't even know I'm here," Jocelyn said, cutting him off. "I have a lot going on at the moment, and being here, reconnecting with where my family comes from, is something I really need right now."

"What do you mean you have a lot going on?"

"Don't worry. I'm not hiding out or anything," Jocelyn said. "I'm in the process of selling my company, and I thought it would be better for the woman taking my place if I weren't around during the transition."

"It's not much of a transition if you already left."

"It's not like I abandoned her. I'm still available by phone and email." Doubt trickled through her, but she pushed it aside. She was selling her company. She was ready to move on and find a new challenge. The sooner she made the break, the better it would be for everyone.

He hesitated as though debating the fastest way to get rid of her. "Maybe we should call your sister and see what she thinks."

"That's a great idea." Jocelyn stood. "I'll get my phone."

"If you don't mind, I'd like to talk to her first." He stood and retrieved his phone from his pocket.

"Fine."

Ty grabbed his jacket and headed out onto the deck before he hit a number on his cell and lifted it to his ear. He turned to face the water so she couldn't read his expression. She wondered if it was deliberate.

Ty paced along the long wooden deck as two questions circled in Jocelyn's mind: who was Ty, really, and how well did he know her sister?

CHAPTER 4

"WHAT DO YOU WANT ME to do?" Troy asked Kristi. He had already replayed his conversation with Jocelyn, noting her lack of a departure date.

"I don't know," Kristi said, clearly exasperated. "I never thought in a million years she would show up unannounced. She hasn't even been out there since our grandfather's funeral."

"She's here now."

"I have to think she's only planning to stay for a few days," Kristi said. "There's no way she can be away from her business for long."

"She said she's selling her business."

"What? You're kidding."

"Nope, and from the amount of groceries she bought, it looks like she's planning to be here for a while," Troy said. "I hate to say it, but you may need to make up an excuse to get her to leave."

"We haven't replaced the broken refrigerator in the bungalow, and there isn't any internet there either, but you'll have to come up with a reason she can't stay in the main house with you. She can be persuasive."

"Don't worry. I can handle it." He glanced over his shoulder. Jocelyn's green eyes locked with his, and she now held her phone in her hand. "I'll let you talk to her first though."

Troy hung up the phone. An instant later, the faint sound of Jocelyn's cell rang out, and she lifted her phone to her ear.

On the other side of the window, Jocelyn settled on the arm of the couch as though she had nothing better to do than hang out on a private island. At least, it would be a private island once she left.

Jocelyn switched the phone from one hand to the other, giving Troy a better view of her face. He could see the resemblance now between the two sisters: ivory skin over high cheekbones, expressive eyes, dark hair with a touch of curl. Jocelyn's hair was shorter than Kristi's, only falling a couple inches past her shoulders, and Troy suspected she was younger by five or ten years.

Jocelyn's relaxed posture and lack of movement gave Troy hope that the woman was listening to reason. As soon as she ended the call, he walked back inside. "Did you talk to your sister?"

"Yeah. She said the refrigerator is broken in the bungalow," Jocelyn said. "I was hoping you'd be okay with me using the kitchen in the main house until I can get a new one brought out."

So much for listening to reason. "No. That's not possible."

"Why not?" Jocelyn asked. "I'll stay out of your way. I'll even feed the dog for you."

"I'm sorry, but there's no way I can function with someone else living here," Troy insisted. "It's not going to work."

"Sure it will. Besides, I won't be living here. I'll be living next door." Jocelyn headed for the kitchen. "I was about to make some breakfast. Do you want some scrambled eggs?"

Troy followed. As much as he'd love the company, conducting top-secret research while having a civilian living so close wasn't a good combination. "Jocelyn, you aren't hearing me. You have to leave."

"Not until I'm finished." She pulled a carton of eggs out of the refrigerator, along with some milk, shredded cheese, and cream cheese.

"Finished with what?"

"Taking pictures."

"Taking pictures?"

"I'm a photographer." Jocelyn retrieved a bowl from the cabinet and cracked an egg. "At least I planned to be."

"And?" Troy prompted.

She cracked two more eggs, added a splash of milk and seasoning salt, and scrambled the eggs with a fork. "With the sale of my company pending, I want to get back to it."

"You can get back to it somewhere else."

"It's not the same. This is where I started taking pictures. It's where I find my inspiration."

"You can find your inspiration next year when your sister is back on the island."

"I'm not willing to wait that long." Jocelyn added some cream cheese and shredded cheese to the eggs and put the bowl in the microwave.

"You're making scrambled eggs in the microwave?"

"It's the best way. Keeps them from drying out." She retrieved a loaf of bread from the bread box and put a slice in the toaster. "Toast?"

"Sure." The word was already out of his mouth before he realized he had responded. What was he doing? He needed her to go.

Jocelyn added a second slice. The microwave dinged. She pulled out the bowl, stirred the eggs, and put it back in for another few seconds.

Troy's mouth watered, but he forced himself to get back on point. "Did you leave a car in the village?"

"No. I did a one-way rental."

"Then you won't have any trouble getting a rental to go home."

"When I'm finished." She stirred the eggs again and put them back in the microwave. "What do you want to drink?"

"Orange juice."

She finished setting the table as though she owned the place. Did the woman not understand English? "Maybe you didn't hear me the first time. You need to leave."

"I don't think you're hearing me," Jocelyn countered. "I'm not done yet."

"So I'm supposed to let you stay here until you decide it's time for you to leave?"

"Pretty much." She stirred the eggs one last time. "Breakfast is ready."

Jocelyn handed him the butter dish and the plate with the toast on it. Exasperated, he took them from her and set them on the table.

They both sat, and Jocelyn scooped some eggs onto her plate before passing the bowl to Troy. "Here you go."

He blew out a frustrated breath. Jocelyn wasn't persuasive. She was downright stubborn. How could he explain to Jocelyn that she needed to leave when he couldn't even tell her why he was here or how important it was to keep his presence on the island confidential?

Jocelyn waved at the seat across from her. "Aren't you going to eat? I'm telling you, these scrambled eggs are the best."

The scent of eggs assaulted his senses. His stomach grumbled. There wouldn't be any harm in eating before kicking her out, right? Besides, who knew when he would have anyone else to talk to.

He took a seat and served himself a small portion before taking a bite. She was right. Eggs were better from the microwave. Or maybe it was all the cheese she added. He scooped more eggs onto his plate, took another bite, and tried to remember why Jocelyn needed to leave.

* * *

Kade followed three different false identities, determined to locate where Gavrie Morozov was now. The Russian operative's appearance in Paris had raised red flags. The presence of Walter Royce in the same city at the same time sent those red flags waving up to the top of the flagpole. Cas, a fellow guardian, had followed Morozov as far as Gare du Nord train station before she'd lost him.

Footsteps sounded behind Kade. His wife walked into the living room, where they had set up their office. "What are you working on?"

Kade glanced at Renee. He loved that tumbled look she always had when she first got up in the morning, her dark hair tousled and her face free of makeup. He noted the workout clothes she wore and the tennis shoes in her hand.

"I'm afraid our morning run may have to wait," Kade said.

"Why? What's going on?" She dropped her shoes on the floor and sat in her desk chair, where she did most of her work as a computer programmer and analyst for the guardian program.

"Gavrie Morozov was spotted in Paris."

"The Russian?" Renee asked.

"Yeah. We finally tracked him to the Brussels airport, where he booked three flights, all to North America."

"What cities?" She turned on her computer.

"Ontario, Philadelphia, and New York–JFK."

"And now you're searching through video feed in those airports, looking for him."

"Actually, I'm trying to find any new reservations with his known aliases."

"You think he's heading somewhere else."

"Yeah," Kade said. "All three airports are on the East Coast. It wouldn't be hard once he's in the US or Canada to rent a car or grab a bus or train to get anywhere else on the continent."

"I'll pull the surveillance in Ontario. It's a smaller airport than the other two, and it will help us know if we're dealing with transportation in Canada or the US."

"Thanks."

"No problem, but once I get done with this, we're going for our run."

"This is national security we're dealing with here," Kade said.

"We deal with national security every day," Renee countered.

"I know, but this is different," Kade insisted. "I've got a bad feeling about this one."

"You're waiting until it warms up outside to go for a run, aren't you?"

"Knowing Morozov could be in the States is making me uneasy. All of the flights he booked landed five days ago. That's a big head start for a guy like him,"

Kade said. When his wife continued to stare at him, he confessed the other half of his reasoning. "It's supposed to get up to sixty degrees in a couple hours."

"Sometimes I don't know how you survived growing up in Russia."

"I stayed inside."

"Right." Renee logged into the guardian database. "Let's see what we can find out while the weather warms up."

"That's a great idea," Kade said. "I'm glad you thought of it."

* * *

Jocelyn took a bite of toast and peered at Ty from under lowered lashes. She wondered how long it would take him to realize she wasn't leaving.

Ty picked up the bowl of scrambled eggs and tilted it toward her. "Did you want any more?"

"No." She smothered a smile. "You can finish them off."

"Thanks." He scooped the rest onto his plate.

"You're welcome." Now certain she was victorious in this little battle of wills, she took a sip of juice and decided it was time to get to know her new neighbor. "You said you do security. What company do you work for?"

"I'm a private contractor."

"And your clients are okay with you working from here?"

"Yep."

"Can you tell me anything about what you do?" Jocelyn asked.

"Nope."

"Are you always this vague?"

"Pretty much." He ate another bite.

When he didn't elaborate, she tried a new topic. "Where are you from?"

"Nowhere in particular."

"You had to be living somewhere before you came here."

"I move around a lot." He reached for the pitcher of orange juice on the table, and his sleeve slid up to reveal a wicked scar on his forearm.

As soon as he set the pitcher back down, Jocelyn gripped his wrist and pushed his sleeve higher to reveal the jagged white line that ran from an inch above his wrist all the way to his elbow. He tried to tug his hand away in what appeared to be an automatic reaction. Jocelyn had little doubt he could have broken free had he wanted to.

"What happened there?" she asked, leaning closer. As though punctuating the injury, three pea-sized red spots ran along the inside of his arm. "Are those burn marks?"

"Yeah." Ty pulled his arm free. "It's from a long time ago."

Jocelyn's eyes narrowed. "Those look like they're from a cigarette."

Ty's gaze met hers, but his expression was blank, almost as though he had raised a shield to make sure she couldn't see who he really was. He pushed back from the table. "Thanks for breakfast."

CHAPTER 5

Troy didn't want to think about his past or the evidence his mother had left on his skin to make sure he could never erase it completely. The scar on his forearm would be easy enough to talk about if Jocelyn were cleared in the guardian program. That particular injury had resulted from a knife fight that hadn't gone quite as he'd planned. The burns were something else.

Shaking off his past, he glanced at the woman still sitting at the table. Vibrant, beautiful, normal. He bet Jocelyn Hartinger had no idea what it was like to wonder where her next meal was coming from or to face the constant battle of whether to sleep in the park or dare to spend the night at home.

Troy collected the serving dishes and his plate and carried them to the sink. As nice as it was to have someone else fix him a meal, Jocelyn obviously wasn't one who would sit by quietly and let him work in peace. No, she was the type who would keep hounding him until he either gave in and told her what she wanted to know or went insane trying to avoid her questions.

Troy loaded the dishes into the dishwasher and debated what tactic he should use next on Kristi's little sister. She would leave here eventually. Now was as good a time as any to nudge her on her way.

She stepped beside him and turned on the hot water. After she slid her plate into place, she said, "I'm going for a walk. Do you want to come?"

"Maybe you should spend some time packing so I can give you a ride back to the village."

"I'm good." Jocelyn breezed out of the room and returned a moment later wearing her jacket and a pair of fingerless gloves. A camera hung from her neck, a black case slung over her shoulder. "I'll be on the beach if you decide you want to join me." She didn't wait for a response. Instead, she walked outside onto the deck and followed the stairs to the yard. She made it only a few steps before she lifted the camera and aimed it at the spot where the water met the rocks below the house.

Watching her through the kitchen window, Troy dialed Kristi's number.

"How did it go?" Kristi asked.

"It didn't. She's determined to stay here and take pictures."

"Take pictures? She's into photography again?"

"Apparently so." Troy wiped down the counter where Jocelyn had prepared their breakfast. "What am I supposed to do? She's refusing to leave."

"I told you she was persuasive."

"She's not persuading me one bit. She's more like a force of nature," Troy countered. He didn't mention that he respected her for going after what she wanted. "It's like she doesn't understand the meaning of the word *no*."

"Oh, she understands it. She just doesn't believe it applies to her. She has no trouble using it herself."

"Regardless, nothing I've said has sunk in. She's convinced she can stay in the bungalow."

"If she's made up her mind about staying, maybe you should just let her," Kristi suggested.

Let her stay. The opportunity to have any source of companionship held an appeal, and Troy could admit that spending time with an attractive woman who challenged his intellect would be an added bonus. Besides, if Jocelyn stayed, he wouldn't have to worry about her telling people he was here. The question was whether he could do his work if she were underfoot.

"How much can I tell her about what I'm doing here?" Troy asked. "I told her I work as a private contractor doing security work."

"That's true enough," Kristi said. "Obviously, we don't want Jocelyn to know that my island is now the home base for a top-secret organization."

"What about the helicopter?" Troy asked. "If she's determined to take photos all over the island, she'll find it eventually."

"You can tell her I agreed to let the Coast Guard park it there."

"And when she asks why?"

"You don't have to know the reasons why. You're just house sitting, remember?"

"I'm also the pilot for that helicopter at the moment."

"Right." Kristi paused. "Okay, what about if you tell her you're a reservist for the Coast Guard. When they asked to leave a helicopter on my property, I agreed as long as you would look after my island for me."

"A private security consultant *and* a Coast Guard reservist? It's a stretch."

"But she won't have any reason to question you," Kristi said.

Troy leaned back against the kitchen counter. "I guess you're right."

"Like Ace always says, rule number one in undercover work is that people will believe what you tell them unless you give them a reason not to."

"You're telling me not to give her a reason to doubt my story."

"That's exactly what I'm telling you. I'm sure you can make it work," Kristi said. "If she stays more than a few days, you'll need to cut some firewood. There are some downed trees near the pond that would be easy to chop up."

"Maybe I should let her stay in the main house after all, especially if she's going to cook for me."

"Jocelyn cooked for you?"

"Yeah. She made scrambled eggs for breakfast. They were amazing."

"I hate to break it to you, but the extent of her cooking skills doesn't go much beyond scrambled eggs, mashed potatoes, and steamed lobster."

"She knows how to cook lobster?"

"She's from Maine. It's kind of a requirement," Kristi said. "Not that it's difficult."

"That's easy for you to say. You're from Maine." Troy turned to the window again, but Jocelyn had disappeared from sight. "I'd better get going. I need to fix the internet so we have our security system up and running again."

"Good luck."

"Thanks. I'm going to need it."

* * *

Walter sauntered into his favorite coffee shop, ready to tackle the world. The vacation to Paris had been exactly what he'd needed: a time to get away from the grind of Washington politics, to reconnect as a family, and to prepare for the many pressures that would undoubtedly arise during the next year as his campaign heated up.

A year from now, that would all be behind him. With the assassination order in place for his main rival in the opposing party, nothing could stop him. The vice president had withdrawn from the presidential race a few weeks ago, after Walter's last attempt to eliminate his competition had failed.

Walter still couldn't believe the drone attack in Helsinki had been thwarted. He had planned each step so carefully. At the Russians' insistence, he had even secretly flown to Europe to oversee the attack.

He had resisted such direct involvement at first, but as his handler had reminded him, his co-conspirators needed to know he was fully invested in the plan or they might not follow through. They followed through, but none of his key people had survived. It was probably just as well. Fewer favors to grant when he finally did make it into office.

Personally, Walter suspected the Russians insisted he fly to Europe because they didn't want to risk his supporters learning of the Russians' involvement.

Had everything gone as they had hoped, the vice president would have died in what appeared to be a terrorist attack. The secretary of state had been the next target on their list.

Of course, the secretary of state was no longer a concern. With the information Walter's sources had discovered about the secretary of state's involvement with the untimely death of his last mistress, Walter wasn't worried about him. The American public might tolerate a lot when it came to politicians, but he was quite certain it would draw the line at electing a murderer.

Walter wasn't going to think about his involvement in trying to end someone's life. After all, he wasn't the one who would pull the trigger, at least not this time. He shuddered at the memory of an isolated trailer, a gun in his hand.

He hadn't had a choice that day weeks ago when he'd killed his accomplice, and he didn't have a choice now. The Russians owned him.

The financial support during his first campaign didn't raise any red flags at the time he was running for office. It wasn't until he was safely elected that his Russian contact came forward with the information that his government had financed much of Walter's campaign.

Walter had faced an unwinnable dilemma. Either he admitted he had unwittingly accepted funding from the Russians and face the end of his political career, or he moved forward and let the extra flow of cash help him rise through the political ranks. He had chosen the latter and, in so doing, had put himself on the road to the presidency. The Russians wouldn't settle for anything less. Nor would he.

Never before had any president enjoyed the unique insight into Russia's goals and objectives for the future. Walter planned to use his knowledge to do what his predecessors had failed to accomplish. He would find common ground between the two nations and open trade and technology sharing that would put them all on top.

Walter had done his part. He was now the top candidate for his party. He still had to suffer through the debates and the campaign trail, but his opponents all had something in their platforms that would keep them from making it to the next level. Only Shawn Hammels concerned him, but his advisors assured him the squeaky-clean candidate was a long shot, at best. Walter was going to win. He was sure of it.

If it weren't for the guardians potentially digging into his finances once he won the primary, he would be worry-free. Unfortunately, the secret organization was diligent in their duties to ensure no president had any ties to another nation. The guardians were also invisible to nearly everyone in the government, even Walter, who sat on the Senate Intelligence Committee.

Walter had managed to eliminate the senator who oversaw the funding of the program almost two years ago. And then it had taken him nearly a year to unearth the man's replacement—Senator James Whitmore, the man who planned to oppose him in his run for the presidency.

Walter took his place in line, the scent of coffee thick in the air. A second later, someone bumped into him.

"Sorry," the man mumbled in accented English.

Walter stiffened when he recognized the man who sometimes passed him information. Walter checked his phone and stepped out of line. He made his way to the restroom, footsteps echoing behind him.

As soon as they were out of sight of the other patrons, the man's voice sounded again. "Sir. I think this is yours."

Walter turned now and looked at the man with medium-brown hair and average build. In his hand, he held an envelope. Walter took it and peeked inside. A series of photos revealed the proof he needed to eliminate the secretary of state as an opponent once and for all. A well-timed leak of the information in late October would help pave his way to the Oval Office.

The only other thing he needed was to get rid of Senator Whitmore. If the assassin did his job, by this time next week, Whitmore would be dead, and nothing would be left to stand in Walter's way.

* * *

Gavrie stroked a finger over the leather of the steering wheel as he watched the flow of traffic pass by. He had chosen to park on this particular access road to give him the flexibility to wait without worrying about someone pulling up behind him. The last thing he needed was to be forced to merge onto the George Washington Parkway prematurely.

For the past four days, he had tracked James Whitmore's movements, analyzed his schedule, and studied his habits. While the older man wasn't prone to many vulnerabilities in his daily routines, his drive to work was predictable. Every morning at seven o'clock, the senator departed his home and began his drive to Capitol Hill. No stops, except for yesterday when he filled his gas tank at the convenience store a few miles from his house.

GPS appeared to be something Whitmore didn't believe in because even when he could have saved fifteen minutes by taking I-66 to avoid a slowdown on the parkway, he hadn't deviated from his usual course. That little tidbit had given Gavrie the final detail he needed to formulate his plan: the long stretch of the parkway that ran along the Potomac River, the steep drop-off, the questionable guard rail in desperate need of repair. Gavrie suspected the guard rail would be replaced soon but not until after the beloved senator from Virginia met an untimely death.

Gavrie checked the time. Six more minutes, maybe seven, until the senator's car would get bumped off the road and tumble down the hill to the river below.

CHAPTER 6

Jim Whitmore turned onto the GW Parkway and wondered how long it would take to get to his office today. He knew he might be able to save time if he took another route into DC from his home in Virginia, but the view along the parkway was worth a few extra minutes in traffic. He'd much rather watch people rowing on the Potomac than stare at a steady line of taillights and pavement.

If all went according to plan, he would deal with this commute for only another fourteen months. If elected, he and Katherine would move into the White House a year from January, and his home would become someplace they would enjoy when they needed to get away from the fishbowl of Washington politics.

Jim merged onto the parkway, pleased to see traffic was moving, even though it was well below the posted speed limit. His cell phone rang, and he clicked on the button on his steering wheel to answer the call.

"Hello?"

"Senator Whitmore, it's Andy. I'm so sorry to bother you, but have you already left for work?"

"I have, but I'm not far from home." Not accustomed to hearing from his neighbor at this time of day, he asked, "Is everything okay?"

"It was until I tried to start my car this morning and nothing happened. I was hoping to get a ride in with you, but if you've already left, I can get an Uber."

"You don't have to do that. I can swing by and pick you up."

"Are you sure? Normally, I wouldn't ask, but I'm not sure I can postpone my meeting with Congresswoman Mead."

"It's not a problem." Jim signaled to take the next exit. "I'll be there in ten minutes."

"Thank you so much."

"You're welcome. I'll see you in a few."

* * *

Gavrie's grip tightened on the steering wheel. Where was he? Even if the senator had hit traffic, he should have been here by now. Gavrie checked the GPS on his phone. No sign of an accident, and the backup that had developed near the senator's entrance wasn't any worse than earlier in the week. So where was he?

He checked the time again. Still no Whitmore.

Gavrie settled back into his seat. He would wait another hour. If he didn't show up by then, maybe he would have to come up with a plan B.

* * *

Jim pulled into Andy's driveway. Andy jogged down the steps of his front porch, briefcase in hand and tie flapping in the breeze. He slid into the passenger seat.

"Thanks again for helping me out." Andy closed the door and clicked his seat belt into place. "I can't believe that today of all days my car wouldn't start."

"I'm happy to help. We both know Congresswoman Mead doesn't tolerate excuses."

"Isn't that the truth."

Jim reversed his course and started toward the parkway. Beside him, Andy tapped on the screen of his cell phone. "It looks like I'll make it on time if we take 66."

"It's worth a try." Jim resigned himself to missing out on his usual morning view of the Potomac. "By the way, I wanted to ask you if you still needed us to look after your horses for Thanksgiving weekend."

"No. I forgot to tell you Helen's parents decided to come here instead."

"That'll be nice to be able to stay in town for the holiday."

"It will. It's hard to believe Thanksgiving is only three weeks away," Andy said.

"Not for me. Katherine finished her Christmas shopping last week."

"Are your kids coming home for the holidays?"

"Matt and his family will come, but Amy's husband is on deployment, so I doubt we'll have them." Jim paused long enough to check his mirrors and merge onto the freeway. "I'm not sure yet about Charlie. He may have to work."

"It's still hard for me to picture Charlie as an FBI agent," Andy said. "I think I'd be a nervous wreck if one of my kids had to carry a gun."

"He's good at his job. We trust the Lord will watch over him." Jim didn't mention the various times his family had survived overwhelming odds. Instead, he asked about Andy's kids and fell into easy conversation to pass the time.

* * *

Jocelyn steadied her camera, a heron framed in her viewfinder. The rumble of a motorboat engine sounded, and the bird took flight. Jocelyn snapped several shots a fraction of a second too late to get the one she wanted.

Annoyance rippled. She wasn't supposed to have to worry about interruptions out here in the middle of nowhere.

The sound intensified, and Jocelyn turned to face whoever had ruined her shot. She recognized the vessel before she saw the man standing behind the wheel. Gil.

Samson darted out of the house, scrambled down the stairs, and raced across the yard until he reached her side.

Gil cut the engine to half and then to quarter speed as he approached the dock.

Jocelyn slipped her camera from her neck and put it in her case to protect it from the water and the dog. Gil lifted a hand in greeting as he cut his engine and grabbed a line to secure his boat.

Samson barked twice, but his wagging tail indicated Gil wasn't a stranger to Heritage Island.

"Gil. What are you doing here?"

"I was on my way into town. Thought you might want a ride in."

"I'm fine, but thanks for the offer."

"Are you sure? I hate to think of you stranded out here by yourself."

"I'm not by myself," Jocelyn said. "A friend is watching Kristi's place while she's out of town."

"I heard someone was staying here. Kristi's mysterious renter."

"What do you mean 'mysterious'?" Jocelyn asked.

"Kristi left town two weeks ago, and he hasn't been into the village once." He nodded at the house. Jocelyn turned. Ty stood on the deck, a cap on his head, the collar of his coat flipped up to protect his neck. Or was it up to hide his face?

"If it's only been two weeks, maybe he hasn't needed to come into town yet," Jocelyn said. "Not to mention, I bought enough supplies to last us both another couple weeks."

"It's odd, though, the way he showed up without anyone seeing him." He leaned closer. "Not even Wally saw him come into town. How do you think your sister's renter managed that?"

"Maybe he didn't come through the village." Jocelyn took a step back. "I'd better get back to work. Thanks for stopping by."

"No problem." He rocked back on his heels but didn't move toward his boat. "Any chance you'd like to hang out tonight? Maybe watch a movie?"

"Thanks, but I have a lot of work to do," Jocelyn said. "Maybe some other time."

His face lit up with hope, and Jocelyn realized the mistake she had made. This guy was going to take her words literally.

"Yeah, maybe this weekend."

"Sorry, that's not what I meant."

Before she could say anything further, he untied the line and hopped onto his boat. "I'll stop by and check on you tomorrow or the next day."

"No, that's—"

The engine started and drowned out any excuse she might have made. Great. Now she would have to find a way to give this guy the gentle hint that she wasn't interested in dating him or anyone else right now.

Footsteps approached. With only one other person on the island, Jocelyn didn't have to guess at the source.

"Who was that?" Ty asked.

"Gil. He's the one who dropped me off yesterday."

"What did he want?"

"He stopped by to see if I wanted to go into town with him."

"You didn't?"

"Not particularly," Jocelyn said. "I was just there yesterday."

"Then why did he think you would want to go into town today?" Ty asked.

"I think he was trying to ask me out."

Ty's eyebrows winged up. "Look, maybe you're not interested in him, but if your being here is going to bring even more people to the island, then you really need to find somewhere to stay in the village. My work requires privacy."

"First of all, I didn't ask him to come visit, and I'm not planning on going out with him," Jocelyn said. "And secondly, I'm not going anywhere." Not waiting for his response, Jocelyn headed for the beach. To her surprise, he fell into step beside her. Neither of them spoke until they reached the sandy stretch of land that lay beyond the cove.

"I'm not trying to be difficult, but having other people on the island isn't what I bargained for," Ty said.

"I could say the same thing about you." Jocelyn stopped and faced him, struck again by his chiseled features and deep blue eyes. "I planned on being here alone."

"But you weren't invited. I was." An edge came into his voice and thickened the hint of Scandinavia in his accent.

"But I belong here." Jocelyn drew in a breath and let it out slowly. "Maybe we should start over." She stopped and offered her hand. "Hi. I'm Jocelyn, Kristi's sister. I'd really love it if you'll let me hang out here for a few weeks while I decide what I want to do next with my life." She sensed his hesitation and added, "I promise, I'll stay out of your way."

Ty was silent a moment longer, and then his eyes met hers. "Promise you won't have anyone over to visit?"

Relief and satisfaction merged. "I promise."

"In that case, what do you have planned for tonight?"

"I thought I would build a fire, hang out, and edit some photos, maybe watch a movie."

"What about dinner?" Ty asked.

"I made breakfast. It's your turn to cook."

"Okay, but only if I get to pick the movie," Ty said.

Delighted at the prospect of spending an evening getting to know her new neighbor, she asked, "Did you have a particular movie in mind?"

"I guess you'll find out tonight."

"I guess I will."

* * *

Jim loosened his tie, collected his briefcase, and walked from the garage into the kitchen. The glorious scent of cinnamon rolls filled the air.

He set his briefcase on a kitchen chair and crossed to the counter where two large trays were covered in tinfoil. Two sticky notes adorned the top, both with identical messages. *Don't eat. Or else.*

The warning slowed his progress. He glanced at the decorative sign on the wall: *With God all things are possible—Matthew 19:26*. He took Matthew's words as encouragement. Unable to resist, he lifted the corner to reveal fat cinnamon rolls with thick icing.

"Jim?" Katherine's voice rang out from somewhere deep in the house. "Don't even think about it."

Jim snatched his hand away. How did she do that? It was like the woman had a sixth sense when it came to baked goods. He tucked the foil back under the pan.

"I knew it." Katherine walked in.

"What?"

"That you would be in the cinnamon rolls within fifteen seconds of walking in the door," Katherine said. "These are for the teacher appreciation breakfast at the high school."

"You realize we haven't had kids in high school for almost a decade, right?"

"I know, but one of the volunteers came down with bronchitis, and Ellen asked if I would help out."

Ellen, the Relief Society president of their congregation of The Church of Jesus Christ of Latter-day Saints. Why was it that he loved his religion completely until baked goods stirred up controversy?

"It's nice to be involved again." Katherine stepped beside him and tucked the foil more firmly under the pan. "Once you're elected president, I won't be able to do things like this very often."

"True." Jim lifted the tinfoil again. "But if the school wasn't expecting you to bring these anyway, they won't notice if one is missing."

Katherine swatted his hand. "Stop that."

Jim snatched his hand back and debated his next tactic. "You know, it doesn't bode well for me if I win the election and I can't even persuade my wife to grant me one little request."

"If you think getting elected president is going to give you free rein in my kitchen, guess again," Katherine said. "If you want to change clothes, you'd better do it now. We need to leave in fifteen minutes."

"The fundraiser doesn't start for an hour and a half."

"I know, but we need to drop the cinnamon rolls off at Ellen's house on our way."

"Katherine . . ." He eyed the cinnamon rolls again. "But . . ."

An impish grin touched her lips, and she waved at the opposite counter. "I set one aside for you. It's over there."

Jim kissed her. "I really love you."

"I know. I love you too." She put her hand on his arm. "Go eat your cinnamon roll. You'll need your energy for when you help me carry all of this to the car."

Jim took a bite and let out a hum of approval. "You're a very influential woman."

"I do my best."

Walter sorted through the stack of messages on his desk. So much for his staff staying on top of things. Through the open office door, the buzz of voices and the ringing of phones carried to him. He wished the familiar background noise could distract him from his task today. He couldn't be sure exactly which line in the budget belonged to the guardians, but he had narrowed it down to six, and though he hated to do it, he knew he had only one choice. He would delete all six and see who came crying about the loss of funds.

His chief of staff passed into view, and Walter called out. "Zack, can you come in here?"

"Yes, Senator?" Zack asked when he reached the office doorway.

"Call Senator Tatum. See if we can reschedule our meeting for Wednesday," Walter said. "I need to keep tomorrow clear to prepare for the debate."

"I'll take care of it."

"Also, do you have the numbers from the latest polls?"

"I do." Zack held up his phone and tapped the screen. "I just forwarded them to you. Right now, you have a twelve-point lead over Peters, eighteen points over Hammels."

"That's not bad, but I'd like a bigger gap. Twelve points could disappear in a heartbeat."

"The debate will give you the chance to widen the margin."

"Let's hope so. In the meantime, I need to spend some time reviewing the intelligence budget before the next committee meeting."

"You have an hour before your next appointment."

Walter held up the stack of messages. "Have you already gone through these?"

"No. Those must be the ones that came in on Friday when I was out of the office."

Walter held them out. "Take care of what you can and bring me the ones I have to deal with personally."

"Yes, sir."

"Close the door on your way out."

Zack complied, leaving Walter alone with the budget and the access code that would allow the Russians to see the expenditures planned for every military and intelligence organization in the US government. He had one hour to complete his task. One hour that could tilt the balance of an entire nation. Make that two nations: the one he loved and the one he worked for.

* * *

Jim thumbed through the latest intelligence budget. He wasn't going to think about how many trees gave their lives each year to support Congress's never-ending effort to make a financial plan. From what he could see, they were still several versions away from coming to an agreement. Cuts in military were one thing, but cutting the intelligence budget was a bad idea for everyone.

He flipped the page and noted several items one of his fellow senators on the Intelligence Committee had lined out as potential cuts. A research project on defensive measures against biological weapons, two classified military projects, a road improvement initiative. When Jim reached the fifth item on the list, his blood chilled. The guardian funding. This particular item was part of a five-year capital improvement program, at least on paper. In reality, most of the money in the budget would be funneled over the next few years into the perpetual fund that would provide for the guardians indefinitely. This specific budget string had passed uncontested last year. Why would someone go after it now?

Turning to his computer, Jim searched through the electronic version to see who had made the change. Walter Royce. Jim's fingers tightened on the thick document, and he picked up the second cell phone Ghost had given him over a year earlier.

The young guardian answered on the second ring. "Yes?"

"We may have a problem with this year's finances."

"Why are you calling me? Isn't that a problem you want to talk to Kristi about?" he asked.

"Usually, but this isn't about how money is being transferred." Jim read the budget line again to confirm the truth. "Walter Royce deleted your funding from this year's budget."

"Then put it back in."

Jim almost smiled at Ghost's ability to get straight to the point. "I intend to, but doesn't it concern you that of all the possible cuts he could make, Royce went after your funding?"

"You think he knows what the money is for?"

"What if he does?" Jim asked.

"How would he figure that out? There are thousands of lines in the federal budget."

"Yet he went after yours." Jim had been so careful in creating the guardians' budget string to ensure it wouldn't trace back to him. "What I've never understood is why he would care to cut off your funding."

"Maybe he doesn't know that we've already found his financial ties to Russia," Ghost said. "If he knows about us, he might also know we're the last line of defense when it comes to vetting presidential candidates."

"Do you have anything new on that front?" Jim asked.

"We can prove Russia funded his first campaign, but we're still looking for evidence that he was involved in the attack in Helsinki."

"Maybe it's time we expose Walter and eliminate his ability to interfere with your program," Jim suggested.

"We've talked about this before. If we expose him now, he has too much time to do damage control," Ghost said. "We need something beyond some dirty funding years ago."

"You want proof he was involved with the assassination attempt."

"Everything points in that direction. We just need a way to prove it."

"I have to say, I would much prefer to run my campaign without having to worry about Walter Royce's illegal activities," Jim said.

"Worst case, you have to beat him, and then we'll expose him."

"Yeah, I'll get right on that."

"While you're at it, maybe you should try to put in a new funding string for us."

"That's not a bad idea." Jim looked over the budget changes again. "Even if Royce pulls yours, I wouldn't mind having a backup. Best case, we get the program fully funded a year early."

"The sooner the better."

"I couldn't agree more."

* * *

Kade didn't like it. First Morozov made it into the country, and now their financing was in jeopardy. Again.

When Jim proposed that a perpetual fund be established to support the guardians outside of the normal budget, everyone had seen the wisdom. Bringing Kristi on board gave the guardians a financial manager and someone to oversee and report to the one person in Congress who knew the guardians were more than a ghost story. If the deletion of the guardians' funding from the budget was deliberate, someone else knew about them. Kade's money was on Walter Royce.

Renee walked in from the kitchen. "Hey, it's getting late. We should get some sleep."

"I don't like this."

"I know, but you know as well as anyone, it takes time to work through this much video feed." Renee put both hands on his shoulders and massaged his tense muscles. "We'll get there."

"But will we get there soon enough? We haven't even identified Morozov's target," Kade said. "If he's working with Royce, the target could be anyone running for president. There are still more than a half dozen viable candidates."

"We'll find him," Renee said with a quiet calm. She pressed her thumb against a knot that had formed beside his shoulder blade.

"Mmm. Right there."

Renee complied. After a minute, she leaned down and kissed his cheek. "We'll pick this up in the morning."

Kade turned his head, their faces now close. He couldn't resist pressing his lips to hers. A bolt of attraction shot through him, and he hooked a hand behind her neck to keep her in place, reveling in her soft lips and the silkiness of her hair beneath his fingers.

When the kiss ended, Renee took his hand and tugged until he stood. "Come on. Time for bed."

"You're getting bossy all of a sudden."

Renee's left eyebrow lifted. "There's nothing sudden about it."

Kade fought back a smile. "Have I told you lately how lucky I am to have you?"

"Not since this morning." Renee leaned forward for another kiss. "But it's okay if you repeat yourself. I don't mind."

"Good to know." He slipped his hand around Renee's waist and guided her toward the stairs. "What are the chances I can convince you to give me another shoulder rub?"

"Fifty-fifty."

"What do I have to do to improve my odds?"

"You could promise to fix dinner tomorrow night."

"But it's your turn to cook."

"Exactly."

CHAPTER 8

Troy slid a disk into the DVD player. If Jocelyn was determined to stay, she might as well know what she was getting herself into. Classic movies, sports themes, and anything that didn't scream chick flick or action movie. He wasn't a chick, and he had enough action in his real life. He didn't need to watch it on a screen.

The scent of popcorn wafted into the room a second before Jocelyn appeared with a huge bowl tucked into the crook of her arm. Samson followed her, sniffing the air.

"Samson, go lie down." Jocelyn pointed at the rug in front of the fireplace that held a fresh log now consumed in flames. Samson sniffed the air again, but when Jocelyn held the bowl out of reach, he circled once and settled on the floor. Jocelyn sat on the couch and grabbed the afghan from beside her. "What are we watching?"

"*Brian's Song*."

"In that case . . ." She stood and disappeared back into the kitchen.

"That was easy," Troy mumbled, a little disappointed that Jocelyn didn't put up more of a fight. She should have at least left the popcorn.

His jaw dropped when she returned a moment later with a box of tissues.

"Okay." She sat back down. "I'm ready now."

"You've already seen this movie?"

"Of course. It's a classic, but I can never get through it without crying," she said without the least amount of embarrassment. She reached over, turned off the lamp beside her, and settled the bowl of popcorn on her lap.

Surprised by her reaction and how comfortable she was in her own skin, Troy hit play and sat on the couch beside her. He glanced at her, but she was already focused on the television, the light from the fireplace flickering over her skin. She really was stunning in that down-to-earth, girl-next-door kind of way.

The opening song started, and Jocelyn scooted closer and held out the bowl of popcorn. "Do you want some?"

"Yeah. Thanks." He grabbed a handful and took a bite. Butter, salt, greasy fingers, along with companionship and safety. This was what he always imagined movie nights would be like when he was a kid. For him, it had more frequently been sneaking into the theater and hiding under the seats in search of fallen treasures that would fill his empty stomach.

"Sorry. I forgot napkins," Jocelyn said.

"I'll get them." Troy went into the kitchen and grabbed the napkins from the holder on the table. When he returned, Jocelyn held the remote, and the movie was paused. It took him a moment to realize she had stopped the movie because of him. He wasn't invisible. "You didn't have to wait for me."

"It's no fun to watch alone."

Troy glanced at her, struck by her comment. He wondered what she would think if she knew he always watched alone. Such was the life of a guardian.

She met his gaze. "What?"

"Nothing." He slid closer to Jocelyn and put his hand on hers. Her gaze whipped up to meet his. He took advantage of her surprise by snatching the remote from her grasp. Suppressing a satisfied smile, he pressed play, and took another bite of popcorn. "The movie's starting."

* * *

Jocelyn had forgotten what it was like to spend a quiet evening with someone. Sure, Ty hadn't said much beyond, "Pass the popcorn," but at least she wasn't alone.

It was ironic, she supposed, that she had to come to a remote island to find companionship. It wasn't that she didn't have friends in Boston, but for the last few years, all of her associations stemmed from work. Her clients and employees only cared about what she could do for them in their careers, not who she was outside the office. Rarely did she have a quiet night like tonight that served no other purpose than to relax and enjoy, at least not since Kristi had moved out.

If Jocelyn had to name a best friend, it would be her sister. She cringed to think of what a lousy friend she had been since their grandfather had died. Between expanding her business and Kristi's decision to move to Heritage Island, they rarely talked more than a couple times a month. If they had spoken more, maybe Jocelyn would have been more aware of her sister's plans and Ty's presence here.

Jocelyn glanced at him now, his strong profile illuminated by the soft light of the embers in the fireplace and the glow of the television screen. Athletic and self-assured, he was exactly the type of guy she had pined to go out with in high school and college. Unfortunately, she hadn't had the best of luck when dating the type she found most attractive.

In recent years, too many men she dated were obsessed with wealth and social status. She missed the simplicity of her teenage years, when people liked each other because they enjoyed spending time together, not because they thought they would look good together. Sure, she knew social climbers had existed in high school, too, but most of those had been in the popular crowd. Jocelyn had always skimmed around the edges, never really diving into the social concerns that came from being entrenched in a clique.

Curious about the man beside her, Jocelyn asked, "What sports did you play in high school?"

"I didn't do sports in high school."

"Really? I figured with your height, coaches would have recruited you into something."

"High school wasn't a good scene for me."

"Why not?"

"It just wasn't."

Jocelyn opened her mouth to press only to close it again. Didn't Ty know that his half answers only made her more curious? How could he be so self-assured and so mysterious at the same time?

The final scene began, and she fell silent. Emotions rose within her as she watched the poignant images of a once-vibrant man dying of cancer while his wife and best friend stood at his bedside. She sniffled. Ty picked up the tissue box and held it out.

"Thanks." Jocelyn took two and dabbed her eyes.

The bond between the two best friends touched her, resonating deeper this time as she considered that beyond her family, she didn't have any friends of such significance.

She swiped at her tears a second time.

The touching hospital scene cut to the narrator, who described the richness of Brian Piccolo's life and the deep friendships he left behind. His life mattered. Jocelyn wanted to be able to say the same thing about hers.

She glanced at Ty, whose gaze was still on the television, his eyes dry. How could he not be moved by this? Or had he seen it enough times that he was immune to the tug at the heartstrings?

Ty stood and opened the fireplace screen. With the poker, he scattered the last remaining embers from the fire.

"What do you have planned for tomorrow?" he asked. "More pictures?"

"Yeah. I have a project I want to work on too."

"I thought you weren't working right now."

"Technically, I'm not," Jocelyn said. "This one is pro bono."

"Who's it for?"

"The Boys and Girls Clubs in Boston. They do so much for the community that when they asked for some assistance setting up their website, it seemed only fair to help them out."

"That's admirable."

"I don't know about that, but it's nice to feel useful." Jocelyn stood. "I'd better head to bed. Thanks for hanging out with me tonight."

"Yeah, no problem." He leaned down to close the flue. Samson took the movement as a signal to stretch and stand.

"I meant to ask, do you have any extra lotion here? I only have a travel size, and I'm almost out."

"I didn't notice any extra in the bathroom in the hall, but you can check the master bath if you want."

"I should have checked in there after my shower this morning." She took a step toward the hall before she stopped and asked, "Aren't you staying in the master bedroom?"

"No. I'm in one of the guest rooms. I wanted to leave your sister's space the way she left it."

"That's nice of you. I'll be right back." Jocelyn went into the master bathroom and looked under the sink. Nothing. The drawers held toothbrushes, toothpaste, and razors. Was that a package of men's razors? Jocelyn pulled the half-empty package out of the drawer. Sure enough, the blue razors inside were intended for men. What were those doing here? Did Ty leave them in here?

Jocelyn replaced the razors in the drawer and crossed to the armoire that occupied the corner of the bathroom. Inside, neat rows of first-aid supplies, shampoo, conditioner, and lotion lined the shelves along with an abundance of toilet paper. She collected a pack of toilet paper, along with a bottle of lotion, and carried them into the living room.

"Did you find what you needed?"

"I did. Thanks." Jocelyn donned her coat and headed for the door. "See you in the morning."

"Do you want me to walk you over there?"

"That's okay. I'll be fine." Jocelyn walked outside into the cold and closed the door behind her before making her way to the bungalow, the porch light she had left on guiding her through the darkness. She opened the door and stepped into the quaint living area with the simple couch and love seat. She set down the toiletries and crossed the cozy living room to start a fire. Only four logs rested in the log holder. It would be enough to get her through tonight and maybe tomorrow night, but she was going to need more wood if she planned to stay here for long.

She laid some old newspaper and kindling in the base and set one log on top. Once she started the fire, she shrugged out of her coat and walked into the bedroom where she had put her luggage. Certain she wouldn't be able to sleep until the cottage warmed up, she opened her suitcases and unpacked her clothes.

When she went to unpack her electronics, she looked around the cottage only to realize she didn't have a surge protector. Not willing to risk her laptop and phone, especially against the uncertain island power supply, she left them in her computer bag and set them aside. Maybe Ty would have one she could borrow.

She moved to the window and looked outside. The lights from the main house cast a shimmer across the water in front of her. A shadow passed in front of a window, and her curiosity heightened. Who was Ty, and where did he come from? One way or another, she was going to find out.

CHAPTER 9

A door opened. A floorboard creaked.

Troy's eyes flew open, and his hand shot under his pillow to grip the gun hidden there, then he whipped back the covers and leapt out of bed. Who was here? Had someone found him?

Predawn light cast soft shadows across the room and chased away the worst of the darkness.

Gun at the ready, he eased the door open and peered into the hall.

The refrigerator door opened and shut. A moment later, the water turned on in the kitchen.

He let his head fall back as his mind cleared. Jocelyn.

He glanced down at the gun in his hand. At least his temporary neighbor hadn't ended up looking down the barrel of his gun for a second time in two days.

At the foot of the bed, Samson lifted his head.

"Don't look at me like that. I didn't plan for her to stay here," Troy said.

Samson stood, his tail now wagging.

"I'm not feeding you. It's only . . ." Troy checked the clock on his bedside table. "Five o'clock in the morning."

The tail wagging increased.

"No." Troy slid his gun back into its spot beneath his pillow and flopped onto the center of the bed.

Samson closed the distance between them and nuzzled his head beneath Troy's hand.

Troy rolled his head to the side so he could see his canine companion and scratched behind Samson's ears. "What?"

Samson barked once in his typical it's-time-to-feed-me response.

"We should still be asleep." Troy closed his eyes.

The memory of last night pushed to the forefront of his semiconscious mind: the contentment he experienced during his evening with Jocelyn, the sense of normal. This wasn't his normal, though, and he couldn't let himself fall into a routine, no matter where he was. He needed to remain alert, to be prepared for anything at any time.

As much as the idea of having someone to talk to appealed to him, he couldn't afford to get too comfortable with Kristi's little sister. Friendship required trust, and that was something Troy had learned early in life was a dangerous thing to give.

The dog barked again.

"You aren't going to let me sleep, are you?"

Another bark.

"Fine." Troy pushed himself out of bed again. Not bothering to change out of his pajama pants, he pulled on a T-shirt and headed for the kitchen.

Jocelyn looked up from where she stood at the stove, her face fresh, her hair slightly damp. "I didn't think you'd be up this early."

"Samson decided we should get an early start today." Troy scooped food into Samson's bowl.

Apology lit her face. "I'm sorry. He must have heard me come in."

"It's all right."

"I hope you don't mind, but I plugged my laptop and phone into the surge protector in the living room. I didn't think to bring one."

"No problem."

The kettle whistled, and Jocelyn turned off the stove. She spooned some hot chocolate mix into a mug and added hot water. "Since you're up, did you want to come out on the dock with me? I thought I'd see if we can catch some fish for dinner."

"I thought you were going to take pictures this morning."

"I can do both."

Curious about how she planned to fish and handle a camera at the same time, he said, "I can spare a few minutes."

"Great." She stirred her hot chocolate and glanced out the window. "The light should be perfect in about twenty minutes."

"Perfect for what?"

"You'll see."

* * *

Jocelyn slid a blank memory card into her camera and glanced out the window at the horizon. A few more minutes and the light would be perfect.

Ty emerged from the hall, his long, lanky body clad in a thick sweater and a pair of jeans. Jocelyn's mouth went dry. The man could make anything look good. She'd about swallowed her tongue when he'd walked into the kitchen this morning in his pajamas. No one should look that good in flannel.

Stubble shadowed his face. His blue eyes pinned hers. "Ready?"

"Yeah." She picked up her camera bag and walked out the door, leading the way to the shed under the stairs to collect two fishing rods from inside, as well as a couple of rod holders, a bucket, and a net.

"Can you take these?" She passed him the two poles, and he gripped them in one hand.

"I can carry those too if you want."

"Thanks." Jocelyn gave him the rod holders and closed the shed doors. She walked toward the spot where the tide reached the edge of the yard, then scooped some water into the bucket and headed for the dock.

Ty followed. He held up the rod holders. "If these are doing the fishing, what are we supposed to do?"

"Wait. Talk. Get to know each other." Jocelyn held up her camera. "And I'm going to take some pictures."

"What are you taking pictures of today?"

"Fishing poles."

"Fishing poles?" His eyebrows rose. "You got up at five in the morning for that?"

"Yeah. It's exactly what I need for the Boys and Girls Club campaign."

"Couldn't you have downloaded something off the internet?"

She stepped onto the dock and cast a smile over her shoulder. "Where's the fun in that?"

"Sleeping can be fun."

"Not really." Jocelyn took one of the rod holders from Ty's hand, leaned down, and clamped it to the side of the dock opposite where the boat was secured. She then baited her hook and cast her line into the water. "Personally, I think sleep is overrated."

"It sounds like you haven't had a lot of nights you've had to go without."

"Are you kidding? I'm the CEO of a successful advertising company." She leaned down and clamped her fishing rod into a rod holder. "I've had plenty of sleepless nights over the past seven years."

"You *were* the CEO."

Ty's words sank in. "Yeah. That's going to take some getting used to. My company has been part of my identity for so long, it's hard to know who I am without it."

"You started your company seven years ago?"

"That's right."

Ty cast off with the ease of someone who was well acquainted with a fishing pole. "You don't look old enough to have been in business that long."

"I started it when I was still in college."

"And now you're taking pictures of fishing poles."

"Yeah." Jocelyn drew her camera out of her bag and took a test shot. The joy of the moment, the freedom, the budding friendship brought with it a satisfaction she hadn't experienced in months. "It's great, isn't it?"

"If you say so." A little smile flashed on his face before he leaned down to secure the second pole into place. "Now what am I supposed to do?"

"You wait." She glanced at her camera's view screen before lifting it again to study her target through the lens: the lines bobbing in the water, the two fishing poles clamped side by side without anyone tending them. Perfect.

"You're really taking a picture of fishing poles?" Ty asked.

"Yep."

"What for?"

"To show people possibilities."

"Possibilities for what?"

Ty's question buzzed over her. The light was perfect. She snapped several shots, adjusted the zoom, and took several more. She stepped to the side to get a different angle. For a while, she worked in silence.

Ty's line went taut, but he didn't move toward the rod.

"You've got one," Jocelyn said. "Aren't you going to reel it in?"

"Only if you promise to put your camera away."

"You don't want your picture taken?"

"No."

"Fine." She lowered her camera.

Ty had barely reached his pole when Jocelyn's line got a bite. She quickly put her camera in its case and rushed forward. She released the pole from its holder and leaned back against the tension in the line.

The muscles in her arms burned as she reeled her fish toward her, the resistance testing her strength. Just when she thought her catch was never going to reach shore, the end of the line came out of the water, a decent-sized mackerel fighting against the hook.

She pulled it in the rest of the way and dumped it into the bucket before freeing the hook. When she turned, Ty was still reeling in his own catch.

"It must be a big one."

Ty only grunted. A few seconds later, his fish emerged from the water. Twice the length of her own and four times the width, the cod floundered back and forth, sending the line jerking as Ty continued to fight it onto land.

"Here." Jocelyn grabbed the net and held it for him.

A minute later, Ty dropped the fish in. "That was a workout."

"Hey, at least it wasn't a halibut. Those things are huge."

"There are halibut in these waters?"

"Yeah, but we'd probably have to go out on the boat to get one. I've never had any luck from the dock," Jocelyn said.

Ty transferred his catch from the net to the bucket. "I didn't think we'd catch anything that size so close to shore."

"The dock is in deep water. You'd be amazed at what a person can catch here." Jocelyn motioned to the bucket. "Did you want to try for some more?"

"With only two of us here, maybe we should stop for the day. We don't have a lot of room in the fridge."

"True." She eyed the two fish. "What are the chances I can get you to clean them?"

"I'll clean them if you cook them."

"Deal."

CHAPTER 10

TROY GATHERED THE TOOLS HE needed from the shed and set them on the table on the patio where Jocelyn had laid today's catch. He filleted the first fish and slid the cleaned pieces into a gallon-sized plastic bag.

"You look like you've done that a lot," Jocelyn said.

"It's not that hard."

"Maybe, but someone taught you well."

Troy gave a noncommittal nod. Someone had taught him well, but he wasn't about to tell her it had been a homeless vet who lived by the pier in Oceanside, California.

"Did your dad teach you to fish?" Jocelyn continued.

"No."

"Who, then? Your mom? Or maybe a grandfather?"

"I spent a lot of time around the water."

"Oh yeah? Where?"

"Lots of places." He finished filleting the last fish.

"Where did you grow up?" Jocelyn asked.

"What is this? Twenty questions?"

"It's called conversation. You know, two people talking, sharing things about themselves."

"I don't have anything to share."

"You have plenty to share," Jocelyn corrected. "You're choosing not to."

"Same thing. I'm going inside to clean up." Troy picked up the bags of fish. "I'll put these in the fridge."

Jocelyn remained silent for a moment before responding. "I'm going to walk to the pond. I'll see you later."

"Yeah. Later." Troy jogged up the deck stairs. After finding a spot for the fish inside the overly full refrigerator, he moved to the sink and washed his hands.

Outside, Samson barked. Jocelyn laughed.

Troy's gaze roamed the yard until he spotted them both at the edge of the woods playing tug-of-war with a stick. An unexpected longing tugged inside him, not unlike seeing a beautiful painting and wondering what it was like to live inside it.

Jocelyn wrestled the stick away from Samson and sent it flying. The dog barked again and raced after it. They repeated the ritual twice more before Jocelyn disappeared down the trail leading toward the pond. Samson bounded into the woods behind her.

Troy watched the trail for a minute longer. She was gone. He was alone. A little pang of guilt pricked inside him, but he knew what he needed to do. She was an outsider, and he had secrets to protect.

With no time to lose, he hurried to the living room, where Jocelyn's phone and laptop lay charging. He unplugged both and carried them into the office. Kneeling beside the window seat, he pressed the hidden lever to open it and proceeded to unlock the safe hidden within.

With a sense of urgency, he retrieved a cell phone and laptop from the neatly arranged equipment inside, along with two devices Kade had invented. One looked like an oversized mouse pad. The other was smaller, about the size of his hand.

Not willing to risk Jocelyn catching him in the act of cloning her electronics, Troy grabbed the appropriate cables and hauled everything to the kitchen. He positioned himself where he could see out the window and set everything on the counter.

He took a quick look outside. No sign of Jocelyn or Samson.

Troy plugged both phones into the smaller of Kade's invention and initiated the program that would clone Jocelyn's cell. He glanced out the window again before he turned to the laptops.

He set the laptop he needed to duplicate on the oversized pad, opened the new computer, and initiated a programming string. He waited for the mirroring program to open on Jocelyn's computer, but nothing happened. He repeated the process, but the screen remained dark.

A quick check of the cell phones indicated that the cloning process was working on that device. He retrieved his phone from his pocket and dialed Kade's number.

"Yeah?" Kade answered,

"Hey, I need your help," Troy said. "I'm trying to clone a laptop, but it isn't working."

"What kind of laptop?"

Troy relayed the details.

"It should work," Kade said. "It must have a security program on it that's interfering."

"Is there a way for you to override it?" Troy asked. "She hasn't tried to access the internet yet, but I doubt she'll last more than another day or two before she asks for the password."

"Who hasn't tried to access the internet?" Kade asked.

"My current houseguest."

"I'm not sure I should even ask what that's all about," Kade muttered. "Let's see what we can do. Did you already clone her phone?"

"I'm doing that now." Troy checked the phones. "It's almost done. How are we going to bypass her security?"

"With any luck, her email account is linked to her phone."

"How does that help?"

"If she paid for her security program, there's probably an email confirming her order."

"Unless she deleted it," Troy said.

"People tend to keep that kind of stuff."

"The phone is all done." Troy picked up the cloned device and clicked on the email icon. "I'm in."

"Do a search. See if you can find any orders for software."

The app opened, and Troy noted the All Inboxes notation at the top of the screen. He tapped the screen to bring up the various email accounts. Two appeared, one for her business and the other for personal correspondence. Inside the business account, he found a list of files sorting Jocelyn's emails into categories. He clicked on the security file and identified the latest renewal notice.

"I found it. The program is called Centurion."

"That's high-end, usually customized."

"Can you hack into it?"

"We'll see soon enough. I'm accessing the cloning drive now."

Several minutes ticked by. Silence hummed over the phone, and Troy continued watching out the window.

"Well?" Troy finally asked.

"I've almost got it." More silence. "There. It's downloading now."

"How long will it take?"

"Ten, maybe fifteen minutes," Kade said.

Outside, Samson darted out of the trees, a stick in his mouth. Jocelyn's voice carried toward him, the words indistinguishable.

"She's coming." Troy stuffed the clone of Jocelyn's phone into his pocket. "We'll have to try again later."

"The download is already in progress. I can't stop it."

Troy moved closer to the window. Maybe he'd get lucky and Jocelyn would play outside with Samson for a while.

Samson circled Jocelyn and dropped the stick at her feet. Jocelyn ruffled the fur on top of the dog's head and walked past him. Samson picked up his stick again and cut Jocelyn off only to be ignored a second time. She continued across the lawn toward the house.

Troy checked the download. Only fifteen percent done.

"I'll call you back." Troy hung up and immediately dialed Kristi's number.

"Hey, how are things going with my sister?" Kristi asked.

"I need you to call her. Tell her you want her to check on something outside," Troy said. "Jocelyn can't come into the house for at least ten minutes."

"Why?"

"I'll explain later."

"Okay. I'll call right now."

Troy's phone went dead, and an instant later, Jocelyn's cell phone rang. Troy snatched it up and answered it.

"I gather Jocelyn left her phone inside," Kristi said.

"Yeah. I'll take it out to her. I know it's asking a lot, but I need you to keep her occupied."

"I'll do what I can."

Troy carried the phone outside and jogged down the steps to the yard. "Hey, your phone kept ringing. I thought it might be important. When I saw it was Kristi, I answered it."

"I'm surprised you even heard it."

"I was in the kitchen when it started ringing."

Jocelyn reached out a hand and took the phone from him. "Thanks for bringing it to me."

Troy waited for Jocelyn to greet her sister before he reversed course and went back into the house. He reached the kitchen and called Kade.

"How much longer?" Troy asked.

"Five minutes. Maybe six."

"Let's hope Kristi can keep Jocelyn occupied that long."

"Jocelyn? Wait, are you talking about Kristi's sister?" Kade asked.

"Yeah."

"Why are we cloning her laptop?"

"Because she's here on the island and refuses to leave."

"And?"

"She's taking pictures all over the place. I need to make sure she doesn't inadvertently share any that could damage our operation."

"Got it," Kade said. "Let me know how it goes."

"I'm surprised you don't want to stay on the phone to see how it turns out."

"Normally, I would, but you're going to need both hands to get everything put away so Kristi's sister doesn't suspect anything."

"Good point. Wish me luck."

"Luck."

"I meant wish me good luck."

"You should be more specific next time." Kade hung up.

"Thanks a lot," Troy muttered. He set his phone down and checked the laptop. Sixty-seven percent. Almost there. He just might make it.

CHAPTER 11

Jocelyn hiked up the hill on the side of the house to where a bank of solar panels had been installed. All she wanted was to get inside and warm up, but her sister insisted something was wrong with the island's power supply.

"I really appreciate you doing this for me," Kristi said.

"I still don't understand how you can tell from Europe that something is wrong here in Maine."

"I've got a monitoring system on the solar," Kristi said. "An alert popped up on the app on my phone."

"Pretty crazy how technology makes the world so much smaller."

"Yes, it is."

Jocelyn reached her objective but couldn't resist taking a moment to soak in the view. In front of her, waves crashed against the cliffs, contrasting with the steady rhythm of the current rolling into the cove and onto the beach on the wayward side of the island. The wind picked up, lifting her hair off her neck and sending an icy chill through her.

"Okay, I'm here. What am I looking for?"

Kristi walked her through the various connections that might have been interrupted. Twice.

"I'm sorry, Kristi, but I don't see anything here. Everything looks like it's connected."

"Maybe the problem is in the junction box in the shed. Can you check there?"

Jocelyn fought back her impatience. "Sure."

She jogged down the hill, rubbed her hands together to work some feeling back into her fingers, and opened the shed door. After she flipped on the light, she crossed to the generator and opened the electrical panel above it.

"All of the circuits show that they're on."

"This is so odd," Kristi said. "Let me reset the system from here and see what happens."

Silence.

Jocelyn turned from the heart of the island's electrical systems and took a good look at the various supplies in the shed. Red plastic containers filled with gasoline lined the shelves on one wall, and her grandfather's tools hung neatly on another above a workbench. She wandered closer to get a better look at a lobster pot that had one side hanging haphazardly off a broken hinge.

"What happened to the lobster pot in here?" Jocelyn asked.

"Oh, I was trying to fix it, but I wasn't able to," Kristi said. "I meant to pick up a new one in town and never got around to it."

"Since I'm planning to stay for a while, maybe I'll go into town tomorrow to pick one up."

"You don't have to do that. There's still one that's in decent shape."

"I'm starting to wonder. I've had it baited for two days and haven't had a single catch."

"That happens sometimes."

"Yeah, but this time of year, I should have caught something."

"Might want to check it out, then. Both of those pots have been around since before Grandpa died."

A wave of nostalgia swept over her. "I still miss him."

"Me too." Another few seconds passed before Kristi spoke again. "Okay, it looks like the solar is online again. You must have knocked something back into place."

"I doubt it. I think your app is messed up."

"Could be. Sorry to bug you about this."

"No big deal." Jocelyn turned off the light and closed the shed. "I'm going inside to warm up. I'll talk to you later."

"Have a good night," Kristi said.

"It's noon."

"Right. Forgot about the time difference."

Jocelyn chuckled. "I'll talk to you later."

She hung up her phone, slipped it into her pocket, and rubbed her hands together. Time to get out of the cold.

* * *

The text from Kristi came only seconds after the download finished. *Out of time.* Troy scooped Jocelyn's laptop and his tools off the counter, tucked the cloned laptop under his arm, and sprinted for the living room. His heart racing, he replaced the laptop exactly as he'd found it.

Canine and human footsteps clicked on the wooden stairs outside.

Moving silently, Troy hurried into his room and closed the door behind him, then flipped the lock and leaned back against the door.

The back door opened.

"That was close," he muttered under his breath.

"Ty?" Jocelyn called out.

He ignored her and stored his tools in his safe, then waited a minute for his breathing to return to normal before he walked into the hall.

Jocelyn stood in the entryway. "Oh, there you are."

"Did you get some good pictures?"

"I think so. Do you have the password for the internet?"

"I'll write it down for you."

"That would be great." She headed back to the living room and retrieved her laptop. Troy went into his office and jotted down the password to the dummy internet account Kade had helped him create. She reappeared in his office doorway. "Do you have it?"

"Yeah. Here you go." Troy held out the sticky note he had written it on.

"Thanks." Jocelyn took it from him. "There's one more thing."

"What's that?" Troy asked.

"I was hoping you would give me a ride to the village."

"Why do you need to go to the village? We have enough food to last for at least a couple weeks."

"I know, but I have a package I need to pick up at the post office."

"You only got here two days ago. Why would you have a package at the post office?"

"I ordered a new photo printer when I was in town on Tuesday. It's second-day delivery, so it should be there by now," she said. "I also need to pick up a surge protector, so I can use my electronics at the cottage."

Troy hesitated. How could he tell her that he didn't want to get too friendly with anyone in town? Going there with her practically guaranteed he'd be noticed.

"If you don't have time, I can call Gil to see if he'll take me."

"I'll take you." The knee-jerk response surprised him, but he didn't bother to ponder why. "We'll go tomorrow."

"Perfect. It's a date." Jocelyn breezed down the hall.

Troy watched her leave, not quite sure how she had manipulated him so easily. It wasn't a date, he assured himself. He was a guardian. He didn't date.

Not anymore. He went back into the living room, where Jocelyn now sat on the couch, the dog snuggled beside her and her laptop resting on her legs.

She glanced up, and her smile was instant. "I had forgotten how beautiful it was here. We should go for a hike later."

Warmth swelled inside him. Was it Jocelyn's infectious smile that gave him the unfamiliar sense of comfort? Or perhaps the novelty of having someone in his life who didn't want anything from him.

"Ty? What do you think?"

"I'd like that."

* * *

Walter watched the recorded debate for the fifth time. With each viewing, he hoped he would experience a different result. How had he let Shawn Hammels get to him? One question after another, Walter had responded as he had rehearsed, but Hammels had picked him apart, twisting his words, citing history to undermine the future he dreamed about, both for himself and for the United States.

Words spoken. Words unspoken. Both had combined to create catastrophic results. The twelve-point lead he had enjoyed yesterday had disappeared during the two-hour broadcast.

How had this happened? Hammels wasn't even supposed to be his main competitor in the primaries. Clearly, his staff had underestimated the man's charisma and wit, as well as his military background and obvious patriotism. As a result, Walter had been ill-equipped to deal with the subtle barbs.

Even when they had agreed on a point, Hammels had done so in a way that ingratiated him to the American public. The polls had proven that.

Anger, frustration, and an underlying streak of fear pulsed through Walter. This was his election. It had to be.

Zack appeared in his office doorway and knocked on the door jamb. He glanced at the television on the wall and held up a file. "I assume you already know the results of the debate last night."

"Where did Hammels come from? The governor of North Carolina? How is he even in the running?"

"No one thought he was," Zack said. "The only thing he had going for him was how he handled the evacuation before the hurricane last year and the cleanup afterward."

"I want a deep background check on this guy. There has to be something in his past that we can use to derail the all-American-boy image he has going."

"I already gave you our initial background on him. So far, he's exactly what he appears to be," Zack said. "Married seventeen years, goes to church every Sunday. No indication of any infidelity or illegal activities beyond a parking ticket in Raleigh, which he paid without argument."

"This is a nightmare."

"I'll have Cindy work up some talking points on emergency preparedness and response. A couple of visits to the local fire department or the Coast Guard might not be a bad idea either."

"Set it up, but I still want that deep dive into Hammels. Even if we can't find any dirt, we will at least be prepared for whatever platform he's going to throw at us next."

"Yes, Senator."

* * *

Light. Contrast. Focus. Filters. The skills learned in her photography classes were all coming back. Jocelyn clicked from one photo to the next, her professional eye contrasting the photos she had taken since her arrival to the professional images she normally sorted through for work. She wasn't there yet, but a few of her photos would at least catch her attention if they were being considered for an ad campaign.

She plucked an apple from the fruit bowl on the kitchen counter and took a bite. Maybe while she was here, she should take some interior photos too. She pushed that thought away. There would be plenty of time for that. She would wait for a bad-weather day to play inside.

She opened the next image and smiled. This was the kind of photo she was hoping for. Samson close to the camera, a stick in his mouth, the background of waves washing up on the beach blurred artistically.

"Take a thousand to find one gem," she said aloud.

"What?"

She turned her head to see Ty standing behind her. He had shed the sweater he'd been wearing earlier, his cotton thermal accenting his muscular chest and arms. Her stomach leapt, and a spurt of attraction shot through her. Where had that come from?

Sure, the man had a long, lean physique she had always been attracted to, and his face certainly wasn't hard on the eyes, but he still hadn't opened up about himself. And she wasn't accustomed to dating men she didn't know.

His eyebrows lifted, and she realized she was staring.

"I thought you were working," she said.

"I needed a break." He crossed to the refrigerator and opened it. After staring inside for a moment, he closed it again and moved to the counter opposite where she sat.

"What are you working on?" Ty asked. He selected an apple for himself.

"Looking through the photos I downloaded," Jocelyn said. "I hope you don't mind my working in here."

"It's not a problem." He motioned to her laptop. "Can I see?"

Jocelyn turned it sideways so both of them could see the screen. "This is my favorite so far."

"It's good. You should send that to Kristi. I know she's missing Samson."

"I'm surprised she didn't take him with her."

"She thought about it, but she didn't want him to be confined to a kennel when she's working over there. Besides, some countries in Europe have ridiculously long quarantine periods for dogs. It would have made it hard for her to travel."

"I envy her the chance to explore Europe. I've always wanted to do that."

"What's stopping you?" he asked. "You're selling your business. You could go spend a few months over there. I'm sure once Kristi gets back, she'll be able to recommend some good places to go."

What he said made sense. She certainly had the resources and the time to travel. "Maybe I could go visit her."

"I'm not sure you'll be able to do that."

"Why not?"

"She's doing some sensitive work over there. I'm not sure she'll even be able to tell you where she is most of the time."

"How do you know that?"

"I overheard her talking to someone she works with before she left."

Jocelyn tried not to regret the lack of contact between her and her sister over the past few years, but she couldn't quite keep the guilt from surfacing. "It's so weird that you seem to know more about my sister now than I do."

"She trusted me to watch after her place and her dog. She wasn't about to do that until she knew me."

An uncomfortable sensation worked through her, and Jocelyn faced the cause head on. "Did the two of you date?"

"Me and Kristi? No. Never."

"Just wondering."

He looked at the wall clock. "Looks like it's about time for you to start cooking that fish. Ready for a break?"

"Sure." While Jocelyn hoped she could figure out how to cook their dinner, she wasn't entirely sure she would have success in any area in the kitchen. She stood and walked to the sink.

"What are you doing?"

"Better safe than sorry." She retrieved the fire extinguisher from beneath the sink and set it on the counter. "I should probably tell you I'm not a very good cook."

"That's okay. I am." He retrieved the fish from the refrigerator. "Grab the big frying pan, and I'll show you how it's done."

Jocelyn fought back a smile trying to form. Finally, she had learned something about him. Was the wall surrounding Ty finally starting to chip away? She wondered how long it would take before he would let her know the man behind the shield.

* * *

Gavrie stood at the back of the restaurant and watched for an opening to perform his task. His failed attempt the previous morning still grated at him. He didn't know why Senator Whitmore had avoided his usual route, but Gavrie suspected someone had alerted him that he was in danger. The question was, How did he know?

It didn't matter. A waiter approached where he stood, and Gavrie slipped into the alcove where the restrooms were located. As soon as he was clear, he moved forward again so he could see the patrons coming and going.

An accidental death. It was going to happen one way or another. Tonight's tragedy would come in the form of a massive heart attack.

Dim lights, linen-covered tablecloths, muted music. The kitchen door opened, and the scent of cooked meat and roasted vegetables wafted toward him. The wait staff bustled from one table to another, taking orders and serving food.

The maitre'd showed a party of four to a table near the center of the restaurant. Finally, the man Gavrie had come to kill had arrived. His target pulled a chair out for his wife and waited for her and the other woman in his party to sit before joining them at the table. The moment the maitre'd handed them their menus, Gavrie walked out of the shadows. Dressed in black slacks and a white button-up shirt to match the rest of the wait staff, he retrieved a water pitcher from the waiters' station and approached the newcomers.

Without a word, he filled the glasses of the two women and then moved on to the man he didn't know. When he finished, he slipped a small plastic bag from his pocket and opened it. In one discrete motion, he emptied the white powder into the water pitcher and pocketed the bag. He then swirled the pitcher with a flick of his wrist and retrieved the presidential candidate's water glass.

The moment he set it down, the man picked it up. "Thank you."

Gavrie nodded and returned the way he had come. He was nearly to the restroom doors when the sound of a glass breaking reverberated over the sonata playing through the overhead speakers.

A woman's concerned voice, a call to 911, a man's plea in search of a doctor. Gavrie pushed the growing commotion from his mind and continued toward the back door, the water pitcher still in his hand.

CHAPTER 12

Jim popped the last bite of banana bread into his mouth and wondered what his chances were of sneaking another piece out of the kitchen. Today's batch of baked goods had been earmarked for some friends from church.

Katherine walked into his office, her face etched with concern. "Jim, did you hear about Shawn Hammels?"

"What about him?"

"He died of a heart attack last night."

"What?"

"He was having dinner with his wife and another couple in DC. Apparently, he was in town, preparing for the next debate." She held out her phone.

Jim took it and skimmed the article Katherine had displayed. "I can't believe this. His campaign really took off after the debate this week."

"I know. Some analysts thought he would take over as the front-runner by the end of the year."

"My campaign manager thought so too," Jim admitted. "Truth be told, if there was anyone I could stomach losing to, it would have been him. I don't always agree with his political views, but he was a good man."

"Yes, he was," Katherine agreed. "Would you like me to send some flowers?"

"I'd appreciate that. I'll reach out to his staff and see if there's anything we can do for the family."

"I'm sure your campaign manager can put you in touch with his people." Katherine paused and tilted her head.

"What?"

"Maybe you should go in for a physical."

"I went in six months ago. I'm fine."

"According to this article, so was Shawn Hammels," Katherine said. "He went on a three-mile run every morning."

"And he died of a heart attack?"

"That's what the article says."

A kernel of unease lodged inside him. "Honey, I'd better make a few calls." Jim handed her phone back. "Thanks for letting me know about this."

"You're welcome." She took a step toward the door. "I'll take care of the flowers now. Unless you want me to bring you another piece of banana bread first."

"I could take another piece of banana bread, but I'll come get it when I'm done." Jim retrieved his phone from his pocket. "I really love you, you know."

"Of that I have no doubt." Katherine left him alone and closed the door behind her.

Jim dialed the number for the guardian stationed in Virginia.

"Is there a problem?" Ghost asked.

"I'm not sure. Did you hear the news about Shawn Hammels?"

"Yes. My wife and I are looking at the data now," Ghost said. "According to the preliminary reports, it appears he died of natural causes."

"What if he didn't?" Jim asked.

"You're thinking like a guardian again," Ghost said. "I find it suspicious that he dies the day after his numbers in the polls put him at the top of his party."

"After the assassination attempt in Helsinki last month, I have to wonder if Royce is trying to eliminate his competition."

"I'll put a bug in the police chief's ear up there to treat this as a suspicious death."

"I appreciate it."

"You can show your appreciation by keeping yourself safe," Ghost said.

"You've been to my house. I don't think we can add much more security."

"Maybe not, but you need to take precautions. Vary your routes during your daily routines, go to church at a different time this Sunday, don't eat at any restaurants you've been to before."

"I can do that."

"I'll let you know when the autopsy report comes in," Ghost said.

"Thanks, Ghost. Give Renee my best."

"I will."

Jim hung up and pocketed the phone. An assassination attempt on one presidential candidate in October, and now one dead of a heart attack only a month later. What were the odds?

Jim pushed back from his desk and walked into the security office where the surveillance cameras for his property were housed. The live feed showed everything outside was exactly as expected. That didn't alleviate the unease his suspicions caused. Maybe it was time to put in a request for a secret service detail. No reason to take any chances.

* * *

Troy scoured through the research amassed on the guardian database about Walter Royce and Gavrie Morozov yet again. The possibility that they were working together had everyone on alert, but where was the assassin, and had Hammels been his target? If so, was he the only one? The secretary of state already had a security detail, but most of the other potential targets still didn't qualify for secret service protection.

The request had been submitted for Senator Whitmore and the other candidates, but Troy had no idea if and when it would be approved. At least Whitmore had enhanced security at his home, or so his colleagues told him.

An alarm popped up on his computer for the island surveillance feed. Troy opened it, expecting to see more deer. Instead, Samson bounded into view. He clicked out of the security screen and pushed back from his desk.

Needing a break after two hours in front of the computer, Troy left his office. The living room and kitchen were both empty, an oddity of late. With no one to talk to for the moment, he grabbed his coat and walked outside. He studied the bungalow, noting the chimney didn't have any smoke coming from it.

The wood supply was low for the little house, so he made his way to the shed. He topped off the fuel for the chain saw and headed toward the pond, where a couple of downed trees lay near the path. Troy fired up the chain saw and went to work. For the next half hour, he cut the trees into pieces small enough to carry back to the house. He wondered if there was a wheelbarrow somewhere.

He set the chain saw aside, and Samson rushed toward him with an excited yip. Footsteps on fallen leaves followed.

"Hey." Jocelyn stepped into view, her scarf wrapped around her neck, a watch cap on her head, and her cheeks rosy. "Do you need some help?"

"That would be great. Do you know if Kristi has a wheelbarrow?"

"I'll go get it."

"I'll come with you. I could use a break." Troy carried the chain saw in one hand and followed her down the path. "What have you been up to today?"

"I've been taking more pictures."

"Are you enjoying it as much as you hoped?"

Her face lit up. "More. It's so liberating to spend my days doing what I want, without worrying about who is behind schedule or what new client I need to meet with."

Her joy tugged at him and made him yearn for something unknown. "What do you want to do with your photography? Are you hoping to see your work in a gallery and try for your own show?"

"I don't know. I guess that's a possibility, but for now, I'm more interested in seeing my art used for other things."

"Like?"

"Ad campaigns, websites, maybe even a book cover." She shrugged. "The artistic thing is great, but I don't know that I want to spend my time trying to get people to know who I am."

"That's unusual for an artist."

"Oh, I don't know. A lot of artists prefer to keep to themselves, but they have to sell in order to make a living," Jocelyn said. "With the sale of my company, I'm fortunate to not need an income from my photos."

"Then there's nothing stopping you from making your dreams come true."

"I guess you're right."

"Maybe you can submit some of your photos to your company."

"That's an idea." Jocelyn ducked under a low branch. "What about you? What's your dream?"

"My dream?" Troy asked.

"Yeah. Everyone has one. You know, if you could change something in your life, what would it be? Or what is that one thing you've always wanted that you've never had?"

Family. The word came into his mind so clearly. Why he would desire that, of all things, he didn't know. He didn't know the first thing about what real families looked like, nor was he in the position to have one of his own.

"Well?" Jocelyn prompted.

"I don't know." Troy followed her into the yard.

"You'll have to give it some thought," Jocelyn said. "Everyone should have a dream."

"Maybe you're right."

* * *

Three nights in a row, Jocelyn had eaten dinner and watched a movie with Ty, and she still knew little about him. Last night, *The Blind Side* had been the movie of choice. For a guy who claimed to have not played sports in high school, he enjoyed watching them, or at least movies about them.

She had seen Ty only briefly this morning, when he'd fixed himself a cup of herbal tea while she had been making herself some hot chocolate. Their conversation had been little more than a cordial greeting before he had disappeared into the office. Jocelyn didn't know what he was working on, but whatever it was, she suspected he was working against a deadline.

How odd to think that deadlines were about to become a thing of the past for her. Other than one project she had agreed to do for free, she didn't have anything she had to do and nowhere she had to be.

Liberated by that thought, she put on her coat and walked outside. She gazed at the thick clouds in the distance and breathed in the crisp air that carried the scent of snow. Not sure if the storm would reach the island or not, she headed downstairs to the shed to get a bucket and a rake. Nothing like her grandma's clam chowder on a cold night.

She wondered if her sister had left the recipe written down somewhere.

The door to the house opened above her. Hoping for companionship, she turned and looked up.

"What are you doing?" Ty asked from the deck.

"I'm going to dig up some clams. Want to help?"

"Are you going to teach me how?"

"You don't know how to dig clams?" Jocelyn held up her rake. "Living on this island, that's a necessity."

Ty jogged down the stairs. "Lead the way."

"You'll need these." Jocelyn handed him the bucket and rake she held and walked back into the shed. She emerged a moment later, carrying an identical set of gear. Oddly pleased to have someone by her side, she started down the path. "Come on."

"You do like clams, don't you?" she asked when Ty fell into step beside her.

"Yeah. I pretty much like all seafood."

"That'll make your time here easier. When the storms come through in the winter, you won't have as much luck with lobster, but until around Christmas, you should have as much as you want if you keep the pot baited, though I haven't had any luck since I've been here."

"The pot?"

"The lobster pot." Jocelyn glanced sideways. "Didn't my sister show you anything before she left?"

"I only got here a couple days before she left for Europe. She mostly showed me around and gave me the scoop on how to work the electrical systems and how to operate the boat."

"That isn't your boat?"

"It belongs to a friend of mine, but he let me borrow it while he's on assignment this year."

"Nice friend."

"Yeah."

Jocelyn handed her rake to Ty. "Here. Hold this for a minute."

He took it, and she stepped onto a fallen tree that stretched out into the water. She used the tree like a balance beam and walked out far enough to scoop water into her bucket. Once she completed her task, she returned to Ty.

"Here. Trade me buckets."

He took the one she offered him and handed his to her. She repeated the process and returned back to his side.

"What's the water for?"

"It helps keep the clams alive while we harvest, and it helps clean out the sand."

"Now what?"

"Now we look for clams." Jocelyn proceeded to show Ty how to find them by looking for the little air bubbles in the sand.

She dug up three and moved a few feet down the beach.

"Hey, I found one." Like a little boy who had discovered buried treasure, he stood with his rake outstretched, a clam balancing on the end, and a delighted expression on his face.

Jocelyn couldn't help but grin. "That's great." She moved closer to examine his find. Her smile faded. Though she hated to squash his enthusiasm, she said, "I'm sorry. That one's too small. They need to be at least this big." Jocelyn held her fingers a couple inches apart. She pointed at a hole in the sand that was as big as her index finger. "Try over there."

Ty followed her instruction and dug in the sand. This time, he came up with a clam that was a good four inches long.

"That's a good one."

He dropped it into the bucket with a splash. "Now what?"

"Now we find a few dozen more."

"A few dozen?" he asked.

"Yeah. I was thinking about making clam chowder for dinner tonight."

His boyish excitement rose again. "New England clam chowder?"

"We are in New England." She grinned and pointed at his bucket. "If you want, we can make it a contest. See who can get the most."

"I think I'd be on the losing end of that one."

"Probably, but it can't hurt to try."

"What do I get if I win?"

"Clam chowder."

"And if I lose?" Ty asked.

"The same."

"You're on. I like my odds."
"I thought you would."

CHAPTER 13

Troy hadn't expected such a sense of satisfaction from harvesting his own food, but he had to admit he enjoyed gaining the new skill. Jocelyn had dug up nearly twice as many clams as he had, but between the two of them, they had managed to gather three dozen before the tide had risen over the clam bed.

"Come on." Jocelyn picked up her bucket and dumped half the water out.

"I thought you needed to keep the clams in water."

"Dump out any extra. It makes it easier to carry." Jocelyn started toward the main house.

"Are you going to teach me to make clam chowder too?"

"Assuming I can find the recipe."

"I thought you didn't cook."

"I don't usually, but this is one thing I've had a lot of practice with. My grandmother used to have me and Kristi help her every time she made chowder. Clam chowder, fish chowder, corn chowder. You name it." Jocelyn glanced at her watch. "Besides, it's still early enough for me to call Kristi if I need help."

"You say that like you expect her to pop over from Europe to help you make dinner."

"Hey, I can FaceTime with the best of them."

"Do you FaceTime with your sister a lot?"

"I used to, but the last few years have been kind of crazy for both of us, with her moving back here and me expanding my business," Jocelyn said. "Before I got here, I think the last time I FaceTimed Kristi was when we had that huge power outage."

"What huge power outage?" Troy asked.

"You must not have been in New England the first weekend in October if you're asking me that question," Jocelyn said.

"No, I wasn't."

"A major snow storm hit the entire region. Kristi called to check on me when she realized how widespread the power outages were."

"How widespread were they?"

"I was lucky. Most of Boston got their power back after a few hours. Maine and New Hampshire weren't as lucky. My parents didn't have power for two days."

"That's rough."

"Yeah, especially during a massive snow storm when it's freezing outside. At least they have a fireplace."

"When was this again?" Troy asked, his mind flipping back in time to the assassination attempt on the vice president in Helsinki.

"First weekend in October."

The same weekend of the attack in Helsinki. "Are you sure? That's awfully early for snow, especially a big storm."

"I know. That's why I remember it. No one thought it would be anything beyond rain." Jocelyn set her bucket down on the edge of the patio beside a water spigot. She turned the knob, but nothing happened. "Is the outside water already turned off?"

"Yeah. I think so."

"We'll use the sink in the laundry room, then."

They walked inside. Jocelyn dumped the remaining seawater from her bucket into the oversized sink, then filled the bucket again with fresh water and set it on the floor.

"Why are you putting the clams in fresh water?"

"It helps clean out the sand." She took Troy's bucket from him and repeated the process.

"How long do you leave them?"

"I'll change the water a couple more times, but they need to soak for at least three hours." She slipped past him and went into the kitchen, where she pulled a wooden box off the shelf beside the window.

Troy edged closer and looked inside. Index cards, scraps of paper, recipes that had been cut out of magazines. Jocelyn riffled through the papers. Delight illuminated her face when she pulled a worn piece of paper from the disorganized mess.

"Found it." She set it on the counter and smoothed it out.

The idea that Jocelyn knew her grandmother well enough to know where she kept her recipes and what this particular one looked like struck him. Did she have any idea how lucky she was to have that connection, those memories?

"I don't suppose you want to help me peel potatoes, do you?" she asked.

"Not particularly. Besides, you won't want to do that until it's time to cook them. You said the clams have to soak for a few hours."

"You have a point."

"I have some work to do, but if I get done early enough, I'll help you with dinner."

"Sounds good," Jocelyn said. "Maybe I'll go take some more photos outside."

"I'll see you later." Troy left her in the kitchen and went into the office. He closed the door and flipped the lock. Even though Jocelyn said she was going outside, he didn't trust that she wouldn't come back and barge into the office without knocking. That was something he couldn't let happen, not with what he wanted to accomplish today.

Spending time on the beach with Jocelyn had given him a much needed break, but now he had a job to do. He logged into the guardian database and checked the latest notes. As had been the case when he checked an hour ago, the search for Morozov continued. Kade and Renee were searching modes of transportation. Cas was utilizing her contacts for clues about the assassin's movements before he left Europe, and Ace was working with his wife to dig deeper into Senator Royce's financials.

Jocelyn's comment replayed in his mind, and he started a search of his own. The data popped up on the screen, and Troy leaned forward. The dates matched.

Jocelyn was right. The weekend of the attack in Helsinki had been the same weekend the power had gone out throughout much of the northeast.

Digging deeper, Troy pulled up the information on Walter Royce's cabin in New Hampshire and cross-referenced the address with the affected areas with power outages. Sure enough, the senator's second home had been without power for over thirty hours. Odd that he hadn't mentioned that during his interview after the attack in Helsinki. Supposedly he had been at his cabin the whole weekend.

Curious, Troy researched the senator's luxury cabin and the various upgrades to it over the years. Five bedrooms, five and a half baths on four acres. Two fireplaces, gas heating as well as a gas water heater and stove. Basic electric ran the rest of the utilities. Troy pulled up the satellite imagery of the house, half expecting to see solar panels on the roof. With the man making a run for the presidency, Troy thought he would have tapped into that resource for political reasons rather than to lower his energy costs.

Leaving the image of the senator's home on the screen, Troy opened a new tab. The rural area had only one main construction company, a company that thankfully kept detailed records of the work it did. New flooring last year, a renovated kitchen four years ago, the installation of a backup generator the year before that.

A generator. Troy let out a sigh. It would have been too easy if he could prove the senator hadn't known about the power outage or that it would have made his cabin uninhabitable during the weekend in question.

Despite the setback, Troy continued his search. He hacked into the senator's security system and pulled up the log for the days in question and read through it, then read it again. Odd. Even though the power at the senator's cabin had only been interrupted for less than a minute, the security system didn't show any activity during the entire weekend. The last log was of the door opening on Friday night at nine o'clock. Had the senator really been home the whole time, or was this proof that he had left on Friday and not returned until after the attack in Helsinki?

A new thought popped into Troy's head, and he started a new search, this time with the gas company. He accessed Royce's account and pulled up the daily activity.

Troy checked the data on his screen four times. He'd found it. Now he just had to find a way to get the proof he needed to stop Walter Royce once and for all.

* * *

Jocelyn slid the diced potatoes into the pot and brought the soup to a simmer. She hoped Ty was hungry. It wasn't until after she'd finished cooking the clams that she realized she should have cut the recipe in half. Too late now. They were going to be eating clam chowder for a few days.

She glanced toward the hall. Since returning from taking photos of the cottage, she hadn't seen or heard Ty. Either he was hard at work in the office or he wasn't here.

A piece of potato dropped to the floor, and Samson gobbled it up before she could stop him. "You shouldn't be eating that."

Samson looked up at her hopefully.

"Are you ready for your dinner?"

His tail wagged.

She stirred the soup and set her spoon aside. "Come on. Let's get you fed."

"Are you talking to me or the dog?" Ty asked from the doorway. "I hope you're talking to me because something smells amazing."

"I was talking to the dog, but don't worry. I'm going to feed you too."

"How long until it's ready?"

"About twenty minutes."

"I don't know if I can wait that long."

His words brought a smile to her face. How many times had a similar conversation played out in her mother's kitchen? "I'm afraid you don't have a choice, unless you like raw potatoes in your chowder."

"Not particularly." He glanced around the kitchen. "Do you need help with anything?"

She pointed at a bucket on the counter. "Would you mind taking the clam shells out and dumping them?"

"Dumping them where?"

"In the ocean."

"Why don't you throw them in the trash?"

"Because we have to haul our trash to the mainland," Jocelyn said. "Didn't my sister tell you about waste management here on the island?"

"She mentioned the compost pile, but throwing stuff away in the ocean is new to me."

"We only throw things in the ocean that came from it in the first place," Jocelyn said. "I usually dump the shells over the cliffs in front of the house. That way they don't all wash back up onto the beach."

Ty picked up the bucket. "I assume the bucket goes back in the shed."

"Yes."

"I'll be back in a minute."

By the time he returned, the dog was fed and the table was set, complete with the oyster crackers she loved to have with her chowder.

"Do you want me to make anything else to go with the soup?" Ty asked. "I can bake some of the fish we caught yesterday."

"This will be plenty for me, but go ahead if you want some."

He leaned closer to the pot so he could see inside. "Looks like there's more than enough to feed us both."

"I may be eating some for breakfast too."

"That's not a bad idea," Ty said. "Of course, if you catch a lobster, that would work too."

"I have some bad news about that," Jocelyn said.

"What?"

"I checked on the lobster pot when I went out to take pictures, and the bait was gone. I think there's a hole in the bottom of the trap."

"That's a bummer."

"Yeah. I told Kristi I would pick up a couple new traps when I go into town," she said. "How was your afternoon? Did you get all of your work done?"

"I made some progress, but it looks like I've got a lot of work to do tomorrow. Are you okay with waiting another day before I take you into town?"

"Yeah, that should be fine."

"Good. I should be able to take some time off on Wednesday afternoon." Troy leaned against the counter. "How was the rest of your day? Did you get some good photos?"

"I think so. I started editing a few of them."

"What was your latest target?" Ty asked.

"The bungalow." She stirred the soup, sampled a bite, and added some Old Bay seasoning. "It's hard to believe my ancestors built it over two hundred years ago."

"It's not often you hear about families staying on the same land for that long," Ty said. "It's like something out of a movie."

"Speaking of movies, did you want to watch one tonight? I found Grandpa's copy of *The Natural*."

"Sure."

"Do you like baseball as much as you like football?" Jocelyn asked.

"I don't think there's a sport I don't like."

"Even ice skating?"

"Even ice skating."

"It won't be long before the pond freezes over, and we'll be able to skate here on the island."

"I didn't bring skates with me."

"I'm sure Grandpa's are around here somewhere. If his don't fit you, we can always order some."

Ty jutted his chin in the direction of the chowder. "Has it been twenty minutes yet?"

Jocelyn poked a fork into a potato. "I don't know, but it's ready."

"Good because I'm starving. Let's eat."

CHAPTER 14

All morning, Troy juggled his research with his new duty of assigning the other guardians tasks based on the various needs around the world. A detained operative in Myanmar, a suspected terrorist in Niger, and the never-ending research into Walter Royce. Troy had handed his findings about the senator's cabin in New Hampshire to Kade in the hopes that the guardian in Virginia would be able to use his computer skills to track down a witness or anyone who could confirm their suspicions that Royce had really been in Europe during the weekend in question.

A door opened and closed, the sound followed by footsteps in the hall. Troy's gaze shifted from his computer to the office door. Despite her inherent curiosity, thus far, Jocelyn had respected his privacy when he was working. Then again, when he was researching, she was usually outside with her camera. He tried not to be jealous of her newfound freedom.

Determined to be useful despite his unexpected neighbor, Troy opened his research on Walter Royce. On paper, the man was the perfect presidential candidate. He had steadily made his way up the ranks, first as a state delegate and then as a congressman. His move to senator had accompanied the birth of his second child.

Beyond the security logs during the power outage and the senator's questionable gas bill, nothing indicated that the man had any ties to criminal dealings or the recent assassination attempt on the vice president of the United States. His questionable campaign finances were another matter.

An alert popped up on the message board about a possible source who could confirm Troy's suspicions. He was halfway through responding when his phone rang. Ace.

"Hey, what's up?" Troy asked.

"Did you see the message from Kade?"

"About the source in New Hampshire? Yeah."

"I need you to meet him tomorrow night," Ace said.

"When and where?"

"Oh two hundred. Wallis Sands Beach in Portsmouth," Ace said. "I'll put the coordinates in the database."

Troy calculated the time and distance in his head. Two hours to fly to Massachusetts, another two hours back. He wasn't going to get much sleep tomorrow.

"I need you to get him secured in a hotel and debrief him," Ace said.

"What intel does he have?"

"He claims to have proof that Walter Royce wasn't anywhere near his cabin in New Hampshire the weekend of the assassination attempt in Helsinki."

"That's huge. Especially if this guy can help us prove Royce was in Europe at the time of the attack." Adrenaline surged inside him. This could be it, the end of the tedious task of searching for clues to bring down the man they knew to be a traitor.

"Call me as soon as you get him secured. The minute we have proof Royce was involved, I want him in custody," Ace said. "I don't want him going after anyone else."

"Is there any way this guy can meet tonight? This is pretty time sensitive."

"Kade tried, but the guy insists he can't slip away until tomorrow."

"Too bad. Do all of the other presidential candidates have protection details?"

"The requests went in, but so far, the secret service isn't buying in to the credibility of the threats against them."

"Do we need to create a threat to get them moving?" Troy asked. It wouldn't be the first time the guardians had taken shots at targets they had no intention of hitting.

"I'll put the request in again. If we don't get a response by tomorrow night, we may have to put you and Kade in motion to get secret service to take us seriously," Ace said. "I'll talk to you tomorrow."

Troy hung up and did another quick check of the guardian message board. Ace, Kade, and their wives were all searching for Morozov and possible ties to Walter Royce. With a mission pending tomorrow, Troy opted for a different type of preparation. He closed down his computer and retrieved a coat from his room. Taking care to move soundlessly, he made his way to the door and slipped outside. Time to prepare the helicopter and make sure he was ready to do his preflight check in the dark tomorrow.

* * *

Senator Walter Royce walked out of the restaurant and approached his waiting car. His driver opened the rear door and waited for Walter to settle into his seat before closing him inside.

Walter glanced at the seat beside him, where a plain manila envelope lay.

"Brendan, where did this come from?"

"A woman stopped by and gave it to me. She said you were expecting this report, but she didn't want to interrupt your dinner."

Uneasy, Walter opened the clasp and slid two sheets of paper out of the envelope. His eyebrows furrowed. Why would someone give him a copy of the security report for his cabin in New Hampshire and a detailed bill for his utilities? He turned both pages over. A message had been scrawled on the back of the gas bill in familiar handwriting: *Vietnam Memorial. Tonight.*

The car started, and the driver merged into traffic.

Walter folded the paper and tucked it into his inside jacket pocket. "Brendan, I think I'm going to take a walk on the mall. Can you drop me off near the Lincoln? Northwest side."

"Of course, Senator."

A few minutes later, they circled between the Memorial Bridge and the Lincoln. When the car rolled to a stop, Walter unclipped his seat belt and opened the car door himself. "I don't know how long I'll be. Go ahead and go home. I can grab a cab."

"Are you sure, Senator?"

"I'm sure. See you in the morning."

"Yes, sir."

Walter started down the sidewalk toward Henry Bacon Drive. He took a moment to look over his shoulder at the massive white columns that made up the front of the Lincoln Memorial. Honest Abe. He had gone down in history as one of the great presidents. If Walter had his way, his name would someday be honored in similar fashion.

Yes, the Russians may have helped him get this far, but who better than he to bridge the mistrust that had existed between the two superpowers for decades? Bringing peace to this nation would be his legacy. By this time next year, the elections would be in full force. Not long after that, he would be making arrangements to move into the White House.

He let that surety settle into his thoughts. He *would* be president.

He slowed his pace when he approached the fluid black wall that made up the Vietnam Memorial. This time of night, it was nearly deserted, and only a few people stood along the brick path in front of it. The wind stung his face, the chill in the November air reminding him why most people chose to see the monuments during the daytime.

He reached the designated meeting place. His eyes instinctively went to the spot on the wall where his father's name was engraved. Walter had been only two years old when his father had died in the war. When he was three, his mother remarried, and his stepfather fulfilled the role of his second parent. He didn't emphasize that to the press, of course. Playing up his legacy served him better if the public saw him as the child who had lost a parent rather than a kid whose memories fell into the normal childhood category.

Someone stepped beside him. Without turning his head, Walter glanced over. Ilina Sokolova, the woman who tied him to Russia and the flow of money that kept his campaign afloat.

"Why am I here?" Walter asked in a low voice.

"Did you see what I sent you?" Ilina asked, her accent well disguised after years of living in the United States.

"Yes, but I don't understand why it's important."

"You didn't look at the date."

"No." Unease bloomed and grew inside him.

"Someone at your security service ran that report yesterday. It was of the activity at your cabin last month."

"So?"

"So it shows that the alarm was on the whole time you were in Europe."

"What does that matter?" Walter was certain Ilina had a point. He wished she would spell it out.

"Where do you keep your woodpile for your cabin?" she asked.

"Outside, under the back deck." Frustration rose within him. "Why all the questions?"

"The day of the attack in Helsinki, a storm came through New England. Your cabin was one of several thousand that lost power for several days."

"I have a generator that turns on automatically when that happens."

"Yes, and it powers the basics, but it doesn't turn your pilot light back on for your heating system," Ilina said. "Your gas bill shows that you didn't use any natural gas for three days. The security report proves you never opened a door during that time to get firewood or refuel the generator."

"That doesn't make sense. My emergency generator runs off natural gas."

"It must have a separate tank it runs off of because the bill didn't record any usage."

Despite the cold, perspiration beaded on Walter's brow. "No one would think to put those two things together. No one would even have access to both reports."

He glanced at the woman beside him again. "How did you even think to look at them?"

"Because I have alerts set up on all of your bills. Like I said, someone ran the security report yesterday. A short while later, you logged in and requested the detailed utility report."

"I didn't do that."

"I suspected as much, but someone logged in as you." She paused. "Who would know you weren't there that weekend?"

Walter thought over his carefully orchestrated alibi. He had flown to New Hampshire, gone to his cabin. He'd left his car and his personal cell phone at the cabin to make sure all electronic signatures would prove he was there. The storm had hidden the tracks from the old jeep he had used to leave his second home and drive to a private airfield where a chartered plane had been waiting.

"No one knew I wasn't there."

"A neighbor? A friend who could have seen your car and stopped by?" Ilina prompted. "Someone knows or at least suspects you weren't there."

"My neighbor. Alec Borgeau lives across the street, and he works for the security company." The pieces fell into place. "He's always outside playing with that stupid drone of his. If he saw my car and no smoke coming from the chimney, he might have stopped to check on me."

"You say he lives across the street from your cabin?"

"Yes."

"That's what I needed to know."

CHAPTER 15

Troy pushed away from his desk. Weeks of searching and he still hadn't found anything to tie Walter Royce to the Russians beyond his first senatorial campaign. He had to be missing something.

Eager to get his body moving and take a mental break, he headed for the refrigerator and the leftover clam chowder Jocelyn had made last night.

Jocelyn. He hadn't heard from her at all today. He knew she had spent at least some time working on her computer because alerts had gone off when she had sent emails to her company. Those alerts had given him a much-needed break from his regular work, but it hadn't taken long for him to clear the content and attached photos so he could push them out of his dummy server and send them on their way.

The cadence of words being spoken carried to him before he reached the kitchen, the mumbling becoming recognizable as he drew closer.

"If I move this here, that should work."

Troy reached the doorway. Jocelyn sat at the counter, her laptop in front of her, a notepad at her elbow, and a scatter of papers beside her.

She didn't acknowledge his presence, and Troy suspected her concentration had blocked out everything beyond what was on her screen.

"Oh, I like that," Jocelyn said.

Troy's lips quirked up, and some of his stress melted away. "Talking to yourself again?"

Jocelyn finished typing something before she glanced over her shoulder. "I'm sorry. Did you say something?"

"I said you're talking to yourself again."

"I was?" A crinkle appeared on her normally smooth brow. "Sorry. I never notice when I do that."

His original purpose forgotten, Troy looked over her shoulder at her computer screen. "What are you working on?"

"Just playing with a couple ideas."

"This looks like an ad campaign, not photos."

"I know. Angela emailed and asked me to look at this."

"Who is Angela?" Troy asked.

"She's my CFO. Or rather, she was. She's replacing me as CEO," Jocelyn said. "The final presentation on this campaign is tomorrow, but something was off."

"And you figured out what it was."

"Yeah. It just needed a couple of tweaks."

"Are you finding it harder to step away from your business than you thought?" Troy asked.

"In some ways. I think once Angela hires a new CFO to take her place, things will settle down. She has the ability, but she needs to learn to trust herself." Jocelyn waved at her computer screen. "She could have figured this out, but I think she was too overwhelmed handling both her job and mine to see through the stress."

"It can't be easy following in your footsteps," Troy said. "You never look stressed."

"Looks can be deceiving."

An alert buzzed on Troy's phone. He pulled it out of his pocket to see a proximity alarm had triggered near the point of the island. He headed for the back door.

"Where are you going?" Jocelyn asked.

"Someone's coming."

She followed him to the door. "How can you tell?"

"Your sister added extra security to the island after the incident last year." Troy didn't mention that the motion detectors covered much of the uninhabited part of the island to protect from someone entering from the areas not visible from the house.

He plucked his coat off the rack by the door and walked outside, not surprised when Jocelyn followed.

"It's just Gil." She stepped beside him on the deck and shrugged her coat on.

"What's he doing here?" Troy asked. "I said I would take you into town this afternoon."

"I'm afraid he isn't taking the hint that I'm not interested in him," Jocelyn said. "He texted me a half dozen times yesterday."

Gil maneuvered his boat to the dock and jumped out to secure it.

"Might want to give him a better clue," Troy said as irritation and a sense of invasion bubbled inside him. "I really can't have neighbors showing up all the time."

"You and my sister never dated, right?"

"I already told you we didn't. Why?"

"Because this would be awkward if you had."

Before Troy could process her intent, Jocelyn pushed up onto her toes and pressed her lips to his.

A jolt shot through him, an electricity he'd never experienced before. His hands lifted to grip her arms, but he wasn't sure if it was to pull her closer or push her away.

When she broke the kiss, she looked more surprised than he was.

"What was that for?" Troy asked.

"If Gil thinks we're together, he'll stop coming by." Jocelyn's head tilted slightly. "You could help chase him off by making it look believable."

Troy caught the glint of challenge in her eyes. The connection between them overrode logic, and he drew her closer. "You want believable, huh?" He lifted a hand to cup the back of her neck, his fingers teasing the silky strands of her hair.

Her eyes darkened, and she drew a quick, unsteady breath.

Amused by her reaction, he drew her closer until their lips were only a breath apart. "I think we can convince him."

The years of working as a guardian, the endless months of avoiding relationships melted away. He waited until her breath shuddered out before he closed the distance between them.

Her lips were even softer than he'd imagined, her sweetness unlike anyone he had ever known. A connection stretched out, enveloped them both, and clicked into place.

Seagulls cried in the distance. Waves washed over the land. Troy's phone vibrated in his pocket. Everything faded into a fog until all he could think about was Jocelyn.

His fingers tightened on her neck, kneading there until her muscles relaxed, and she leaned closer still. He caressed the side of her neck, his fingers trailing along the softness of her jaw. He kissed her again, losing himself in the heady sensation of holding a woman close. And not just any woman. As much as he didn't want to admit it, he'd already come to admire Jocelyn. Her quick wit, her dry humor, her intelligence.

When he drew away, her eyes fluttered open, dazed and disoriented. He understood both sensations. The world wasn't quite steady under his feet either.

He was living in a fantasy world, one that included a beautiful, unattainable princess who could make him forget about the trials of real life. But he couldn't have a real life. He had been broken long before he'd become a guardian. He didn't know anything about the life normal people lived, and Jocelyn deserved more than normal. She deserved exceptional. Even as that thought struck him, he leaned down to give her one last kiss.

A few seconds passed before he remembered their audience and managed to find his voice. "I think that should do it."

Her confusion deepened. "Do what?"

"Convince your friend to stop coming by unannounced." Even as regret took hold, Troy took a step toward the door. "I'll let you get rid of him. I'll be inside."

Not waiting to see if their intended audience was still on the dock, Troy walked inside and willed his heartbeat to steady. From the moment he met Jocelyn, he suspected she would be trouble. Little had he known she had the ability to turn his entire world upside down. The woman was downright lethal.

* * *

Jocelyn took a moment to gather her senses. Her idea to use Ty as a deterrent for Gil's interest had been a good one, but she hadn't expected an instant attraction to fill her the moment she kissed him. Her cheeks warmed when she thought of being in his arms, of the sensation of having him hold her close.

It's just been too long since I've been in a relationship, she told herself. That must be why she had experienced that unexpected connection. Sure, Ty was good-looking, but she had gone out with attractive men before. Not once had any of their good-night kisses created that lightning-bolt effect.

A boat bumped against the dock and reminded Jocelyn she had an objective to accomplish. She walked down the steps and crossed the yard to the dock. Gil stood beside his boat, his weight shifting from one foot to the other.

"I didn't expect to see you today," Jocelyn said.

"I . . . You . . ." He swallowed and started again. "I heard you had a package at the post office and thought you might need a ride to go get it."

"How did you hear that?"

"My cousin works there. She saw a package addressed to your sister's P.O. box and asked if I knew if anyone was picking up her mail."

"Thanks for checking on me, but my boyfriend is going to take me into town this afternoon."

"Oh." He glanced at the deck where Jocelyn and Ty had been standing and hastily looked away. "I didn't realize you were dating anyone."

"Yeah." She put her hand on his arm in an effort to ease the blow. "Thanks for stopping by though and for letting me know my package arrived."

"No problem." He took a step back. "I guess I'll see you later."

Jocelyn nodded. "Maybe I'll see you in town."

"Yeah. Maybe." He untied his boat and stepped back on board. A moment later, the engine started.

When Gil looked at her, she waved. He gave her a halfhearted nod and then turned his attention to the water in front of him.

Jocelyn watched him until he reached the open water. Poor guy. He was nice enough, but their brief boat ride together had already proven he was not her type. She liked to travel and explore new things. Gil had never left New England, and she suspected he preferred the slow, easy cadence of life in Maine. As much as she was enjoying some downtime, she wouldn't ever be content to stay still for long, not unless there was something challenging her in her everyday life.

She made her way inside, where Ty was standing by the fire. Her stomach fluttered at the mere sight of him. This wasn't good. She had come to Heritage Island to simplify her life, not complicate it.

Determined to dispel any awkwardness between them, she shrugged out of her coat and crossed to him. "Hey, I'm sorry if I made things awkward," she said. "Gil wasn't going to stop coming around unless he thought I was involved with someone else."

"It's no big deal."

No big deal? Ty's kiss had knocked her completely off-balance, and he was standing here pretending like it hadn't affected him. She wasn't buying it. What was going through his mind? What was he feeling?

Jocelyn swallowed those questions and asked another. "What time did you want to go into town? The post office closes at four thirty."

He looked at the clock on the wall. "We can go now if you want."

"Yeah. I'd like to get that errand taken care of as soon as possible."

"I'll get the key to the boat."

Jocelyn watched him disappear down the hall, and a hollow sensation settled in her stomach. "No big deal," she muttered under her breath, unable to fight the stabbing frustration that pierced through her. She didn't believe the attraction she'd experienced was one-sided, but he was clearly holding his emotions in check. Or perhaps he was someone who treated all relationships as inconsequential. She hoped that wasn't the case, because she doubted she would be able to look at him quite the same way again.

CHAPTER 16

The village was even smaller than Troy had imagined. He'd managed to make it past the harbormaster with a nod of the head, but already, two townspeople had greeted Jocelyn with a wave and a cursory hello.

"How do you know so many people?" Troy asked as they continued up Main Street.

"I don't, but I'm sure word has already gotten around that I'm Kristi's sister."

"Word doesn't have to get around for people to know that," Troy said. "You two look a lot alike."

She kept her eyes on the sidewalk in front of her. "I guess."

"Is something wrong?" Troy asked when she let the conversation drop.

She didn't answer. Now that he thought about it, Jocelyn hadn't said much of anything since they'd left the house. Their kiss flooded his mind. He rubbed his lips together and tried not to think about what it was like to hold Jocelyn close. He needed to keep things uncomplicated between them. Work gave him enough challenges without trying to juggle a relationship with someone who didn't have clearance to know who he really was.

When they talked after Gil left, he thought they were good, but now he wondered if he had misread the signals.

They reached the post office.

"I'll wait out here," he said.

"Fine."

He reached for the door to open it, but Jocelyn beat him to it. The short answers, the lack of eye contact. Yeah, she was annoyed at something.

The woman behind the counter greeted Jocelyn with enough volume that her voice carried to Troy, even though the door was closed between them.

"Where's your boyfriend?" the woman asked. "I heard you were seeing the fellow your sister has looking after things on her island."

Jocelyn must have responded because the woman paused for a moment.

"You bring him in with you next time so we can meet him."

Another pause.

The conversation switched to small talk about Kristi and Heritage Island. Down the street, a woman walked out of the bakery, juggling a pastry box in one hand and pushing a stroller with the other. A baby fussed from inside the stroller, and a little boy who couldn't have been more than three walked beside his mother, a ball in his hands.

Troy turned away from the young family to keep his face hidden. With any luck, they would walk away from him.

"Mommy! Get the ball!" a little voice demanded.

"Wait here. I'll get it."

Troy glanced back at the woman long enough to assess the situation. The boy had dropped his ball, and it had bounced into the street. In the distance, a car door slammed and an engine started.

The woman engaged the brakes on the stroller and said something to the little boy.

The post office door opened, and the postal worker's voice spilled out. "You're welcome. You enjoy the rest of your day."

Troy grabbed the handle to hold it open for Jocelyn. She emerged holding a good-sized box.

"I can carry that for you," Troy said, but before he could reach for it, he assessed the scene down the street once more: The bright red ball in the middle of the street. The young mother stepping off the curb. The sound of a car picking up speed.

Troy reacted. "Watch out!" He sprinted forward and grabbed the woman around the waist just as the car whipped around the corner.

The woman screamed. Jocelyn cried out.

Troy pulled the woman back to the curb a fraction of a second before the driver hit the brakes and skidded past them.

Troy steadied the woman before he released her. "Are you hurt?"

She didn't respond other than to stare at him and gasp for air.

Jocelyn appeared beside him, her arms now empty. She put a hand on the little boy to keep him on the sidewalk.

The driver had come to a stop and was rushing toward them. "I'm so sorry. I didn't see her there."

"I'm okay," the woman finally managed to say. She checked on her children, and her eyes filled with tears before she spoke to Troy. "Thank you. If you hadn't been here . . ."

"I'm glad you're okay." Troy gave her arm a squeeze, then glanced at the box Jocelyn had put down on the sidewalk by the post office. He walked the few steps to retrieve it and asked Jocelyn, "Are you ready to go?"

She spoke to the woman instead of answering him. "Are you sure you don't need help?"

"Yes." She took a deep breath. "Thank you."

"You're welcome." Jocelyn smiled at her then held out her hands to take the box from Troy.

"I've got it," Troy said. Remembering that Jocelyn had mentioned stopping by the store, he added, "I'll put this on the boat while you take care of whatever else you need to get while we're here."

Eager to put some distance between himself and the small crowd forming, he headed for the harbor and hoped today's incident would quickly fade from memory.

* * *

Jocelyn's preconceived idea of shopping with Ty and maybe popping into the diner for a meal dissolved. She watched his retreating figure for a moment before she turned her attention back to the woman who had nearly been run down by the car.

The driver, a post office worker, and the two old guys who had been playing chess outside the barber shop now crowded the sidewalk. Seeing that the townspeople were tending to the young mother and her children, Jocelyn excused herself and made her way to the general store.

The scene from moments before replayed in her mind. She didn't know Ty could move that fast. Thank goodness he had, or those two little kids might not have a mother anymore. Jocelyn shuddered at the thought.

With some effort, she forced herself to focus on her reason for being here. She found a surge protector and then made her way to the section where fishing equipment lined one wall. In the corner, a dozen lobster traps were stacked nearly to the ceiling. She was debating whether she could carry two lobster pots by herself when someone called her name.

"Hey, Jocelyn."

She turned. Gil stood directly behind her.

"Hi, Gil. I should have expected to see you here."

"It's a small town." He stuffed both hands into his pockets. "Did you already pick up your mail?"

"Yeah, thanks." She tried to pick up a lobster trap with one hand, but it was too heavy.

"Do you need some help with that?"

"I don't want to pull you away from your errands."

"It's no problem." Gil took the trap from her. "How many do you need?"

"Two, but I can make two trips. It's fine."

"I'm heading to my boat anyway." Gil reached for a second trap.

Jocelyn took it from him. "I can take one of them."

"I'll carry this up to the front for you," Gil said. "Give me a minute to grab what I came for, and I'll carry this down to the harbor for you."

"Thanks. I really appreciate it."

He nodded and proceeded to take the trap to the currently unoccupied checkout counter. "Be right back." Gil disappeared down a nearby aisle.

A display of work gloves caught her attention. She set down the trap and browsed through them. She selected a pair in her size and a second that she thought would fit Ty. With any luck, they would need gloves once they got the new traps laid. It had been too long since she'd had a good lobster dinner.

A man in his fifties approached from the opposite side of the store. "Are you ready to check out?"

"Yes. Thank you."

He stepped behind the counter. "You must be Kristi's sister."

"I am."

"I heard you were in town. It's Jocelyn, right?"

"That's right."

"Next time you talk to your sister, tell her Ned said hello."

"I'll do that." She paid for her purchases and tucked the surge protector and the gloves into her purse to make them easier to carry.

Gil approached and held up an extension cord. "This is your last hundred-footer back there."

"Thanks. I'll get some more ordered."

Gil completed his purchase, set his new extension cord on top of the lobster pot, and picked them up. "Take it easy, Ned."

"You too."

As soon as they were outside, an icy gust of wind whipped through Jocelyn's hair and stole her breath.

"Smells like snow is coming," Gil said.

"It's a good thing we both came into town today, then."

They walked in silence for two blocks. "What's the story with your boyfriend? Have you been together long?"

"A while." Jocelyn tried to believe "a while" could be applied to a few hours. She exaggerated further when she added, "I like how things are going."

"He's a lucky guy."

"That's sweet of you to say." They reached the harbor. "I appreciate your help."

"Happy to do it. What slip are you in?"

"The boat's over there." Jocelyn pointed. She caught a glimpse of movement that was so brief she wasn't sure what had caused it.

They carried the lobster pots to the side of the boat. When she didn't see Ty anywhere, she called out, "Ty? Are you here?"

No response.

"He must have gone to the store," she said. "You can set that on the dock. He can help me load it later."

"That's okay. I don't mind." He stepped toward the boat only to stop when the hatch opened.

Ty emerged from below deck, his appraising gaze meeting Gil's before he turned his attention toward her. "Hey, hon. I thought I heard your voice."

Hon? The oddity of hearing Ty refer to her with an endearment caught her off guard and brought with it new hope. She swallowed. "Ty, I don't think you've met Gil. He helped me carry the lobster pots down from the store."

"Sorry." Ty reached out and took the one she was carrying. "I didn't realize you were getting two, or I would have stayed to help you."

With the way he had rushed away earlier, Jocelyn wasn't sure that was true.

Ty set the first trap down and reached for the second one. "Thanks for your help." Ty secured the pots. "Jocelyn, are you ready to go?"

"I am, unless you want to stop by the diner for something to eat."

"No, I'd rather get back. Besides, we have that fish we still haven't cooked up." Ty offered his hand, and she took it before climbing aboard.

"Gil, thanks again for your help," she said.

He nodded. "See you later."

Jocelyn waited for him to leave before she turned to Ty. "Why did you rush off like that?"

"I don't like crowds."

"This town isn't big enough to form a crowd."

"It looked big enough to me." He tossed her a life jacket. "Weather is moving in. Let's get home."

Jocelyn slipped the life jacket over her head. Home. She wondered how long it would take her to figure out exactly where that was.

CHAPTER 17

Troy fastened his life jacket and stared at the man walking away. What had Jocelyn been thinking bringing Gil to the boat? Troy's jaw clenched. Their kiss this morning was supposed to have chased him away.

It was bad enough that he couldn't get that kiss out of his head. The last thing he needed was for Gil to get his hopes up again and open Troy up to making more memories with Jocelyn, moments together that would stir up feelings best left buried.

Jocelyn made him yearn for what he couldn't have: a normal life, a woman to share his future, a family. He had given up on those things when he had faked his own death. His fate was sealed. For Jocelyn, the opportunities were endless. As much as he enjoyed spending time with her, someday, their time together would end.

That thought had barely formed when Gil stopped to talk to an older man and glanced in his direction.

A twinge of irritation crept through Troy. Or was it jealousy? Whatever it was churning inside him, it was time to get rid of that guy once and for all.

Jocelyn stepped beside him. "Are you ready?"

Rather than move to the helm, Troy slid his arm around her waist. Her eyes went wide. He leaned closer and whispered, "Don't look now, but we have an audience." Jocelyn started to turn her head, but Troy stopped the movement by putting his hand on the back of her neck. "I said don't look now."

Her gaze lifted to his and held. The breeze tugged at her hair. Whether Gil was still watching, Troy didn't know nor did he care. He leaned down and brushed a kiss across her lips. It was the same as before—the instant connection, the softness of her skin beneath his touch, the little sigh that escaped her.

The bright afternoon sun, the smell of fish that permeated the village, the sting of the wind against his cheeks. Everything faded away except the softness of her lips and the sizzle of attraction.

This was an act, he reminded himself. He didn't need to confuse things between them. That thought came and went, but he only drew Jocelyn closer.

Her arms wrapped around his neck, her fingers skimming across the exposed skin above his sweater. A shudder worked through him, and he grasped at the thought that told him this wasn't right. It wasn't right, but it was perfect at the same time. He ignored the thought for a minute more before he pulled away and slid his hands down her arms and released her.

"We should get back to the island." Troy cast off and started the boat.

Jocelyn waited until he navigated out of the harbor before she spoke. "You called the island home a few minutes ago."

"That was a slip of the tongue. It isn't my home. It's your sister's."

"But it's yours for now."

Troy cast her a sideways glance but didn't respond.

"Where was home before you came here?" Jocelyn asked.

"Nowhere really."

"Tell me one place you lived."

"Why?"

"Why not?" she countered.

Because he couldn't tell her. She wasn't cleared. She didn't even know she needed a security clearance to know where he'd lived or why he needed to keep his past private or even why she couldn't call him by his real name.

"I know you've lived in Europe."

Surprise flashed, along with his wariness. "How do you know that?"

"I can tell by your voice. You have an accent."

"No, I don't." Even as he spoke the words, he heard the slight cadence that had become so familiar during his years in Scandinavia. "Okay, maybe I have a little bit of an accent."

"So you did live in Europe."

"Yes."

"Where else?"

"Maine."

Her head tilted, and Troy could almost see the wheels turning in her head. Jocelyn might not be the best interrogator, but he couldn't fault her determination.

"You're impossible. You know that?"

"Yeah." He increased speed. "I do know how to cook though."

"Good, because I had planned to eat at the diner so I could avoid that particular chore tonight."

"We still have leftover clam chowder."

"Yeah, but I had that for breakfast. I need some variety."

"I'll bake the halibut. I might even make some potatoes."

"Sounds good." She fell silent for a moment, but Troy wasn't surprised when the questions started again.

"Since you won't tell me where you're from, will you at least tell me where you learned to cook?"

"Europe."

"You're such a fountain of information."

His lips twitched into a half smile. "I try."

* * *

Jocelyn tossed and turned beneath the heavy down comforter. No matter how many times she tried to clear her mind and fall asleep, the events of the day wouldn't stop repeating over and over in her head.

Kissing Ty should have been nothing more than a simple ploy to keep Gil from stopping by unannounced. So much for simple. Her lips were still tingling from the last time he kissed her, and that had been hours ago. She looked at the clock and rolled onto her back. Almost midnight. She had followed Ty's lead and gone to bed early tonight. She wondered if he was sleeping any better than she was.

A rumble sounded, and the bungalow shook. She sat up in bed. The storm that hit earlier had dissipated within an hour. Had the wind kicked up again?

Unsettled, she pushed her covers off and grabbed a robe to ward off the chill, then moved to her window as the sound increased before fading. She caught a glimpse of light before she recognized the retreating source of the sound. A helicopter. What was a helicopter doing around here at this time of night?

Deciding she wasn't going to sleep anytime soon, she belted her robe and made her way into the kitchen, where she poured herself a glass of water and wondered if Ty had woken up too. She stared out the window at the main house, but it remained dark.

She set her glass aside and turned off the light. It was time she stopped letting Ty invade her thoughts. If he could sleep despite the connection they had shared, so could she.

* * *

Troy made his approach to the meeting spot from over the Atlantic. Though the beach was closed for the night, so no one was on it, residential homes surrounded the parking lot. The last thing he needed was a crowd forming to figure out why a Coast Guard helicopter had landed in their neighborhood in the middle of the night.

He flipped on the spotlight to illuminate the terrain below. A sandy beach, a building of some kind, and a large, empty parking lot beyond the structure. Make that an almost empty parking lot. A pickup truck was parked on the far edge beside a grassy field and some picnic tables.

From above and in the dark, he couldn't make out the color, much less the make and model, but the information Kade had given him had indicated his contact would be driving a vehicle consistent with what he saw below.

Troy circled the parking lot to ensure they didn't have any unwanted visitors. No other nearby vehicles, except for a snowplow parked at the corner of the adjoining neighborhood and an assortment of other cars and trucks parked in front of the nearby houses. Troy angled the helicopter so the spotlight illuminated the building and the beach, then lowered altitude until the skids bumped against the pavement.

In the wash of light, he could see into the truck. Empty. The surrounding area remained still, as did the building in front of him. Signs for men's and women's restrooms were painted on the outside wall of the one-level concrete structure.

Troy waited for a moment, hoping his contact would approach upon his landing. No such luck. After a couple minutes passed without any sign of movement, Troy shut down the engines. Time to find the man who might very well be able to end Walter Royce's deception as well as his run for the White House.

Troy removed his helmet and secured the aircraft. Though his instinct was to draw his gun for protection against the unknown, he didn't want to scare off his potential source.

He skirted along the wash of light and approached the truck. "Alec?"

No response.

Troy reached the vehicle and put his hand on the hood. Still warm.

"Alec?" he called again.

When he was again met with silence, he circled the truck. He reached the tailgate, and a low voice called out. "Who are you?"

"Ghost. Are you Alec Borgeau?"

"Yes." A man stepped out of the darkness of the beach. Troy could barely make out a few benches on the edge of the sand, all angled to face the water.

"I understand you have information."

"Yes, but first we have to go somewhere safe."

"That's what I'm here for. To ensure your safety." Troy tilted his head toward the chopper. "Come on. Let's get out of here."

"I need to get my bag."

"Is this your truck?"

Alec stopped midstride. "Who are you really?"

"I told you. I'm Ghost."

"The man I talked to told me to rent a car so I couldn't be tracked through my GPS."

"That was my associate," Troy said. He should have known Kade would have taken such precautions, but during his years in Europe, a car rental was rarely a first choice for transportation.

"You can trust me." Troy stepped forward.

Alec jerked back as a gunshot rang out followed by a second.

"Get down!" Troy dove forward and tackled Alec to the ground.

"Get off me!" Alec pushed at Troy to break free.

"Stay down," Troy demanded even as Alec's elbow connected with his ribs. "Someone is shooting at you."

"Shooting at me?" Alec's eyes widened.

Troy grabbed the back of Alec's coat and pulled him behind the truck. Ignoring the throbbing in his side, he drew his weapon and pressed against the vehicle. He peeked around the back of the truck for a split second. No sign of the gunman.

Troy hadn't managed to pinpoint the shooter's location, but from the general direction of the sound, he was sure whoever was on the other end of the gun had to be hiding by the bathhouse. Unfortunately, with the helicopter parked only a hundred feet from the building, getting to their ride wasn't going to be easy.

Troy had been out in the open when he had approached Alec. It hadn't been until Alec came into view that the shooter had opened fire. No doubt about it. His source was the target.

"Do you have your cell phone with you?"

"No. I left it at home."

"What about an exercise tracker? Or an Apple watch?"

"No."

"Have you used any credit cards tonight?"

"I had to use a credit card for my rental car."

"That must be it," Troy said.

"You think someone followed the GPS on my rental car?" Alec asked. "How would anyone even know to look for that?"

"Someone was either following you or they were monitoring your credit card."

"What are we going to do now?"

"I'm going to get you out of here," Troy said. "Trust me."

CHAPTER 18

Jocelyn startled awake, the ad copy for the Boys and Girls Club vivid in her mind. Why was it always in that brief transition between consciousness and sleep that ideas formed with such clarity?

Bleary-eyed, she checked the time. Three fifteen in the morning. She rolled onto her back and tried to convince herself that she could go back to sleep and that she would remember her idea when she woke up in the morning. She knew better. How many times had she found the solution to a problem only to fight the entire next day to solve it a second time?

Too bad she hadn't also received revelation on what to do about her sister's handsome house sitter and the distracting effect he had on her.

She flipped on the bedside lamp and squinted against the sudden brightness. "I swear, I'm not going to get any sleep tonight."

Keeping most of her body beneath the covers, she rolled onto her stomach and stretched out her hand so she could retrieve her laptop from where it was charging on the floor. Using her lap for a desk and two pillows against the headboard to protect her back, she opened the correct file.

A few notes and a new background photo brought her inspiration to life. She could easily see how the graphics could be modified for her client's web page, brochures, posters, and any number of other marketing tools. Her instinct to share her idea with someone surfaced, and it took her a moment to realize that she no longer had a staff to run things by, nor was anyone on this continent awake at this unreasonable hour.

A smile escaped almost instantly. Her sister wasn't on this continent. She did the mental math. Five hours ahead would make it eight fifteen in London. No way her sister wasn't up by now.

She grabbed her phone and hit the button on her favorites list to FaceTime Kristi. No answer. Jocelyn was debating calling again when her phone rang. She hit a button on her phone, and her sister's face filled her screen.

"Hey, sorry I missed your call," Kristi said. "Is everything okay?"

"Yeah. I couldn't sleep and wanted to talk to someone."

"You got an idea for a campaign again, didn't you?"

"Maybe." Jocelyn pulled her computer closer. "Tell me what you think."

Jocelyn flipped the screen on her phone toward her laptop so Kristi could see her work in progress.

"I like it. It reminds me of your old work, when you first started," Kristi said. "Fun, fresh, different."

"Thanks." Jocelyn flipped the phone back to face her. "I didn't realize how much I missed creating until I started working on this one. It's been too long."

"Are you having second thoughts about selling your company?"

Jocelyn let that thought mull through her mind for a moment. "No. It's time for something new."

"Have you decided what that something new is?"

"Not exactly. It's only been a week since I agreed to sell. It'll take time to plan for what comes next."

"That has to be driving you crazy. You love to plan."

"No, I don't."

"Are you kidding me?" Kristi asked. "Not that I want to give you a swelled head or anything, but you're one of the most organized people I know."

"You must be confusing me with someone else," Jocelyn said. "I like to go with the flow. Me, my camera, and nothing but a blank canvas."

"When you're taking pictures, that's true, but the rest of the time, you like to organize everything, including your life and everyone else's around you."

Jocelyn couldn't deny that for most of her adult life, she had spent far too many hours arranging her calendar and juggling obligations. Rarely did relationships make the calendar, family or romantic. "Maybe that's one of the things I need to change."

"Maybe so."

"Since I'm awake anyway, tell me how you like Europe so far. Is it fabulous?"

"I love it. It's everything I hoped it would be." Kristi's face glowed with contentment. "How are you doing? Are you and Ty getting along okay?"

"Yeah, but he doesn't talk about himself at all. It's so frustrating."

"He's a pretty private guy," Kristi said.

"I guess, but for someone who spends his days working on a computer, you'd think he'd want some adventure in his life."

Kristi chuckled. "I'm sure living on the island with you is all the adventure he needs."

* * *

Troy opened the driver's side door, gripped his pistol, and studied the building across from him. Where would he hide if he were the one targeting them? The lights on the exterior of the building would reveal anyone hiding at the front of the building, which left the back corner. Unfortunately, if Troy was right, the gunman had a clear line of sight if they made a run for the helicopter or if they tried to get into the truck.

"Give me the key to the truck."

"It's keyless. The fob is in the cupholder."

"Good. As soon as I tell you, get in the truck on the driver's side," Troy said. "Keep your head down."

"Are you sure about this?" Alec asked.

"Trust me," Troy said, even though he wasn't sure he trusted himself. "Are you ready?"

"I'm ready."

"Now!" Troy squeezed off three shots, and Alec scrambled into the truck.

Another shot rang out, a flash of light accompanying the sound.

"Move over," Troy commanded. He fired off two more shots, scrambled into the driver's seat, and closed the door behind him.

A bullet crashed through the back window, shattering glass.

Troy started the car. He rolled down the driver's side window, squeezed off two shots, and gunned the engine.

"What are you doing? You're driving toward the shooter."

"I'm driving to the helicopter," Troy corrected. He ducked when bullets impacted the hood. His gun now gripped in his left hand, he returned fire.

He slammed on the brakes as soon as he reached the spot between the bathhouse and the chopper, the front of the truck facing the helicopter, leaving the back to protect them from gunfire. "Stay down. As soon as I open the door to the chopper, follow me inside. Get out of the doorway as fast as you can."

Alec gulped. "Even if we make it, what's to keep him from shooting us down?"

"This is a military helicopter. He can't shoot it down using a handgun." Troy put his hand on the man's arm. "You can do this. I'll tell you when."

"Okay." He let the word out with a shaky breath.

Troy took a deep breath of his own, then pushed open the door. Immediately, more shots fired. He waited for a split second. Then in one fluid motion, he stepped free, squeezed off two shots and sprinted the few meters to the chopper.

He yanked open the hatch, took position inside, and fired again. He quickly released his clip and reloaded.

"Now!" Troy shouted. He laid down cover fire, and Alec ran toward him, his suitcase in hand.

A bullet clanged off the metal skid, and Alec's bag dropped.

"Leave it!"

Alec complied. He dove through the open hatch, and Troy closed it as soon as he pulled his feet inside.

"Strap in." Troy pointed at a seat in the back. He started the engines, the rotors coming to life above him.

He glanced behind him to make sure Alec had indeed buckled in. Bullets ricocheted off the bulletproof glass of the cockpit, and Troy pulled on his helmet. Time to get out of here and get this man to safety.

* * *

Kade fought against his rising frustration. Five days and nothing. He and Renee had already gone through the security feed at the airports but hadn't identified Gavrie Morozov anywhere. Apparently, ghosts weren't the only people who knew how to stay invisible.

Early-morning light filtered through the window above the workspace Kade shared with his wife. The tension the uncertainty caused had woken both of them before dawn, the uncertainty of knowing Morozov was on the continent as well as the lack of contact from Troy. He should have checked in by now.

Kade's phone dinged.

"Is it Troy?"

"Yeah. He just landed at the Coast Guard station on Cape Cod. He said he's going to check out a car and get our source settled into a hotel. He'll update us once he debriefs him."

"Sounds good." Renee turned her attention back to her computer. Several minutes passed in silence. Then she reached out and grabbed his arm. "I found him."

"Morozov?" Kade rolled his chair closer to his wife. The image on her computer screen revealed a man wearing a ball cap and glasses, only part of his face visible in the image from the security feed. He was dressed casually, in jeans, his shirt hidden by a Philadelphia Eagles jacket.

"You sure this is him?" Kade asked.

"We don't have any clear shots of his face, but he's the only person in any of the airports I can't identify," Renee said. "His height and weight match our suspect's, and with the way he avoids the cameras and has his face hidden, it's got to be him."

"What airport is this?"

"Philadelphia."

"Any idea where he went from here?"

"He took a hotel shuttle."

"Then we know where he is."

"Not exactly. He checked in using an alias, but I don't think he stayed there." She pulled up a new screen, the image of a hotel entrance replacing the airport feed. "Look at this."

A couple entered, followed by a family of five. A moment after the new arrivals disappeared inside, a man walked out alone, wearing khakis and a sport coat. The ball cap was blue this time, and the sunglasses now had wire rims instead of plastic, but the man moved with the same determination and purpose as the man from the airport.

"Do you have a shot of the parking lot?" Kade asked.

"Yeah, but the license plate was a temporary tag that belonged to a Honda Civic." She switched screens again. "This is a Honda CR-V."

"One of the most popular vehicles on the road."

"Yeah."

"Put a BOLO out. Let's see if the locals can help us track this guy down."

"Already did. I'm searching through traffic cameras now, but he has over a week head start on us."

"We'll catch up to him."

An alert sounded from the guardians' automated search program.

"Got one." Renee retrieved the latest report. "I have a sighting from nine days ago of him on I-95 heading south."

"Toward Washington."

"Talk about a target-rich environment."

"Yeah."

"The last sighting was at a rest area in Maryland," Renee said.

"There should be more sightings than that."

"Maybe he switched cars."

"It wouldn't surprise me."

Renee pulled up a map to show where Morozov was seen last. "There isn't much around here except this rest stop."

"Check the cars going in and out. See if you can find our guy." Kade pushed back from the desk. "And put an update on the guardian message board. Maybe with this new information, we'll have more luck finding him and identifying his target.

"Where are you going?"

"To get the truck ready."

"This video feed is over a week old. I have to think if he's in Washington that he was the one behind Shawn Hammels's death. I don't believe for a minute Hammels died of a heart attack, no matter what the doctors say."

"Yeah, but Morozov is a pro," Kade said. "He would have cleared out of DC as soon as his target was dead. No one has found any evidence of him leaving the country."

"It took us almost a week to track him this far. Maybe we just haven't found him leaving."

"Or his job isn't done yet."

"I hope that's not the case."

"Me too," Kade said. "Either way, I want to know if Morozov was anywhere near Shawn Hammels."

CHAPTER 19

Troy unlocked the hotel room door and ushered Alec inside. The two-hour flight from New Hampshire to the Cape wouldn't have been so bad had Alec not gotten airsick less than ten minutes after they took off. He hoped the crew at the Coast Guard station could do something about the smell.

Troy had checked the helicopter in for maintenance with the story that shots had been fired at him while assisting with a drug bust off the coast. He'd leave it to Kade to create the electronic trail that would back up his story.

"Nice room." Alec stopped by the window. "Great view."

"I'm glad you like it because you're going to be here for a while."

"How long is a while?"

"At least a week. Maybe two."

"Then what?"

"It depends on what you can tell me about Senator Royce and if you have proof."

"I had proof. It was in my bag," Alec said.

"The bag you dropped when running for the helicopter."

"I'm afraid so. All of my clothes were in there too. Any chance you can help me pick up a few things before you leave?"

"We'll take care of that when the stores open," Troy said. "Did you have another copy of this proof of yours?"

"I emailed a copy of the security logs to myself, but the file for the video feed was too large to send as an attachment."

"We'll try to retrieve your files, but the guys after you have probably already wiped your computer," Troy said, fighting disappointment. "For now, tell me what you know."

"I work at Ellis Security, which is the company the senator uses for his security system at his cabin. I live across the street from him."

"And?"

Alec sat in the office chair. "We had a power outage a few weeks ago, and I was tasked to see which clients maintained uninterrupted service so we could analyze where the weaknesses are. When I noticed Senator Royce's report, it looked off, so I dug a little deeper."

Though Troy suspected this man had uncovered the same anomaly he had, he asked, "What do you mean it looked off?"

"His generator kicked in automatically, so his interruption in service lasted only thirty seconds, but not once during the power outage did the system get turned off, nor did he ever open a door to go outside."

"You said it was a storm that knocked the power out. Could he have decided to stay in?" Troy asked. "Or is it possible he wasn't in New Hampshire that weekend?"

"Normally, I would have thought that was the case, but I saw him on the news only a couple days later. He was making a statement about the assassination attempt on the vice president, and he mentioned that he had been at his home in New Hampshire when he heard the news. How could he have heard the news when we didn't have electricity or internet service?"

"He could have received a phone call or checked the news on his phone."

"Maybe, but I had my drone out several times that weekend," Alec said. "Walter's car was outside, but not once did I see smoke coming out of the chimney, and he keeps his woodpile out back. The lows were below freezing."

"That is interesting. The question is whether there's a way to prove he wasn't there."

"You think he was involved with the assassination attempt, don't you?"

Troy didn't answer his question but, rather, asked one of his own. "Why do you think he was involved?"

"Someone was shooting at us a couple hours ago. I think that's proof enough."

"But what made you suspicious?" Troy clarified.

"It was something he said at the country club one night. I was having dinner with my boss, and the senator was at the next table talking to one of his political advisers. When they mentioned the vice president as a possible rival, Walter said that one good scare would be all it would take to get the VP to drop out of the race."

"That doesn't prove anything."

"I know, but when I started putting everything together, it all made sense. Besides, it wouldn't be the first time Royce used his place in New Hampshire to hide where he really was."

"What do you mean?"

"He keeps an old jeep at his place, as well as a motorcycle and a couple of snowmobiles. There's a trail at the back of his property that leads to a back road. More than once, he came up here on his own only to disappear for the weekend, even though stories in the news would say he was here the whole time."

"How far is his place to the Canadian border?"

"Forty, maybe fifty miles."

Troy checked his watch. "Are you ready for a trip to the store?"

Alec looked out the window again. "Yeah. Let's get this over with while it's still early."

"My thoughts exactly."

* * *

Jocelyn slept through breakfast, finally waking to Samson's scratching at her door. Why was he bothering her? Ty had fed him almost every day since she'd arrived.

The dog barked, and Jocelyn rolled out of bed. "Fine. I'm coming." She pulled on her robe, slipped her feet into her boots, and opened the door. "You want to come in?"

Samson barked again and wagged his tail, darting several steps toward the main house.

"You want breakfast?"

The tail wagging increased, and the dog barked yet again, this time jumping into the air.

Resigned to follow him, Jocelyn hurried to the main house. She walked inside to find the lights off and the fireplace cold.

"That's odd." Maybe Ty had had a late night too. She fed the dog, then returned to the bungalow and stumbled back into bed.

When she could no longer sleep because of the light streaming into her room, she showered and dressed for the day. The moment Jocelyn walked outside, Samson raced toward her and barked twice.

"You want to go for a walk?"

He barked again.

"Let me grab my camera." She was having a conversation with a dog. She supposed she should be grateful she had someone to talk to, especially when Ty was working. She retrieved the battery she had charged and slid it into place. A rumble sounded overhead, the windows and walls vibrating.

Curious, Jocelyn put on her coat and went outside, camera in hand. The sensation was the same as last night when she'd woken in the middle of the night.

She looked at the skyline. Nothing but open water and sky. The sound grew louder for a moment and then stopped completely.

Samson raced through the orchard toward the path leading to the cliffs. Jocelyn followed.

A razorbill in a tree caught her attention, and she stopped long enough to take a few pictures. When the black-and-white bird decided to find a new perch, Jocelyn resumed her walk. She reached the natural clearing at the high point of the island and stared.

A helicopter. And not just any helicopter but a Coast Guard rescue helicopter. That wasn't exactly the type someone could pick up at an auction.

She stepped out of the woods and approached the aircraft. The last thing she had expected was for the grassy clearing to be used as a landing zone.

She knew the Coast Guard had been instrumental in rescuing her sister from nearly drowning last fall. Was Ty one of the men who had rescued her? Was that why he was here? If so, why would the Coast Guard let him hang out on an island by himself, with a helicopter? And why was he so secretive?

Jocelyn snapped a couple photos of the unlikely scene. It was magnificent, really. The woods, the grass, the cliffs, and the helicopter in the middle of the rugged terrain.

"What are you doing?"

Jocelyn whirled and lifted a hand to her heart. Ty stood behind her, eyes narrowed, his jaw clenched.

"You startled me."

"What are you doing?" he asked, repeating his question.

Jocelyn lifted her camera since he apparently hadn't figured out the obvious on his own. "Taking pictures."

"I don't want you taking pictures of the helicopter. This is a restricted area."

The tension in his voice caught her off guard nearly as much as his words did. "You have a restricted area on my sister's property?"

"The Coast Guard has a restricted area on your sister's property."

"Wait. I thought you worked as some sort of security contractor. Why would you have anything to do with a Coast Guard helicopter?" Jocelyn asked.

"I do work security, but I'm also a Coast Guard reservist."

Jocelyn studied him in a new light. "You're a pilot?"

"Yes." His demeanor relaxed slightly.

"Does this helicopter being here have anything to do with last year's rescue?"

"That and her application to have her island recognized as its own municipality," Ty said. "Letting the Coast Guard park a rescue chopper here strengthens her claim that she receives federal support rather than local support on her island."

"I guess that makes sense," Jocelyn said. "I'm kind of surprised no one in town mentioned it though. I would have thought the harbor master or Gil would have told me you had a helicopter here when I was looking for a ride."

"They don't know the helicopter is parked here."

"That won't last long. In that town, everyone lives for the latest gossip."

"Do me a favor and keep this to yourself. I don't want you to start the gossip chain," Ty said. "I'd rather not feed any village rumors."

"Why would it matter?"

"Your sister doesn't want any new structures built on the property, and the Coast Guard doesn't want to dedicate more staff here to keep this aircraft secure."

"You think the locals are going to come onto the island and mess with it?"

"Locals were sneaking onto this island last year."

"True." Jocelyn remembered all too well when her sister had nearly died after a run-in with one of the locals. Nothing had ever scared Jocelyn more in her life.

"Besides, the military isn't in the habit of announcing its operations to the public."

"You and your helicopter are classified?" Jocelyn asked.

"It's more accurate to say I'd prefer to stay out of sight."

* * *

Troy left Jocelyn and her camera on the cliffs. He didn't know if she would abide by his request to leave the helicopter out of her viewfinder, but he could take care of any trouble photos later. For now, he needed to get back to the house and check on her latest phone activity to make sure she wasn't sharing anything that might compromise him or the guardians.

He hated spying on her, especially after the tender moments they had shared, but as much as he craved more time together, he wasn't sure he could handle it. Already, he couldn't imagine this island without her, but he couldn't expect her to stay with him indefinitely, especially when he couldn't be honest about his true purpose here.

He went into the office, where he had left the clone of Jocelyn's phone. A quick check revealed she hadn't communicated with anyone in the last hour. In fact, except for a message from a woman named Angela and a middle-of-the-night call to her sister, she hadn't talked to anyone since yesterday.

Though Troy would have preferred to work in the kitchen, where he could watch the harbor, he pushed aside his original plans and closed the door to his office. The possibility of Jocelyn turning up behind him and inadvertently seeing classified information was too great.

He settled into the office chair and glanced out the window. The view of the cliffs was stunning, but he would prefer to know when Jocelyn was coming and going. He'd have to start monitoring the island's security cameras more often, if for no other reason than to protect national security from her curiosity.

Another wave of disappointment rose. Too bad her curiosity couldn't be used to help the guardians instead of creating a risk for them.

He logged into the guardian database. An alert flashed across the top of the screen, and he read the urgent messages from Renee and the update that she and Kade were heading to DC.

He read through the responses until he got to the one saying their head programmer, Hannah, was already searching for the assassin's current whereabouts. Renee, Kade's wife, was focused on identifying a possible target, while Cas, the guardian based in Paris, was doing her own search for images of Gavrie Morozov getting on the plane to Philadelphia.

Troy grabbed his phone.

Kade answered with his usual greeting. "Yeah?"

"What's the latest on Morozov? I saw you're heading to DC."

"Intel still lines up that Morozov may have met with Royce in Paris. Our best guess is he may be after one of his opponents."

"Are you sure he hasn't completed his mission? Shawn Hammels is already dead."

"It's possible, but that's assuming he only had one target."

"The VP has already withdrawn from the race. If Royce is going after the opposing party, his targets would have to be either the secretary of state or Senator Whitmore or both."

"We both know the secretary of state wouldn't be able to beat Royce if his past comes out," Kade said.

"If we're right about Royce knowing that . . ."

"Whitmore could be his target."

"It would have to be either Whitmore or Peters," Troy said. "Peters is his main competition now in the primaries."

"Evidence pointed at Royce trying to frame Whitmore for the attack in Helsinki. It's likely he still sees Whitmore as a threat."

"We need to get him to safety until we locate Morozov."

"I'm headed to Whitmore's house now," Kade said.

The phone went dead, and Troy could only hope Kade got to the Whitmores before Morozov got to them first.

CHAPTER 20

Jim glanced out the front window at the wide lawn and the road beyond the trees that lined the front of his property. For anyone passing by, the beautiful house he and his wife had made into their home looked like one of many along a street lined with mansions. Only a select few people knew of the extraordinary security measures that had been installed.

He was still hoping a secret service detail would be assigned to him soon, but he was starting to wonder if he should hire extra security until his request went through. He knew firsthand how quickly life could change if he wasn't careful. Jim also couldn't deny that Shawn Hammels's death had him rattled.

Footsteps sounded in the hall, and Jim turned as Katherine walked in carrying a large box.

"What's that?"

"Some old clothes that need to go to Goodwill." Katherine set the box down on the coffee table. "I want to clean out as much as possible so the house is ready for someone else to stay here after the election."

"You're pretty confident about me winning, considering we still have a year to go."

"You'll win."

"And if I don't?" Jim asked.

"Then we'll have clean closets without the stress of moving."

"Always an optimist."

"It's part of my charm."

Jim looked out the window again.

"Is everything okay?" Katherine asked.

"Yeah, just an uneasy feeling I can't shake." He turned back to his wife. "It's silly. We have a security system designed by the best operatives the government has to offer, and I still keep wondering if there's a way for someone to get through to us."

"You've been on edge for the past couple weeks. Are you going to tell me why?"

"I got wind of some rumors that a candidate or two might be willing to take unorthodox measures to pave their way to the White House."

"You're the target of an assassination attempt?" Katherine asked.

"I never said that."

Katherine stared at him for a moment. "I understand you can't talk about classified information with me, and you've been in this business long enough for me to know when not to ask questions, but I want you to make me a promise."

"What's that?"

"Don't ignore those promptings. If something doesn't feel right, do something about it."

"You're right." Jim pulled his phone from his pocket.

"What are you doing?"

"Taking your advice." He dialed the number for the guardian who lived closest to him and was debating how to start the conversation when Ghost's voice came on the line.

"Senator, where are you?" Ghost asked with a clear sense of urgency.

"At home. Why? Is something wrong?"

"We aren't sure, but Renee and I are heading your way," Ghost said.

"Why?"

"We've been tracking an assassin who entered the country two weeks ago," Ghost said. "A few days before he left Europe, Walter Royce was in Paris."

"You think Walter . . ." Jim sensed his wife's gaze on him, and he let the words trail off.

"I don't know if he's coming after you or if he is looking to frame you for someone else's murder, but I don't want you exposed until we get a handle on this."

"What do you want us to do?"

"Stay where you are for now, and make sure your security system is engaged. We'll be there in forty-five minutes."

"The alarms are already on," Jim said. "What do you want us to do while we wait?"

"I don't know if you and Katherine keep go-bags, but if you don't, it may be time to reconsider."

"We'll pack bags just in case."

"See you in a bit."

Jim hung up the phone and faced his wife. "We need to pack."

"Pack? Where are we going?"

"I have absolutely no idea."

* * *

Troy started a new search, this time focusing on the traffic cameras around the Whitmore home in northern Virginia. He didn't know how long he'd watched cars coming and going, but he suspected Kade's rig should pass into view within the next half hour.

Samson barked. A moment later, a knock sounded on the office door.

He minimized the browser on his screen and crossed the room to unlock the door. He pulled it open. Jocelyn stood on the other side of the threshold, her hair windblown, her eyes bright. The tug of attraction was instant, and it took every ounce of willpower to keep from leaning forward and capturing her mouth with his.

She pressed her lips together as though she shared his thoughts. "I'm going to make some lunch. Did you want anything?"

Troy glanced at the wall clock, realizing for the first time that it was already one o'clock.

"Thanks, but I've got a lot more work to do before I can take a break." He sat back down at his desk.

Jocelyn nodded and disappeared back the way she had come, the door clicking shut behind her. A few minutes later, another knock sounded, but this time, it opened before Troy had the chance to respond.

Jocelyn walked in carrying a tray with a bowl of chowder, some crackers, and a glass of water.

"What's this?" He minimized his search program. "I said I had to work."

"You have to work, but you need to eat." She set the tray on his desk and gave his hand a squeeze that sent another bolt of attraction rippling through him. "Let me know if you want seconds." As she had before, she left the room and closed the door between them.

Troy trained his eyes on the screen again. He managed to focus for nearly three minutes before the scent of the chowder got to him. Losing the battle against his willpower, he picked up the spoon Jocelyn had put on the tray and took a bite and then a second.

Deciding he was hungry after all, he pulled the bowl closer so he could eat while watching the screen.

When he finished, he let the spoon clatter into the bowl. He couldn't remember the last time a woman had done something like this for him. His heart softened. Though he couldn't fathom how he could pursue a real relationship with Jocelyn, maybe he needed to reconsider how he spent the next few weeks. After all, he might never get another chance to spend time with anyone quite like her again.

* * *

Jocelyn scrolled through the photos she took this morning. Samson splashing through the water on the beach, waves rolling over sand, a deer poised at the edge of the woods, a warning buoy off the coast of the island.

She paused when her first shot of the helicopter filled the screen. The image awoke her creative juices—a military aircraft set against nature at its best. The battle of water and wind against the rocks below, and the helicopter perched in the grass as though it were posed to show it could handle anything nature could throw at it. The red and white of the helicopter, and the water caught in midair as it bounced off the unforgiving cliffs. Add a pilot in the foreground, and it would make the perfect recruiting photo.

She clicked forward until she reached a different angle, this one with the helicopter against the backdrop of virgin forest. She loved that the helicopter was parked on grass rather than a landing pad, not that Kristi would ever agree to let anyone interfere with the untouched portion of the island. She was surprised her sister had agreed to let the Coast Guard park the helicopter on the island in the first place.

Jocelyn's eyes narrowed when she thought of Ty working in her grandfather's old office. Why was a pilot camped out on an island by himself? And why was he spending his time on the computer rather than in the air? Then again, what did she know about how pilots spent their days? Or people in the military, for that matter.

She pushed back from the kitchen table and carried her dirty dishes to the sink. After she rinsed them and slid them into the dishwasher, she made her way back down the hall to see if Ty wanted seconds.

She lifted her hand to knock, but when she heard Ty's voice, she hesitated and leaned closer.

"I just talked to Ace. We're sending in some secret service agents, but I think you'll get there before they do." He paused and then cursed under his breath. "I've got an unidentified pedestrian visible on the back side of the senator's property. You'd better step on it." Another pause. "I'll call him. You just get there."

Jocelyn took a step back. She shouldn't be eavesdropping. Heaven knew she would have been furious if she'd found someone listening to a private conversation outside her office.

"Senator. This is Ghost."

Ghost? Her curiosity piqued again, and she edged forward. Why was Ty calling himself Ghost, and who was he talking to?

* * *

Jim gripped his cell phone and pressed his finger to his other ear to block out the blaring of the house alarm. The alarm, the call from a guardian whose voice he didn't recognize. Something was terribly wrong. His gaze landed on his wife, a sense of urgency pulsing through him.

"Our alarm tripped. Can you see anything?" Jim asked Ghost.

"Intruder approaching from the back side of the property near the stables. The local authorities have been alerted."

"What's our safest exit?"

"Stand by."

Jim took Katherine's hand and tugged to lead her to the bedroom door.

"The suitcases?" Katherine asked, raising her voice only enough to be heard over the alarm.

"Leave them."

Ghost's voice came over the phone again. "The police are only three minutes away. Go into the bedroom next to yours and hide in the closet."

"Shouldn't we try to leave? If we can make it to the garage—"

"I only see one intruder, but I can't tell if anyone is on the street waiting to take a shot when you leave."

Fighting against the instinct to flee and get Katherine away from the threat, Jim followed Ghost's advice and hurried into the room that belonged to their daughter, Amy. He opened the door to the walk-in closet. "In here."

The skepticism on Katherine's face mirrored his own, but she complied. Jim picked up his daughter's basketball so he would have a place to stand beside his wife. He closed the door, enveloping them in darkness.

"We're in the closet," Jim whispered. "Now what?"

"Stay there, and stay on the line," Ghost said. "I'll guide the police to you."

"I'm trusting you."

"We'll keep you safe."

Another alarm sounded, this time the shrill ringing that indicated the house had been breached.

"He's inside."

Katherine gasped.

Ghost's reassuring voice came through the line. "Try to stay calm and be silent."

Jim wrapped his arm around his wife's shoulders and pulled her close. "Shhh."

Her arm lifted to his waist, and her fingers dug into his shirt.

Be still, and stay quiet. Those words echoed through his head. He prayed Ghost's advice would be enough to keep them hidden and keep them alive.

* * *

Kade didn't bother to hide from the public eye when he reached the Whitmore home. He parked the tractor trailer on the street, threw open the door, and drew his pistol. Sirens rang out. "Move our rig out of sight and coordinate with the police."

"Troy just texted," Renee said. "The house has been breached. Back door."

Kade raced toward the front door. He tried to open it, but it held firm. Locked. He punched numbers on the numerical lock on the door, entering the override code known only to a few select members of Whitmore's inner circle, and the lock clicked open.

With one hand, he pushed the door open slowly and held his pistol at his side with the other.

The blaring alarm greeted him.

He slipped inside. His hand flexed on the grip of his pistol. Though his heart pounded, he kept his breathing slow and even.

He glanced into Jim's office. Empty. A floorboard creaked. Kade whirled toward the sound and ducked when he saw the flash of movement. A gunshot rang out, and a bullet whizzed by his head.

Kade darted into Jim's office. Another shot fired, this one impacting the door jamb. Kade lowered to his knee before he peeked out and led with his gun. "Drop it!"

Another shot.

Pinned down and with no way to return fire without exposing himself, Kade held his position. As long as the assassin didn't make it to the stairs, he couldn't get to the Whitmores.

The intruder fired again, this time taking three shots spaced in between rapid footsteps on the stairs.

"Freeze! Federal agent!" Kade called out only to be ignored.

A stair creaked near the second floor.

Kade drew a deep breath. He did a quick count in his head and dove into the entryway.

A bullet whizzed by him as he somersaulted across the floor and came up firing.

Kade squeezed off two shots as the intruder dove for the landing at the top of the stairs. Both bullets impacted the photo above his target in the hall and sent glass flying.

The intruder put both hands down on the floor and sprinted like a runner exploding from the blocks. He disappeared into the upstairs hall and out of sight.

Though Kade's instinct was to race after him, he ducked to the side of the stairs. Another shot fired, this one hitting the hardwood floor where he had been standing a moment earlier.

Again, Kade returned fire and put a bullet in the Whitmores' wall. Katherine was not going to be happy. Of course, she needed to survive the day in order to yell at him.

The intruder's footsteps pounded down the upstairs hall. Kade's heartbeat quickened, and he raced up the stairs two at a time.

A door opened and closed an instant before Kade reached the top landing. His gun still raised, he listened for any sound that would lead him to the shooter. Nothing.

He tiptoed past the broken glass, droplets of blood smeared on the carpet. Two more drops beaded on the floor by the corner of the wall where the shooter had taken cover.

Silently, Kade hurried forward.

Another drop of blood outside a bedroom door.

Two shots fired, and Kade's heart leapt into his throat. Quickly, he turned the knob and prayed the senator and his wife were still alive.

CHAPTER 21

Jim's body jerked when more gunshots sounded. His hold on Katherine tightened. The closet door flew open.

Jim turned so his body shielded his wife. Then he looked up and saw Ghost. Relief spilled out of him in the form of a sigh.

Ghost held up his hand, signaling them to stay where they were, then he closed them in again.

Katherine's body trembled against his.

"It's okay," Jim murmured. "It's going to be okay."

Rapid footsteps. Ghost's shout. Another gunshot. Blaring sirens.

Jim prayed Ghost would win whatever battle he was waging and that the authorities would arrive before someone managed to take a shot at him or Katherine.

More footsteps approached.

Jim held his breath when the closet door opened again.

"Sorry," Ghost said, holding the door open wide. "He got away."

"How?" Jim asked. He was certain his heartbeat would return to its normal rhythm eventually.

"Out your bedroom window. He rappelled down the side of the house."

"He had a rope?"

"Yeah. One of those compact climbing ropes. He must have planned to use it as his escape all along."

The sirens grew louder and then stopped.

Jim stepped out of the closet and drew Katherine out behind him. "Did the police see him?"

"I doubt it," Ghost said. "He was already to the tree line when I shot after him."

Katherine's fingers pressed into Jim's side. "What now?" she asked.

"You're going to give a statement to the police," Ghost said.

"And then?" Jim asked.

"Then you're going to finish packing. Renee and I will take you someplace safe until we find the people who want you dead."

A knock sounded at the front door, followed by a shout. "Fairfax County Police!" The door opened a moment later.

"Call me as soon as you're done with the police."

"Where are you going?" Jim asked.

"I'll be back."

"But . . ." Katherine started.

"Remember, I wasn't here," Ghost said. "All you know is that someone chased the gunman off. You don't know my name."

"We don't know your name," Jim reminded him.

"It's safer that way."

Another shout sounded from downstairs. "Senator Whitmore? Fairfax County Police. We are entering the premises."

"Let them know you're okay." The moment the words were out of Ghost's mouth, he disappeared into the hall.

"Up here," Jim called out.

Footsteps pounded on the stairs. A moment later, a uniformed police officer appeared in the bedroom doorway.

"Sir, ma'am, are you okay?"

Jim drew a deep breath and nodded. "We're okay."

* * *

Kade darted through the trees until he reached his rig at the back of the Whitmore property. Renee sat behind the wheel, the engine off, the window rolled down.

"Lock it up," Kade said when he reached her. "We have work to do in the back."

Renee rolled the window up and joined him outside. "Is everyone okay?"

"Yeah, but I need to put in a witness report, and we need to set up a safe house for the senator and his wife." Kade ducked under the trailer and opened the hatch that led into the living room of their customized mobile home.

"What did you have in mind?" Renee followed him inside and closed the hatch behind her. "The Whitmores aren't the kind of clients you can drop off at a hotel and leave for a few weeks."

"Is Brent in town?" Kade asked, referring to the Whitmores' son-in-law, who served as a Navy SEAL.

"No. He and Amy are in the Med right now." Renee moved to her desk on the far side of the room. "What about having them stay with one of their sons?"

"Too obvious." Kade sat at his desk and opened his laptop. "The senator is the target. His family should be safe as long as he isn't with them."

"What do you suggest? I'd say we could take them home with us, but we can't be sure our rig wasn't spotted," Renee said. "Even if we switch out the plates . . ."

"It's risky," Kade finished for her.

"Right."

Kade logged in to the guardian database and accessed the FBI server.

Renee sat beside him. "You'll want to mask our IP address before you file your report."

"I'm putting in an anonymous tip through the FBI. It's easier to tap into their server directly since we already have access."

"That'll work," Renee said. "Although you'd better let Charlie Whitmore know what's going on. Since he's FBI, you don't want him to stumble onto the report without knowing his parents are safe."

"True. I'll call as soon as I finish this."

Beside him, Renee tapped the keys on her keyboard. "Our safe house in Maryland is open. We can change vehicles and take Senator Whitmore and his wife there."

"I was thinking about somewhere more remote."

"Like?"

"The Whitmores talked about visiting Kristi and Ace in Maine."

"Kristi and Ace aren't in Maine right now."

"I know, but their guest house is, and so is a guardian who isn't currently handling any other cases."

"A guardian who can fly the senator back to DC if we need him to."

"Exactly." Kade finished his report and hit Submit. "Look for a landing zone where we can make the handoff."

"Do you want me to call Troy while you talk to Charlie?"

"Yeah. The sooner we get him in the air, the better."

Kade dialed Charlie's cell number.

"Whitmore."

"Charlie, it's Ghost," Kade said.

"What's wrong?"

"Everyone is okay, but someone breached your parents' defenses at the house."

"How is that possible?"

"Someone had to know a lot about the security system to get as far as he did," Kade admitted. "I put in a witness report through the FBI database. Can you make sure it gets forwarded to the Fairfax County Police?"

"Yeah. What else can I do?"

"Make sure you and the rest of your family are safe. I suggest getting everyone off the grid. We can't be sure the assassin won't go after one of you to draw your dad out."

"There's got to be more that I can do than that."

"You can coordinate with the police. We're pretty sure we know who's behind this, but we still have to find a way to prove it."

"Who?"

"As soon as I can prove it, you'll be the first to know."

"You've got to be able to give me more than that."

"Sorry. We both know that if you and Brent know who we're investigating, you'll start poking around on your own."

"This is my father we're talking about."

"I know, which is why we can't afford to tip off the mastermind behind this," Kade said. "Let me do my job. It's the only way I can be sure to keep your parents safe."

"I really hate this."

"I know," Kade said. "Focus on the assassination attempt. I'll even send you the file on the shooter."

"That's a start," Charlie said. "Keep my parents safe."

"I will. Let me know if the cops give you anything."

"We both know you'll read the report before I get the chance to call."

"That's okay. Sometimes the report doesn't tell you everything."

"Don't I know it."

* * *

Troy monitored the police activity, his phone in his hand, his eyes glued to the security feed on his computer. He had input the details of the intruder's path when the man had left the Whitmores' house, but Troy had yet to get a report of what had happened inside. Had the Whitmores survived? Or had the guardians failed to protect the man who could be the next generation of leadership in this country?

Troy's phone rang. He pulled it free and glanced at it. Renee. "Status?"

"The Whitmores are safe," Renee said.

"And Kade?"

"He's fine, but we need you to meet us."

"Where?" Troy pushed back from the desk.

"Delaware. I loaded the coordinates into the database. If you leave soon, you should get there around the same time we do."

Troy leaned over the computer and pulled up the information. He jotted down the coordinates and the radio frequency Renee had provided. As much as he hated to leave Jocelyn here alone, he said, "I'll be in the air in twenty minutes."

"Good. And fair warning: Kade is planning to send the Whitmores home with you."

"He's planning what?"

"Sorry, I've got to go. I'll see you in a couple hours."

"Renee—" Troy started to protest, but the line went dead. Apparently, Kade had forgotten about Jocelyn's presence on Heritage Island. Either that or the concern for the Whitmores' safety outweighed the possible security implications of having a civilian know their whereabouts.

Not willing to take any chances of a security breach from his side of things, Troy disabled the internet and shut down his computer. He then rushed down the hall to his bedroom, changed into his flight suit, and grabbed his go-bag before he ran toward the back door.

Samson barked.

"Stay," Troy ordered. He yanked the door open and was halfway outside when Jocelyn appeared from the kitchen.

"Where are you going?"

"Emergency." Troy motioned to the dog. "He gets two scoops of food twice a day."

He made it to the bottom of the stairs before Jocelyn called after him. "Wait. When will you be back?"

He glanced up, struck by the oddity that someone would care when he came and went. "I don't know."

"Be careful."

"I will." Troy picked up his pace again and jogged the quarter mile to the helicopter landing area. He did his preflight check of the aircraft, seconds ticking by in his head. Having Kade drive the senator and his wife to the planned landing site in Delaware would reduce his flight time, but picking up the senator and his wife without being noticed wasn't going to be easy.

Once his preflight check was complete, he climbed into the aircraft, strapped himself in, and started the engines. With no control tower to report to, he checked his radar. When he was certain the area was clear, he lifted off, taking the path away from the mainland. He glanced to his left, where the house perched atop the hill, its lights glowing from the windows.

The fleeting thought that this was home for now crossed his mind. Following that thought was the question, How was he going to explain Senator and Mrs.

Whitmore's presence on the island while ensuring Jocelyn didn't share that information with anyone? And where was he going to have everyone sleep?

Details. He could deal with those later. For now, his priority was to get to the meeting spot in Delaware and pick up the man and woman who could very well become the next president and first lady.

CHAPTER 22

He should have heard something. Walter paced his home office, the television in the corner tuned to the local newscast, the national news feed playing on his computer, and his phone gripped in his hand. Why hadn't he heard anything? Jim Whitmore should be dead by now.

"Walter?" Marcia called from the living room.

"In here." Walter forced himself to sit behind his desk and set his phone down beside the computer.

"We're leaving for Emma's soccer game in a little over an hour. Are you coming with us?" his wife asked.

An excuse formed on his lips, but he reconsidered before he managed to speak the words. As much as he wanted to be among the first to receive the news that a US senator had been murdered in his own home, what better place to be than with his family in front of dozens of witnesses? "Have you already eaten?" Walter asked.

"Not yet. I thought we could pick up a pizza on the way."

"We haven't gone out to eat as a family since we got back from Europe. Why don't we leave now and I'll take everyone out for a dinner that isn't fast food?"

"We would love that, but are you sure you have time?" Marcia asked.

"Yeah. Let me go change, and we'll leave as soon as you and the kids are ready."

Pleasure seeped into her expression. "I'll tell the kids."

Walter followed her into the hall and headed for their bedroom, taking a quick peek at the television as he left. He changed clothes and returned to his office, but the newscaster was now talking about a drive-by shooting in southeast Washington. Like that was anything new.

Another check of his computer and a glance at his phone. Still nothing.

"Walter," Marcia called out. "Are you ready?"

"Coming." He picked up the television remote and turned off the TV. He drew a deep breath and straightened his shoulders. He was a family man, a US senator, and a presidential candidate who was above reproach. That was how his family knew him. That was how the country knew him. By the end of the night, the man who had access to the truth would no longer be alive, and Walter would once again pretend that his image was his reality.

* * *

Jocelyn stood on the front porch, with Samson by her side and her camera raised as the silhouette of the helicopter disappeared from sight.

The familiar task of seeing the world through her viewfinder allowed her to fight back the concern that had been surging through her since Ty had left the house.

An emergency, he'd said.

The urgency and tension in his voice played in her memory. She didn't think she had ever seen someone move so fast or with such an intense sense of purpose. When she'd first met Ty, she never would have guessed him to be a military guy. Sure, his hair was cut short, and his posture was excellent, but until she'd seen him in uniform, she hadn't been able to visualize him in the cockpit of the helicopter she'd found. Then again, his reflexes when he'd saved the young mother in town had been impressive.

What was today's emergency? Was he going to rescue someone else, or was he flying into some kind of danger zone? Jocelyn reminded herself that he did this for a living. He was trained, and he would come back.

She lowered her camera and scrolled through her most recent photos. Her concern faded, and her stomach leapt with pleasure. Stunning. The lighting, the shadow of the fading aircraft. Truly, this might be her best work.

A trio of squirrels scampered around the base of a nearby hardwood tree, and Jocelyn lifted her camera again.

Samson barked and chased after them, sending all three critters racing into the branches. Jocelyn shifted her focus from the squirrels to the dog. Samson pressed his front paws against the base of the tree trunk as though he couldn't figure out why the squirrels wouldn't come down to play with him.

Jocelyn captured the moment, snapping several more photos. Then her phone rang, interrupting her solitude.

She lowered her camera and glanced at the caller ID. "Hey, Angela. How's everything going?"

"Everything was going great until an hour ago."

"What happened?"

"Demetrius emailed me his resignation."

"Seriously?"

"Yeah, and get this. He's going to work for Design Central."

"Our biggest competitor."

"Jocelyn, I'm not sure what to do. The Diamond Brothers ad campaign is due in two weeks."

"I don't suppose Demetrius gave two weeks' notice."

"No. He's coming back tomorrow to get his things, and then he's done."

"First thing you're going to do is call IT. Have them back up everything on his desktop and copy the files in his online server."

"Okay. Then what? He's the project manager on that account. With Sophie out on maternity leave, that team is already working shorthanded."

"Then I guess I'll have to pitch in."

"Are you sure?"

"Yeah, I'm sure," Jocelyn said. "When you talk to IT, have them send me everything the design team has so far."

"I'll call right now." Angela's sigh sounded over the phone. "Thanks, Jocelyn."

"No problem." She looked out at the now-dark horizon. "I don't have anything better to do."

"We both know you never have trouble finding something to do."

"This will be a fun challenge for me," Jocelyn said. "And don't forget, you've got this."

"I hope so."

"Trust me. I'll talk to you tomorrow." Jocelyn hung up the phone. "Come on, Samson. We have work to do."

The dog returned to her side, and Jocelyn ran her hand over his head. "What do you think, boy? Do you want to model for me?"

He barked, and Jocelyn laughed. "Well, come on, then. Let's turn Kristi's living room into a photo studio."

She led the way inside, amazed at how different the island felt now that she was truly alone. Her gaze landed on the back door. What was Ty's emergency? And when would he be home?

* * *

Jim escorted the police officer to the front door. "Thank you for your help, officer."

"We'll let you know as soon as we have anything on the intruder."

"I appreciate that."

"Are you sure you don't want us to have a unit park outside your house for the next day or two?"

"No, we're fine," Jim said. "We're going to stay with some friends for a few days."

"You have my card. Give me a call if you think of anything else."

"I will. Thanks again." Jim closed the door as soon as the officer walked outside. The moment he turned, Katherine was in his arms.

"Hey, it's going to be okay."

Katherine tucked her head beneath his chin. "What do we do now?"

"I'll give Andy a call to see if he'll look after the horses for us."

"What are you going to tell him?" Katherine asked. "We don't know where we're going or how long we'll be gone."

"I'll tell him the truth."

She pulled back so she could see him. "You're going to tell him that a secret government operative wants to relocate us?"

"I may leave out a few details." Jim sent a text to his neighbor. The response came back a moment later. "Andy said they'll feed the horses for us until we get back."

"At least we know the horses will be okay," Katherine said.

"Hey, we're going to be fine." Jim gathered her close once again. "Ghost will make sure of that."

"I hope you're right."

Jim's cell phone buzzed. "Maybe that's him."

Katherine stepped from his embrace, and Jim read the message.

"Ghost wants us to drive to the rec center." Jim moved toward the stairs. "I'll go get the suitcases."

"I'll come with you." Katherine followed him upstairs into the bedroom.

Together they gathered a few last items, took their suitcases downstairs, and loaded them in the backseat of the car. Jim waited to open the garage until both he and Katherine were seated and ready to go.

He pulled out of the garage and noted the police car still parked at the side of the road. Ghost and Renee weren't anywhere in sight, but he supposed he should have expected that.

Struggling to keep his emotions steady, he pulled onto the street and headed to the rec center. Five minutes later, he parked at the edge of the lot.

He had barely turned off the engine when a tractor trailer headed toward them. The truck stopped between the rec center and where Jim had parked.

The driver's side door opened, and Ghost climbed out and walked to the passenger side of the car to open Katherine's door.

"Go get in the cab," Ghost said.

Katherine followed his instructions.

Jim retrieved their suitcases and locked the car. Ghost took the bags from him. "Get in. I'll pass these up to you."

Jim climbed into the cab. His wife sat on one of the bunk beds built into the back of the cab, but Renee wasn't anywhere in sight.

Ghost passed the suitcases to him, and Jim set them behind the driver's seat. He slid over into the passenger seat to make room for Ghost.

"Where's Renee?" Jim asked.

"She's securing our transportation." Ghost waved to the back. "You'd better go back there with your wife. You don't want to be seen."

Jim slipped onto the bunk beside Katherine. Ghost settled into the driver's seat and started the engine. Jim leaned forward. "Where are you taking us?"

"For now, we're heading to a truck stop where I can leave my rig without it being noticed."

"And then?"

"And then you're going to meet your next guardian."

"Is he the one who called me a while ago?" Jim asked.

"That's right."

"Another ghost?" Katherine asked.

"Yes. Another one."

CHAPTER 23

Nothing. How was this possible? Walter kept his smile in place through dinner and his daughter's soccer game. He bit his tongue when the ref made a bad call on his daughter that had resulted in a penalty kick that lost the game for her team. Any idiot could see that the handball had been incidental.

Walter checked his cell phone at regular intervals. After all, everyone knew he was a senator. Someone as important as him couldn't be expected to go for over an hour without someone needing him. Yet, no one did. Not his campaign manager or anyone from his party headquarters. Not any of his aides or his chief of staff. And more specifically, not Gavrie Morozov. Surely, he or Ilina would have sent him a coded message once the task was complete.

The two teams lined up and shook hands.

His wife leaned closer and whispered in his ear, "She's going to be upset. Do you mind if we stop for ice cream on the way home?"

"That's fine."

A black SUV pulled into the parking lot, and a man wearing a dark suit climbed out. Was this it? Had secret service sent an agent to protect him and give him the news?

The passenger side door opened, and a teenage boy climbed out wearing a blue soccer uniform. Not secret service. A parent bringing his son to the game after work.

His daughter approached and threw her arms around Marcia's waist.

"Hey, honey. Don't be upset. You played great."

"It's my fault we lost."

"You didn't do anything wrong," Marcia insisted.

"It was just bad luck." Walter put his hand on Emma's shoulder. He swallowed the instinct to blame the referee. "It could have happened to anyone."

"Yeah, but it happened to me."

"Let's go get some ice cream," Walter said. "I'll bet a hot fudge sundae will help you shake off your bad mood."

Twelve-year-old indignation appeared on her face. "Dad, I don't think a hot fudge sundae is going to make everything better."

"Maybe not, but it can't hurt to try, can it?"

She shrugged. "I suppose it can't hurt."

Walter guided her toward the car. He only wished dessert could chase his troubles away so easily.

* * *

Jim held his wife's hand and watched the headlights of the cars passing them on the two-lane road.

After Ghost had picked them up at the rec center, they had driven to a truck stop, where Ghost had parked his semi in the midst of several other tractor trailers. Within minutes, they had switched vehicles and were on their way. To where, he still wasn't sure. Though the question burned on his tongue, the constant communication between Ghost and someone else made him wonder if the guardians even knew where they were going to end up for the night.

Renee had taken over driving when he and Katherine had switched into the simple sedan. Ghost, on the other hand, had spoken to the police, another guardian, the FBI, and someone else Jim wasn't sure about.

The logistics of how he could do his job while in hiding played through Jim's mind, but for the past two hours, with Katherine by his side, he couldn't discount the necessity of keeping his wife safe and trusting the guardians to do the same thing for him.

Could politics really be the cause of the attack tonight? And if so, who was behind it?

Katherine squeezed his hand. "You're wondering if it's worth it, aren't you?"

"It's hard not to ask whether we want to put our family at risk. My political aspirations aren't worth it if I can't ensure our family's safety."

"We've been through this kind of thing before," Katherine said.

"Yes, but never because of a choice I made."

Ghost hung up from his most recent phone call. "We're all set. Your ride is refueling at the nearby Coast Guard station. He should get to our meeting spot within a couple minutes of us."

"You're sending the helicopter to get us?"

"Yes." Ghost turned to face them more fully. "It's for search and rescue. You two needed to be rescued."

"This isn't quite what I had in mind when I arranged for the guardians to have it."

"We're adaptable."

"Where is it going to take us?" Katherine asked.

"Maine."

"To Kristi's house?" Jim asked. "She and Ghost aren't even there right now."

"That's right. The guardian who is house-sitting for them is the one picking you up."

"You know, it's getting hard to keep all of you guardians straight."

Renee cast a glance over her shoulder. "It may get worse before it gets better."

"That's not very promising," Jim said.

Ghost pointed at the upcoming intersection. "Turn here."

Renee followed his directions until they came to a stop beside an open field, rolls of hay stacked along the edge from a recent harvest.

"Where are we?" Katherine asked.

"Our landing zone."

The rumble of an engine sounded overhead. A moment later, a Coast Guard rescue helicopter lowered into view.

"Let's go." Ghost pushed the door open, and Renee popped the trunk. By the time Jim and Katherine were out of the car, Ghost already had their luggage.

Ghost led the way, ducking as he approached the helicopter. Jim and Katherine followed his lead.

Within minutes, their bags were stored, and they were both strapped into the seats behind the pilot, headsets protecting their ears.

A voice came over the earphones. "All set back there?"

Jim pulled down the microphone attached to the headset. "All set."

The helicopter lifted off, and Katherine's hand slipped into his. The simple connection was all it took to remind him of what was most precious to him. Could he really justify risking his family's safety for a chance at the White House? After today, he wasn't sure.

* * *

A dozen scenarios ran through Troy's head about how to explain the Whitmores' presence on the island, and he still didn't know what to do.

The lights of his landing zone came into view. He was out of time. They were nearly back to the island.

He decreased his altitude, a strong wind causing him to circle before making his landing.

He turned off the engines, pulled off his helmet, and climbed out. When he opened the back, he got his first good look at the senator—tall and athletic, despite his age, looking closer to fifty rather than sixty-one, which Troy knew him to be.

The man climbed out and extended his hand. "Thank you for coming to get us."

"Happy to help."

The senator turned to help his wife climb down from the helicopter. "This is my wife, Katherine."

"It's good to meet you, Ghost." Katherine pulled her coat tighter around her and stuffed her hands into her pockets.

"You can call me Ty."

"You're giving us your real name?" Senator Whitmore asked.

"No, I'm giving you the alias I've been using with my new house guest."

"House guest?" Jim asked.

Troy unloaded the luggage. "Kristi's sister showed up after Kristi and Ghost left for Europe. I tried to get her to leave, but I wasn't very successful."

"Does she know about us staying here?"

"Not yet. I'm not sure what to tell her." Troy secured the helicopter and picked up the two suitcases. "She thinks I'm a security specialist and Coast Guard reservist who is staying here to watch Kristi's place while she's in Europe."

"In my experience, the truth usually works the best." Senator Whitmore took one of the suitcases from Troy.

"Truth is a luxury I can rarely afford." Troy turned on the flashlight on his phone and started down the path to the house. "Watch your step."

"Do you think Kristi's sister can be trusted?" Katherine asked as she and her husband fell into step behind Troy.

"I don't know. I believe she's a person of integrity, but I don't know whether she can be trusted to the level of security we require. I barely know her." Troy said the words, but he wasn't sure he believed them. Their evenings spent in front of the television, their walks on the beach, the kisses they'd shared. Despite the walls he had erected between them, Jocelyn had wormed her way into his thoughts and emotions.

"I think our best bet is to stick with your Coast Guard story," Senator Whitmore said. "We can say you're hiding us out while the authorities investigate an assassination attempt."

"That could work," Troy said, considering. "Especially since I'm censoring her outgoing messages and emails."

"Why would you keep her from emailing?" Katherine asked.

"She took photos of the helicopter. I couldn't chance her sharing those," Troy said. "I think we can trust her to protect your location, but I'll keep her off the internet and monitor her phone usage for at least a day or two until we're sure she understands the seriousness of the situation."

"This could be an interesting few days," Jim said.

Troy didn't comment. He led the way to the main house.

Lights burned from the kitchen windows, but the living room was dark, except for an occasional flicker. He couldn't tell if it was from the television or the fireplace.

Samson barked and exited through his doggie door. The dog barked again.

"Samson. Quiet."

Troy turned off the flashlight on his cell phone and led the way upstairs to the deck. Samson approached, his posture alert. As Troy had seen Kristi do, he announced, "Friend."

The dog sniffed at the senator and his wife.

"Sorry about him. He's protective of the property."

"We don't mind protective." Katherine extended her hand and let the dog sniff her. Jim followed suit.

"Let's get in out of the cold." Troy ushered them into the empty living room. A fire burned in the fireplace, and the television was on, the picture paused.

Jocelyn appeared in the doorway leading from the kitchen, clad in a pair of flannel pajamas and silhouetted in the wash of light.

An unfamiliar warmth flowed through Troy.

She stepped forward. "You're back."

"Jocelyn, meet my house guests." Troy set the suitcase down. "Senator and Mrs. Whitmore, this is Jocelyn Hartinger."

"Senator. It's good to see you again." Though curiosity and confusion appeared on her face, Jocelyn extended her hand.

"Jocelyn Hartinger." Jim turned to his wife. "Katherine, Jocelyn is the one who helped with the ads on my last campaign."

"Oh, yes, of course." Katherine shook Jocelyn's hand. "So good to meet you."

"You too. Your husband has told me so many wonderful things about you."

"Oh, really?"

"Jocelyn may have been the beneficiary of those oatmeal raisin cookies you sent with me to my campaign meeting a couple years ago."

"Jim is the epitome of the saying 'The way to a man's heart is through his stomach,'" Katherine said.

Troy watched the friendly exchange, not sure what to think. "Senator, Mrs. Whitmore, let me show you to your room." Troy guided them to the master bedroom and opened the door. "Here you go. I hope this is okay."

"This is fine." Jim set down the suitcase he carried. "Thank you."

"You're welcome." Troy motioned toward the main part of the house. "Please make yourself at home."

"Thank you again for everything," Katherine said.

"You're welcome." Troy headed back toward the living room and wondered what other surprises Jocelyn had in store for him tonight.

* * *

Jocelyn wrapped her fingers around her mug and sipped hot chocolate as questions raced through her mind. What was one of the top presidential candidates doing here on Heritage Island? And in what capacity was Ty involved in the situation?

She had been debating whether to sleep here in her old room, not sure when Ty would get back. Work had dominated her time since Ty had left, so she'd stayed in the main house to have access to the internet. Unfortunately, connectivity problems had derailed her efforts and prevented her from being able to view the few files Angela had managed to recover from Demetrius. Jocelyn had been forced to start the project over from scratch. Relying on a phone call to get the details about the campaign had been frustrating, but she had to admit, she rather liked working from a blank canvas.

The movie on the television droned on. She had put it on more for background noise than for entertainment.

She set her hot chocolate aside and picked up her laptop. The rough idea for the next Diamond Brothers ad was taking shape, but even after an hour of scouring through the stock photos on her hard drive, she still didn't have quite the right shot for the background.

Her photos from this morning came to mind. The solitude and rhythm of the water, the purity of the untouched landscape. That was what she needed for this campaign. She pulled up her photographs from today and smiled. That was it. The perfect shot.

Ty's voice broke into her thoughts. "I didn't expect you to be over here so late." He approached her.

"I had some work to do." She took another sip of her drink. "The water in the kettle is still hot if you want some hot chocolate."

"I'm good, but thanks." He sat in the chair beside her.

"Are you going to tell me why Senator and Mrs. Whitmore are here?" Jocelyn asked.

"Remember how I told you I work security?"

"Yeah."

"They need security."

"Why? Did something happen?"

"Someone broke into their house tonight," Ty said. "It was a possible assassination attempt."

"Oh my gosh!" It seemed too unlikely to be true. "I can't believe they were so calm just now."

"They put on a good front, but they're both pretty rattled," Ty said. "Obviously, we need to keep their presence here a secret."

"I wasn't planning on announcing it on social media."

"I'm not just talking about social media. Except for your sister, no one can know they're here." His voice grave, Ty continued. "It's a matter of safety for them and for us."

"Don't worry. I won't tell anyone."

"Thank you."

"It's no big deal. In my business, I deal with confidential information all the time."

"I never thought about advertising as being something that would require a lot of secrets."

"Are you kidding? Corporate espionage is alive and well, and design and marketing firms are often the first targets," Jocelyn said. "Companies trust us with the details of their new products that sometimes are months or even years away from hitting the market."

"I guess that would require a certain degree of secrecy."

"I spend as much on security for the computer systems at my company as I do for office space," Jocelyn said. "Speaking of which, something is wrong with the internet. I haven't been able to access my email at all today, but it was working fine yesterday."

"I've had a few glitches, but if you need to send something out, let me know, and I can probably email it from my computer."

"How do you have internet when I don't?"

"That's classified."

"But you're asking me to trust you."

"I guess I am." Ty's eyes met hers. "Then again, I'm already trusting you to not tell anyone the Whitmores are here."

"Like I said, I know how to keep a secret."

"So do I." Ty stood and walked across the room. "I'm going to bed. I'll see you in the morning."

"Good night." Jocelyn watched him disappear down the hall. A sense of comfort washed over her at the thought that she wouldn't be on the island alone. Odd that she had spent most of her time over the past few years enjoying the solitude that came with living by herself. She had come here searching for more time alone to rediscover herself, yet she could no longer fathom what it would be like to stay here without Ty nearby.

She shook her head and reminded herself that she had a job to do. She mentally calculated the number of hours it would take her to complete this project. With Kristi's house filling up and no internet at the bungalow, she might have to find a way to create her own office space.

CHAPTER 24

Troy caught the aroma of something baking and rolled over in bed. In his semiconscious state, he imagined himself in San Diego, in the little apartment where he had lived as a boy. The scent of freshly baked bread and pastries coming from the bakery downstairs had offered a daily reminder of the food he hadn't had.

His eyes still closed, he sniffed the air. Something was baking all right. Something with apples.

Troy took a deep breath and suddenly noted the lack of stench that had always accompanied the smell of baked goods. He wasn't in San Diego. He was in Maine. He was safe.

The memory of the months and years since his childhood skipped through his mind as he came more fully awake. He wasn't the kid who had to dumpster dive for his survival anymore, nor was he the teenager who had slept in the park more often than not to avoid the drug-infested hovel he had lived in with his mother and whichever friends could offer her a few bucks for her latest score.

He opened his eyes and scanned the tidy room. His room. An image of Jocelyn surfaced. His life.

Startled that he had joined those two thoughts into one, he let the events of the past few days roll through his mind. She was getting to him. The constant energy humming through her, her innate optimism, her absolute certainty that every problem had a solution.

Unfortunately, she didn't have a clue what problems she would face if he gave in to his desire to pursue a relationship with her. Who was he kidding? Whether he kissed her again or not, they had a relationship. He didn't know how to define it, but he had little doubt that her absence would leave a hole unlike anything he had experienced before.

He pushed the comforter off and climbed out of bed. Trusting that the scents coming from the kitchen meant that Jocelyn, the Whitmores, or both had made themselves at home, Troy grabbed clean clothes and headed for the shower. Five minutes later, he walked into the kitchen to a sight he had never before witnessed, except in movies.

Senator Whitmore stood by the kitchen table, holding a stack of plates. Katherine balanced a baking sheet in one hand and closed the oven door with the other. Jocelyn closed the refrigerator and set a carton of juice on the counter. Family. He was pretty sure this was what it looked like.

Jocelyn glanced in his direction. "Ty, I was wondering if you were awake."

"What's all this?" Troy asked.

Katherine set the baking tray on top of the stove and picked up a spatula. "I hope you don't mind my using your kitchen. Baking relaxes me."

"Are those apple scones?"

"Yes." Katherine transferred the scones to a large plate.

"I don't think there's anyone alive who would mind waking up to the house smelling like this," Troy said.

"My sentiments exactly." The senator set four plates on the table.

"I told Katherine I didn't think you would care." Jocelyn set the juice down and returned to the cabinet to get glasses.

"Here. Let me help." Troy took two glasses from her, set them in their proper places, and reached for the fruit bowl on the counter. He moved it to the table and asked, "Is there anything else I can help with?"

"I think we're ready." Katherine added the plate of scones to the table and claimed a seat beside where her husband stood.

Following the senator's lead, Troy waited until both women were seated at the table before he sat.

"Do you mind if I offer a blessing on the food?" Senator Whitmore asked.

Though surprised by the request, Troy nodded. "Go ahead." Again, Troy followed the senator's lead and folded his arms.

He expected a simple, recited prayer. The senator's prayer was neither. He spoke like he was talking to a cherished friend or mentor. He expressed his gratitude for their safety and for Troy's efforts in protecting them. He mentioned his appreciation to renew his association with Jocelyn, as well as his gratitude for the food and for Katherine's efforts in preparing it. He then went on to ask for the continued health and safety of all of them and their families.

When the prayer ended, Troy managed a whispered amen. Who in the world were these people? Had they dropped out of a Norman Rockwell painting or a

1960s sitcom, or was this really their normal? Or, at least, their normal for when hiding from a potential assassin?

Katherine took a scone for herself and passed the plate around the table.

Troy took one and sampled the warm pastry. Apple, cinnamon, and a hint of sweet, all inside the dense pastry. "Oh, that is amazing."

"Thank you." Katherine took a bite. "They didn't turn out too bad."

"Mrs. Whitmore, these are a huge step above 'not too bad,'" Jocelyn said.

"Please, call me Katherine."

"And while we're at it, you should both call me Jim," the senator added.

"I don't know if I can do that," Jocelyn said. "It's weird to call you by your first name, knowing that you could be our next president."

"We're on a remote island. This isn't a place for formalities."

"But still . . ."

"Jim's right. We're guests in your home, not Senator and Mrs. Whitmore."

"Okay, but once you get elected, I'm calling you Mr. President."

"Fair enough."

Troy noted a brief hesitation in Jim's response. "You are still planning to go through with the election, aren't you?"

"We'll see," Jim said. "Katherine and I haven't had much time to talk about the implications of someone trying to kill me."

"You'll have time to yourself today, but I don't think you should jump to any quick decisions," Troy said. "Give the authorities time to search for the culprit."

"Jim has never been one to make rash decisions," Katherine said.

"That's good to know," Troy said. "It's an excellent quality for a president to have."

* * *

"What do you mean you don't know where he is?" Walter demanded, his voice lowered to a whisper so as not to be overheard if someone came down the path from the Jefferson Memorial. "How could you fail?"

The man sitting on the bench behind him spoke in a low voice. "They saw me coming, and they had help."

"You knew they had a top-of-the-line security system."

"This wasn't top of the line. This was military grade."

"I thought you could get through anything."

"I can, but not when there's a security force I don't know about."

"What now?" Walter asked.

"They disappeared," he said. "I didn't see them leave, but I also haven't seen any evidence of them being home."

"Maybe they're hiding out at their house."

"No. A neighbor came by and fed the horses. Besides that, if the senator were still there, he'd have some kind of security outside. Secret service, a hired security team, someone."

Walter couldn't argue with that. Whitmore certainly had the financial means to hire a bodyguard.

"How do we find them?" Walter asked.

"We wait."

"Wait? For what?"

"James Whitmore is a US senator running for president. He won't be able to stay in hiding for long."

"And if he does?"

"If he does, you won't have to worry about him winning his primary. He'll come across as a coward who isn't connected to the people."

Walter let that concept seep in, but a niggle of doubt remained. "I want your assurance that you will finish the job when he comes out of hiding. The liability of letting Whitmore live exists whether he runs for president or not," Walter said. "He has to die."

"I understand. Give me his schedule before he went into hiding."

"I'll have it for you by the end of the day." Walter sensed movement and glanced behind him, but all he saw was the back of a man walking away. Their meeting was over. The question now was how and when Jim Whitmore was going to die. Morozov was right. Whitmore couldn't hide forever. He would have to come out into the public eye eventually. When he did, his political career and his involvement with the guardians would end forever.

* * *

Jim helped Katherine clean the kitchen. The simple routine gave him some semblance of normalcy. Of course, he would much prefer to be in his own home, helping Katherine in their own kitchen, but first they had to ensure they would survive such a scenario.

"You're awfully quiet." Katherine rinsed the baking sheet and handed it to him so he could dry it.

He glanced at the living room, where Jocelyn was currently sitting on the couch, a laptop resting on her legs. He wasn't sure where Ty had disappeared to after breakfast, but at the moment, he was living up to his other name of Ghost.

"What are you thinking?" Katherine asked.

Jim dried the baking sheet and set it on the counter. "I don't know if this is all worth it."

"Running for president?"

Jim put his hand on the small of her back. "I don't think I could live with myself if something happened to you because of a career choice I've made."

"None of this is your fault."

"If I weren't—"

That was as far as he got before Katherine set aside her dishrag and held up a hand to stop him. "This country needs honest men in politics. We can't change how things are without some level of integrity in the White House and in Congress."

"I want to make a difference, but I can't do that if I'm dead, and I wouldn't want to try if something happened to you."

"What happened yesterday is going to take some time to put in our past." Katherine dried her hands on a kitchen towel. "I can't imagine right now going home and feeling safe."

"Which is exactly my point. You should always feel safe in our home."

"We have to trust the guardians to take care of the threat." Both hands gripped his arms, and her eyes met his. "You also need time to pray about what to do next."

"You're right." Jim looked out the kitchen window. "Maybe we should go for a walk. I could use some fresh air."

"I would love to go for a walk." Katherine made her way into the living room. "Jocelyn, do you have a coat I can borrow? I don't think the one I brought with me is heavy enough for Maine."

Jim followed her. "I guess we should have found out where we were staying before we packed."

"We had other things on our mind," Katherine said.

Jocelyn stood. "I saw one of my sister's in the hall closet the other day. I'll grab it for you."

"Thank you," Katherine said.

"It can get a bit chilly, but if you want a nice place to walk, follow the path on the other side of the dock," Jocelyn suggested. "It leads to the beach."

"Do you want to join us?" Katherine asked.

"No, thanks. I have a lot of work to do." Jocelyn motioned toward the hall. "I'll get that extra coat for you."

She disappeared and returned a moment later carrying a knee-length overcoat. "Here you go."

"Thank you."

"You're welcome. Senator, if you need a heavier coat, I'm sure there's one in the laundry room. That's where my grandfather kept his."

"Thanks, but remember, you can call me Jim."

"Right. By the way, you might want to take Samson with you."

"Afraid we'll need him to guide us back?"

"That, and he'll chase off any wildlife that might bother you."

"What kind of wildlife?" Katherine asked.

"Mostly it's just deer and squirrels," Jocelyn said. "They're harmless enough, but I wouldn't want you to get surprised by something jumping out at you."

"Neither would I," Jim said. "We had enough surprises yesterday to last a lifetime."

CHAPTER 25

Jocelyn stood on the deck of the main house, a mug of hot chocolate in her hand. The boat swayed in the gentle waves by the dock, and the sunlight shimmered on the water. At the edge of the cove, the Whitmores followed the path toward the beach. Married for more than thirty years and they were still holding hands. What would that be like?

A sense of longing churned inside her. She wanted that magical connection the older couple shared. She wasn't naive enough to think every marriage was like the Whitmores', but they set a standard worth striving for. Love, friendship, loyalty, support. She hadn't realized how much she longed for all of those things until the older couple had arrived and reminded her firsthand what a successful relationship looked like.

An image of Ty burst into her mind. Even though she had tried to pretend things were the same now as before they'd kissed, nothing she did completely blocked those images from her mind. The more time she spent with him, the harder it was to deny her growing attraction.

Little by little, he had let some of his walls come down, but when it came to his profession—or rather, professions—he rarely said anything. When he did, it was never beyond needing to get some work done.

Doubt surfaced as she replayed her conversation with him from last night. How had he come to be the person the Whitmores had chosen to trust in their time of need? And why had he brought them here instead of handing them over to the police or FBI or secret service or whoever normally protected senators after an assassination attempt? Did he often protect high-ranking government officials? Is that why he was so secretive when it came to his work?

As much as she wanted to know more, she supposed she would have to respect his privacy in that area of his life. After all, it wasn't like she ever would have been able to confide in anyone about her upcoming ad campaigns or their new products.

Even as that thought bloomed, she corrected herself. Surely if she loved someone, someone she could trust completely, that would change things. Maybe someday she would be able to open her heart to a man she could trust with any secret, no matter how big or small.

* * *

Kade sat in the coffee shop at a table by the window. If Walter Royce followed his usual routine, he should be here any minute for his morning latte. How anyone could drink the same thing every day and spend ten dollars to do it was beyond him. Then again, Kade had been trained long ago to avoid routines and predictability. In his business, such weaknesses could be deadly.

The senator's car pulled into the lot. In Royce's case, the habit provided Kade access.

"Are you ready?" Renee's voice came over his earpiece.

"Yeah." Concern rose within him. "Make sure you don't let the senator see you."

"I wish I could tell you the same thing."

"This isn't a hide-in-the-corner type of situation." Kade knew his wife was thinking about the Russian mob who had put a price tag on his head, but the Russians weren't here. He hoped. Even if they were, they thought he was dead. He was safe. Renee wasn't.

From the clues the guardians had pieced together, Walter Royce may very well have been involved in the attempt to kill Renee last year. Kade wasn't taking any unnecessary risks where she was concerned.

"Are you sure the phone you have is identical to the senator's?" Renee asked.

"Positive."

"Good luck."

As expected, the senator climbed out of his car, his eyes on his cell phone rather than on what was in front of him.

Kade pushed back from his seat and headed for the door. He pulled a cell phone from his pocket and activated an app he had developed.

The moment the door opened, Kade "accidentally" ran into the senator. Both cell phones dropped to the floor.

"I'm so sorry," Kade stepped between the senator and the phones. "Are you okay?"

"Yeah." Senator Royce brushed at his suit.

Kade leaned down and scooped up both phones. He handed his to the senator. "Here you go." Kade pocketed the second phone. "I really am sorry."

"Just watch where you're going next time."

Kade nodded, amused. Leave it to the arrogant types to assume they were in the right, even though the senator was the one not looking at what was in front of him.

Kade left the coffee shop and looked down at the cell phone screen. He activated the file-sharing feature on the phone.

"Did you get it?" Renee asked over his comm unit.

"Yeah."

"I'm sharing the cloning program with you now."

A new file popped up on the screen. Kade loaded it onto the senator's phone and promptly hid it in the background so it would run undetected.

"Status?" Kade asked.

"I've got it. I can see everything on his phone."

"Roger that." Kade glanced into the coffee shop, where the senator was punching in a code to access what he thought was his cell phone.

Kade walked back inside and approached the older man. "Excuse me, but I think this is yours."

The senator looked down at the phone Kade held. "That explains why I can't get this one to open."

They traded phones, and the senator punched in his passcode. The screen opened.

"That's better. Thanks."

"No problem. Have a good day." Kade headed for the door. If all went as planned, today would be a very good day for the guardians.

* * *

Troy couldn't stand it anymore. He had spent all morning searching for proof that Walter Royce had left his place in New Hampshire the weekend of the VP assassination attempt, but so far, all he had were utility bills and security logs that raised suspicions, plus a neighbor's persuasive observations. He had logged all of the intel he'd gathered into the guardian database with the hope that one of his colleagues would have more luck.

Needing a break from the confines of his office, he went into the living room, where Jocelyn was sitting alone, her feet on the coffee table, her laptop on her thighs, and a mug of hot chocolate cooling on the occasion table beside her. He stepped behind her and watched as Jocelyn manipulated the image on the screen to the desired size and added some graphics. He had to admit, the woman had talent. He could easily imagine the ad she had created in a glossy magazine or popping up as an internet ad.

She set her computer aside and rolled her shoulders. He suspected she, too, had spent many hours working. The woman was tireless. She was also stubborn and consistently upbeat. The combination was more appealing than he'd expected.

Admiration welled inside him, along with a spark of attraction. He stepped into her line of sight so he wouldn't startle her. "You look like you could use a shoulder rub."

"Are you offering?"

"Maybe."

She smiled. "I wouldn't say no."

Troy moved behind her, put his hands on her shoulders, and began to knead at the tight muscles.

She leaned her head forward. "That feels so good."

"It's supposed to." He pushed her hair aside and rubbed her neck. The softness of her skin, the human connection, the simple pleasure of having someone to talk to. He had missed such things—he'd missed the enjoyment of being in the company of a beautiful woman.

Of course, before stepping into his role as a guardian, he had always opted to date women who were simple, uncomplicated. Jocelyn was neither. Not for the first time today, he contemplated what it would be like to let himself fall into a relationship with Kristi's little sister. Challenging, certainly, but he suspected he might enjoy going toe to toe with her on a regular basis. Even with the chaos of the past few days, she always seemed to hover on the edge of his thoughts.

He gave her neck one last squeeze. "How was that?"

"It was just what I needed." She rolled her head from side to side. "Thank you."

"You're welcome." He waved at her computer. "How's your work going?"

"I'm almost done with this piece of the campaign," Jocelyn said. "I think I can get it finished on time."

"That's good. I'm going to walk down to the beach. Did you want to come?"

"Sure."

Troy put on his coat before he held hers out and helped her put it on.

"Thanks."

He opened the door and breathed in the salt air.

"I love being so close to the ocean," Jocelyn said. "There's nothing quite like watching the spot where ocean meets land."

He couldn't have expressed his feelings better himself. There was something about the soothing rhythm of the waves coming in, the movement of the water.

Maybe it was because he had so often escaped his childhood home and spent his time on the beach, with the ocean lulling him to sleep.

He doubted Jocelyn would understand his former life, but that didn't stop him from asking about hers. "Did you come here a lot when you were a kid?"

"All the time. Sometimes we would spend the whole summer here with our grandparents."

"What was that like?"

"What? Spending our summers on the island?"

"That and having grandparents."

"You didn't know your grandparents?"

Troy shook his head. "I never even knew my father."

"That's too bad," Jocelyn said, sympathy carrying in her words. "At least you had your mom, right?"

"That's debatable." As quickly as he'd opened the door into his childhood, he slammed it shut. "Did you want to get the rakes and dig some clams?"

"I probably don't have time to do that today," Jocelyn said. "We could bait the lobster pots though."

"I'm game," Troy said. "Are you going to teach me how to do it?"

"It is one of the most important skills you can learn while living in Maine."

Working together, they pulled the trap by the dock out of the water and replaced it with one Jocelyn had bought in town a couple days ago. She showed him how to place the bait inside and close the trap properly.

After they repeated the process with the second trap, she said, "That's all there is to it."

"How long do you think it will take before we catch one?"

"This time of year, we've got a good shot to have one or two by tomorrow."

Troy glanced at his watch. "I should probably get back to work."

"Me too." They walked across the yard together. "I have a few things to finish before the sun goes down."

"Why would it matter if you get work done before it gets dark?" Troy opened the door for her and followed her inside.

"Because I want to see if I can get some good sunset photos this evening that I can use for my campaign."

"What constitutes a good sunset photo?"

"I have one I took yesterday that isn't bad, but the angle of the shot isn't quite what I'm looking for." Jocelyn went into the living room and retrieved her laptop. She opened her photos and clicked on one to maximize it.

"Wow." Troy leaned closer. "I knew you took pictures, but I didn't realize you were such a talented artist."

Her eyes lifted to meet his, and her cheeks warmed. "Thanks."

"May I?"

"Yeah. Go ahead." Jocelyn angled the laptop toward him.

Troy sat at the table and clicked through the images. A sailboat on the water, the water splashing against the cliffs, a buck posed majestically in the woods, golden leaves on the forest floor, Samson ready to pounce at a squirrel, another where the dog looked like he was smiling at the camera.

"These are amazing." He clicked to the next screen, and the image of his helicopter appeared in front of him. In the top corner, he noticed two symbols: a red heart and a black square. "What do these mean?"

"The hearts mark my favorites."

"And the square?"

"A black square means I'm missing permissions. Green squares mean the images can be used."

"This is a great photo. I'm sorry I can't let you use it."

"I understand. It's not like it would work for the ad campaign I'm working on anyway."

"How long will it take you to finish this project of yours?"

"I'm not sure. If you can help me access the internet, I'll send everything to one of my designers and let him do the heavy lifting," she said. "Do you have any idea why the internet stopped working?"

"I'm pretty sure I know what the problem is."

The back door opened, and the Whitmores walked in.

"Hey there." Jocelyn straightened. "How was your walk?"

"It was good, thanks." Katherine shrugged out of her borrowed coat and hung it on the rack by the door.

Jim followed suit. "What are you two up to?"

"Just looking through some photos." Troy handed the laptop back to Jocelyn. "I'd better get some work done." He took a step toward the hall and stopped. He motioned to the photo on the screen. "I know I said you can't use that image publicly, but is there any way you might be willing to print me a copy? That would look great hanging on a wall."

"Yes, of course."

"Thanks." Troy headed to the office and sat at the desk. He would put the photo right there beside his computer. Maybe a few personal touches would make him feel more at home.

* * *

Jim gave Ty a five-minute head start. As soon as Katherine settled by the fire with her latest book and Jocelyn returned to her work, he made his way to the office and knocked.

"Come in."

Jim opened the door. "Do you have a minute?"

"Of course." Ty waved at the chair across from him. "Have a seat."

Jim closed the door behind him and sat in the chair opposite Ty. "Any news on our intruder?"

"Nothing definitive yet, but our investigation is moving forward."

"I don't suppose you're going to explain that to me."

"No, sir."

Jim wasn't surprised by the answer, but that didn't lessen his frustration with having so little control over his current situation. "Any idea when you'll have more definitive information?"

"Not yet."

"What do I do now?" A battle waged within him, the fear for his safety and the safety of his wife contrasting against the decision to run for the top office in the country. He let his questions spill out. "How do I balance my family's safety with my job? Congress is in session. I'm supposed to meet with my campaign manager on Tuesday. I have a presidential debate scheduled for Thursday."

"I can arrange for you to have a teleconference with your campaign manager. The debate may be a bit trickier. Where is it supposed to be?"

"New York City," Jim said. "It's at one of the television studios."

"How would you feel about doing your debate remotely?" Ty asked.

"I like that idea a lot better than the possibility of being a target again," Jim admitted. "How would we work that?"

"I think we can set up camera equipment here and patch you through to the network."

"Would someone be able to trace the signal?"

"I'll talk to Ghost to see what he can arrange."

"Renee's ghost?"

"That's the one."

Jim leaned back in his seat. "That takes care of two of my three issues. What do I do about my work in the Senate? I have several votes coming up."

"Can you have someone else stand in as your proxy?"

"No. I have to be present to vote." Jim ran over his schedule in his head. "With any luck, nothing will come up for at least a week or two, but I need to be in committee to make sure your funding gets pushed through."

"You know, if Congress did their job, we'd already have a budget."

"You aren't telling me anything I don't already know. Unfortunately, even though passing the budget is our main responsibility, politics get in the way."

"For now, I think our best bet is to keep you here. If I need to fly you to DC for a session, I can do that and have Ghost help me with security," Ty said. "Is there anything else that can't be handled remotely?"

"The biggest issue besides my day job is figuring out how to manage my campaign."

Ghost drummed his fingers against the desk. "You mentioned yesterday that Jocelyn helped with one of your previous campaigns. What about having her work with you?"

Jim considered the possibility. He had opted to use a marketing company in DC because of the closer proximity. "I guess I can brainstorm with her to see if she has any ideas of how to manage things from here."

"Her presence could prove to give you a much-needed buffer until we have more information about the shooter," Ty said. "If your campaign manager knows you are working with her, she can call and speak to him freely."

"What if someone tries to trace her here?"

"I already made a clone of her phone. I can add a scrambler to make sure her signal can't be pinpointed."

"Sounds like Jocelyn and I need to have a talk." Jim pushed out of his chair.

Ty stood as well. "I assure you, Senator, we're doing everything we can to eliminate the threats against you."

"I know you are," Jim said. "Honestly, if I hadn't prayed so much before making this decision, I would probably walk away from the election. Katherine and I prayed about it again today, and we keep getting confirmation that this is what I'm supposed to do."

"What does prayer have to do with you running for president?"

"You don't really think I'd take on this challenge without asking for the Lord's blessing, do you?" Jim asked. "A presidency is more than the man in the position. It's also the inspiration he lets guide him in his decisions. I can't imagine trying to do the job without the Lord's help."

"I never thought of it that way."

"I'll let you get back to work." Jim was halfway down the hall before a new thought struck him. Maybe Ty didn't know what it was like to have the Lord involved in his daily life. After all, the man had been living for who knows how long as a dead man.

CHAPTER 26

Jocelyn leaned back on the couch and tried to imagine the ad with the proper graphics in place. If one of the other artists on the team could use her work as the background, they would have plenty of time to work their magic before the deadline.

Sitting on the couch opposite her, Katherine set her book aside. "Are you all done?"

"I'm done for now anyway." Jocelyn slid her computer off her lap and onto the cushion beside her. "As soon as Ty fixes the internet connection, I'll send my latest proofs off to the graphic designer."

"I understand you're selling your company," Katherine said. "What's next for you?"

"I'm not sure. For now, I'm having fun getting reacquainted with my camera." Jocelyn waved toward the office. "Even though Ty hates having his picture taken."

"I think it's a guy thing. Jim isn't fond of cameras either."

"Our future president doesn't like cameras? This could be interesting."

The senator emerged from the hall. "Is my wife telling stories about me again?"

"Maybe." Jocelyn grinned. "Want to come join us? You can give me the real inside scoop."

"I'm not very complicated," Jim said. "What you see is what you get."

"I've learned over the years that that sentiment is rarely true," Jocelyn said. "People are complex, especially those in the public eye."

"I suppose you would know that well with your career," Jim said.

"Most of what I've done over the past seven years is try to help companies create an image," Jocelyn said. "You were one of the few I worked with from the political world."

"Any chance you're interested in stepping into my world again?" Jim sat beside his wife. "I hoped you could help me design the next stage of my political campaign."

"Seriously?" Jocelyn looked at him skeptically. "I thought you were working with a DC-based firm."

"I am, but with everything that happened yesterday, I need someone to help me figure out how much to leak to the media and how to best spin why I'm off the campaign trail for the moment."

"I'd love to help," Jocelyn said. "Did you have anything in particular in mind?"

"The PR firm I'm working with was getting ready to shoot some photos of me in my office on Capitol Hill."

"They wanted to show you in action?" Jocelyn asked.

"Something like that."

Katherine put her hand on her husband's knee. "I thought you wanted your campaign to be more about letting people know who you really are."

"The public sees me as a senator."

"But you're more than that," Katherine countered. "I think you'll do better if you let the country see the man behind the position."

"I don't know. Maybe."

The campaign the senator's team proposed merged with Katherine's suggestion in Jocelyn's mind. She could already imagine it. "It'll take me a couple days to get the photos I need, but I think we can come up with something unique that will let Americans know who you really are."

"I appreciate that," Jim said. "Where do we start?"

"First things first. Do you like to fish?"

"I used to, but it's been years."

"Come on. We're going to go catch some dinner." Jocelyn grabbed her camera. "Katherine, want to come?"

"I'd love to. Should we see if Ty wants to join us?"

"Sure. I'll go check with him." Jocelyn stood. "I'll be back in a minute. You two might want to grab some gloves and coats." She walked down the hall to the closed office door. She lifted a hand to knock but hesitated when she heard Ty's voice carry to her. The words were muffled, but she was quite certain he wasn't speaking in English. Was that Russian?

Footsteps approached from inside, and Jocelyn took an instinctive step back. The door swung open. Surprise lit Ty's face. He spoke into his cell phone. "I'll call you back later."

"I'm sorry, I didn't mean to interrupt," Jocelyn said. "I'm taking the senator and Katherine fishing. I thought you might want to join us."

A brief flash of uncertainty appeared on his face. "I'd like that."

"Great. Grab your coat. We're heading down to the dock now."

"I'll meet you out there in a few minutes."

"Okay. See you then." Jocelyn returned to the living room, her curiosity piqued. Who had Ty been talking to? Why had he switched from Russian to English as soon as he'd seen her? And how had he learned to speak Russian in the first place?

* * *

Troy finished updating his notes in the guardian database and pushed back from his desk. He had touched base with both Kade and Ace, but neither of them had made any more progress on locating Gavrie Morozov or connecting him to Senator Royce.

At least he had been speaking to Kade in Russian when Jocelyn had been at the door. The last thing he needed was to have her or Katherine overhear a classified conversation. Honestly, he preferred to avoid letting Jim get involved in the discussion until they made more progress toward getting him safely home.

The senator's comment about praying for guidance in his decision to run for president played over in Troy's mind. Did people really think God could give them answers? In his experience, God looked out for other people. Not him. Surely, if there were a Supreme Being, He wouldn't send children to someone like his mother.

Absently, he rubbed a hand over the burn marks on his arm. Those particular scars had come from a night when he had arrived home empty-handed, the scent of chili on his breath from his meal at the local soup kitchen. He had tried to tell his mom that the cops had been patrolling behind the mall where he'd normally gone dumpster diving. She had been too stoned to listen. He'd been six years old.

Shaking the memories away, he left his office and grabbed his jacket. He reached the deck and took in the scene before him.

Jim Whitmore stood at the edge of the dock, a pole in hand. Samson lay at his feet. To anyone who might pass by, Jim looked like an ordinary man enjoying a leisurely pursuit. Or was he the lone man against the world?

A few meters away, Jocelyn took a few steps to the side, her camera raised. After a moment, she motioned to Katherine, who stood behind her.

Carrying a fishing pole of her own, Katherine joined her husband.

While Jocelyn continued to take photos, Jim traded poles with his wife. At first, Troy thought he was going to cast off for her. When Jim reached into a bucket of fish remnants, baited the hook, and traded rods again, Troy couldn't help but smile. Mrs. Whitmore didn't like slimy things.

Jim stepped to the side while Katherine cast off. She apparently wasn't satisfied with her first effort because she reeled her line in and cast off a second time.

Jocelyn continued to work the angles and take more photos.

Samson's head lifted. He must have sensed Troy's presence because he abandoned the Whitmores and loped to the yard. He picked up a worn tennis ball and deposited it at the base of the stairs.

He barked twice—Samson-speak for "Come play with me."

Troy jogged down the stairs, picked up the ball, and sent it flying toward the woods.

An excited yip and Samson was off. A moment later, he raced back to Troy and skidded to a stop. The ball dropped.

Troy threw it again, repeating the process several more times before he crossed to where Jocelyn stood. She was bent over at the waist, her eye pressed to the viewfinder of her camera. Her fingers alternated between taking photos and manually making adjustments to the lens.

She was every bit as intensely focused as a soldier taking aim on the battlefield. With that image in mind, Troy waited for her to straighten and lower the camera before he spoke.

"Did you get what you wanted?"

She held her camera out and scrolled through her recent images. "I think I can work with these."

"Can I see?"

"Sure." She handed him her camera and showed him which button to push to view the previous shots.

He expected to see a bunch of images of the senator standing by his wife, but these were so much more. Little moments illuminated the screen. The senator's hand on his wife's back, their hands holding fishing poles, a net and bucket at their feet, the two standing together in perfect harmony, their lines in the water.

"These are amazing."

"Thanks."

He clicked to bring up the next image, and his heartbeat quickened. Without him noticing, she had captured him midway through throwing the ball for Samson. Troy hit the delete button.

"What are you doing?" She snatched the camera from him.

"I told you I don't want my picture taken."

"I wasn't going to share it with anyone."

Katherine's delighted squeal rang out. "I got one!"

Jocelyn's camera lifted, and she once again manipulated her lens.

Katherine leaned back against the pressure on her line.

"Reel it in," Jim encouraged. "You can do it."

Slowly, Katherine turned the reel.

"Bring it in faster," Jocelyn said.

"Jim, help me."

Jim set his pole aside and wrapped his arms around his wife, placing his hand over hers on the reel. "We've got this."

Troy fought his instinct to help the senator and his wife. He couldn't step back in front of Jocelyn's lens.

Seeming to read the reason for his hesitation, Jocelyn lowered her camera. "Go help them." She waved at the dock. "I won't take any of you."

Troy took only one step before the fighting red-striped bass emerged from the water. Jocelyn's camera came back up, and she went back to work.

"I've got it," Katherine announced. "Grab the net."

Jim did so, and together the Whitmores wrestled the fish out of the water and into the net and then into the bucket.

Katherine let out a relieved sigh. "As hard as this one fought, I thought I'd caught a shark."

"That would have made some headlines," Jocelyn said.

"We may want to wait on making headlines, at least for a few days," Jim said.

"You're going to be in the headlines whether you want to be or not," Jocelyn said. "An assassination attempt on a US senator is going to keep the press buzzing, especially while you're in hiding."

"She's right," Troy said. "We need to use this press to your advantage."

"How do we do that?" Katherine asked.

"I'm sure the senator's staff and PR team are already working on it." Troy motioned to the fish. "I assume that's what we're having for dinner tonight."

"Absolutely." Katherine jerked a thumb at her husband. "I'll cut it into fillets right after Jim cleans it."

"Me? It's your fish."

"I know, but you're so much better at this than I am."

"Where have I heard that before?" Jim asked.

"I don't know. Maybe last month when Andy gave us those catfish that he hadn't cleaned yet," Katherine said.

Jim cast a hopeful look in Troy's direction.

"Don't look at me. I have work to do," Troy said.

"And I'm going to preserve the moment for your posterity." Jocelyn held up her camera.

"I'm starting to think I'm surrounded by three master manipulators," Jim muttered.

"Come on, honey. Let's see if you can catch one too." Katherine took her husband's hand and led him back to the bait bucket. "First, I need you to bait my hook though."

Amused at the interplay between the senator and his wife, Troy watched a moment longer. It wasn't until he glanced at Jocelyn that he noticed the tense set of her jaw.

"Hey, I'm sorry about deleting the photo, but I told you I don't want my picture taken."

"Yes, you've made that abundantly clear," Jocelyn said icily.

"What do you expect? That I'm okay with being your subject as long as I don't know about it?"

"No, but I would hope you'd trust me to be professional enough to not share an image without permission." She faced him more fully. "When you were playing with the dog, it was the first time I'd seen you so relaxed, so carefree. I wanted to be able to remember it. I wanted the chance to have something to remember you."

"You don't need a picture to remember me."

"Don't I? You hardly ever talk about yourself. You never give any hints of who you are or where you came from." Jocelyn blew out a frustrated breath. "It's like you don't want anyone to even know you exist."

Her words only served to emphasize the truth. He didn't exist, at least not in traditional society. If he did, maybe he'd have found the courage to explore the attraction simmering beneath the surface every time he was near Jocelyn. His chest tightened, and he stuffed his hands into his jacket pockets. The hard truth glared at him. She was high class. He came from the slums. She was a civilian. He was a ghost. End of story.

Troy took a step back and waved at where the Whitmores now stood on the dock. "I'll let you get back to work."

Without waiting for a response, he crossed the yard. This time, when Samson ran up with the ball in his mouth, Troy ignored him. Ty Dodson didn't exist, he reminded himself again. It was best not to forget that no matter what name he was using, he didn't live in the real world.

CHAPTER 27

The Whitmores caught four fish, and Jocelyn took more pictures than she cared to count.

As much as she wanted to go inside to download her photos, her annoyance with Ty hadn't faded, and she wasn't sure she was ready to face him alone. How dare he delete a photo without asking her first.

She had taken the shot instinctively. The half smile on Ty's face and the dog's excitement had been irresistible. Apparently, when Ty and her camera were in the same place, Jocelyn would need to learn some restraint.

He was right. She should have asked first before taking his picture. That fact grated on her, but she had long ago adopted the "shoot first and ask questions later" approach. It had served her well until now.

"I need some hot chocolate," Katherine announced when they returned the fishing equipment to the shed. "Does anyone else want some?"

"That sounds great. Thanks." Jocelyn retrieved a fish scaler, a large cutting board, and a knife from the shed. She put the tools on the table at the edge of the patio. "Senator, we can clean the fish over here."

Jocelyn laid the first fish on the cutting board and removed the head, pulling the spine along with it.

"You've obviously done this before." He retrieved a striped red bass and picked up the scaler.

"My grandfather was a true believer that we should know how to take care of ourselves while on the island." She wrinkled her nose. "As much as I hate cleaning fish, I'd much rather do this than process venison."

"You processed your own deer meat?"

"We have deer on the island, so we have to thin out the herd to keep the numbers under control," Jocelyn explained. "Grandpa didn't believe in letting us kill the deer and leave the dirty work to someone else."

"You know how to fish and hunt?"

"Yeah. Not exactly skills I needed in the business world."

"I don't know. If any of your competitors saw how you handle that knife, they'd all think twice about trying to poach your clients."

"I never thought of that." Jocelyn skinned and filleted the first fish and retrieved the second. "I have to admit, though, it's kind of nice knowing I'm pretty much done with those kinds of problems."

"It's a big change for you," Jim said. "Are you ready for it?"

"I think so. What about you?" Jocelyn asked. "If the polls are right, you've got a good shot at the White House."

"Assuming I can live that long."

"I'm sure the authorities will find whoever came after you." Jocelyn finished with the second fish and moved on to the third. "How did you end up here though? Do you know my sister, or were you already friends with Ty?"

"Your sister, actually. We met about a year ago."

"You meet a lot of people, but I doubt you trust many of them with helping you hide out."

"True, but she's someone I've come to trust."

"Don't tell me she's your financial adviser."

"Not exactly, but I've consulted with her on some financial matters in the past," Jim said. "I knew she had a helicopter pilot living here, so it made sense to take advantage of the situation."

"Does your family know where you are?"

"No, but they know to take extra precautions."

"You don't think someone would go after your children, do you?"

"I would hope not, but whoever is behind this has proven ruthless so far." Jim swallowed hard. "What better way to draw me out than for a family funeral?"

"You know that's a possibility, and you're still going through with the election?"

"Katherine and I prayed about it again last night. We both received the same answer as we did before. It's the right thing to do."

"Your faith is admirable, but I doubt believing in God is going to protect your family from an assassin's bullet."

"Maybe not, but He has a way of putting the right people around me to keep us safe."

Jocelyn fell silent, not sure what to think of the senator's comment or his surety that God would preserve his life. She finished cleaning the third fish and handed the knife to Senator Whitmore so he could finish with the one he had scaled.

"I'm being outdone by the women on this island today," Jim said. "First Katherine catches three fish to my one, and now you clean them three times as fast. I may need to up my game."

"Will it make you feel any better if I kill a deer and let you dress it?"

"No."

"Okay. Let me know if you change your mind."

* * *

Troy read through the latest entries in the guardian database and then read them again. The words continued to blur before him while the memory of Jocelyn's reaction outside played over and over in his mind.

He didn't want to care about Jocelyn's annoyance when he'd deleted his photo, but he did. No matter how many times he laid out the facts that they came from incompatible worlds, he couldn't change the truth: she mattered. Still, she'd taken the photo without his permission, and he had every right to destroy the evidence of his presence here. Sure, she didn't know the risks involved or the truth that if certain people knew he was alive, he wouldn't stay that way for long.

It was ludicrous, really, that the members of a gang in California would still care about whether he was dead or alive, but he had spent enough time in their world to know how reputations were made. To the brotherhood, he was a traitor. He had turned in one of their own. Murdering him would bring his killer legendary status within the ranks.

What that particular brotherhood didn't understand was that he had never been one of them. He had done what he had to in order to survive, but the minute he'd found a way out, he'd taken it.

A visit to the Marine recruiter, advancement through officer candidate school, flight training, his first post with the Marines. Everything would have been perfect had he not been assigned to Camp Pendleton, only ten miles from his old neighborhood. He still wasn't sure if Rafael had run into him by chance on his day off or if he had somehow planned it. Regardless, Troy had been offered two choices: smuggle drugs for the brotherhood or die. Troy had opted for a third choice. He'd turned Rafael in to the authorities. The first attempt on his life had come less than two hours later.

Troy pushed back from the desk and crossed to the window. Waves crashed against the cliffs below, the swirling water mirroring his emotions. He shouldn't care about Jocelyn or what she thought, but he did. Whether he wanted to admit it or not, her opinions mattered. And he couldn't deny he looked forward to seeing her every day, even though it had taken tremendous willpower to keep things platonic between them.

The Whitmores' presence had helped reduce his time alone with Jocelyn. Unfortunately, seeing the senator and his wife interact, seeing the tangible connection between them, made him yearn for what he couldn't have. This wasn't like the situations when some of his fellow guardians had met their wives. In each of those instances, the guardian had developed feelings for someone who understood who he was. The women they ultimately married also had some intelligence background. Jocelyn was a civilian in every sense of the word.

The back door opened and closed, and voices carried toward him.

Troy forced himself to return to his desk and read through the latest messages one last time. Once he was assured there wasn't any news of significance on the database, he logged out and headed for the kitchen. The scent of fish assaulted him.

Katherine set a baking sheets on the counter with a clatter and riffled through the spice cabinet until she found the Old Bay seasoning.

Jocelyn stood at the sink, the water on full blast, her back to the room.

"Where's the senator?" Troy asked.

"He went to take a shower," Katherine said. "He didn't want to smell like fish all day, for some reason."

"I don't blame him." Troy spotted the large Ziploc bags filled with filleted fish. "Looks like you were successful."

"Yeah. We have two more bags in the refrigerator."

"I guess we don't need to go fishing again for a couple days."

Jocelyn finished washing her hands, flicked off the faucet, and grabbed a hand towel. "Katherine, did you need any help before I go shower?"

"No, you go ahead."

Without another word, Jocelyn exited through the door to the dining room as though she didn't want to even look at Troy.

Troy watched her go, and his heart sank. Whether she knew his real identity or not, he needed to make things right between them.

* * *

Jocelyn grabbed her grandfather's rifle, a box of ammunition, and a bag of apples. When she walked out of the mudroom into the kitchen, she found Katherine standing at the counter, an assortment of baking supplies scattered around her.

Katherine looked up from the batter she was stirring. "Going hunting?"

"Not exactly. I just need to get some fresh air," Jocelyn said. "I'll be back in a little while." She donned her coat, pocketed the ammunition, and headed out the door but stopped on the deck and took a deep breath. Solitude. She needed this and time to think and work off her mad. She hated it when her emotions got the best of her, and she was furious that Ty had brought out her anger. She was mad he'd made her mad. Yeah, that was logical.

Since yelling at Ty wasn't going to solve anything, she would opt for the next best thing: shooting something.

Ty and the senator had disappeared into the office twenty minutes ago. She didn't know if the two men had work to discuss or if Ty was hiding from her. Either way, it was probably best that everyone stay out of the danger zone. She supposed she could have locked herself in the bungalow, but without internet, there was nothing to do there besides sleep.

She made her way to the beach where she and her sister had learned to shoot when they were kids. Using the apples for targets, Jocelyn lined five on top of a fallen log and paced along the sand until she was fifty yards away. Taking aim, she fired off her first shot. Miss. Annoyed, she aimed again. This time an apple exploded into the air.

One by one, the other four apples disintegrated onto the sand.

She set up more apples only to destroy them into unrecognizable bits. She repeated the process until she set up the last six apples.

She destroyed four before she missed again.

"Four out of five isn't bad," Ty said from behind her.

Jocelyn turned to face him. "I suppose you can do better."

"I didn't say that." He waited until Jocelyn pointed the barrel of the rifle at the ground before he continued. "Are you still mad?"

"Yes, I'm mad."

"Look, I said I was sorry, but I can't have my picture floating around for whoever might want to put it online."

"I wasn't going to share it."

"How was I supposed to know that?"

"You could have asked. Even better, you could have trusted me." Jocelyn turned back to the target and shot twice more. Fruit exploded. She opened the chamber and made sure the gun was out of bullets before she turned back toward the house. "I'm going inside."

Ty took her by the arm to keep her from passing him. "You don't strike me as the kind of person to run away from trouble."

"You don't strike me as someone who wants to mess with a woman holding a gun."

"It isn't loaded."

A new volcano of emotions heated inside her. "I don't get you. One minute I feel like we have this special connection between us, and the next you act like I'm some criminal who can't be trusted."

The hand on her arm dropped to his side. "Sorry I don't trust as easily as you."

"Why not?"

"Look, I don't come from a place like this." He waved a hand to encompass the island. "Your normal is foreign to me."

"This isn't exactly my normal either," Jocelyn said. "What does that have to do with you deleting my photo?"

"I'm not talking about living on an island. I'm talking about all of this. This isn't how I grew up: sitting down for meals together, having food in the refrigerator and pantry, having a bed to sleep in without having to worry about some junkie waking me up in the middle of the night."

Something softened inside her. Jocelyn saw the change in Ty's expression when he realized what he had said, when he realized he had shared a piece of his past he had thus far kept to himself.

"Tell me about where you come from. Help me understand."

She sensed him wavering, but she couldn't tell if he didn't want to expose his demons or if he didn't trust her with them.

"What were your days like? Tell me about your mom."

"She gave birth to me, but that's about all she gave me besides a few scars."

"Like the burns on your arms."

"Yeah." Ty swallowed. "She only cared about where her drugs were coming from. It was my job to bring home food and scrounge for money however I could."

"I'm so sorry."

"It was all I knew until I joined the military."

"And you became a pilot."

"I did," Ty said. "My past is something I survived. It's not something I'm proud of."

Jocelyn took his hand in hers. "Who you were in the past doesn't define who you are now. Your life is whatever you want to make of it."

"I wish that were true." Regret flashed on his face. His eyes met hers, a storm brewing in the deep blue as though a fierce battle were being waged inside him. Then the clouds cleared, and his free hand lifted to caress her cheek.

Jocelyn's stomach leapt when he leaned closer and his lips settled on hers. The jolt of attraction sparked, simmered, and settled into something new and yet somehow familiar. Her hand tightened on the rifle she held, the rigidity of the wooden handle contrasting with the warmth seeping through her.

Ty's fingers slid into her hair, and a shiver worked through her. This kiss wasn't like the ones they had shared before. They didn't have an audience, and it had nothing to do with make-believe.

Jocelyn's heart and mind opened, both expanding to make room for this man who continued to tug at her heart. The image he painted of his past made her want to protect and nurture. When his muscular arms drew her closer, their roles reversed in her mind as she found a sense of safety she had never before experienced.

Ty drew back and caressed her cheek once more. "I'm sorry I deleted your picture. Forgive me?"

"I was planning on staying mad at you for at least another day or two."

"Maybe you could change those plans?"

"I'll think about it."

"Good." He took a step back. "If you're finished destroying apples, do you want to go on a walk with me?"

"I think I can be persuaded."

Ty leaned forward and captured her in another kiss. "Good."

CHAPTER 28

Troy still wasn't sure what had possessed him to share details about his past, but he had to admit the dark shadow of his childhood didn't seem quite as heavy as it usually did since clearing the air with Jocelyn.

Hand in hand, they made their way through the now-dormant orchard and up to the cliffs before they reached the patch of ground where the helicopter was parked.

"Did you always want to be a pilot?" Jocelyn asked.

"Honestly, all I wanted was to get away from the life I grew up in," Troy admitted. "The military let me do that."

"You said you never knew your dad. Do you know anything about him?"

"Yeah." Even the single word of truth dredged up emotions long since buried. He wasn't sure why he didn't hide behind his security clearance, why he let himself give her a piece of the truth. "My father was a dealer. He was in and out of prison most of my life."

"Where is he now?"

"I don't know, and I don't want to know."

"And your mother?"

"If she wasn't drunk, she was high." He moved to the edge of the cliffs and watched the water spray into the air.

Jocelyn released his hand and slipped her arm around him. "I'm so sorry. I can't imagine growing up in a situation like that."

Eager to change the subject, he said, "Tell me about your parents. I know you and Kristi grew up here in Maine."

"Yeah. I guess we were the typical live-in-the-suburbs kind of family," Jocelyn said. "Kristi is nine years older than me, but she and Ace used to let me tag along with them a lot."

It took a moment for Troy to remember that he wasn't supposed to know who Ace was. "Ace?"

"He was my sister's best friend growing up," Jocelyn said. "They started dating in high school. Or maybe it was after Ace left for college. I can't remember."

"Your sister must have been pretty amazing to let her little sister tag along when you had such a big age gap."

"Yeah, she was. She still is, actually," Jocelyn said. "I was thinking the other day how she's been my best friend for as long as I can remember. Maybe that's why I wanted to come back here. I needed to reconnect with who I was before my company took over my life."

"Have you decided what you're going to do next?"

"I don't know. The more I work on Senator Whitmore's campaign, the more I think I want to stick with photography. It's been so much fun creating the artwork that will fit the ad concept instead of having to search for something that might work."

"Maybe you should try finding an agent for your photos," Troy suggested. "You have a lot of talent."

"That's sweet of you to say, but I think I'd rather put my photos up on one of the photography sites and see if I get any bites."

"Or you could create your own website."

Her eyes lit up, and Troy could almost see her processing the possibilities. "That's not a bad idea. I don't know how successful it would be . . ."

"There's only one way to find out."

"Maybe you're right."

* * *

Jocelyn retreated to the bungalow as soon as she finished dinner. Her evolving relationship with Ty brought butterflies to her stomach every time she thought of him, but she had work to do so she could once again enjoy her time here.

A call to Angela and a teleconference with one of the graphic designers gave her the insight she needed to finish her part of the Diamond Brothers project. Now she needed to go to the main house to figure out how to regain her internet access so the rest of the design team could finish their part of the campaign. As much as she wanted to be involved in the final presentation, that wasn't her job anymore. She had to trust her former employees to take it from here.

She had expected to stay on the project through completion, but the truth was, she needed to let the other designers do their job, and she had new fish to fry, so to speak.

The Whitmore campaign was an opportunity she hadn't expected, and it was also one that could establish her not only as a graphic artist but also as a photographer.

The shots on the dock had turned out even better than she expected. If the Whitmores' morning routine worked the way she hoped, she suspected she would have the next images she needed before noon.

But right now, it was one in the morning. She really needed to work on getting to bed at a reasonable hour.

She grabbed her coat and shoes. As soon as she collected her laptop bag, she headed outside. The wind whipped through her hair, and she caught her breath. Moving quickly, she hurried to the back door and pulled on the handle. Locked. Fumbling, she dug through her bag and fished out her key. A shiver worked through her as she finally slid the key into place and slipped inside.

A lamp had been left on beside the couch, but the rest of the house was dark. She set her bag on the coffee table and padded to the office. Time to figure out what was going on with the internet. She had a project to send off and a warm bed waiting for her.

She slipped into her grandfather's office and closed the door behind her before she turned on the light. She supposed she should think of the office as Ty's now, or at the very least, Kristi's, but it was hard to imagine this room without her grandfather in it, even knowing he had been gone for three years now.

She pushed aside the feeling that she was intruding in someone's personal space. After all, had Ty followed through on his promise to fix the internet, she wouldn't have to take care of it herself. She did a quick search for the internet router. When she didn't find it, she sat in the desk chair. Surely the router was in the office somewhere.

"If I were a router, where would I be?" Jocelyn asked in a low voice. Spinning around, she turned to the credenza and opened the lower cabinet to reveal several pieces of electronic equipment. "Finally."

She leaned down to figure out which one was the router. Before she had touched anything, a shrill alarm rang out, and Jocelyn startled.

To her surprise, the computer screen on the desk lit up, eight boxes popping up in quick succession, each one revealing a different view of the island.

Heavy footsteps approached. The dog barked. Jocelyn stood and took an automatic step back when the office door swung open.

"What happened?" Ty demanded, Samson following at his heels. "What did you do?"

"I didn't do anything. I was just looking for the router so I could connect to the internet."

Ty pushed past her and stepped in front of the computer screen. From where she stood, Jocelyn saw a shadow of movement on the edge of the image on the lower left.

"Is this an alarm system for the island?"

"Yes. Did you see anything when the alarm went off?" Ty asked.

"No." Jocelyn's gaze lowered to his hand, and she noted the gun gripped there. "Do you sleep with that thing?"

"Stay here and keep the doors locked," Ty said. "Call me if you see anything on the monitor."

"I don't have your number."

Ty reached into a drawer in the credenza and handed her a cell phone. "I'm listed as T in this phone."

"Be careful."

"I will." When the dog started to follow, Ty pointed. "Samson, stay." Ty disappeared down the hall. A moment later, the door opened and closed with a quiet click.

Samson pressed against Jocelyn's leg, and she stroked his head as she lowered herself back into the chair. She watched the monitors, expecting to see Ty show up on the screen, but he never did. Was the man deliberately trying to remain unseen? And what or who had set off the alarm? For that matter, why did her sister have such a sophisticated alarm system in the first place?

* * *

Troy moved through the darkness, each footstep deliberate to ensure what little sound he made would be swept away by the sound of the wind and surf. He circled the house. No sign of an intruder. Based on the security feed on his computer, the alarm had triggered on the wayward side of the island, near the bungalow.

He flexed his hand on the grip of his pistol, the cold stinging his skin. He should have grabbed some gloves, but his concern for Jocelyn and the Whitmores had taken precedence over his comfort. At least he'd grabbed a jacket before he'd slipped outside.

Who or what had tripped the alarm? Ace mentioned the wildlife sometimes caused one to go off, but he hadn't seen anything on the screen when he'd reached the office. Surely Jocelyn would have noticed if it was a deer, wouldn't she? Maybe she wouldn't. After all, she wasn't trained in surveillance or in anything else related to the military or intelligence.

Troy glanced at the main house. The knowledge that Jocelyn might not understand the full gravity of the dangers facing the Whitmores and anyone near them caused Troy to quicken his pace. His search of the bungalow and the surrounding yard didn't reveal anything, nor did his sweep of the dock.

Though part of him wanted to check out the beach to make sure there wasn't a boat tethered there, he wasn't prepared to put that much distance between himself and Jocelyn. Or rather, he couldn't put that much distance between himself and the Whitmores. Katherine and Jim were trusting him to keep them safe.

Taking a different path than the way he had come, he circled back to the house. Again, he didn't see anything that should have set off the alarm. He used his key to let himself back inside.

He made it only halfway to the office before he heard Samson's growl.

"It's just me," Troy said, his voice low.

Jocelyn was sitting in front of the computer in the office, Samson standing protectively beside her.

The dog's ears perked up for a second before he growled again.

"Is something out there?"

The rumble continued in Samson's throat.

"Has he been growling the whole time I was gone?" Troy asked.

"No. He only started a couple minutes ago," Jocelyn said. "I don't know what set him off."

Troy flipped the light switch, leaving them in the dark.

"What are you doing?" Jocelyn asked.

"I want to make sure no one is out there."

"Why would anyone come on the island in the middle of the night?"

"I can't think of a good reason." *Except to assassinate a presidential candidate.* He crossed to the window and peeked through the blinds. Nothing but water and rock.

Another growl from Samson.

"Something's got to be out there for him to be acting like this," Jocelyn said. "Maybe raccoons are getting into the trash."

"If they were, they would have run off when I checked the yard," Troy said. "I'm going to make sure the house is secure. Wait here."

"In the dark?"

"You can use the flashlight on the cell phone if you want some light, but keep it pointed at the floor," Troy said.

"If I can use a flashlight, why can't I just turn on the light?"

"If someone is out there, turning on a light gives the intruder a target. The beam of a flashlight, if you keep it pointed down, is small enough to go unnoticed."

With his gun still in hand, he moved back into the hall. Time to find out if the problem was a something or a someone.

* * *

Jocelyn fumbled with the phone to turn on the flashlight. She swiped at the screen, but instead of the shortcuts popping up, a faint ringing sounded, and the screen lit up with an outgoing call, the letter *A* visible above a phone number.

"Oh no."

Before she could hang up, a man's voice came over the line. "Is everything okay?"

"Sorry. I didn't mean to wake you up," Jocelyn said.

"It's daytime where I am," he said. "Is that an alarm I hear?"

"Yeah," Jocelyn said. "My friend went outside to see what's setting it off."

"Your friend?" he asked. "Who is this?"

A familiarity in the voice struck her, but she couldn't place it. She started to answer the question, but with how Ty had been acting, she fought against her normal response. "I'm not sure I should answer that question. Who is this?"

"You're calling off a guardian's phone. Why?"

A guardian? "Sorry, it was an accident. I was trying to turn on the flashlight on the phone."

The alarm continued to sound from the computer.

"What's going on there?" he asked.

"I don't know. The alarm went off, but there isn't anything visible on the video images."

"Tell your guardian to call me when he comes back."

"How can I give my friend a message? I don't know your name."

"Give him the phone. He can press redial."

In an instant, Jocelyn was transported back to her childhood when she used to race her sister to the phone. The phrase "give him the phone" brought with it a sense of déjà vu only, in her mind, *him* switched to *her*. "Ace?"

"What?"

Jocelyn shook her head. She was hearing things. "Sorry, you sound just like my sister's old boyfriend." A boyfriend who had died over twenty years ago.

The dog barked.

"Samson, quiet."

Silence hung over the line for a moment before the man spoke again. "Is your friend back yet?"

"No, not yet."

"Stay on the line until he gets there."

Jocelyn opened her mouth to respond, but she swallowed her words when the door opened and Ty walked in.

Jocelyn held out the phone. "Someone wants to talk to you."

CHAPTER 29

Troy took the phone. Who was calling him at this hour of the night?

"Hello?"

"What was my sister-in-law doing with a guardian-issued phone?" Ace asked.

"I needed a way for her to call me while I was outside checking out the reason for the alarm."

"Did you find anything?"

"Nothing." Troy leaned down and reset the alarms, the buzzing that had accompanied them now silent. "I'll stay up tonight in case there's someone out there."

"Keep me informed."

"I will."

"Also, you'll need to make up a story about who I am. Jocelyn recognized my voice."

"What?"

"I hung out at her house all through high school. Her sister was my best friend, even before we started dating. Not to mention I called Kristi every day when I was in college. Jocelyn almost always answered."

Troy turned to Jocelyn, who was staring at him. "I'll do what I can. Talk to you later."

"Who was that?" Jocelyn asked as soon as he hung up.

"A friend."

"He said something about that being a guardian's phone. What's that all about?"

"That's classified."

"Seriously?"

Troy debated briefly how much he could say without opening the guardians up to unwanted speculation. "Please don't repeat it to anyone. It's a code name for the unit I work with."

"You can trust me."

"I hope so. You're already privy to information that is being hidden from the general public."

Jocelyn waved toward the bedroom where the Whitmores were apparently still sleeping. "You mean where the Whitmores are hiding?"

"Yeah. I'm kind of surprised they didn't wake up."

"The sound of the surf is so loud, you can hardly hear anything in the master bedroom." Jocelyn pointed at the computer where the security feed was still visible. "Besides, that alarm isn't very loud. I'm surprised my sister didn't have it set up in her bedroom instead of in here."

"She has a laptop she uses that duplicates the desktop."

"I guess it's a good thing she wasn't looking at it tonight." Jocelyn hesitated before she corrected herself. "I guess it would be today for her."

"Yeah, it would."

"Are you really going to stay up all night and watch the monitors?"

"I'll do a couple more security sweeps outside, but yeah," Troy said. "I can't take any chances with the Whitmores' safety."

"I can't imagine anyone would be able to find them here." Her eyebrows drew together. "Unless they brought their cell phones with them. I've seen that on TV before, where someone gets found through the GPS on their electronics."

"The Whitmores are clean," Troy said. Kade had ensured they didn't bring any electronic signatures with them, and the senator was well-versed enough in intelligence to know how to avoid such a scenario.

"While you're up, can you help me access the internet? I need to send out the file for work."

"Yeah. Grab your laptop."

Jocelyn took a step toward the door.

"Actually, you wait here," Troy said. "Where is it? I'll get it for you."

"It's on the coffee table."

Troy couldn't explain why he felt the need to keep Jocelyn tucked away in the office, but he didn't fight his protective instinct. He retrieved her laptop and returned a moment later. "Here you go."

"Thanks." She settled into the chair across from the desk.

Troy debated briefly how to give Jocelyn access to the internet without her realizing that all of her correspondence was being cleared by him. He opened his laptop and set it between them so Jocelyn couldn't see his screen. Once he granted Jocelyn access to the dummy server, he said, "You should be good now."

"Thanks." Jocelyn proceeded to tap on her keyboard. A moment later, her outgoing email popped up on his screen.

"All done," Jocelyn said.

"Which project was this? The Boys and Girls Club?" Troy asked as he opened up the email to ensure she hadn't inadvertently exposed classified information.

"No, I sent that in a couple days ago," Jocelyn said. "This one is for Diamond Brothers."

"I thought you weren't taking on any more work from your company."

"I wasn't going to, but my replacement called when you went to pick up the Whitmores," Jocelyn said. "A rival company poached one of our top graphic designers, so I offered to help out."

"Gotcha." Troy scanned the text of her note to someone in her company. Even though her email stated that she was turning over the rest of the ad campaign to her employees, he asked, "How much longer will you be working on this project?"

"My part is done. Angela and the other designers can put on the finishing touches." Jocelyn stood. "I'm going to make some hot chocolate. Do you want some?"

His uneasiness at having Jocelyn in the main living area of the house surfaced again. He glanced at Samson, who now lay quiet on the floor.

"That would be great, but do me a favor and take the dog with you."

"Why?"

"Because if someone is outside, he'll let you know."

"I think you're being paranoid."

"That's my job."

"One of these days, you really need to tell me more about this job of yours." Jocelyn took a step toward the door. "Come on, Samson."

Troy waited for her to leave before he opened the attachment she was sending to her old company. Time to get it cleared and send the email on its way so he could focus on more important things, like if someone else really was on the island.

* * *

Jocelyn carried two mugs of hot chocolate down the hall. Sugar wasn't going to help her sleep, but after the events of the past twenty minutes, she doubted her mind was going to shut down for at least another hour or two.

Her conversation with the man on the phone kept playing through her mind. Who was he? Had she not attended Ace Samson's funeral with her family, she would have sworn she'd been talking to her sister's old boyfriend. Jocelyn had only been eight when Ace died, but she had been old enough to always be the first to answer the phone when it rang, even though nine times out of ten it had been for her sister. Ace had been Kristi's most frequent caller. He had also spent nearly every weekend at their house.

Jocelyn's heart ached for her sister. Even though Kristi had dated over the years, never had she found someone she loved the way she had loved Ace. Jocelyn suspected that Kristi's loss was the reason she was still single.

Samson, Ace's canine namesake, led the way into the office, where Ty currently sat in front of the desktop.

"Here you go." She handed him one of the mugs. "Have you seen anything out there?"

"No."

Jocelyn settled into the chair across from him. "The alarm that went off, how does it work?"

"It was an exterior motion sensor."

"Maybe it was a deer or a bird that set it off."

"It's possible."

"Does this happen a lot?"

"This is only the second time since I've lived here."

"With as much wildlife as we have on the island, I'm surprised the sensors don't go off all the time."

"Only the cameras and motion sensors closest to the house and by the helicopter pad are on all the time. Your sister replaced the one near the garden with a security light because it kept going off."

"That's not surprising," Jocelyn said. "What about by the water? You knew Gil was coming before he got here."

"Kristi has a sensor on the buoy near the cove."

"What about the rest of the island?"

"From what I understand, if any of the main sensors trip, it will activate a secondary system that has other sensors around the island. Those are really only used to try to locate an intruder once a problem has been identified."

"I can't believe my sister went to all of this expense," Jocelyn said. "Of course, if she hadn't had the extra security, who knows if she would have survived that intruder last year."

"It was a scary time, from what I understand."

"It was." Jocelyn blew on the dark liquid in her cup before she took a sip. "What are you watching for now?"

"Anything that moves."

"That sounds extremely boring."

"If you need help sleeping, you can watch with me for a while."

"I don't think there's any way I'm falling asleep anytime soon." She set her mug on the edge of the desk and picked up her laptop. "Is it okay with you if I work here for a while?"

"If you want. I'd prefer you stay in the main house tonight anyway." Ty took a swallow of his hot chocolate and leaned back in his chair. "What are you working on?"

"The Whitmore campaign." Jocelyn opened her latest photos and scrolled through her favorites. She stopped when she reached one of Jim and Katherine standing side by side, their fishing poles in the water. She angled her laptop toward him. "What do you think of this one?"

"I like it. I think my favorite, though, is the one where you zoomed in on their hands."

"That one did turn out well," Jocelyn said. "I think if I mix in a couple of the Whitmores in the kitchen together, the only thing I still need are some shots of the senator at work."

"What do you mean?" Ty's posture stiffened as though suddenly uncomfortable. "I thought your idea was to portray him in more natural settings."

"Well, yeah, but I also don't want the public to forget where he's worked for the past twenty years."

"I'm sure his campaign manager has some photos you can use."

"I wasn't impressed with the pictures the PR firm used for his last ad," Jocelyn said. "He looked much too stiff, too presidential."

"Don't you want him to look presidential?"

"I want him to look like the man everyone wants to have in the White House without appearing too arrogant to remember he represents the people." Jocelyn settled her computer back on her lap and started building a mock-up ad. "How long do you think it will be before the senator and his wife get to go back home?"

"I don't know," Ty said. "He's going to do the debate from here. Maybe you can take some photos of him then. I'm sure he'll dress in a suit for that."

"I guess that will have to do for now."

CHAPTER 30

As soon as the sun came up, Troy scoured the grounds around the house, looking for any sign of an intruder. Tracks for deer, raccoon, and squirrels were mixed with Samson's, but no matter how hard he looked, the only footprints evident on the island were those that appeared to come from him, Jocelyn, and the Whitmores. And none of those crossed through the area where the alarm had triggered last night.

He had watched the security monitors all night, fueled by hot chocolate and leftover scones. Jocelyn had stayed up with him until dawn when he'd finally escorted her back to the bungalow. At least he had managed a couple hours of sleep before the security system had woken him.

If the evidence in front of him was accurate, whatever had triggered it had been a creature of the four-legged variety.

Footsteps approached, and Troy whirled, his hand instinctively going to the grip of his handgun.

"It's just me," Jim said. "Katherine is making pancakes and wanted to know if you'd like some."

"Maybe later. I need to walk the coastline."

"Is something wrong?"

"Something tripped an alarm last night. I want to make sure no one came onto the island," Troy said.

"You don't really think someone could have tracked us here, do you?"

"It's highly unlikely." Jocelyn's comment about tracking electronics flitted through his mind. "You and your wife didn't bring any kind of electronics with you, did you?"

"No. Ghost made sure of that," Jim said. "The only things we have with us are our clothes and the cell phone Ghost gave me."

"Is it the one you had from before the intrusion?"

"No. Even though he said that phone is secure, he switched it out for another one."

Troy waved in the direction of the sensor that had tripped. "Everything I'm seeing here looks like last night's guest was probably a deer or a raccoon."

"That's good news," Jim said. "I'm surprised I didn't hear the alarm go off."

"It's only rigged to sound on the computer in the office and on the relay I have set up on my laptop and my cell phone," Troy said. "With this island being so remote, the last thing we want is some random person showing up to visit Kristi and finding out she has a high-tech alarm system."

"I guess that would look suspicious to the neighbors."

"Yeah."

"How extensive is the security system here?" Jim asked.

Troy gave him the same explanation he had given Jocelyn earlier.

"Sounds like it's a decent system considering how much land is here." Jim took a step toward the house. "I'll let Katherine know to save you some breakfast. Have you seen Jocelyn yet this morning?"

"She was up all night. I doubt we'll see her before noon."

"We'll save some breakfast for her too."

"I'm sure she'd appreciate that."

* * *

Walter Royce stood with his wife as Shawn Hammels's brothers and uncles escorted the casket out of the church. An abundance of top government officials were in attendance at the service. Walter had hoped for a spotlight moment as Hammels's main competitor, but the president's presence stole that from him. Too bad.

Walter lingered long enough to chat with a few of his fellow senators before making his way out to his car. The driver opened the door. Walter waited for Marcia to slide into the back seat before taking his spot beside her.

"It's so hard to believe Shawn Hammels is dead," Marcia said. "He was so young."

"Yes, he was." Young enough to still have three kids in elementary school. Young enough that he could have been instrumental in US politics for decades to come. Young enough that the Russians had been unwilling to let him see his future.

Though Walter couldn't prove it, he suspected Ilina or Gavrie had something to do with Hammels's death. He wasn't buying the natural causes story. The timing had been too convenient.

Walter's gut clenched. It was one thing to help eliminate candidates who had already experienced the prime of their lives, but someone so young? He didn't think he could have condoned such a death. Hammels's kids were even younger than his were.

Emotionally exhausted, Walter fought the urge to lean his head back. Had it only been a week ago that he had been counting down to when his main competitor would be eliminated and the guardians' resources crippled? Now, instead of moving forward with a sense of security, he woke every morning wondering if that day would ever come.

Even though Shawn Hammels was no longer a competitor, Walter needed his campaign to pick up traction soon. If the Russians kept killing off his competition, eventually someone was going to point a finger at him.

Walter's cell phone chimed. He glanced at it, and a text popped onto the screen. He opened it, and new hope took flight.

"Who was that from?" Marcia asked.

"Another one of those travel deals I keep getting."

"You should block the number."

"Sometimes they're worth looking at," Walter said.

"Did you want to join the procession to the cemetery?" the driver asked.

"Yes, thank you." Walter stared out the window as they left the church in the heart of DC and crossed the Potomac River to Arlington National Cemetery. When they arrived, he took his spot with the host of VIP attendees and their significant others.

The graveside service was thankfully brief.

As soon as the mourners began dispersing, Marcia took his arm. "Are you ready to go?"

"I want to stay for a little while."

She glanced at her watch. "I'm sorry, but I need to get home to pick the girls up from school."

"You go ahead," Walter said. "Brendan can take you home and come back for me."

"Are you sure? I can wait a few minutes."

"I want to visit my father's grave, and I think some time alone will do me good."

"Are you worried you're going to be next?" Marcia asked.

"What do you mean?"

"Someone tried to assassinate the vice president last month, then Jim Whitmore this month. Shawn Hammels is dead." Marcia took a deep breath. "It's scary."

"Don't worry. I'll be fine."

"Okay." She leaned in and kissed him. "Call me if you're going to be late tonight."

"I will." Walter watched her disappear into the departing crowd, then made his way to his father's gravesite. A woman stood by the next marker over.

It took only a brief glance to recognize her as his handler.

"Is Shawn Hammels dead because of you?" Walter asked.

"Don't worry," Ilina said. "No one will ever be able to prove it was anything other than a heart attack."

Walter took a moment. "I could have beaten him without your help."

"We saw an opportunity and had to take it."

Walter tried to push aside the little flicker of guilt that Hammels had been killed because of the threat he was to Walter's campaign. Instead, he tried to focus on his real foe. "Any luck finding Whitmore?"

"No. He's hidden himself well."

Frustration rose. "I think it's more accurate to say the guardians have hidden him well."

"Either way, we have no idea where he is."

"There has to be some way to find him," Walter insisted.

"We're trying," Ilina said. "We're monitoring secret service assignments, his PR firm, his neighbors, his family. So far, we haven't found anything."

"Have you even found his family?"

"No. They're all in hiding, just like the senator," Ilina said.

"If you don't have any new information for me, why am I here?"

"It's time we see how committed James Whitmore is to his responsibilities as a senator."

"What do you mean?"

"I can't imagine he isn't monitoring the budget changes somehow from wherever he is. If a few more key programs disappear from the budget . . ."

"Do you really think he would risk his life for his country?"

"I think it's worth finding out."

* * *

Jocelyn didn't bother to check the time when she stumbled out of her room and headed for the shower. She couldn't remember the last time she had pulled an all-nighter. Four years ago? Maybe five? And that certainly hadn't been because she was hanging out watching security cameras. Not that she had spent much time doing that. Ty had stared at cameras. She had stared at her laptop.

At least he had chatted with her while they'd stared at their respective screens. He hadn't opened up about his past like he had before, but favorite movies and foods had been safe enough topics. Although, how the man could like liver was beyond her.

As soon as she dressed, she went over to the main house, but she was alone. Where was everyone? Had there really been someone on the island, and if so, why hadn't Ty woken her?

Maybe something had happened to him and the Whitmores. Jocelyn peeked out the window. Nothing. No Ty. No Samson. No senator. No Katherine.

Her uneasiness increased, and she retrieved her grandfather's rifle. She loaded the gun and pocketed some extra ammunition.

She checked out the window again. Seeing nothing, she made her way to the back door. The cabin cruiser was docked where it always was, and she didn't see any sign of a visitor. If she was going to sneak onto the island, where would she secure her boat? Other than Ty's helicopter, a boat was the only way onto the island. The helicopter. Maybe Ty and the Whitmores went somewhere.

Questions and scenarios continued to flood her mind as she made her way through the orchard and up the path to the helicopter. All the while, she listened for any sound out of place. She wondered if she would even notice.

She found the helicopter exactly where it was supposed to be.

The boat was here. The helicopter was here. So where was everyone?

She crossed to the cliffs and looked out at the ocean. The water stretched out before her, mirroring the blue sky. A few boats dotted the water between Heritage Island and the mainland.

The leaves behind her rustled. Jocelyn's grip tightened on the rifle, and she whirled toward the sound.

Ty stepped into the clearing. "Hey, what are you doing up here?"

Her free hand lifted to her chest, where she could feel her heart pounding. "I was looking for you. I woke up, and no one was in the house. I got worried."

"Sorry about that." He closed the distance between them. "The Whitmores went for a walk on the beach."

"And Samson is with them?"

"Yeah."

"What about you? What have you been up to?"

"I was checking out the island to see if I could figure out what set off the alarm last night."

"Any luck?"

"No. It must have been some sort of wildlife. I couldn't find any sign of anyone being here."

The tension in her shoulders eased. "That's good news."

"Yeah, it is." He nodded at the rifle. "Unless you were planning on more target practice, I don't think you'll be needing that."

"Better safe than sorry."

"Yeah." He took her free hand and tugged. They started toward the house, and he asked, "Want to help me decide what to fix for dinner? I told Katherine I'd cook tonight."

"Dinner? I'm ready for breakfast."

"I'm afraid you have your days and nights mixed up."

"It's not the first time that's happened," Jocelyn said. "Did you get any sleep?"

"A couple hours. I took a nap after I did my first check of the island," Ty said. "Do you want to watch a movie tonight?"

Delighted at the prospect, she smiled. "Are you asking me out on a date?"

"It will probably be a double date with the senator and his wife."

"I'd like that." Anticipation fluttered in her stomach. They continued down the path to the house. "Want to check out the lobster pots with me?"

"I wouldn't say no to a lobster dinner."

Jocelyn stopped at the shed and took the time to unload her grandfather's rifle before she set it inside and traded it for gloves and a large bucket.

"You're looking optimistic today," Ty said. "We haven't caught a single lobster since I've been here."

"Yeah, but the new traps have been out for a couple days, and I didn't check them yesterday." Jocelyn led the way to the buoy and pulled on the rope until the first pot surfaced. One lobster was inside, barely over the legal limit.

"You caught one."

"He might make an appetizer for us." Jocelyn tugged on her gloves and filled the bucket halfway with saltwater. The lobster's claws snapped as she moved it from the trap into the bucket and put the lid on to keep it from climbing out.

"Hopefully, we'll have more luck with the other one." Jocelyn moved to the second pot and smiled. "This is more like it."

"Did you get another one?"

"Four more." She proceeded to transfer their catch from the pot to the bucket, pausing when she checked out the third one, which had a notch in its tail. She tossed it back into the water.

"What did you do that for?"

"It was a female with a notched tail."

"So?"

"So, it means she's a good egg bearer. We can't keep her." She retrieved the last lobster, checked it for size, and tossed it into the water as well.

"What was wrong with that one?"

"It was too big." She closed the trap. "Three will be plenty, especially if we dig up a few clams to go with them."

"What do we do with these while we get the clams?"

"There's a holding tank in the shed. We'll need to get some more salt water for it, but that'll hold them until we're ready to fix dinner."

"I think you're the one making dinner tonight."

The simplicity of his comment, along with the expectation that they would dine together warmed her. "I'll cook the seafood. If you want anything else on the table, that's on you."

"Does macaroni and cheese go with lobster?"

"Macaroni and cheese goes with everything."

"Good. We have a plan."

* * *

A lobster dinner with Jocelyn and the Whitmores, a movie with Jocelyn snuggled beside him on the couch. The walls Troy had built around his heart continued to chip away. He suspected it wouldn't be long before they crumbled entirely.

The night couldn't have been more perfect. Of course, Jocelyn and Katherine had insisted they watch a romantic comedy for their movie night. It really was like a double date. At least, he was pretty sure this was what dating was supposed to feel like.

With the exception of a few short-lived relationships in high school, his social life had been centered around life on base and taking college classes. Looking back now, he supposed he owed his recruiter for pushing him to get his degree and apply to officer candidate school. He'd gone straight from OCS into flight training. He'd worked hard to earn his wings, determined to open another door for his future. If only he had been assigned to the East Coast or Okinawa for his first post instead of California.

Water under the bridge, he reminded himself. The events that had led to his fictional death had brought him to this point, for better or for worse.

The couple on the television screen kissed, and Jocelyn snuggled closer. Troy couldn't resist brushing the hair off her face and pressing his lips to her forehead.

The movie ended, and the credits started rolling. On the other couch, Jim stretched his arms over his head and stood. "I'd better get to bed. I have a lot of prep work to do tomorrow to get ready for the debate on Thursday."

"Thanks for hanging out with us tonight." Troy pulled away from Jocelyn, not sure what the senator would think about him getting romantically involved with an uncleared civilian.

"I think I'll head to bed too." Katherine stood. When Troy started to stand, she waved at him. "Don't get up. We'll see you in the morning."

"Good night," Jocelyn said.

"Night." Katherine took her husband's hand, and the two disappeared down the hall.

"I really like them," Jocelyn said. "I hope the senator wins the election."

"Me too." Troy picked up the remote and turned off the TV before he settled back on the couch beside Jocelyn. He slipped his arm around her shoulders again. "Are married couples usually like Jim and Katherine?"

"What do you mean?"

"They've been married for at least thirty years, and they still always seem to want to spend time together. They even hold hands."

"I don't think my parents are quite as in tune as the Whitmores are with each other, but I think any marriage can be good if both people are willing to work at it," Jocelyn said. "My mom always says that being a wife and a mother are the two hardest jobs she's ever had, but they're also the most rewarding."

"I guess I never thought about marriage as being work."

"Nothing worth having is ever easy," Jocelyn said.

"I guess you're right."

CHAPTER 31

Jim straightened his tie and stepped in front of the camera set up in the living room. The national debate for his party would start in a matter of minutes, and he was a nervous wreck. Instead of interacting with his opponents in front of a live crowd, tonight, he would have an audience of three.

Was this really worth it? He and Katherine had been on the island for four days, and the authorities still hadn't made any progress on finding the man who had broken into his home.

"Are you sure about this?" he asked Ty. "Maybe I should skip the debate."

"Trust me. Ghost made sure the signal won't be traced," Ty said.

"Who's Ghost?" Jocelyn asked from where she stood behind where she had mounted her camera to a tripod, the video feature ready to go.

"A mutual friend," Ty said as though he had anticipated the question. "Are you sure you're okay operating the camera? If you want to take regular photos, I can do it."

"It's fine. I already took a bunch of the senator getting ready for the debate." Jocelyn adjusted the headset she wore and motioned to the tripod. "Besides, everything is all set up. All I have to do is hit record as soon as the studio gives us the word."

Jim took a deep breath. "This is even more nerve-racking than when I'm with the other candidates."

"You'll be fine," Katherine said. "All you have to do is be honest and speak from the heart."

"That's easy for you to say," Jim muttered.

"Trust your wife," Jocelyn said. "She's a smart lady."

"I knew I liked you." Katherine crossed to Jim and fixed his tie herself. "There. Perfect."

Jocelyn held up a hand. "Okay, we're going live in two minutes."

Jim fought the urge to mess with his tie again. He straightened his shoulders and looked at the camera.

"Katherine, come over here." Jocelyn motioned to the spot beside her. After Katherine complied, Jocelyn continued. "Okay, Senator, don't worry about looking at the camera. Just talk to Katherine. Give her your answers. That will make it feel more natural."

Jim took a deep breath. "I can do that."

"I'm sure you can." Jocelyn held up a hand. "We're live in five, four, three . . ." Jocelyn signaled two and one without the accompanying words. The moderator's voice came on over the earpiece Jim wore.

"Senator Whitmore, can you hear me?"

"Yes, I can."

"Excellent. Then let's get started."

* * *

Troy jogged along the beach, Samson racing beside him. Since the day of the false alarm, he had made a habit of taking a daily run around the island. A light dusting of snow had fallen overnight, leaving an undisturbed shimmer of white on the ground.

Between his growing confidence in the security on the island and the results of last night's debate, Troy suspected Jim Whitmore was well on his way to the White House. Or he would be once the guardians neutralized the threat against him and proved the Russians were pulling Royce's strings.

Troy took the path to the house and emerged by the yard, where Jocelyn stood on the dock, gloves on her hands and a bucket at her feet.

His heart stuttered at the mere sight of her.

"Hey, Samson." Jocelyn set down her tools and scratched behind the dog's ears. "What trouble are you getting into this morning?"

Troy slowed to a walk, not surprised by the dog's excitement about Jocelyn's presence. He couldn't blame him.

She looked up and saw him. "I was wondering if you were out here."

"Yeah. Samson came on my run with me." Troy reached her, and Jocelyn leaned in for a kiss. The naturalness of the gesture and his instinctive response struck him. Her lips on his chased away the worst memories of his past, and he couldn't resist pulling her closer.

How had they gotten here? Meals together, movie nights, long walks, and their all-night adventure watching security footage. Somehow, it had all combined to create something unique and precious. He had been so hesitant to let Jocelyn stay here on the island when she'd first arrived, yet now he wanted nothing more than for her to stay on Heritage Island for the duration.

Shaken by the thought, he pulled back and tried to gain his footing. The presence of the bucket with a lid on it gave him an easy conversation starter. "Looks like you're planning to fix dinner again."

"I only caught one. I'm hoping Katherine can help me make lobster bisque."

"That sounds good."

"I thought so. We both know it'll be better if someone else cooks it though."

Troy didn't dispute her claim. "Do you need help carrying anything?"

"Yeah, if you can put the lobster in the holding tank, that would be great. I want to bait the lobster pots again."

"I can do that." Troy's phone rang. He checked the number to see Ace calling. "I'll see you inside."

"Okay."

Troy carried the bucket with one hand and answered the call with the other. "Hey. What's up?"

"Can you talk?"

"I'm outside right now. Can I call you back in a couple minutes?"

"Sure. Talk to you in a bit."

Troy transferred seawater and the lobster into the holding tank, stored the bucket, and jogged up the stairs. When he reached his office, he closed the door and dialed Ace's number. "Okay, I'm good now."

"Was Jocelyn around?"

"Yeah. She caught a lobster and wanted some help."

"Sounds like the two of you have figured out how to get along."

"You could say that." Troy tugged at the neck of his sweater that suddenly felt too tight. "She's been working with Senator Whitmore on his campaign. It's made things easier now that he's the subject of her photographic exploits."

"What is she doing on Jim's campaign?"

"I'm not completely sure, but she has pictures of him and Katherine fishing on the dock and more of them together in the kitchen," Troy said. "There's one of Jim working at the kitchen table that's really good."

"Glad she found something to keep her busy. She can be a pest when she gets bored."

"From what she said, you should know that well."

"What did she tell you?"

"She told me how you and Kristi used to let her tag along with you when you were in high school."

"I'm surprised she even remembers that. She couldn't have been more than six or seven."

"Apparently, you made a good impression."

"I guess."

"I assume you didn't call to talk about Jocelyn. What's up?"

"I wanted to let you know that we finally have a lead on Walter Royce."

"What did you find?"

"A private plane was chartered out of a little airfield in Vermont. It's about a sixty-mile drive from Royce's place in New Hampshire, but the timing fits when he would have left, if we're right about him being in Europe the weekend of the attack in Helsinki."

Troy sat at his desk. "Do we have any proof he was on the plane?"

"Not yet, but I'm sending a forensics team in to pull prints and any fibers that might tie him to the plane."

"Even if we can tie him to it, that won't prove he was on it the weekend he was supposed to be in New Hampshire."

"Actually, I think it will," Ace said. "This particular aircraft is usually parked in Lithuania. The flight from Vermont was a return trip."

"So?"

"So, we found it odd that the plane made another trip to Vermont only thirty-six hours after it got back home."

"That is odd."

"Not only that, but Kristi and I have also gone over the flight plans for the past two years. The only time that plane was anywhere near where Royce was supposed to be was the weekend we're trying to place him in Europe."

"How long until the forensics team gets there?"

"Should be within the hour."

"As careful as Royce has been, you know it's possible that they scrubbed the aircraft down."

"It is, but I'm also having Kade make a trip to Vermont to talk to the staff at the airport. It's a mom-and-pop operation. There's a good chance someone saw Royce when he got there."

"It's worth a try. We're due for a break in this case."

"We'll get one. It's just a matter of time."

CHAPTER 32

Jim sat at the kitchen table and read through his emails, each one painting a bigger problem than the last. His request to restore the budget items Walter Royce had deleted had gone unheeded, and from the looks of things, even more funding in the intelligence budget was now in jeopardy of being cut. He needed to get back to Washington. Soon.

Jocelyn walked in, a stack of paper in hand. "Senator, do you have a minute?"

"Call me Jim, remember?"

"After last night's debate, I'm tempted to skip straight to Mr. President."

Jim couldn't help but smile. The debate last night had gone far better than he had anticipated, and his lead in the polls had increased by nearly seven points. Afraid to jinx his early success, he said, "Let's hold off on that for the next twelve months or so, shall we?"

"Okay, Mr. Soon-to-Be-President." Jocelyn held out the stack of paper. "I need your opinion on these."

"What are they?"

"The mock-ups for the commercial your PR firm will start running early next year."

Jim picked up the top sheet. A sketched outline of the Capitol Building had been overlaid with a half dozen images. He and Katherine standing on the dock, another of their hands on their fishing poles.

Jim hadn't realized Jocelyn had taken photos of him and Katherine doing the dishes the night before, but she had captured the moment beautifully, right down to the towel on his shoulder and Katherine's smile when she'd laughed at something he'd said. "These are incredible."

"Thanks." Jocelyn's cheeks flushed. "I did several mock-ups so you can see some different layout ideas and a bigger selection of photos. I have more, but I think the ones I used were the best to show you as the man behind the office."

Ty walked in and stopped when he saw what Jim was holding. "That turned out great. I was hoping she would use the one of you and your laptop at the kitchen table."

"I guess we should put that one on the list of photos to keep in the ad." Jim set the top sample aside and looked at the next. One by one, he laid them out on the table. "You have enough here for me to do a whole series of ads."

"That was the idea. You'll want to freshen up your commercials as your campaign progresses," Jocelyn said.

"Katherine is going to love what you've done."

"Where is she?" Jocelyn asked.

"Putting away laundry." Jim gathered the pages again and handed them to Jocelyn. "You should show these to her. She'll love you forever if you give her an excuse to take a break."

Jocelyn grinned. "I can do that."

As soon as she left, Jim turned to Ty. "I hate to tell you this, but I've got to get back to work on the Hill. Royce lined out some more critical projects. I think he's looking for your funding."

"He must not know that he already deleted it," Ty said. "How soon do you need to get back?"

"Monday."

"I'll work with Ghost to see what we can do to increase security."

"Anything else on proving Royce's involvement?"

"We have a new lead that's promising. I hope to hear back from Kristi's husband soon."

"I'll pray for that."

* * *

Three days. That was all Troy had until he would need to escort Senator Whitmore to DC. Dealing with the potential security issues at the Capitol Building would be bad enough, but trying to do so with Walter Royce within the same walls was going to be a nightmare. For every person the guardians could plant to protect Whitmore, Royce could bring in another potential assassin.

They already knew the name and face of one assassin. Capturing him would go a long way in ensuring Jim's safety, but until Royce was arrested and his power limited, Troy wasn't going to rest easy.

Leaving Jocelyn here on the island didn't sit well with him either. He also didn't know whether to risk leaving Katherine here or if he should consider bringing her to Washington.

He checked the message board for updates. Nothing. He checked the time. Too late to call Ace, but Kade was still in the same time zone.

Troy dialed his number. "Any luck finding a witness in Vermont?"

"Nothing so far," Kade said. "Flight logs show the plane in question landed at twenty-one hundred the day before the Helsinki incident. It refueled and left three hours later."

"Did you talk to the airport employees working that night?"

"Yeah, but the airport runs on a skeleton staff after five. No one remembers anything."

"Do they have security cameras of the parking lot?" Troy asked. "Royce would have had to get there somehow."

"They do, but the airport isn't cooperating."

"Makes me wonder if someone there is covering for him."

"That was my thought." Determination vibrated in Kade's voice.

"How long will it take you to hack into their system?"

"I've been at it for three hours so far. I'll let you know when I break through."

"Thanks. We're on a bit of a time crunch. Jim Whitmore said he needs to get back to DC by Monday. Royce is going after critical projects in the budget."

"Trying to get us to tip our hand."

"That and bring Jim out of hiding," Troy said. "I'm not thrilled with the idea of taking him back there."

"I can get to DC by Sunday, and I'll have Renee drive up and start surveillance."

"That'll help, but a staff of three isn't a lot against Morozov," Troy said. "No offense against the Capitol police, but they don't know who they're dealing with."

"Maybe it's time we clue them in."

"What do you suggest? We can't tell them we suspect a US senator of being involved with two assassination attempts."

"For all we know, it was two assassination attempts and one assassination."

"What?"

"The autopsy results just came back on Shawn Hammels. Officially, he died of a heart attack, but the coroner couldn't find any evidence of a heart condition that would explain the sudden death."

"Sounds like he was poisoned."

"Nothing popped up on the tox screen, but get this. The restaurant where Hammels was killed had a new waiter that night, but he didn't come back to work the next day. According to the manager, the man said he was hired by the restaurant owner, but the owner denies hiring anyone."

"Let me guess. Brown hair, average height, average weight."

"With a Russian accent," Kade said. "It had to be Morozov."

"I have to think he's still in DC."

"He's waiting to finish what he started," Kade agreed. "I think it's time to bring in reinforcements. I'll call Ace to see if he can come help out for a few days."

"That's a good idea."

"I'll let you know what the forensics team comes up with."

"I thought we would have had something by now," Troy said.

"I thought so too, but I talked to Ace a little while ago. They can't find the plane."

"They can't find it?"

"No."

Troy's stomach sank. "So much for finding proof."

CHAPTER 33

Jocelyn turned on the TV and logged into her Netflix account. Or she tried to. Every time she entered her username and password, an error message popped up. Internet Connection Failed.

"Problem?" Katherine asked from where she sat on the couch across from her, a book in hand.

"It's not letting me log in. I thought everyone might want to watch a movie."

"I think I'm going to read in bed for a little while." Katherine closed her book and stood. "I'll see you in the morning."

"Good night." Jocelyn tried to log in again unsuccessfully. Resigned that she would have to limit her options to DVDs, she crossed to the cabinet and flipped through the movies her sister had left behind.

"Find anything interesting?" Ty asked.

"I didn't hear you there." Jocelyn stepped toward him. "You're working late."

"Yeah. I have some logistics I need to work out, but I probably won't get the information I need until tomorrow."

"Does that mean you have time for a break?"

"Yeah. Did you find a movie you liked?"

"Not really. Want to do a puzzle instead?"

"A puzzle?" His eyebrows drew together as though she were speaking a different language.

"Yeah. You know. You take the pieces, fit them together, and create a picture?"

"I don't think I've done a puzzle since I was in elementary school."

"Seriously? Time to remedy that. Puzzles are perfect for a lazy evening at home." She leaned down and opened the lower section of an occasion table. After a brief debate, she selected a puzzle she hadn't done before. "Here's one we can do."

"Where are we supposed to do this puzzle? Is it something we can finish in one night?"

"I doubt it, but Grandma used to keep a puzzle board in the laundry room."

"What's a puzzle board?"

"You put it on the table so that you can take your time on the puzzle but still be able to move it aside when you need to use the kitchen table," Jocelyn said. "I'll see if it's still there."

She found the felt-covered board exactly where her grandmother had kept it when Jocelyn and Kristi used to come visit. Jocelyn carried it to the kitchen table. "Here we go."

"Now what?"

"Now we make a picture." Jocelyn opened the box and dumped the pieces onto the board. She turned several over so the color was showing.

Ty sat across from her and followed her lead. His lack of conversation caused her to study him.

"Is everything okay? You've been quiet all night."

"I have a lot going on with work."

"Does this have anything to do with Jim going back to DC?"

"How did you know about that?" Ty asked.

"I overheard the two of you talking." She noted his concerned expression and quickly added, "Sorry, I wasn't trying to eavesdrop."

"Don't tell anyone, but he has to be back at work on Monday."

"Is he still in danger?"

"Yes."

"Then how can he go back?" Jocelyn asked.

"He has work to do that can't be done by anyone else." He looked up from the puzzle. "If I could find a way for him to work remotely, I would."

"What about Katherine? Is she going too?"

"We haven't talked about it yet, but I'm assuming he'll want her to stay here," Ty said. "I know if it were me, I wouldn't want you to be anywhere near potential danger."

The concerned way Ty spoke of her safety brought a bevy of butterflies to her stomach and drove home the reality of how much their relationship had changed in the last few days.

"I assume you're flying Jim to DC. Will you be gone long?"

"I'll stay with him until he does what he needs to," Ty said. "We'll be back by Friday at the latest."

"Are you going to give me your number so we can talk while you're gone?"

"No, but I'll give you a phone you can call me on."

"Why would you want me to use a different phone to call you?"

"Because my phone is government issued. Using it for personal calls can get me in trouble."

"I guess that makes sense," Jocelyn said, although she wasn't sure it really did. She turned over the last piece of the puzzle and started gathering blue pieces that made up the ocean. She tested a few of the middle pieces until she found two that went together. She repeated the process until she had six pieces attached.

Ty also fit several pieces together, but all of his were part of the edge. "Why are you starting with the middle?" he asked. "I may not know much about puzzles, but I at least know to do the outside first."

"That's how Kristi does it."

"But you don't?"

"Sometimes. Not always."

"You really are one of a kind, aren't you?"

"I could say the same thing about you," Jocelyn said. "I'm going to miss you next week."

Ty put his hand on hers. "I'm going to miss you too."

* * *

Seven hours to hack into the airport's security system. Kade was losing his touch. Then again, what regional airport used a military-grade, encrypted computer system?

From the hotel room he had turned into his current center of operations, he downloaded the surveillance footage and scanned through the files on the airport's server. Might as well see if anything else might point a finger at Royce or the Russians being involved. He copied everything: financials, personnel rosters, billing, correspondence.

He added it all into the guardian database and sent a text to Kristi with the request to search the billing and financials. After he tasked Ace with the other computer files, he dialed his wife's number.

She answered with a groggy hello.

"Hey, sorry to wake you."

"That's what you always say," Renee said.

Kade envisioned her in a hotel room, her hair tumbled and her face free of makeup. "Okay, so, I'm sorry I'm not there to wake you in person."

"Honesty. That's a good quality." Humor laced her voice. "What's going on? Did you find anything?"

"Not yet. I need some help going through the surveillance feed."

"How many cameras?"

"Four. The front gate, the entrance to the main building, the hangar, and the runway."

"Going through the images shouldn't take long since we've already narrowed the window of when Royce could have arrived."

"That was my thought, but we'll need to widen the time frame in case he has a handler or anyone else we can tie back to him."

"Let's see if we can even prove Royce was there first," Renee suggested. "I'll start with the front gate and the main building. You take the other two."

"Deal. Call me if you find anything."

"You know I will. When are you back in DC?"

"I'll catch a train in a few hours."

"Are you sure you don't want to fly?"

"We don't have time for me to sit around in airports waiting on a flight," Kade said. "I booked a private compartment on the train so I can watch video on my way to DC."

"I'll get started on what you sent. You should take a nap."

"I'll sleep after we find what we need," Kade said.

"We've been trying to prove Royce's involvement for over a month."

"We're going to find something this time. I can feel it."

"I hope you're right, because we're running out of time. Senator Whitmore returns to Washington in two days."

"I know. I'll talk to you soon."

"Love you."

"Love you too." Kade hung up and set an alarm for when he would need to leave for the train station. Then he opened the first surveillance video and hit play. Maybe, for once, they would find what they needed in the first few hours instead of after viewing every available minute of security feed. Maybe.

* * *

Jocelyn tapped on her keyboard with one hand and held her phone with the other. Early-morning sunlight filtered into the living room, where she sat alone.

Troy had taken Samson out for a run twenty minutes ago, and the Whitmores hadn't yet appeared from their bedroom. The early-morning call from Jim's publicist had taken her by surprise, but even more surprising was the fact that he hadn't received the proofs she had emailed six hours ago.

"I don't know why you wouldn't have received my email by now," Jocelyn said. "I sent it out last night."

"I checked my email again, and they aren't here."

"Let me make sure I have your email address right." Jocelyn spelled it out for him.

"That's it," Shane said.

"I've had some problems with my internet service here. Let me try again."

"Sounds great. Thanks."

"No problem. Can you let me know when you receive them?"

"I can do that."

She resent the email with the link to her photos. A moment later, Ty walked in the door.

"You have perfect timing," Jocelyn said.

"Perfect timing for what?" Ty asked.

"I need to give Jim's PR person access to these photos and proofs, but he isn't getting my email with the link. Can I send it from your computer? Or can you email it for me?"

"I'll do it for you. Do you have his email address and the link info?"

"Yeah. Thanks." Jocelyn handed him her note with the information.

Ten minutes after Ty disappeared into his office, her phone rang again.

"Jocelyn, I'm looking over your proofs now," Shane said.

"I know it's a little different from what you and the senator talked about originally, but—"

"These are even better. I love the approach you're taking. We can do a lot with these."

Satisfaction and a sense of accomplishment flowed through her. "I'm so glad."

"I have to admit, I was skeptical when the senator told me he brought you on board as a photographer. Politics is a lot different from what you normally do, but you clearly have an eye for this," Shane said. "We'll have to do this again soon."

"I'd like that." Jocelyn leaned back on the couch. Maybe she could make a career as a photographer after all.

CHAPTER 34

Kade was almost to New York before he noticed the anomaly in the security feed. With the train rumbling beneath him, he dialed Renee.

"I was about to call you," Renee said. "These videos are fake."

"I know. It should have been snowing at the airport that day, but these images show a clear night."

"The time stamps have been altered. Someone clearly replaced them after the fact," Renee said.

"Can you tell who did it?"

"I'm working on that now."

"I'll go over the personnel files. It's a small airport. It shouldn't be hard to figure out who was involved."

"This wasn't an employee who did this."

"How can you be so sure?" Kade asked. "If no one at the airport was involved, why wouldn't they have given me access to the security feed?"

"Because they didn't want you to see the drug-smuggling operation they have going through there."

"Again, how can you be sure it wasn't an employee who swapped out the videos?"

"Because I checked the flight logs against the planes on the runway," Renee said. "These were clearly from a week afterward."

Kade caught up with her logic. "If someone on the inside was involved, they would have used feed from the past to override the days Royce was there."

"I'm trying to trace the security breach now, and I sent a message to Hannah to get her help," Renee said, referring to the guardians' lead programmer.

"Good luck."

"Thanks." After Kade said goodbye, he opened the list of files he had downloaded. Time to start a new search for a senator in a snowstorm.

* * *

Walter hated the constant cloak-and-dagger meetings of the past few weeks. The last thing he needed was to be spotted alone with a woman who wasn't his wife, especially late at night. And on a Saturday, no less.

The World War II Memorial was the chosen meeting place this time. Walter made his way past the fountain in the center and stopped beside the pillar for New Hampshire. He was there only a moment before Ilina stepped beside him.

"Someone was asking questions at the airport in Vermont."

"Who?"

"We think it was one of your elusive guardians."

"We?"

"One of my associates was concerned when we found out your security and utility records were accessed. He replaced the surveillance feed at the airport with a different week to make sure you weren't seen."

"Then we shouldn't have a problem," Walter said in a low voice. "Why am I here?"

"I need to know if there is anything else that can cause problems," she said. "Did anyone see you when you were at the airport?"

"No. Nobody," Walter insisted. "The gate attendant was already gone when I got there, and I drove straight to the hangar like you told me to."

"What about on your way there?" Ilina asked. "Did you stop for gas? Run a red light? Anything?"

"No." A flash of memory broke through. "Wait. There was one person."

"Who?"

"The snow had already started when I left for the airport. The roads were too slick for me to drive my motorcycle, but there wasn't enough snow for me to use the snowmobile. I took the jeep I keep in New Hampshire instead."

"So what's the problem?"

"I spun out and got stuck in a ditch on one of the back roads right after I crossed the border into Vermont," Walter said. "I had to get a tow truck to pull me out."

"You called a tow truck?" A flash of her Russian accent sharpened her tone. "Did you use your credit card?"

"I used my burn phone to call, and I paid cash," Walter said. "The driver doesn't even know my name."

"Someone saw you. If he knows who you really are . . ."

"It was a tow truck driver in rural Vermont. What are the chances that he follows politics in a state that isn't his own? Besides, if the guy had recognized me, he would have come forward before now."

"Do you know who the man was?" Ilina asked.

"I'm not sure. He was with A&M Towing."

"I'll check out the driver and make sure we don't have a problem."

"Shouldn't you be more concerned about finding the senator?"

She smirked. "I've already found him."

* * *

Jim climbed into bed beside his wife, his mind crowded with worry. Was he making the right decision, going back to work on Monday? Would Ty be able to keep him safe? More importantly, would Katherine be safe here in his absence?

Katherine rolled onto her side and stretched her arm across his chest. "What are you thinking?"

"Too many things."

"You're worried about going back to DC."

Jim didn't try to deny it. His wife knew him too well. "I keep asking myself, Is all of this worth it?"

"I know. I pray about it every night, but I never get any inspiration to contradict the decision we made together two years ago," Katherine said. "You're supposed to run for president. You're supposed to be president."

"But why?" Jim pushed up on one elbow so he could see her more clearly. "Can one man really make that big of a difference?"

"You already know anyone is capable of making a difference, even if it's only creating the ripples that will allow others to see those changes through." Katherine sat up and propped her pillow behind her. "How much longer do you think I'll have to stay here?"

"I don't know. Another week or two." Jim pressed a kiss to her forehead. "I know this isn't easy, being away from our house and not being able to talk to the kids and grandkids."

"That's as hard on you as it is on me. I know this might sound crazy, but do you think there's any way we could go to church tomorrow?"

"Ty isn't going to like that."

"I know, but I keep getting this feeling that it's important we go."

The thought of going out in public should panic him, but instead he experienced the opposite effect. A sense of calm settled over him, giving him a peace he hadn't experienced in days.

"I'll talk to Ty in the morning."

"We should turn in. I have no idea how long it will take for us to get to the nearest church building."

"Knowing how the guardians work, we won't be going to the closest one, but I'm sure we can come up with enough options that we can convince Ty to take us somewhere."

"I'll pray for that."

* * *

Troy stared at the couple across from him. He couldn't be hearing them right. "You want me to take you where?"

"To church." Jim straightened his tie.

"Someone wants you dead, and you want me to fly you to the mainland so you can go to church."

"That about sums it up."

Troy glanced at the clock on the mantel. Seven o'clock in the morning. Maybe he was dreaming.

Jocelyn emerged from the hallway wearing a gray sweater dress and tall black boots. "I'm ready."

"You're ready for what?" Troy asked.

"Katherine invited me to go to church with them."

"What about security?" Troy asked, directing his comment to the senator. "I can't make sure you're safe with only an hour's notice."

"There are a dozen different places we can go to church that are within a half hour of here," Jim said. "Or we can take the boat and go to the branch in the village."

"The branch?"

"Yes. There are a few members of our faith who meet in a small building a couple blocks off Main Street."

"I'm not letting you go into the village. That's too close to home," Troy said.

"Where would you suggest?" Jim handed him a list of addresses scattered all along Maine's coast.

"This is crazy. We're supposed to be leaving for DC tonight."

"We can still leave for DC tonight, but first, I'd like to take my wife to church."

"Can't you skip going this week?"

"We thought about it." Jim glanced at Katherine, who gave him a subtle nod. "Both of us keep getting this feeling that we need to go to church today."

"Are you both willing to take the risk of being found?"

Katherine put her hand through her husband's arm. "It may not sound logical, but we've learned to follow promptings when we get them."

"We won't be at the church for long." Jocelyn crossed to Troy and put her hand on his arm. "Don't you think it's unlikely anyone will figure out where the Whitmores are staying?"

Three sets of eyes stared at him, and Troy wavered in his resolve. "Do the services at all of these churches start at nine?"

"Most of them will have congregations meeting at several times during the day," Jim said. "Most will be at nine and then ten thirty or eleven. Some may start as late as twelve or one."

"Find one that starts later that's in the Boston area."

"Why Boston?" Katherine asked.

"Because I don't want you seen in Maine, and I know I can set down the helicopter at the Coast Guard base and check out a car to take you into the city," Troy said.

"Will we be allowed on base?" Jocelyn asked.

"I can put you all in for visitor passes."

"Then it's settled. When do we leave?" Katherine asked.

"We'll leave in an hour," Troy said. He headed for his room to change into his flight suit. For the first time in his life, apparently, he was going to church.

* * *

Gavrie tugged his knit cap lower to cover his ears. An island. Why did the senator have to hide on an island?

It had taken him a full day to find a helicopter pilot who wouldn't ask questions and several hours in the air to fly from Boston to reach the location tagged by the photos he had accessed through the senator's PR firm. After a whole week of no contact between the senator and his publicity team, Gavrie had started to wonder if Whitmore was going to drop out of the race.

But from what he saw in the emails Whitmore's photographer sent, Whitmore not only intended to run, but he also intended to win.

The campaign mock-ups were brilliant, and Gavrie suspected that Royce wouldn't stand a chance against the classic all-American image Whitmore possessed in spades. Which left the election in Gavrie's hands. Once he took care of Whitmore, the balance in the polls would tip again in Royce's favor.

"These are the coordinates," the pilot said over his headset.

"Circle the island. I want to see what's down there."

The pilot complied. A windmill on the tip of the island appeared to be the power source. Large rocks lined one side of the island, finally giving way to a stretch of beach. When the helicopter rounded the tip, a house came into view. Perched on a hill, the structure overlooked a little cove, where a boat was currently docked. As they continued, Gavrie noted a second, smaller house nestled into the trees.

The woods appeared to dominate the interior of the decent-sized piece of land, which would make it impossible to reach, except by boat.

"Let's take a look at the other side," Gavrie said.

The pilot nodded. He swept wide over the water and brought the helicopter around to reveal a wall of cliffs below the house and stretching out along the entire windward side of the island.

They were nearly back to where they'd started when a clearing came into view. Gavrie pointed. "Can you land there?"

"As long as the wind isn't too strong."

"Take us down." A sense of anticipation simmered. Time to finally get this job behind him so he could move on to something new.

CHAPTER 35

Kade was so focused on finding who had altered the airport's security feed that he almost missed the change in flight plan. The plane that he believed took Royce to Europe had been scheduled to depart at twenty-three hundred hours but instead hadn't left until midnight. Why?

Only two other flights departed that night. One of them had been only fifteen minutes before the suspect plane's scheduled departure, so Kade discounted the idea that weather had been the reason for the delay.

The refueling log showed a completion time of twenty-two hundred, leaving a full hour to spare before the scheduled departure. No maintenance reports were included in the log nor was a mechanic on duty. Could the delay have been because Royce had been late to arrive?

Kade scoured through local police reports to see if any accidents had occurred along the senator's likely route. He then searched for any traffic citations. Nothing.

The idea that he might find the senator on a traffic camera disintegrated when he discovered the area was so remote that there weren't any cameras near the airport.

Taking a different approach, Kade went through Troy's notes in the database on the source he had located in New Hampshire. He retrieved the phone number for the burn phone Troy had assigned him and dialed the number.

"Hello?"

"Alec? This is Ghost."

"Any chance you're calling to tell me I can go home now?" Alec asked.

"No, but you may be able to help me make that happen," Kade said. "You said the last time the door opened at Royce's house was around nine o'clock on October 2. Is there any reason it would take more than two hours to drive sixty miles into Vermont?"

"The roads weren't too bad when he left, but there are a couple of spots that get pretty slick during a storm."

"Where?"

"The five miles before the border and about ten miles once you cross the state line."

"If someone were to get stuck, who would they call for help?"

"You can call the cops to help pull you out," Alec said.

"Let's assume you don't want to call the cops."

"Dawson's Towing runs up that direction on the New Hampshire side. I'm not sure about once you get into Vermont. I think A&M works in both states."

"Thanks. I appreciate it."

"Let me know if there's anything else I can do to help out. I'd really like to get home."

"I'll do my best to get you there."

* * *

"Wait here," Gavrie told the helicopter pilot.

"How long?" he asked. "The wind is picking up. I doubt we have more than an hour or two before we won't be able to fly."

"I'll be back in an hour." He hoped.

Gavrie climbed out of the helicopter and noticed a solar light a short distance away. He scanned the field. Lights surrounded the landing zone. They weren't the only ones using this field to park a helicopter.

The wind whipped over him, stinging his cheeks. He stepped behind an oak tree, a glare catching his eye. A security camera. He bypassed it and worked his way through the woods beside a well-worn trail. Whoever lived here came to the cliffs frequently.

He sidestepped a motion detector and two more security cameras. The positioning and quality of the equipment, the nearly undetectable landing zone—the security measures were impressive and well-planned, but they weren't going to keep the senator from Virginia alive for much longer. Too bad. This island made the ultimate safe house. If Gavrie hadn't been trained in countersecurity, he doubted he would be able to go undetected. And what better place to hide someone than in the literal middle of nowhere?

Gavrie wasn't sure what this island was called, much less who owned it, but he suspected it belonged to the US government.

A squirrel scampered up a nearby tree. Gavrie waited a moment for his pulse to settle before he moved to the edge of the clearing where the two dwellings were located. He checked the small one first, peeking in windows. Darkness greeted him. Even the fireplace was empty.

On a day this cold, there was no way they wouldn't have a fire going.

Keeping to the edge of the woods, he made his way through an orchard and up a hill to what appeared to be the front door of the main house. He tried the doorknob. Locked. He retrieved his lock-pick kit from his pocket and went to work. Less than a minute later, he opened the door slowly, slipped inside, and closed the door behind him.

A dog barked. Paws clicked against the wood floor.

Gavrie darted into the dining room to his left and made his way into the kitchen. No sign of human life anywhere. He reached the living room the same time the dog did.

A quick sweep of the room revealed what Gavrie didn't want to see: a cold fireplace, the lights off. Where was everyone?

A deep growl rumbled in the animal's throat.

Gavrie grabbed the poker from beside the fireplace. He shoved it between himself and the four-legged aggressor. Using the poker to maintain the distance between them, he edged past the dog into the hall. No lights, no sign of life.

He peeked into the first bedroom, which was currently being used as an office. Empty. He reached the next one and stepped inside, closing the door to keep the dog out. He checked the closet, under the bed, out the window. Still nothing. He repeated the process with each room, the dog crowding him each time he came into the hall. When he reached the master bedroom, he stopped at the bedside table and smiled. A framed photo of Senator James Whitmore with his wife and family. The man had been here. Judging from the open suitcase by the door and the clothes in the closet, he was still staying here.

Gavrie finished his search of the master bedroom and confirmed his suspicions. The house was empty.

With the dog still following, he hurried back to the front door and headed outside. As soon as he closed the door between him and the dog, he sprinted through the woods toward the helicopter.

Less than a minute passed before he heard the dog bark again, this time the sound coming from outside.

Gavrie hurdled a motion detector on the ground and ducked beneath a camera mounted in a tree. He listened for the sound of pursuit, but the only footsteps crunching on the leaves were his.

He emerged into the clearing and slowed his pace to avoid tripping any of the security measures at the landing pad.

When he climbed into the helicopter, the pilot asked, "Did you find what you were looking for?"

"Not exactly." He strapped himself in. "Fly over the island. I want to see the center."

"You got it."

The engines started up, and a moment later, the helicopter lifted off. They hovered briefly before the pilot headed farther inland. Woods, a pond, the path from the orchard to the landing pad. Gavrie saw it all.

They reached the two houses, a wide yard situated between them, and the dog in the center of it.

If the dog was here, where was the owner? And when were the inhabitants coming back?

CHAPTER 36

Troy stepped into the church and looked up. The roof hadn't caved in. So far, so good.

Organ music started.

"Perfect timing." Jim headed for a set of open double doors. "That's the opening hymn."

Though it went against his instinct, Troy let Jim and Katherine lead the way. "Look for a seat by the door."

They entered a chapel, and Jim found a row with enough seats for all of them in a side pew. Troy analyzed the exits—all eight sets of doors—before his gaze swept over the congregation.

No one knew the Whitmores were here. Certainly no one from Troy's former life would be this far east.

The Whitmores and Jocelyn slid into the pew, and Troy took the spot beside the aisle. He wasn't sure what to do a few minutes later when a teenage boy said a prayer and then a younger boy, who couldn't have been more than twelve or thirteen, offered him a tray with broken pieces of bread on it.

When he noticed a little girl across from him eat a piece of bread off an identical tray and then pass the tray down her aisle, Troy followed suit. He handed the tray to Jocelyn, who then offered it to Jim and Katherine. The ritual was repeated a few minutes later with miniature cups of water.

Troy hadn't known what to expect for the sermon, but he wouldn't have guessed the main part of the service would include a teenage girl speaking from the pulpit. Her message about following divine inspiration was simplistic and foreign to everything Troy had experienced in his life. How did one know what they were receiving was a message from God instead of a gut feeling?

Another song, followed by another speaker, this one a man in his forties. Unlike the girl's talk, the man offered examples of inspiration and promptings he and others had received in their lives.

Troy glanced at Jim and Katherine. Did they believe their impression to attend church today was a prompting? And how could they know for sure?

After the closing prayer, Jim said, "See, that wasn't so bad."

Troy stood and checked the ceiling. Still no cracks or signs of it caving in.

"Is it okay if we stay for Sunday School?" Katherine asked.

Before Troy could answer, a man approached. Troy recognized him as one of the men who had been sitting up front during the meeting.

"Hello. I'm Bishop Everton. Are you visiting?"

"Yes. We're only here for today." Jim shook the man's hand.

"Glad to have you."

Troy's phone buzzed, and he glanced at the screen. Kade. "I need to take this."

"We'll be fine here," Jim said.

Troy walked to the front of the chapel, where there was some open space, and answered the phone. "What's going on?"

"We think we know where we can find proof about Royce going to the airport, but I need you to leave right now to investigate," Kade said. "Royce's phone was turned off for an hour earlier. I don't want to take a chance he's tying up loose ends."

"What about Ace? I thought he was on his way here."

"He won't arrive for a couple more hours. The source is in Vermont. It won't take you long to get over there and back."

"I'm in Boston right now . . ."

"Even better. That's only about an hour away."

"I'm with the Whitmores."

"What? Why do you have them there?"

Troy opened his mouth to explain but couldn't get the words out. He couldn't very well lie about the reason he had brought them here, not while standing in a chapel, and he doubted Kade would understand the Whitmores' insistence on going to church. "It's a long story."

"Check them into a hotel. They'll have to hide out until you can go back and pick them up."

"Okay. Send me the details."

"Already did."

Troy ended the call and walked back to where Jocelyn and the Whitmores were still chatting with the bishop. "Sorry to interrupt, but we have to go."

"Go where?"

"I have an urgent matter to take care of," Troy said. "I'll have to check you into a hotel until I can come back to pick you up."

"How long will you be gone?" Katherine asked.

"I'm not sure. I should be back tonight."

"If you want to stay for Sunday School, I'm sure my wife or I can give you a lift to a hotel after," Bishop Everton said. "In fact, we can do one better. You can come home with us. Worst case, we have a couple of spare rooms if you need to stay the night."

"I don't think that's a good idea," Troy said.

"My apartment is only about forty-five minutes from here," Jocelyn offered. We could always go there after church."

Troy leaned down and whispered in her ear. "You've been working on Jim's campaign. We can't let him go anywhere he could be traced."

"Right. I forgot about that," Jocelyn said. "I guess my apartment won't work after all."

"Ty, can I speak with you a minute?" Jim asked.

"Yeah." Troy stepped back to the front of the room, and Jim followed.

"What's going on?"

"A possible witness could be in danger," Troy said in a low voice.

"Let us stay with the bishop," Jim said. "No one knows we're here, and it'll let you get to where you need to be faster than if you have to take us somewhere first."

"I don't know anything about this guy."

"You don't need to. I do."

"What can you possibly know about a man you just met?" Troy asked.

"I know the qualities needed to be an active member of my church, and Bishop Everton qualifies. We can get his address and contact information before you leave. Trust me. Besides, it sounds like time is of the essence." He nodded to where Jocelyn and Katherine waited with the bishop and added, "Don't worry. We'll take good care of her."

A warmth spread through him. "Okay. You win. Let's get that address and phone number."

* * *

Gavrie sat in the back of the helicopter and waited for the aircraft to be refueled at the public heliport while he considered his next move.

The presence of the dog on the island spoke volumes. Someone was going to be back on the island within the day, and he had to assume the lights surrounding the landing zone meant the current inhabitants had used a helicopter to fly to the mainland. Gavrie would have to use another mode of transportation next time, and unfortunately, that meant renting a boat.

He was debating his options when his phone rang. Ilina.

"Are you still in Maine?" Ilina asked

"Yes. The pilot is refueling. I should be in the air within the hour."

"Did you accomplish your task?"

"Not yet. No one was there, but it looks like they'll be coming back," Gavrie said. "I found some of the senator's stuff there."

"Maybe they got tipped off you were coming."

"I don't think so. It looked more like everyone went out for an afternoon helicopter ride," Gavrie said. "I plan to rent a boat and try again tonight."

"I need you to take care of another problem while you're waiting."

"Where?"

"Vermont."

"Send me the information."

"I put it in an email a minute ago," she said. "This needs to be done today."

"I'll leave as soon as my pilot comes back."

"Don't leave any witnesses."

"I never do."

Gavrie hung up and opened Ilina's message. Another witness. More evidence to destroy.

He shook his head. He certainly hoped Walter Royce didn't plan to conduct his presidency the way he was managing his campaign. Otherwise, he would be impeached or arrested before he would be of any benefit to Russia or the people trying to put him in power.

CHAPTER 37

Troy waited until he was in the air before he radioed Kade for more details. While his fellow guardian had given him the coordinates of where he should be able to find the man he was looking for, Kade had left out one important detail: where to land.

"ETA?" Kade asked as soon as he answered Troy's call.

"Fifteen thirty," Troy said. "I need a landing zone and ground transportation when I get there."

"Already taken care of." Kade relayed the updated coordinates.

Troy plugged them in. "Are you sending me to the airport our suspect flew out of?"

"Yeah. It's the only adequate landing zone in the area."

"What about ground transport?"

"Our witness is coming to you."

"Does he know why?"

"No," Kade said. "He's a tow truck driver. I put in a call that you needed a tow."

"How is he supposed to find me if I don't have a car?"

"He'll meet you in the parking lot beside the red Dodge Ram."

"Whose truck is it?"

"The air traffic controller's," Kade said. "He'll be on duty until nineteen hundred tonight."

"Roger that." Troy signed off and envisioned the task before him. The possibility of finding another eye witness was huge, but even combined with Royce's questionable campaign finances from his first campaign and the anomalies in his utility bills the weekend of the Helsinki attack, Troy wanted more. Was it too much to ask for a smoking gun?

He switched frequencies, cleared his landing with the control tower, and put in a request for refueling. A few minutes later, the thick blanket of trees below him gave way to open space, and the airport came into view.

Several small planes were parked near a row of hangars. Troy identified the helicopter landing pad and checked in with the control tower.

As soon as he was on the ground, he signed off on the fuel order and made his way to the airport's parking lot. With less than half of the thirty spaces occupied, it took him only a minute to locate the vehicle he would soon pretend was his.

Less than ten minutes after he arrived, a red tow truck pulled into the lot. Troy waved to get his attention.

The driver parked and climbed out of the cab. Dark hair with a dusting of gray and a waistline that carried a few pounds more than a doctor would consider healthy, the man appeared to be in his early fifties. "What seems to be the trouble?"

"Actually, I needed to ask you a few questions," Troy said. "Are you Hal?"

The man's bushy eyebrows drew together. "Questions about what?"

"Do you keep track of your calls?" Troy asked.

"Yeah. I keep my log in my truck. What's this about?"

"I'm investigating an incident from October 2. It would have been a Friday night."

"Why is the Coast Guard investigating something that happened in Vermont?"

"I'm working with the FBI," Troy said. "The Bureau didn't have anyone in the area with a helicopter, so they sent me. Apparently, this is an urgent matter."

"Doesn't seem so urgent since whatever they're looking into happened over a month ago."

"That's what I said, but those are my orders."

"You got some ID?" Hal asked.

"Yeah." Troy flashed his Coast Guard credentials.

Hal leaned closer to inspect them before he looked up. "Thanks. Can't be too careful these days."

"Now, about your log—do you keep track of the vehicle make and model you service?" Troy asked.

"Sure do." He opened the door to his truck, leaned into the cab, and straightened with a tablet in his hand.

"Do you have anything for October 2? I'm looking for something after nine and before midnight."

He tapped on the screen. "Oh yeah. That was a busy night. A snow storm came in and left all sorts of folks stranded."

"How many calls did you take in the window I gave you?"

"Four. Two tows, a dead battery, and a car I had to pull back onto the road."

"Can I see?" Troy held his hand out, and Hal passed him the tablet. Troy read through the log. The two tows had both been pickups in Vermont with the end destination of the local repair shop. The dead battery had been at a house a few miles outside the nearest town. The last one listed only a number as the address, and the spots for the vehicle information were blank. "What does this mean? And why isn't there any vehicle information in here?"

"That's the highway number where the car was serviced," Hal said. "I can't remember why the rest of the log wasn't filled out."

"Is this the road you'd take to get to New Hampshire?"

"One of them."

Troy fished his phone out of his pocket and pulled up a photo of Walter Royce. "Any chance this is the man you helped?"

Hal leaned closer. "Yeah. I remember that call now. The guy's jeep slid into a ditch. I got him back on the road, but when I brought him the paperwork to fill out, he said he was in a hurry and gave me two hundred dollars for my trouble."

"He paid in cash?"

"Yes."

"You sure this is him?"

"I'm sure."

"And you're sure it was from this night?"

"Yeah. The star next to that line means I was paid in cash," Hal said. "No one pays in cash anymore. Most of the time, I get paid through AAA or through the repair shop."

"Would you be willing to testify to what you just told me?"

"I can do you one better." Hal tapped on the laptop and opened a list of files. He clicked on one. "Would this help?"

An image started playing of a vehicle on the side of the road.

"What is this?"

"I have a dash camera on my truck."

The driver of the vehicle on screen climbed out of his jeep and walked toward the tow truck. He turned his head and looked straight into the camera. Walter Royce. Stamped across the bottom of the screen were the time and date of the recording.

"Can you email this to me, with your logs? You can use my hot spot if you need it."

"That's okay. I can use mine."

Troy gave him the email address he had set up for when he was corresponding with civilians. Hal activated the hot spot on his phone and forwarded the files.

Troy watched his screen until the email popped up on his phone. "I got it. Thanks."

"No problem."

"I know this may sound like an odd question, but do you have a family?"

"Yeah. A wife and two teenage boys. Why?"

"How would you feel about taking your family on a vacation for Thanksgiving?"

"Thanksgiving isn't until next week."

"I know, but the people I'm investigating are dangerous. In case they realize you have evidence, I'd like to put you into protective custody until we have this resolved." Troy saw the flash of uncertainty on the other man's face. "I know this sounds far-fetched, but your testimony could save a man's life."

"I don't know . . ." Hal's phone rang. He glanced at the screen. "It's my wife."

"Go ahead and take it."

"Hello?" He paused. "Who was he?" Another pause. "Did he say what he wanted?" Hal lowered his phone but didn't hang up. "Some guy was at my house asking where I was. Said he needed to talk to me, but he wouldn't tell my wife what he wanted."

"Does your wife park in a garage?"

"Yeah."

"Good. Tell her to pack a bag and bring your sons here," Troy said. "She needs to make sure no one sees their luggage though."

"How do I know I can trust you?"

"For one thing, I already showed you my credentials."

"IDs can be faked."

"That's true, but helicopters can't." Troy pointed at the airfield. "I'll be flying you out of here in that."

Hal's gaze landed on Troy's ride. "Honey, I need you to do something for me." Hal proceeded to relay Troy's instructions. As soon as he hung up, he said, "She'll be here in twenty minutes."

"Good. In the meantime, we need to go for a ride."

"Why?"

"We need to disable your GPS, but we want to do it somewhere else in case this guy is trying to track you."

"You sure you're one of the good guys?"

"I'm on your side. Trust me," Troy said. "Right now, my only job is to keep you and your family safe."

"Climb in. I know just the place we should go."

CHAPTER 38

Gavrie made three detours before he finally made the correct turn to take him to the tow truck's location. From what little the wife had told him, Hal was the only operator of A&M Towing within fifty miles. A little accident, followed by an explosion of the tow truck, would take care of any lingering evidence against Royce.

Gavrie continued down the road, his eyes sweeping the shoulders for his target. He drove for ten minutes but didn't see a single car, much less the bright-red tow truck. Where was it?

Gavrie glanced at his tracker. According to the signal, he should have passed the truck over a mile back. Gavrie slowed and did a U-turn. He traversed the mile again and went a mile beyond. Still nothing.

He did another U-turn, this time pulling over on the shoulder when he reached the spot where the truck was supposed to be parked.

Not sure why the signal would send him here when the truck was clearly somewhere else, he pulled up the GPS data on another vehicle, this time for Hal's personal vehicle. It was in motion. Where was the wife going on a Sunday afternoon?

Hopeful that she would lead him to her husband, Gavrie put his car in gear. Time to have another chat with the missus.

* * *

Jocelyn checked the time on her cell phone and looked out the window of the bishop's living room. Almost seven o'clock and not a word yet from Ty. Even if he showed up right now, they wouldn't get back to the island until at least ten. Surely Ty would convince the senator to wait until tomorrow to fly to DC. Wouldn't he?

Bishop Everton and his family had been beyond kind to them. An early dinner after church, followed by a religious discussion and board games.

"Nothing yet from Ty?" Jim asked.

"No." She glanced behind her at the empty living room. "Is everyone else still in the dining room?"

"Yes. They're playing Apples to Apples."

"Do you think we'll have to stay the night?"

"I hope not."

"I'm sorry we can't stay in my apartment," Jocelyn said. "Although it's hard to believe someone would know I'm helping on your campaign, much less that I'm with you and Katherine."

"You sent photos to my PR firm. That connects us."

What he said made sense, but it also didn't seem quite real. "It's hard to believe you have to live with such a high level of security. Are you ready for that when you're president?"

"If I'm elected, I'll have the added resources of the secret service."

"I thought the secret service also protected senators."

"Only if there's a threat."

"You qualify."

"Now I do, but circumstances dictated that I secure my safety outside of the usual channels."

"I don't suppose you're going to explain that, are you?"

"No." Jim waved toward the dining room. "You should come play. It will help take your mind off Ty."

An approaching car engine sounded outside. Jocelyn looked out the window again. Relief flowed through her when a car turned into the driveway. "He's here."

"I'll get Katherine."

Jocelyn opened the door.

Ty climbed out of the car but remained next to it. "Are you ready?"

"Yeah. Let me say goodbye." Jocelyn went into the dining room and, with Katherine and Jim, thanked their hosts.

Once they were all in the car, Jim asked, "Are we staying in Boston tonight?"

"No. As soon as you get your suitcase and I make sure the island is secure, we'll leave for DC."

"Are you sure you don't want to leave first thing in the morning?" Jim asked. "If we leave early, we can get there before my first session."

"That's too risky. We have weather moving in. If the winds get too bad, we'll be grounded."

"I guess we're going tonight, then."

"Do you have somewhere to stay?" Jocelyn asked.

"I secured military housing tonight at the base where I'll park the helicopter," Ty said. "We'll likely stay there until we come back to Maine."

"I'm sorry it's been such a crazy day for you." Jocelyn put her hand on Ty's shoulder and rubbed at the tension centered there. "You must be exhausted."

"I'm okay."

"I'll be glad when you have this week behind you."

"Me too."

* * *

Virginia. New Hampshire. Maine. Vermont. Now Maine again. Gavrie's impatience simmered as he drove the rented SUV through the woods in Maine.

It was bad enough that his plans for James Whitmore had failed multiple times, but the back-and-forth travel up and down the coastline was beginning to wear on him. Not to mention that he wouldn't get the second half of his fee until he completed his task. This job was starting to interfere with other potential contracts.

Gavrie had followed the GPS signal on Hal's personal vehicle until he'd found it abandoned at the airport. According to the flight logs, only a private charter to Philadelphia had left after he had spoken with the tow truck driver's wife. Gavrie didn't know if the man and his family knew there was a reason to hide out or if they'd had prior plans to take a vacation. Regardless, he wasn't about to chase them all the way to Pennsylvania when his primary target should be back on the island in Maine by the end of the day.

He slowed when he turned onto the street of the house he had rented two hours ago. The gray cape cod was situated on a bluff above a rocky beach. He parked in the driveway and collected his binoculars and the grocery bag of food he had picked up at a gas station fifty miles back.

He punched in the code on the door and turned the knob. Success.

He walked inside, but the temperature in the house wasn't much warmer than outside. He found the thermostat, cranked it up to thaw, and continued through the hall until he reached the windows on the back wall of the living room.

He lifted his binoculars. With the sun already sinking deep beyond the horizon, he could barely make out the faint glow of the solar lights where he had landed earlier today. He would have preferred to have a clearer view of the landing zone, but this would have to do.

He called Ilina.

"What's your status?" she asked as soon as she answered.

"The tow truck driver isn't in town. Looks like he and his family either knew I was coming or they went on holiday together."

"Where are you now?" she asked.

"Back in Maine. I rented a place where I can watch the island, but I need radar support," he said. "I did another flyover before I picked up my rental car, but I can't be sure the target's helicopter didn't land while I was driving."

"I'll check and get back to you," she said. "What are your plans?"

"The place I rented has a boat. As soon as we confirm the target has returned, I'll complete the contract."

"Remember, no witnesses."

"With the way I've spent the last two weeks, I could hardly forget."

* * *

Troy reveled in having solid ground beneath his feet again. After spending so much time in the air today, he was ready for a break. Ace had already texted him that he was waiting to be picked up at their safe house in the village. Thank goodness. Troy didn't think he could manage flying four more hours today on so little rest. Once he completed his current task of securing the island, he would pick up Ace and let him take over at the controls.

Jim started to climb out behind him, but Troy signaled for him to wait. "Let me check everything out before I bring Katherine and Jocelyn down to the house."

"I still need to grab my suitcase."

"I'll get it for you," Troy said. "Is it in your room?"

"It is."

"I'll be back in a few minutes. There are some blankets in the back if you get too cold." Troy glanced at Jocelyn briefly before he headed down the path to the house.

He hated leaving her here unprotected. Two women alone on an island. Two capable women, he amended. Besides, no one knew they were here, and Jim was the target, not them.

He was probably being paranoid to insist on checking everything out before he let them return to the house, but better safe than sorry.

He liked to think he always took such care with those he was tasked with protecting, but he couldn't deny that Jocelyn's presence made him wish he could stay here and let Ace transport Jim to DC on his own.

Too risky, he reminded himself. Even with Ace, Kade, and Renee helping him with protection duty, Jim wasn't safe as long as Walter Royce had access to the Capitol building. Then again, with the new video evidence he had discovered today, they had enough proof to at least start an investigation. Soon Royce's access to Jim and the other candidates would be severely limited.

Samson barked when Troy approached. He bolted out of his doggie door, took a protective stance, and let out a low growl.

"Hey, boy. It's me."

Samson's posture relaxed, and he raced down the stairs. Troy rubbed the dog's fur. "Did you miss us?"

Samson barked again.

"Come on. You can help me check out the bungalow." Troy used his flashlight to guide the way across the yard. He unlocked the front door, ensured the bungalow was empty and secure, and locked it back up.

He entered the main house through the back door and did his cursory search to make sure everything was as he'd left it. Once satisfied, he zipped up Jim's suitcase and carried it into the hall.

Samson growled.

"What's the matter, boy?" Troy asked. "You're acting like you don't know me. I'm the one who feeds you, remember?"

The mention of food prompted another bark. Even though Troy was eager to get back to the helicopter, he went into the kitchen and checked Samson's food dishes. The extra food Jocelyn had put out this morning was gone, and the water dish was almost dry.

"All right. I'll give you some more." He scooped some food into the dish and filled Samson's water bowl.

Samson lapped up the water.

"Come on, boy. Come with me to get our friends."

Samson lapped up more water and lifted his head.

"Come on." Troy carried the suitcase to the back door and walked outside. As he hoped, Samson followed.

A few minutes later, he reached the clearing. Jocelyn pushed the door of the helicopter open.

"Everything okay?"

"Yeah. Everything's fine." Troy took her hand to help her climb down. "Come on. I'll walk you down to the house."

"You don't have to do that. I can find my way," Jocelyn said. "I've been coming to this island my whole life."

"Are you sure?"

"I'm sure."

"Take my flashlight, then." He handed it to her.

"Thanks." She went up onto her toes and gave him a quick kiss. "Be careful this week."

"I will. You too."

Katherine climbed out of the helicopter. Even in the darkness, Troy could see her concern and the moisture on her eyelashes.

"Can you let us know when you arrive in DC?" she asked.

"I'll text Jocelyn."

"Thanks." Katherine leaned toward her husband and gave him a goodbye kiss. "Be safe."

Jim gave his wife's hand a squeeze. "I'll do my best."

"Make sure your best is good enough." Katherine took a step back until she was standing beside Jocelyn, the dog nuzzling in between them.

Troy climbed into the pilot seat, a hollow sensation settling in his stomach. He didn't want to leave. He didn't have a choice.

He drew a deep breath and started the engines. The sooner they picked up Ace, the sooner they could start their journey. If what he'd learned in church today was true, maybe the Lord would help them all return home soon.

* * *

Gavrie cut the motor and let the surf carry the boat the last fifty meters to shore. His chosen spot to hide his boat couldn't be more perfect. The little section of beach that curved around the wayward side of the island gave way into a little inlet invisible to both the houses and the helicopter landing zone. With the tide rising, whatever sound he made would be lost beneath the roar of the crashing waves.

He had left the rental house as soon as word had come that the helicopter had been spotted on radar. Though the pilot had stayed above the mainland until he'd been within a few miles of the island, the moment he'd changed his heading to his true destination, Gavrie had set out, armed with night-vision goggles, a thermal scope on his rifle, and heat-sensor equipment, should he need to pinpoint the location of the island's current guests.

The boat bumped against sand and listed to the left. Another wave rocked the boat and sent it another few meters farther onto shore.

Gavrie shouldered his rifle and moved to the bow. Another wave rolled onto shore, and he gripped the side to steady himself. He grabbed the rope used to secure the vessel, waited for the next wave to recede, and climbed onto the beach. Frigid water splashed over his boots.

He tied the boat off, stretching the rope to a nearby tree, then slipped into the woods. He had two hours until high tide. Just enough time to eliminate his target and get back to the boat before the ocean would wash away any footprints he might leave.

An engine rumbled in the distance. The helicopter?

Gavrie looked up, but the trees obscured his view. If the helicopter was leaving, did that mean Whitmore was here alone? It didn't matter. He had enough ammunition to take care of the senator and anyone else who might be here to protect him. No witnesses. That was part of the job.

Gavrie patted the pistol holstered at his waist. If his geography was correct, a few hundred meters through the woods was all he needed before he'd be in the perfect spot to pick off the senator and his security team when they traversed the path between the helicopter pad and the house.

He adjusted his night-vision goggles and sprinted forward until he reached his chosen spot, a bluff that overlooked the orchard. He dropped onto his stomach and took aim. He was ready, and the senator was a dead man.

CHAPTER 39

An unfamiliar tension settled in Jocelyn's chest as she stood beside Katherine and watched the helicopter lift into the sky.

Katherine sniffled, and Jocelyn put her arm around the other woman's shoulder. "Jim will be okay. Ty will make sure of that."

"I know. I keep telling myself not to give in to the fear, but it isn't easy."

"Come on. Let's get out of the cold." Jocelyn rubbed her gloved hands together and aimed the flashlight down the path.

Katherine fell into step with her, Samson sticking close to Jocelyn's side.

When they reached the edge of the orchard, Samson stopped. The fur on the back of his neck stood straight up, and he lowered his head and growled.

"What's wrong, boy?" Jocelyn rubbed a hand over his neck. "Is something out there?"

Another growl.

"Maybe we should go in the front door," Katherine suggested.

"Good idea." Jocelyn stepped onto a large stump situated in the midst of several tall oaks that separated the orchard from the house. Now nearly a foot taller than her usual, she turned back to Katherine. "Watch your step. The trees are thick through here."

As if on cue, Katherine stumbled. Instinctively, Jocelyn leaned down to steady her.

The sound of an engine backfiring carried over the roar of the ocean. Jocelyn fell from the stump and landed beside Katherine. The sound repeated.

Samson barked.

"Quick, behind the tree." Katherine grabbed Jocelyn's arm. Instead of Jocelyn helping Katherine, the older woman dragged Jocelyn forward.

"What . . . ?" The flashlight fell from Jocelyn's hand and rolled to the edge of the trees.

Another engine backfire. Wood splintered above them.

"Someone is shooting at us."

"What?" Jocelyn repeated.

"We need to hide." Katherine pulled her deeper into the woods.

Another shot.

Jocelyn ducked.

Samson barked.

Disbelief cut through her mind, followed by fear and then reality. Someone really was shooting at them. Whoever had tried to kill Jim in his home was here now. The ramifications of that crashed over her. She and Katherine were alone on an island with someone who had a gun, someone who wanted them dead.

"Jim isn't even here. Why are they shooting at us?" Jocelyn asked.

"I don't know." Katherine moved deeper into the woods, and yet another gunshot rang out, this one sending bark flying.

The dog stopped and growled, but Jocelyn pulled at his collar to bring him to her side behind a tree.

"You know this island," Katherine said. "We need to get away and call for help."

"This way." Jocelyn kept her head down and moved deeper into the woods toward the cliffs.

The gunfire stopped, but the silence was every bit as threatening as being shot at.

They reached the cliffs that ran along the windward side of the island.

"Why did you bring us here?" Katherine asked. "We're trapped."

"If we stay in the woods by the cliffs, whoever is out there won't be able to hear us."

Katherine looked up at the sliver of moon in the sky. "I can barely see where I'm going."

"Stay right behind me. I don't need light to find my way." Jocelyn turned away from the house and started toward the point of the island.

"The house is that way. We need to get to a phone."

"That's the first thing someone would expect us to do." At least, that was the first thing Jocelyn would have expected someone to do if the roles were reversed.

"What if we work our way along the front of the house?" Katherine suggested. "Maybe we can get to the boat."

"I don't have the key." Awareness flashed in her mind. "Maybe we can find the other boat though."

"What other boat?"

Jocelyn started forward again, weaving her way through the trees. "Whoever is out there had to get on the island somehow."

"That's assuming there's only one person. What if he has a driver waiting for him?"

"I didn't think of that." Jocelyn skirted past the next tree, the dim glow of lights from Ty's landing zone filtering through the trees. "I have an idea."

"What?"

"My sister has a bunch of motion detectors on the island. Maybe we can set them off."

"What good will that do?"

"A couple weeks ago, Ty knew someone was here because an alert went off on his phone. He said there are sensors near the house and the helicopter landing site that are always active, but once they go off, they activate the other system," Jocelyn explained. "If we can get a bunch of the alarms to go off, maybe when he lands, he'll notice it."

"It'll be hours before they get to DC."

"Then we'd better find a good place to hide until then."

"I hope you have someplace in mind."

"I have a couple of ideas," Jocelyn said. She wasn't going to admit that none of them would keep them from freezing if they sat still for too long.

* * *

Gavrie shouldered his rifle and adjusted his position. His prey was out there, and he had no interest in playing hide-and-seek. Using his night-vision goggles, he crept to the orchard. At least the goggles gave him better clarity than the scope on his rifle. His targets had been at the edge of his range, and he hadn't been able to make out much beyond two people's presence.

The oddity that he had spotted only two targets struck him, as did the fact that no one had returned fire. Was it possible that Whitmore's protectors were so confident in his hiding place that they hadn't left any guards with him?

Gavrie followed the faint tracks in the leaves until he reached the cliffs. The rocky path masked the direction the Whitmores had taken, but he had to think they would try to get to the house. People always thought they could find someone to help them, but it never worked. Even if they managed to call, no one would be able to get here before it was too late.

He made his way to the house, opting to enter through the front door. The hinge creaked.

He tensed and waited for the dog to appear. When silence met him, he continued inside. He did a search, but the house was empty. He left the way he'd come and sidestepped the motion detector between the main house and the smaller one by the dock. He picked the lock and checked out the interior, again finding himself alone.

Where were they?

Not willing to spend any more time on this island than necessary, he pulled out the handheld heat sensor. He activated it and gritted his teeth. While the high-tech equipment could sense body heat for nearly a quarter of a mile, he hadn't anticipated the density of the wildlife here.

Heat spots at the center of the island. More at the edge of the orchard. Still more at the point of the island. Even though the equipment could show him where living beings were currently located, it couldn't identify the difference between animal and human.

Fighting back his frustration, he scanned the area again. The majority of the heat signatures were stationary. His targets would undoubtedly be in motion. In less than a minute, he found what he was looking for. Three specks of movement along the cliffs. He wasn't sure why he hadn't spotted the third member of the party sooner, but that had to be them.

Target acquired.

CHAPTER 40

Troy set the helicopter down in the yard of the waterfront farmhouse. The guardians had purchased the property several months before as a mainland safe house and a landing zone when they needed quick access to the village and a vehicle.

Ace lowered his head and ran toward them. Rather than wait for Troy to get out of his seat, Ace climbed in opposite him. He put on his flight helmet and spoke into the microphone so he could be heard over the engines.

"Senator, you need to get out and wait here."

"Why? What's wrong?"

"Alarms are going off all over Heritage Island."

"What?" Troy couldn't be hearing him right. "I checked the island out myself before we left. Maybe Jocelyn and Katherine set some off when they walked back to the house."

"Negative. Someone else is on the island with them," Ace said. "I caught a glimpse of someone with a rifle on two different cameras."

"Then I'm coming with you," Jim said from the back seat.

"You need to stay where you'll be safe."

"My wife is over there. I'm coming."

"We don't have time to argue," Ace said.

"I'm coming," Jim said again.

Ace gritted his teeth and signaled Troy. "Take her up."

Though Troy's training demanded they leave Jim here, he couldn't fight the sense of urgency that cascaded over him. He lifted off and reversed his heading.

"What do you know?" Troy asked. "How many intruders?"

"I've only seen the one, but alarms have gone off at the landing site, along the cliffs, in the woods, and by the pond."

"What about by the house and the bungalow?"

"None there."

The oddity that there wasn't any activity by the logical place of refuge sent alarm bells ringing in Troy's head. "Why wouldn't the intruders check out the house?"

"I don't know. Maybe it's Jocelyn and Katherine setting off the alarms."

Memories flashed through Troy's mind. The alarm that had tripped when Gil had come to visit, the night Jocelyn had stayed up when motion sensors had triggered in the woods. "That's exactly who is triggering the alarms. They're doing it on purpose."

"I don't follow," Jim said over his headset. "How would they know to do that?"

"If they knew it wasn't safe at the house, this would be the only way to alert me," Troy explained. "Jocelyn knows the sensors are on the island."

"That's brilliant," Jim said.

Troy nodded. "It is if we can find them."

"We'll find them."

* * *

Wind stung Jocelyn's cheeks, and her heart continued to pound in her chest. When they reached the cliffs and realized the shooter wasn't behind them, Jocelyn's stark terror subsided into a mere bone-jarring fear. Her decision to visit Heritage Island could very well cost her her life because she was in the wrong place at the wrong time.

For generations, her family had been born and had died on this island. As much as she appreciated her heritage, she didn't want to join her ancestors as the next name in that legacy.

For the past fifteen minutes, she had crisscrossed in front of half a dozen spots on the island that matched the images she had seen the night she had stayed up with Ty. The helicopter landing area, the path by the pond, the woods near her grandfather's old hunting blind. She pushed aside the branches of a sapling to reveal several pieces of wood that had been nailed to the side of a tree.

"What are those there for?"

"They work as a ladder." Jocelyn pointed at a wooden platform mounted to the tree ten feet above them. "We're going to hide up there."

"What about the dog? If he's down here, they'll know we're close by."

Jocelyn looked down at Samson. Katherine was right. Having the dog with them limited their options. The possibility of him growling or barking was yet another concern. The very thing that had saved their lives in the orchard could lead to their deaths.

Flee or fight. With hours until any help might arrive, maybe it was time to try a combination of the two.

"I have another idea. You go up there." Jocelyn pointed. "I'm going to see if I can get to the house after all."

"Why?"

"Because that's where my grandfather's rifle is."

"We should stay together."

Jocelyn debated, then shook her head. Their progress had been painfully slow when they'd passed out of the lighted area by the cliffs. Jocelyn knew these woods. Katherine didn't. "No offense, but I'll be able to move faster on my own."

"You're right."

Grateful that Katherine didn't argue, Jocelyn shrugged out of her coat. "Here. You can use this as a blanket to fight the cold."

"What about you?"

"I'll be moving to keep warm. You'll have to sit still."

Katherine accepted the offering, draped it over her shoulders, and put her foot on the bottom rung. She climbed to the blind and disappeared over the side.

"I'll be back as soon as I can," Jocelyn said.

"Be careful."

"I will." She shivered. "Samson, come."

Jocelyn crept through the brush to an overgrown path, the dog following. A deer startled and bounded through the trees. Jocelyn followed its path in the general direction of the house.

What were the chances the shooter was waiting for her there? And if she did manage to get her grandfather's gun, would she actually need to use it?

Her breath puffed out in front of her. She didn't know if she wanted the answer to that question to be yes or no. All she wanted was to survive the night and for this nightmare to end.

* * *

Gavrie looked up from his monitor and checked his surroundings. The rash of movement near the center of the island had finally subsided into three unidentified creatures heading on a parallel path toward the beach. After weaving in and out of the trees, one of the beings had stopped, while the other two veered off toward the dock. Had the senator taken refuge in the woods while his bodyguards tried to get to the boat? Or was it the senator's wife hiding out and the senator forging forward? The only way to be sure was to get close enough to make out their shapes so he would know for sure if they were his prey.

Decision time. Gavrie debated for a brief moment. A moving target or a stationary one. He'd take the stationary one. With any luck, he'd get the senator on the first try. If it was the man's wife, no doubt the senator would rush to the rescue. From his intel on James Whitmore, the senator was just dumb enough to try to save the woman he'd been married to for over thirty years.

Gavrie studied his heat sensor again and noted the location of his primary target. Six hundred meters. So close.

He took his time moving forward, the night-vision goggles giving him the advantage of seeing the protruding tree roots and low branches despite the lack of light.

He reached a spot two hundred meters away and removed his goggles. He lifted his rifle and looked through the thermal scope and confirmed someone was still huddled in the same spot. He lowered his rifle and put on the goggles again.

The terrain in that particular spot was hard to decipher. Thick brush, trees that appeared to rise out of thin air, the bottoms of their trunks not visible.

Realizing his target must have taken refuge on the edge of a bluff, he traded his goggles for his rifle again. He checked the location of his prey, took aim, and fired.

He shouldered his weapon, replaced the night goggles, and drew his pistol.

A rumble sounded overhead. He looked up but couldn't see the sky beyond the trees. It didn't matter. If the helicopter was returning, whoever was on it was too late.

He rushed forward, gun drawn.

Time to finish this.

CHAPTER 41

Jocelyn made it to the bungalow before a second gunshot rang out, followed by two more. "Katherine." The word escaped Jocelyn, and tears sprang to her eyes. Despite her best intentions, her plan had failed. Jocelyn was still alive, but Katherine had been found. "Please let her be alive," Jocelyn whispered.

She leaned over and struggled to catch her breath. Her lungs burned; her muscles ached. The quarter-mile trek through the woods had pushed her physically, but that was nothing compared to the worry that consumed her.

Samson nudged her leg, and she stumbled forward a step. She was alive, she repeated in her mind. No matter what else was happening in the woods, she needed to stay that way, if for no other reason than to make sure the people hiding in the woods were brought to justice.

Who was she kidding? She was a graphic artist and a photographer, not a cop. What business did she have thinking she could make a difference?

Samson barked, and a light from overhead passed over the yard.

She looked up. Ty!

Samson darted forward as though trying to catch the spotlight, but he couldn't quite reach it. The helicopter continued over the center of the island.

The hope that Katherine would survive her wounds pushed Jocelyn into action. She followed the woods along the edge of the yard and hesitated briefly when she reached the clearing where the path to the orchard connected to the yard.

In an effort to gather her courage, she mentally counted to three.

Her body burst into motion. She sprinted forward and raced up the back steps, even as she expected to hear bullets flying toward her. None came.

She tried the doorknob, but it didn't turn. "Great."

Beside her, Samson stood protectively. His presence sparked a new idea. She squatted down and squeezed through the doggie door. Samson followed.

Down the hall, the faint ringing of an alarm carried to her. She didn't have to check the computer monitor to know the threat tonight was real. She retrieved her grandfather's rifle and a box of ammunition.

The helicopter buzzed overhead. What was Ty doing?

* * *

Troy made another sweep of the island, guilt eating at his stomach. Why had he let Jocelyn stay? Her presence could very well get her killed, assuming she was even still breathing.

He pushed that thought aside. The very possibility of her life getting cut short hurt beyond description.

Beyond the proximity alarms and motion sensors going off, their first look at the island had revealed a boat on the northwest side.

"I don't see anyone," Troy said. "Do you see anything on the heat sensors?"

"There's too much wildlife down there to distinguish between human and animal," Ace said. "I have movement near the beach and inside the house."

"I'm taking her down." Troy approached the landing zone. "What are we going to do with the senator? We can't take him out here if there's a shooter."

"One of us goes looking for the shooter," Ace said. "The other can fly cover with Jim."

"You fly cover."

"Are you sure?" Ace asked.

Was he sure he needed to find out for himself if Jocelyn was okay? "I'm sure."

Troy put the helicopter down. As soon as he was on the ground, he unclipped his harness and hurried to the back of the helicopter. He opened the weapons locker and selected a spare pistol, extra clips of ammunition, and a communication headset.

He slipped the headset on. "Test. Test."

Ace's voice came through a second later. "You're good. Sensors don't show any sign of life within a fifty-meter radius."

That was all Troy needed to hear. He did a quick look of his own and exited the helicopter. As soon as he reached the trees, the helicopter lifted into the air.

Troy gripped the pistol in his hand and pushed into the woods. The house or the beach? Where should he look first?

He wasn't alone, he reminded himself. Even though the guardians rarely worked together in person, when they did, they had a reputation of being invincible. He hoped tonight would prove that reputation accurate.

* * *

Gavrie fired another shot and pushed the brush aside. His jaw clenched, and anger boiled inside him. A deer. He'd shot a deer.

James Whitmore had more lives than a cat. It was like the man had an invisible shield around him that protected him from harm. No more. One way or another, the senator from Virginia would take his last breath before the night was through.

Gavrie checked the heat sensor again, and new hope ignited inside him. Someone was moving fast from the cliffs toward the residential part of the island. Another in or near the house. Now he was getting somewhere.

Donning his night goggles again, he plotted an intercept course. He would take care of whoever was running to the house, and then he would kill whoever was inside.

If neither of them was the senator, he would kill every living thing on the island if he had to, but tonight, Jim Whitmore was going to die.

* * *

Jim stared at the screen in front of him, endless prayers repeating in his mind. He couldn't imagine life if something happened to Katherine. They had left her here to keep her safe. How was it possible that they had been found?

He blinked back the tears that welled in his eyes. No time for fear. He had a job to do.

After Ty left the helicopter, Jim had moved to the copilot's seat so he could watch the heat sensors.

Ghost had shown him how to identify movement when Ty had left the landing zone and headed down the path toward the house. Most of the other heat spots remained stationary, presumably deer bedded down for the night.

A single heat spot became two, one of them now in motion. "I think I have something."

"Where?"

"On the eastern side of the island. The signal is moving toward the houses."

"Ghost, did you copy that?" Ghost asked.

"Roger." Ty's voice came through the communication headset. "Can you light him up?"

"Moving to target."

A new fear enveloped Jim. "What if it's Katherine or Jocelyn?"

"Don't worry. Ghost won't shoot until he knows who it is."

"Good to know."

* * *

Jocelyn hurried to the deck, loaded rifle in hand and extra ammo in her coat pocket. Samson followed.

"Where are they, boy?" Jocelyn whispered.

Samson didn't respond, not that Jocelyn had expected him to. She chose a spot at the corner of the deck where the house would protect her from anyone approaching from the cliff side of the island but where she could see anyone coming into the yard.

She steadied her gun, watching, waiting.

The thought that maybe she should go hunting for the people after her popped into her mind only to be discounted. She'd been taught to hunt deer, not people. She wasn't trained for this.

Even as that thought surfaced, memories of her grandfather's lessons filtered through her mind. Stay still. Keep quiet.

She shivered, a reminder of the below-freezing temperature. She wiggled her fingers to keep feeling in her hands.

Samson growled low and deep in his chest.

Jocelyn tensed, and her gaze swept over the edge of the woods. In the faint moonlight, she glimpsed movement near the path to the orchard. The shooter was back.

Jocelyn adjusted her aim.

The sound of the helicopter grew louder, its spotlight filtering through the trees, her target now taking shape.

Jocelyn took a deep breath and settled her finger on the trigger. She squeezed it at the same instant Samson bumped into her, sending her shot wide.

The dog barked and darted toward the stairs.

"Samson!" Jocelyn took aim again as the helicopter came into view, the spotlight illuminating the yard and the man in the trees. Ty? How could he be on the ground if the helicopter was in the air?

Her eyes narrowed, confirming the truth. She'd nearly shot Ty. Her heart squeezed into her throat, blocking her air.

If he had been the cause of the movement she had seen, where was the person who had shot at her, the person who had found Katherine?

Samson reached the bottom of the stairs and made it a third of the way across the yard before he stopped and growled again.

Recognizing the dog's warning, Jocelyn quickly looked in the direction Samson was facing. There on the path to the beach, a figure emerged.

Afraid it might be Jim, Jocelyn fired a warning shot over his head.

The spotlight angled toward the man, the man with a rifle aiming at her. It wasn't Jim. It was the enemy.

Samson barked.

Ty shouted. "Take cover!"

Jocelyn dropped to the deck as a shot rang out, her rifle still gripped in her hand. She rolled onto her stomach in time to see the man dart behind a tree.

Ty fired off a shot and raced to the side of the house. Samson raced after him.

Jocelyn held her position, afraid to move.

A minute passed. Then two. Where was the shooter? And where was Ty?

CHAPTER 42

Troy burst through the front door, the dog following. He slowed long enough to slam the door behind him.

"Katherine? Jocelyn? Where are you?"

When no one answered, Troy rushed to the back door.

"Status?" Ace asked over his headset.

"I'm in the house. I don't see either of them." He peeked out the window but was unable from this angle to see if Jocelyn was still outside. "Can you tell if Jocelyn is still on the deck?"

"I don't have a visual."

"What about the shooter?" Troy asked.

"Searching now." The spotlight from the helicopter swept over the area where the shooter had been moments ago.

Troy opened the back door. "Jocelyn?"

"I'm here."

"When I tell you, come inside."

"The shooter is still out there."

"I know. I'll lay down cover fire," Troy said. "Are you ready?"

"Ready."

"Now!" Troy stretched his arm out the door and sent a spray of bullets into the woods.

Jocelyn's footsteps pounded toward him. When she reached the door, he ceased fire and stepped back to let her through.

Another shot rang out. Jocelyn tumbled forward, and she and her rifle dropped to the floor.

"Jocelyn!" Troy dropped beside her.

"I'm all right."

Troy kicked the back door closed. Glass shattered. Jocelyn cried out.

"It's okay. Stay low and move into the hall."

She crawled forward, collecting her rifle when she reached the spot where it had landed by the couch. Troy followed.

When they reached the hall, he helped her to a stand. An instant later, she was in his arms.

"I'm so sorry. I almost shot you."

"It's okay."

"How are you down here if the helicopter is up there? Who's flying it?"

"A friend. Where's Katherine?"

"I had her hide in my grandfather's old hunting blind." Tears sprang to her eyes. "I'm so sorry. I think those guys found her."

"How do you know?"

"Right before you got back, I heard gunshots."

Troy absorbed Jocelyn's words. If Katherine was dead, Jim would withdraw from the presidential race, not that Troy could blame him. The man had married an incredible woman who deserved more than to be gunned down in the woods.

Ace's voice interrupted his thoughts. "Status?"

"I'm with Jocelyn."

"And Katherine?"

"Jocelyn left her in a hunting blind in the woods."

"I know where that is," Ace said.

"Be advised, shots were fired."

Ace's voice didn't sound quite steady when he responded. "Understood."

* * *

Jim couldn't breathe. All of his prayers, all of his pleas for guidance had brought him to the same decision repeatedly. The Lord couldn't have brought him down this path toward the presidency only to take away the one thing he held most dear.

Tears threatened, and he fought them back. She wasn't dead. Until he had proof to the contrary, she was alive and whole. "We have to get down there."

"I'm sorry, but it's too risky," Ghost said. "It's my job to keep you safe."

"My wife's safety is more important," Jim insisted. "You know where she is?"

"I know where she was the last time Jocelyn saw her."

"Then let's find her."

"We won't be able to see her from the air," Ghost told him. "The blind is built into the side of a tree. It blends in with the surrounding woods."

"Then we have to go down there."

Ghost glanced in his direction, and Jim could read the resistance in the other man's eyes.

"If that were Kristi down there, you know you wouldn't be able to stay up here if she might be injured or worse," Jim pressed. "I need this."

Jim sensed Ghost's internal debate, but after a moment, the guardian nodded. "Fine, but you stay with me and follow my instructions to the letter."

"Agreed."

"Hate to break this up," Ty said over the headset, "but do you have a location on the shooter?"

Jim studied the monitor. "It's hard to tell. There's a lot of movement."

"The gunfire probably startled the deer." Ghost circled the open space of the yard and flew over the trees where the gunman had last been seen.

Jim tried to discern which of the heat spots in motion was closest to where the shooter had been last but couldn't narrow it down.

Ghost spoke into the headset again. "Ghost, we don't have a visual. We're putting down to look for Katherine."

"Roger that," Ty said. "I'll check the security feed and advise."

Ghost changed his heading and swept the spotlight over the woods in the center of the island. Three minutes later, he reached the landing zone and lowered the helicopter to the ground.

* * *

Troy tugged on Jocelyn's arm and led her into the office.

"What do we do now?" Jocelyn asked, the light from the monitors illuminating her face.

"We search for the shooter." Troy studied the images on the screen. "Did you get a good look at any of the intruders?"

"No. We were cutting through the woods to the front of the house when someone started shooting at us."

"How many people were shooting?"

"I don't know." Jocelyn's eyebrows drew together. "I think all the shots came from the same direction."

"Then we could be dealing with a single gunman."

"Do you really think whoever is after Jim would only send one person?"

"Most assassins work alone. It prevents plans from getting leaked, and a single person is more likely to stay invisible when trying to breach a security system."

"You sound like you know a lot about this."

"More than I ever cared to."

"I don't see anything." Jocelyn motioned to the monitors. "Do you?"

"No." On one screen, Ace and Jim came into view as they left the helicopter. "Are any of these cameras in the area by where you left Katherine?"

Jocelyn studied the images for a moment. "This one on the far side of the pond is close."

"Where exactly is this hunting blind located?"

"It's on the wayward side, between the pond and the windmill."

A new alarm sounded. Troy checked the location and spoke into his headset. "A sensor tripped north of the pond. Is that you?"

"Affirmative."

Another alarm rang out.

"If this was Jim and your friend, who is this over here?"

"That's our shooter." Troy identified the location where the second alarm tripped. "Ghost, be advised, you've got someone on an intercept course."

"ETA?"

"Three minutes. Maybe four."

"We're almost there."

"What's happening?" Jocelyn asked.

"My friend and Jim are looking for Katherine."

"If she didn't make it, they could be walking into a trap."

Despite sharing her concern, Troy said, "My friend can stay invisible."

"That's good for him, but what about Jim?"

On the screen, movement crossed through the corner of the image on the bottom left. "There he is."

Jocelyn's hand gripped his arm. "You need to go help them."

"I don't want to leave you here alone."

"If you're right and there's only one person, I'm not the one in danger right now."

Troy's duty to the Whitmores and his fear for Jocelyn's safety battled inside him. As much as he hated to admit it, Jocelyn was right. She was safe for now. If he and Ace could neutralize the shooter, she would be fine in the house alone.

Troy opened the window seat and retrieved a communication headset. He tuned it to the correct frequency and handed it to Jocelyn. "You stay here and watch the screen. Tell me if you see any movement."

Jocelyn put her hand on his. "Be careful."

Troy nodded. He cast one last glance at her, checked the monitors, and forced himself to leave her behind. The guardians had to win tonight's battle. Jocelyn's future, his future, the Whitmores' future, and the future of their country depended on it.

CHAPTER 43

Gavrie held his position for several minutes. Deer had scattered when the gunfire had started, and he needed time for them to settle again so he could see past them to acquire his target. Not to mention, he hadn't wanted to move with the helicopter overhead. The spotlight had come within a few meters of him several times, but he had used the trees and fallen leaves to hide himself from view.

Now that the helicopter had flown off, he could move freely.

He crept forward and headed for the landing zone. Something rustled in the trees, and once again, he took off his night-vision goggles so he could look through the scope on his rifle. A buck bounded between two trees and continued inland. Gavrie scanned his heat sensor again, and anticipation took flight. There in front of him, only a few hundred meters away, were two distinct figures moving with purpose deeper into the woods. If they were Whitmore's security team, they might lead him right to the senator.

He replaced his night goggles, and with his rifle over his shoulder and his pistol in hand, he started toward his objective once again. A few more minutes to take care of the targets outside. Then finally, he would be able to get out of the cold.

* * *

The words spoken between the two guardians repeated in Jim's mind over and over again. His family had experienced so many miracles over the years. Had he blinded himself to the possibility that the Lord might have plans for him that included a life without Katherine?

A new pain speared through him as he fought against the fear. "How much farther?"

"We're almost there." Ghost ducked under a low-lying branch and came to a stop beside a tall oak. He looked up and called out in a low voice. "Katherine?"

Jim saw it now, the edge of a wooden platform protruding from the tree several feet above him.

"Katherine?" Ghost called again.

No answer.

Silence dragged on for several seconds, the hole inside Jim ripping wide.

Ghost pushed aside some brush to reveal wooden planks nailed to the side of the tree trunk. Then he held out his pistol. "Cover me. I'll see if she's up there."

Jim shook his head. He was tired of waiting for others to give him news. "I'll go."

"Are you sure?"

Jim nodded. He put a hand on an upper rung, placed his foot on a low one, and climbed upward. He reached the top and peered over the top of the platform. His gut clenched when he saw Katherine curled on her side, her eyes closed, her dark hair spilling out of the hood of her coat. "Katherine!"

Jim pulled himself onto the platform and hurried to her side. He put his hand on her neck, her exposed skin cold to the touch. He searched for a pulse. Relief shot through him when the slow beat vibrated against his fingers.

Katherine's eyes fluttered open. "Jim."

"I'm here, honey." Jim helped her sit up.

"Is she okay?" Jocelyn's voice sounded over the headset.

"I think so," Jim said. He cupped Katherine's face in his hands. "Are you injured?"

"C-c-cold." She shivered.

Jim wrapped his arms around her.

Ghost appeared at his side. "Katherine, can you walk?"

She nodded, but her head moved in slow motion.

Ghost took off his glove and pressed a finger against her neck. "Her pulse is too slow. She's got the beginnings of hypothermia."

"What do we do?"

Ghost's hand came up to silence him. He crept to the side of the platform and peered over the edge.

He spoke, his voice so low Jim could only hear him over the communications headset. "We have a problem. Movement fifty meters to the west."

"On my way." Ty's words puffed out as though uttered between steps.

"ETA?" Ghost asked.

"Not sure."

Jocelyn interrupted. "He's about three or four minutes from the blind."

Ghost pulled away from the edge the same instant a shot fired.

"Better get here sooner than that. We're trapped in the tree."

"Coming."

* * *

A hunting blind. Gavrie had passed within a few meters of that tree less than thirty minutes ago and had never seen the camouflaged platform. No matter. He saw it now.

He circled to his left in search of a better angle, but whoever was up there had pressed back against the tree, and the platform was too high for him to get a visual.

He had two options: climb a tree opposite his target or shoot through the platform and hope his bullets found their mark.

He identified a tree with a clear line of sight and branches low enough for him to climb. He tested a low branch to make sure it would hold his weight. Satisfied it would, he put his hand on it and pulled himself up.

A shot rang out, and a sting ripped through his thigh. Gavrie released the branch and fell to the ground.

His hand went to the spot where his leg didn't feel quite right. He looked at his fingers. Blood.

He rolled behind a tree and examined the spot where a bullet had torn away skin. A flesh wound. Irritating but not enough to stop him.

With plan A no longer viable, he pushed to a stand and kept the tree between himself and the blind. He gripped his pistol, rolled around the edge of the tree, and fired off his entire clip at the blind.

His target returned fire.

Gavrie pressed himself against the tree while bullets sparked around him. He reloaded, holstered his gun, and traded it for his rifle. If the bullets from his pistol hadn't penetrated the platform overhead, maybe it was time to see what his rifle could do.

* * *

Jim pulled Katherine closer as bullets tore through the wood in front of them.

"Quick. Help her stand." Ghost fired twice. He hurried to Katherine's side and helped Jim pull her to her feet.

Katherine leaned against him, not able to support her weight fully.

"Come on, honey." Jim adjusted his hold so his arm was around her waist. "Try to stand."

Another gunshot rang out. The bullet ripped through the platform and impacted the edge of the tree. Bark flew.

Another shot.

Katherine's body jerked, and she cried out.

"Katherine!" Jim angled toward her, searching for an injury but seeing none. "Are you okay?"

"What's wrong?" Ghost asked.

"I don't know." Jim put his hand against Katherine's cheek so she would look at him. "Are you hurt?"

"My arm," she whispered. "Hurts."

Ghost leaned closer and examined both of Katherine's arms. He was searching her left when Jim saw the small tear in her coat.

"Be advised, Katherine is injured."

"Almost there," Ty panted.

Another gunshot.

"Hurry. We're out of time."

* * *

Troy pushed through the woods toward the gunfire. Even though he didn't have the gunman in sight, he fired off two shots, aiming low to make sure he didn't inadvertently shoot a friendly. He passed two more trees and took cover when return fire sparked near his previous position.

"Do you have the shooter's location?" Troy asked.

"Thirty degrees southwest of the blind," Ace responded.

"I don't know where the blind is."

"Fire off two shots, so I know where you are," Ace said. "I'll guide you in."

"Roger that." Troy fired off two more shots, this time taking cover rather than continuing forward.

"You're almost under us," Ace said. "Circle to the north twenty meters, and we'll have him between us."

"Give me some cover fire."

"On three," Ace said. "One, two, three."

Gunfire flashed, this time coming from above him. Troy sprinted northward. He made it halfway to his intended destination before his foot caught on a rock. He stumbled forward and landed in a clump of bushes.

More shots whizzed overhead.

The lessons drilled into him during basic training flooded his mind. Keeping his head down, he crawled past two small trees and took cover behind a thick tree trunk.

"Status?" Ace asked.

"Halfway there."

More gunfire, but this time, it wasn't aimed at him. Troy estimated the shooter's location and fired before rushing forward again.

Another set of footsteps mirrored his own. "He's on the move. Do you see him?" Troy asked.

"Affirmative. Looks like he's retreating toward his boat."

"What's Katherine's condition?"

"Took a bullet to the arm, and she's suffering from hypothermia."

"Let's get her and Jim to the helicopter," Troy said. "We can call the Coast Guard to intercept our guy."

"Agreed."

Jocelyn interrupted the conversation. "Do you want me to call?"

"Yes," Troy said. "Tell them the boat is a twenty-footer, and it's currently on the northwest side of the island."

"Okay."

"Ghost, do you need help?" Troy asked.

"Make sure our shooter doesn't circle back while I get everyone down."

"Roger." Troy scanned the nearby woods but didn't see anything beyond Ace and Jim helping Katherine climb to the ground.

CHAPTER 44

RETREAT. GAVRIE HATED THE WORD, but sometimes it was a necessary tactic to lure his prey into his trap. He zigzagged his way toward his boat for a hundred meters until he was sure no one was in pursuit.

He couldn't be sure, but he suspected he had wounded at least one person in the hunting blind. That would slow them down and force their hand. If they chose to leave, their logical choice of transportation was the helicopter. Fortunately, Gavrie knew where it was.

He changed course, this time taking a direct line for his objective. He reached the landing pad and took a moment to locate the perfect spot to hide.

He dropped to the ground and stretched his rifle in front of him. He looked through the scope and smiled. Perfect. A few leaves for camouflage, and he would be set. The Whitmores and their would-be protectors would have to cross through his scope to get to their ride. This would be like shooting targets in an arcade. He was ready to win his prize.

* * *

Jocelyn plugged one ear while she held her cell phone to the other. The brief glimpse she caught of a man running through the woods had heightened her anxiety. The alarm that had started a minute ago wasn't helping.

She finished her call with the Coast Guard operator and put her headset back on. "The Coast Guard is on their way."

"How long?" Ty asked.

"Thirty minutes."

"He'll be to shore by then," a man said.

Jocelyn had heard his voice several times over the past few minutes. He was obviously the friend Ty had mentioned, the same friend Jocelyn had accidentally called the night of the false alarm.

"Can you see him on any of the monitors?" Ty asked.

"I saw him a minute ago."

"Where?"

"It was in one of the wooded areas, but I can't tell where."

"What's the camera number?" the man with the familiar voice asked.

"Eight."

"That doesn't make any sense. Are you sure?"

"I'm sure," Jocelyn said. "I don't know if it's related, but an alarm started right after I saw the guy on camera."

"Look on the screen," the man said. "Is it alarm four?"

"Yes. How did you know that?" Jocelyn asked.

"Ghost, hold your position." The man was speaking again. Why was he calling Ty "Ghost" instead of using his name?

"What's wrong?"

"The gunman isn't leaving the island. He's waiting for us at the helicopter."

"Why would he do that?" Jocelyn asked.

"He's trying to finish what he started," Ty said. "What now? We have to get Katherine to the hospital."

"Go to my boat. We can call for an ambulance to meet us in the village."

"Roger," Ty said. "Jocelyn, let us know if you see anything else on the monitor. When we're close, be ready to meet us at the boat."

The thought of going outside again sent a new wave of apprehension through her. She drew a deep breath and forced herself to respond. "Okay. Tell me when."

* * *

What was taking so long? Gavrie fought the urge to scan the area again for fear that his prey would emerge from the woods at the exact moment he moved, but they should have been here by now.

Frustrated, he kept his eye to his scope and searched the area by the helicopter and the nearby terrain. Nothing. He pushed to a stand and expanded his search. Several heat signatures moving in and out of the trees as they made their way toward the residential side of the island.

Did they think they could take refuge in the house? No lock was going to keep him from getting what he wanted.

He expanded his search farther. Another person at the house. Or was that two? He was too far away to have a clear line of sight.

No matter. If the house was where they wanted to make their last stand, he would accommodate them.

* * *

Troy followed Ace and Jim as they helped Katherine through the woods. They hadn't dared stop long enough to evaluate the gunshot wound. If they didn't get her warmed up soon, the hypothermia would threaten her life more than the bullet in her arm.

They reached the edge of the woods, Ace's boat now visible at the dock.

"Jocelyn, any sign of movement?"

"No. I don't see anything."

"Good," Ace said. "With any luck, we can get off the island and have the Coast Guard intercept the boat when this guy tries to leave."

"Should I meet you at the boat?" Jocelyn asked.

"Wait until we get Jim and Katherine on board," Ty said. "I want to make sure it's safe before you cross the open yard."

"Okay," Jocelyn said. "We're bringing the dog too, right?"

"Yes. We'll bring the dog."

"Ghost, get the boat ready to cast off," Ace said.

"You sure you don't want me to cover you?" Troy asked.

"You can cover me from the boat." Ace spoke into his comm gear. "Jocelyn, are you ready?"

"I think so."

"Go to the back door. When I tell you, run for the boat. Call Samson, and he'll follow you."

"Okay."

Troy slipped through the shadows and onto the dock. He climbed aboard the cabin cruiser, made his way to the controls, and retrieved the key from the drawer compartment where Ace kept a spare hidden.

He inserted the key, opened the hatch to the below-deck compartment, and returned to the dock to prepare to cast off. He untied the line securing the boat to the dock cleat by the bow, leaving the one by the stern until everyone was aboard.

Troy drew his weapon and scanned the darkness. "Ready."

"Coming your way." Ace and the Whitmores started toward him, Katherine still struggling to walk. As soon as they reached the edge of the dock, Ace drew his weapon and took up a sentry position.

"Jim, can you take her the rest of the way?"

"I've got her."

With his arm around his wife, the senator continued forward. He was nearly to Troy when Ace said, "Jocelyn, now."

The back door opened and closed. Troy glanced toward the house, where Jocelyn was now running down the stairs, her rifle in her hand and the dog behind her. They reached the yard, and immediately, Samson stopped in the yard and barked.

If the dog was barking at the shadows, something or someone was hiding there. Jocelyn must have had the same thought because instead of continuing forward, she darted below the deck and disappeared behind the shed as a gunshot rang out.

"Samson, cover!" Ace lifted his weapon and fired off several shots into the woods. The dog raced to Jocelyn's side, and Ace jerked his head toward the Whitmores. "Get them on board."

Troy took a step forward and had to fight instinct to process Ace's command. Jocelyn was out of the line of fire. The senator and Katherine weren't.

"Hurry." Troy took Katherine's arm with his free hand and helped her onto the boat. Jim followed.

Another volley of gunfire sparked around them. Ace returned fire and raced toward the woods.

"Quick. Through the hatch." Troy leaned down and unfastened the rope from the dock cleat. "Jocelyn, are you okay?"

"I'm okay, but I'm not moving until that guy stops shooting."

"Ghost, what's your position. I'll help you flank him."

"Negative. Get the Whitmores to safety."

"But—"

"That's an order. Secure the senator. I'll get Jocelyn and fly her out of here."

"How are you going to take on the shooter alone?"

"I'm not alone. I have Jocelyn and Samson. The three of us know this island better than anyone," Ace said. "Trust me. I'll keep her safe. You need to do the same for the Whitmores."

Troy's stomach clenched, but as much as he hated to admit it, Ace was right.

Troy cast off, hurried to the controls, and started the engine. Fighting every instinct to stay with Jocelyn, he powered the boat away from the dock and turned toward the mainland.

* * *

A new sense of panic bubbled inside her. Jocelyn couldn't have heard them right. Ty was leaving her alone with a gunman and a man she didn't know.

"Jocelyn, can you hear me?" Ty's friend came over her headset.

She took an unsteady breath. "Yes."

"I'm going to keep you safe, but I need your help."

"I'm listening."

"When I tell you, I want you to fire one shot at the tree to the right of the bungalow. Wait a second and then fire again."

"What are you going to do?"

"I'm going to see if I can flush him out," he said. "If you see him, shoot."

The memory of Ty in her scope, of the moment she could have killed him, erupted with a vengeance. "I can't."

"You can. It's just like how your grandfather taught you."

The oddity that he would know that intimate detail struck her but was quickly lost in the gravity of their situation. "Grandpa taught me to hunt, not to kill people."

"If someone was threatening one of his little girls, you can bet he would have shot him."

Jocelyn couldn't argue with that. "How can I be sure I won't be shooting you?"

"Because I'm not going to be the one running from the trees. Are you ready?"

Jocelyn took a deep breath and gripped her rifle. "Ready."

"Now."

She swung around the edge of the shed, took aim, fired two shots, and ducked back into her hiding place.

Bullets sparked, two hitting the side of the house only six inches from where she stood.

The gunfire stopped for a brief moment, long enough for someone to expel the clip of a pistol and reload.

She squeezed her eyes shut. This couldn't be real. It had to be a bad dream.

More gunfire.

"Get ready."

"I don't know if I can do this."

"Just like when you were a kid," he said in a calm voice. "Steady, aim, and shoot."

Steady her weapon. Aim. Shoot.

Gunfire started again, but this time, it wasn't aimed at her.

"He's coming your way."

Mustering every ounce of courage, Jocelyn peeked around the corner of the shed. She lifted her weapon. Steady.

A man appeared at the edge of the trees and took cover beside one, his face angling toward her, a rifle over his shoulder and a pistol in his hand.

Aim.

"Do you have a rifle on your shoulder?" Jocelyn asked.

"No."

Him or me, Jocelyn reminded herself.

Shoot.

Jocelyn squeezed the trigger. The man's body jerked, and he whirled toward her, his hand now pointing a gun at her.

Before Jocelyn could react, another man emerged on the other side of the bungalow and fired three shots.

The first man's body jerked again, and this time, he fell to the ground.

"Hold your fire." The second man ran across the yard, kicked the shooter's pistol clear of his hand, and confiscated his rifle. He then leaned down and checked the man for a pulse.

Jocelyn remained where she was, afraid to move forward, afraid to see what she had done.

After a moment, Ty's friend stood and crossed to her. The sense of familiarity she had experienced when hearing his voice pricked at her again.

"Are you okay?" he asked.

"Yeah. Is he . . . ?" she asked.

"He's dead." The man reached out and put his hand on her arm. "You didn't kill him. I did."

Jocelyn took a step to the side so she could see the man's face more clearly in the moonlight. For a second, he looked and sounded exactly like Ace Samson. Light played over his face, and she drew an astonished breath. "It can't be . . . You can't be . . ." She put her hand on his shoulder and nudged him farther into the light. "Ace?"

"Yes."

"How is this possible? You're dead."

"Sometimes *dead* is a relative term."

"Does my sister know?" Her hand gripped his arm tighter. "I hope so, or you really will be dead when she finds out."

The corners of his lips curved into a smile. "Your sister knows."

"She didn't tell me?"

"She can't tell anyone."

"Why not?"

"Because I'm a ghost."

CHAPTER 45

Troy read the text message from Ace for the thirtieth time. Jocelyn was safe. He had received the news moments before he had reached the mainland. He only wished his relief would overshadow the guilt for leaving Jocelyn in harm's way. Or perhaps it was the guilt that he had chosen to accompany the Whitmores to the hospital rather than return to Jocelyn on the island.

He could admit that he had been more than tempted to turn Jim's security over to the local authorities, but protocol and his training wouldn't allow it. Senator James Whitmore wasn't an ordinary citizen, and the guardians had promised to keep him safe. For now, that duty belonged to Troy alone.

Since arriving at the hospital, Katherine had steadily improved, now able to speak without slurring her words. Her shivering had stopped, and her early prognosis was a mild case of hypothermia. The concern now was the gunshot wound in her arm.

The X-ray technician entered and proceeded to take pictures of her arm from varying angles.

Now alone with the Whitmores again, Troy leaned against the wall inside the door of the treatment room. Jim reclaimed his spot beside Katherine's bed and took her hand in his.

The simple gesture brought out a deep yearning for what the Whitmores shared: the love, the commitment, the connection. Had the bond between the Whitmores brought those dreams to life within him, or was it Jocelyn's presence these past few weeks?

A doctor entered the room and approached Katherine's bedside. Jim stood.

"What's the prognosis?" Jim asked.

"The good news is the bullet didn't do any permanent damage."

"And the bad news?"

"We're going to have to do surgery to remove the bullet and put pins in her arm to reinforce the bone while it heals."

Katherine's grip on Jim's hand tightened. "When?"

"As soon as possible. I took the liberty of reaching out to a surgeon in Bangor who specializes in this type of operation. He can be here in two hours."

"Thank you, Doctor," Jim said.

The doctor shook his hand. "We'll take good care of her."

As soon as the doctor left, Troy approached Katherine and repeated the sentiment he had already expressed several times. "I'm so sorry this happened to you."

"You did everything you could to keep us safe, and for that, we're grateful," Katherine insisted.

"Anything new from Ghost?" Jim asked.

"Not yet," Troy said.

"Maybe you should give Jocelyn a call and see how she's doing," Jim said.

Troy retrieved his phone from his pocket. "That's a good idea."

* * *

Jocelyn sat in front of the fire, her brother-in-law at her side. "This is all so surreal. You're alive, my sister is secretly married, and now you're telling me that I can't tell anyone about it, not even my parents."

"I'm afraid so." Ace leaned forward and rested his elbows on his knees. "I know it may not make sense to you, but the people who tried to kill me when I faked my death are still out there. If they find out I'm alive, they'll come after me. I can't risk your sister getting caught in the crossfire."

"The way I almost did tonight."

"I am so sorry about that," Ace said. "The reason my friend tried to get you to leave when you first got here was as much to protect you as to maintain his privacy."

"And I wouldn't leave." Snippets of memory surfaced. "You called him Ghost when you were in the woods. Is he like you? Someone pretending to be dead?"

"I'm sorry, Jocelyn, but that's classified information."

"Which means yes."

Ace's silence spoke volumes.

Memories of her time with Ty flooded her mind. He had finally opened up about pieces of his past, but she had never before considered that he was censoring what he shared because of necessity rather than choice.

All this time she had been falling for a man who didn't really exist. A secret government operative. Was Ty really the kind of person who she thought only existed in spy movies and in novelists' overactive imaginations?

Ace had called him Ghost, but what did that mean for her and Ty? Did their time together have an expiration date, a set ending he had neglected to tell her about?

The cell phone Ty had given her rang. She looked down, the letter T illuminating the screen. Jocelyn held the phone out to Ace. "Maybe you should take this. I need some time to let this all sink in."

Ace took the phone and answered. "Hold on a sec."

"I'm going to fix some hot chocolate."

Before she could leave, Ace stood. "While you're processing everything I told you, there's something else you should know."

"What's that?"

"You're going to be an aunt. Kristi is pregnant."

More pieces clicked into place. Kristi's move to Europe, Ty discouraging Jocelyn from visiting, the men's razors in the master bathroom.

She forced aside her tangle of emotions and considered her sister's situation. The man she had loved for decades had come back into her life, and finally, she had the chance for a family.

Jocelyn put her hand on Ace's arm. "Congratulations. I'm really happy for you."

"Thanks." Ace waved toward the kitchen. "Are you going to make me hot chocolate too?"

Transported back to her childhood, she gave a slight smile. "Maybe."

* * *

Troy itched to get back to the island and talk to Jocelyn face-to-face. She had yet to answer any of his calls or texts, and Ace's presence had already exposed her to far more information than a civilian should ever have access to.

Troy stood outside the surgery waiting room and replayed the scene on the dock over and over as he tried to rewrite the ending. If he had been the one to stay with Jocelyn, she never would have known Ace was alive. She wouldn't have learned about the guardians, and she would still think he was normal.

Ace had replayed his conversation with Jocelyn. While he hadn't admitted that Troy had faked his death, Jocelyn had connected the dots until she understood enough to know the truth.

Now what? Would her new understanding of his life give them the chance to build on what had started between them? Or would she run away from the possibilities and leave him broken?

His phone rang, and his heart leapt in his chest. Disappointment rose when he read the caller ID. Kade.

"What's the latest?" Troy asked. "Do you know how Morozov found the island?"

"We think it was through the geotagging on some photos Jocelyn sent to Jim's PR firm."

Guilt bloomed. "Then it's my fault. I sent the email with those photos."

"It was a mistake any of us could have made, but that isn't why I'm calling," Kade said. "We got him."

"Gavrie Morozov? Ace already told me. He killed him on the island."

"Not Morozov. Walter Royce." Troy could hear Kade's excitement and satisfaction. "Ace accessed Morozov's cell phone. With the clone I made of Royce's cell phone, I was able to recover a message between them. I also found evidence of a money transfer from a bank in Russia into an offshore account."

"Is there enough proof to hold up in court?"

"The message will prove he was working with Morozov to go after Whitmore and Hammels."

"But not that the Russians have been pulling his strings."

"Not yet, but with any luck, the money transfers will connect those dots. A judge signed the warrant for Royce's home and office fifteen minutes ago," Kade said. "I think once they start digging and interview our witnesses, they'll be able to piece together the truth."

"I hope they find the proof they need."

"We'll find out soon enough. The FBI should be at his house any minute."

"Let me know when they have him in custody."

"I will. Also, a couple of secret service agents are headed your way. They can oversee Jim's protection while he's in the hospital."

"I thought you didn't want anyone but the guardians protecting him."

"Now that Royce won't be able to use his influence to get to Jim, we can bring in some help. Besides, you aren't going to do anyone much good if you don't get some sleep," Kade said. "As soon as you get back to the island, Ace will trade places with you. He's grabbing some shut-eye now."

"Thanks. I'll head back over there once secret service gets here," Troy said. "Send me their names though, would you?"

"Will do."

Troy hung up and went into the waiting room, where Jim was pacing from one end of the room to the other.

"Any news on Katherine yet?" Troy asked.

"Not yet." Jim glanced at his watch. "I thought they would be done by now."

"I'm sure we'll hear something soon," Troy said. "I do have some good news. The FBI is on their way to search Walter Royce's house."

"What?"

"The guardians found proof that Royce was behind your assassination attempt. They also found a money trail between him and the assassin."

"It's over?"

"It will be soon."

The door on the far side of the room opened, and a man in scrubs walked in. "Senator Whitmore?"

"Yes."

"I'm Dr. Preston. Your wife is out of surgery and is on her way to recovery."

"Did everything go okay?" Jim asked.

"She did great. The bullet broke the bone and caused some damage there. We inserted two pins to hold the bone together while it heals, but in time, she will regain full use of her arm."

"That is wonderful news." Jim shook the doctor's hand. "Thank you for everything."

"My pleasure," he said. "We'll talk later. As soon as your wife is awake, the nurse will come get you so you can sit with her in recovery."

"Thank you."

The doctor nodded and disappeared through the doorway.

Jim rubbed his hands over his face. "She's going to be okay."

"Yes, she is. You both are," Troy said. "What now? Are you going to continue with your campaign?"

"I am." Jim looked at him with an expression of humility rather than ambition. "Even after all that's happened, the answer to my prayers hasn't ever changed. For whatever reason, the Lord wants me to do this."

"Our country would be lucky to have you as our president," Troy said.

"Thank you. I do have a favor to ask though."

"What's that?"

"Can you get me access to a phone? With all that's happened and with the pending charges against Walter Royce, I need to make some phone calls and request the upcoming votes be postponed."

"The other ghost will be trading places with me within the next couple hours. I'm sure he can take care of that," Troy said. "Do you think you can get the vote postponed?"

"Yes. As soon as I make the claim that Royce has been making changes on behalf of a foreign power, all of his actions will be scrutinized before anything moves forward."

"As they should."

Two men entered, both wearing dark suits.

"Senator Whitmore? I'm Agent Doherty. US Secret Service." The dark-skinned man motioned to his partner. "This is Agent Hall. We've been assigned as your protection detail."

Troy stepped forward. "May I see your identification please?"

They both pulled out their credentials. Troy verified that they were who they said they were. "I thought there were four of you."

"The other two agents are waiting with Mrs. Whitmore."

"Sorry. After two assassination attempts, we can't be too careful."

"We understand," Agent Doherty said.

"I'm fine," Jim said. "You go back and check on Jocelyn."

"Call me if you have any problems." Troy leaned forward and whispered, "Ghost will be here shortly."

"I'm not going anywhere."

CHAPTER 46

Walter stumbled out of bed and grabbed his cell phone off his night stand. Who in the world was stupid enough to pound on his door at this ungodly hour of the night? He glanced at his watch. Make that morning. Didn't they know who he was?

He belted his robe over his cotton pajamas and looked out the side window. Two men in suits. Secret Service maybe?

"Who is it?" Walter demanded.

"FBI. Senator, open the door please."

A streak of fear pulsed through him. They knew. Somehow, he had been discovered. He fought that thought aside. He'd been too careful. No one could prove he was working with the Russians. No one would connect them.

He yanked the door open and adopted his most indignant look. "What is the meaning of this? It's three o'clock in the morning."

"We're well aware, Senator." The older of the two agents held out a folded piece of paper. "We have a warrant to search the premises."

Walter absorbed the slap of reality. His first assumption was correct. He had been discovered. "May I see that?" He took the warrant from the agent. The words blurred together. "If you don't mind, I'd like to call my lawyer."

"That is your prerogative; however, we are exercising our legal right to enter the premises." The two agents pushed their way inside. "You will also need to hand over your cell phone. It is one of the items specified on the warrant."

The agent took Walter's phone out of his hand. A new sense of dread shot through him. "How am I supposed to call my lawyer if you take my phone?"

"I'm sure your wife has one you can borrow."

His wife. What would Marcia think when she found out? And his children. What of them?

Marcia appeared at the top of the stairs. "Walter, what's going on?"

"I'm not sure." Walter stared up at the woman who had been by his side through everything without even knowing the hole he had fallen into. She deserved to be the woman the nation looked up to, but now she would be known only as the wife of a traitor. He swallowed and forced the words out. "The FBI has a warrant to search our house."

"What in the world for?"

Walter couldn't answer her question. Instead he asked, "Where's your phone? I need to call our lawyer."

"It's in our room."

"Gentlemen, if you'll excuse me." Walter didn't wait for permission to be granted before he went upstairs. He stopped at the top landing, where his wife stood and lifted a hand to her cheek.

"What is this all about?" she asked.

Walter leaned down and kissed her. "I love you. Never doubt that."

"Walter . . ." Her voice trailed off when he disappeared into the bedroom.

He drew a deep breath, went into his closet, and retrieved the emergency kit Ilina had given him. He opened it to reveal a pistol, cash, a fake passport, and a pouch with cyanide tablets. All he had to do was swallow one pill, and this would all be over.

He debated his options. What was worse? Ending his life or facing the accusations of what he had done? Would anyone understand that he could have made a difference? He picked up the cyanide tablets only to put them back down. He couldn't do that to his family.

He moved to the bedside table and picked up his wife's phone. Could anyone help him? Would the Russians protect him after all he had done for them, or would they see him as a risk they could no longer afford?

He dialed the number he had long ago memorized.

Ilina answered on the second ring. "What happened?"

"The FBI is here. They want to search my house."

"You know what you have to do."

Walter's stomach curled. "I can't. There has to be another way."

"Where are you now?" Ilina asked.

"In my bedroom."

"Go to your window. I'll get a ladder and put it up so you can escape."

"You're here?" Walter asked incredulously.

"I heard the FBI might come to your house," Ilina said. "I'll get you out of there. Trust me."

A heavy-handed knock sounded on his door. "Senator Royce, open up."

"They're at my bedroom door."

"Go to the window," Ilina repeated.

Walter forced himself to cross the room. He pushed the curtains aside and slid the window open. He scanned the yard and the street below, searching for any sign of Ilina. He caught sight of a woman sitting in a car across the street. He looked closer. Was she holding a rifle?

A gunshot rang out. He'd been right. This would all be over soon.

* * *

Jocelyn held up her phone and spoke to her sister's image on the screen. "I can't believe you didn't tell me any of this."

"Don't be mad," Kristi said. "Ace isn't kidding when he told you that keeping his presence a secret is a matter of life and death."

"What about when you have the baby?" Jocelyn leaned back on the couch and propped her feet on the coffee table. "What are you going to tell Mom and Dad?"

"I'm going to tell them I had a great opportunity to adopt a baby while I was in Europe."

"Don't you think they'll notice when the baby starts looking like you?"

"He or she might look like Ace."

"Still cause for suspicion."

"People usually see what they expect to see," Kristi said. "Enough about me. How are you doing? That had to be so terrifying for you, having an intruder on the island."

"I don't think I've ever been so scared in my life."

"I hate to tell you this, but it may take a while before you feel safe again."

"Ace has been with me ever since he shot that guy," Jocelyn said. "He even helped me write out my statement for the police and met with the authorities when they got here so I wouldn't have to."

"He's good at dealing with that kind of stuff. Where is he now?"

"Taking a nap."

"I'm surprised you aren't sleeping. It's been a while since you've pulled an all-nighter."

"Actually, I pulled one with Ty last week when an alarm went off." The thought of that night, of the quiet moments they had shared during their time together, tugged at her.

"Sounds like you've enjoyed spending time with him."

"Yeah, I have." Regret surfaced.

"Now that you know the truth, are you going to stay on the island?"

"I don't know. I planned to stay here until I decided what to do next."

"Have you decided?"

"I think so. Ty actually gave me a few ideas."

"Like?"

"I'm going to start a photography business."

"You've loved taking pictures for as long as I can remember," Kristi said. "Any idea what kind of photography?"

"I'll put up a fee schedule so I can take on clients, but my main focus will be to build a website to feature my photos and make them available for ad campaigns."

"That's a great idea."

"I hope it works out."

"You've already had a ton of success with your company. Maybe it's time to enjoy life in the slow lane for a while," Kristi said. "You don't have to take on clients if you don't want to."

"You're right. Honestly, after tonight, I'm not sure I'll want to go out in public for a while anyway."

"You've been through a traumatic experience. It takes time to get your sense of normalcy back."

"You should know."

A cell phone rang in the other room.

Jocelyn yawned.

"You should get some sleep," Kristi said. "I'll talk to you later. Love you."

"Love you too." Jocelyn hung up her phone.

Footsteps sounded behind her. She jumped up and whirled around.

"It's just me," Ty's voice soothed. An array of emotions appeared on his face: apology, regret, hope, fear, and myriad others she couldn't identify.

Relief and heartache tangled inside her. "I didn't know you were back."

Ace walked in before he could answer. "I just got word. Walter Royce is dead."

"Dead?" Jocelyn stood. "How?"

"Shot right through his bedroom window," Ace said. "He was alive when the FBI served the warrant at his house, but they heard a gunshot a few minutes later. He was dead when they reached his bedroom."

"That's awful," Jocelyn said.

"At least we know the immediate threat against the Whitmores has been neutralized," Ty said.

"You say that like you expect someone to come after him again."

"We can't be sure what will happen in the future, but he will have the secret service to protect him, at least through his campaign."

Ace opened a cabinet and took out a couple protein bars. "I'm flying to the hospital to check in with the Whitmores. I'll see you two later."

"Check your fuel levels before you take off. We put in a lot of flight hours yesterday," Ty called after him.

"Will do." Ace grabbed his coat and walked out the door.

As soon as they were alone, Ty took a step toward her. "I am so sorry I had to leave you here."

Whatever resentment she had experienced earlier eased beneath his apology. "Ace told me he ordered you to leave."

"Yeah, he did." He took another step. "What else did Ace tell you?"

"He told me he had to fake his own death." Jocelyn gathered her courage and asked the question that had been burning inside her since she learned of Ace's secret life. "Did you do that too?"

Troy skirted around the coffee table and closed the remaining distance between them. "I want to tell you everything about me. Really, I do."

"But?"

"It's classified."

"That's too bad."

Samson stood and stretched.

Needing distance from this man who held such a big piece of her heart, a man who wouldn't ever be able to share anything about himself, she leaned over and scratched Samson behind the ears. "I'd better feed the dog, or he's going to wake us up in an hour. Come on, Samson." She left the room, chunks of her heart chipping away until all that was left was rubble.

* * *

Troy watched her go, the now-familiar battle waging inside him. He wanted to invite Jocelyn into his inner thoughts, to let her see the battle scars that had helped forge him into the man he was today. For the first time in his life, he could imagine letting someone into the private horrors he had endured as a child, even if he couldn't explain the daily life he currently lived.

Though his body demanded sleep, he stared out the window into the darkness. The faintest light in the distance turned the horizon from black to deep blue. Dawn would break in another hour or so and chase away the demons of last night. Or so he hoped.

He could have lost Jocelyn. Numerous times, she had been shot at and chased. It was a miracle she had survived. It was a miracle all of them had.

Several of his fellow guardians had been through similar situations with the women they loved.

Love. Troy doubted he had ever experienced the emotion before, but this connection he felt for Jocelyn had to be something like it. He wanted her with him. Always.

The realization startled him enough to contemplate his friends' relationships.

Kade had been the first guardian to marry, Ace the second. Nolan, the guardian he trained last year, planned to marry within the year. Troy couldn't say he was ready to make that level of commitment, but Jocelyn gave him the desire to take a step in that direction.

He dialed Ace's number.

"I haven't even left yet," Ace said. "What's up?"

"What do I have to do to gain permission to bring Jocelyn into my circle of need-to-know?"

"As in, who you really are?"

"Yes."

Silence filled the line for a moment. "What are your intentions toward my sister-in-law?"

"I'm not sure yet, but I want the chance to spend time with her without the walls of secrecy between us." Anticipating resistance, Troy added, "She already has a basic knowledge of the guardians because of you, and she's seen us work firsthand. You should know better than anyone that she can be trusted."

"I do know she can be trusted."

Hope bloomed. "Well?"

"She can't have access to missions or the other guardians."

"Does that mean . . . ?"

"You can tell her who you are."

"Thank you."

"Keep in mind that I watched Jocelyn grow up. She's like a sister to me. If you hurt her, you will be sorry."

Troy grinned. "Understood." He hung up, and a moment later, Jocelyn walked into the room. She cast her eyes toward the floor as she walked along the far side of the room.

"Jocelyn."

The single word stopped her, but she kept her back to him. He drew a deep breath, not sure how to read her reaction. He crossed to her and put his hand on her arm. Gently, he turned her toward him. "I just got off the phone with Ace."

"So?"

"He gave me permission."

"Permission for what?"

"To tell you who I am." His hands slid down to link with hers. Their eyes met, and he let the truth come. "Jocelyn, given half a chance, I could fall in love with you. I hope you will stay here so we can see who we can become together."

She blinked in quick succession before she managed to speak. "Who are you? Or who were you before you died?" Jocelyn asked. "You did die, didn't you?"

"Yes." Troy let the memories surface. "A gang from my old neighborhood wanted me to sell drugs on base. I turned them in to the authorities."

"And they came after you?"

Troy nodded. "If they knew I was alive, they would come after me again."

"How did you meet Ace?"

"I met Ace when he recruited me into the guardian program," Troy said.

"The guardian program. That's who you work for."

"That's right. We help people, but we stay invisible to the world around us."

"That's why you ran off after you saved that woman in the village." Jocelyn squeezed his hand. "You didn't want to be noticed."

"The fewer people who know who I am, the better." Troy drew a deep breath and let his dreams pour out in his words. "I want you to know me. What do think, Jocelyn? Are you willing to take a chance on us?"

She smiled. "It just so happens that I don't have anywhere else to be at the moment."

"Really?" He couldn't stop his own smile from forming. "I can't tell you how happy I am to hear you say that."

She brushed a light kiss across his lips, then pulled away and retrieved her house key from her pocket. "Here. You need to take this."

"Why?" he asked, a seed of panic sprouting within him. "I thought you were willing to give us a shot."

"I am, but I'm also old-fashioned. I can't have a key to a man's house."

His eyebrows lifted. "You've had that key for the past few weeks. What's changed?"

"Before, I was visiting. If I'm moving here for the year, I'm going to be your next-door neighbor, which means I'll need to get a new refrigerator and my own internet."

"So you'll stay?"

"I'll stay."

"This is your family's home. Maybe you should move in here, and I should take the bungalow."

"No. You need to stay here. This house has a nicer kitchen, and we both know you're a better cook." Jocelyn retrieved her phone and scrolled through her contacts.

"Jocelyn?"

"Yeah?"

"Don't you think you should get some sleep before you worry about buying new appliances?"

"That's probably a good idea." She tilted her head as though studying him from a new angle. "For the record, Ty, I think I could fall in love with you too."

"I hope so, but it would be even better if you fell in love with the real me." Troy took her hand. "My name isn't Ty. It's Troy."

"Troy," she repeated. Her lips touched his before she smiled once more. "It's nice to meet you."

REDEMPTION

A SAINT SQUAD NOVEL

TRACI HUNTER ABRAMSON

COMING IN SEPTEMBER 2021

PROLOGUE

Perspiration beaded on Eric's forehead. The plan had been so simple. Find the gun, go to school, get to his father's classroom. What came next blurred in his mind. His father wasn't here. Why wasn't he here?

The pistol trembled in his hand.

Twenty-nine terrified teenagers stared at him. Someone whimpered. A whisper of compassion stirred within Eric, but he stamped it out. These people didn't care about him. They only cared about themselves. They didn't even know his name.

He took a step back, pushing the pain from yesterday's beating out of his mind.

Mrs. Cunningham, his special ed teacher, sat at a nearby desk. Why was she here? And why did she keep talking to him?

"You don't have to do this, Eric." Her voice trembled, but she kept going. "Tell the police the truth. If you do that, you can get the help you need. You won't have to go home again."

She had spoken those words before. She had filed a report with the counseling office, but the counselor hadn't believed the truth. The principal hadn't believed it either, so why would the police? His father had them all fooled. He was Mr. Popularity when it came to high school teachers. Eric was an outcast, a nobody, a never mattered.

He gripped the gun in his right hand, the weight of it reminding him why he was here. He had a reason for being here. What was it again? His father. Right.

"Why isn't my dad here?" Eric had asked the question before, but he still couldn't understand the answer.

"I told you he didn't show up for work today." Mrs. Cunningham's hands shook. "Did you see your father this morning before you left?"

"No." The single word came out in a derisive snort. He never saw his father in the morning, if he could help it. Even though they went to the same place every day, Eric always walked the ten blocks to school. It could be sleeting outside or pouring rain. It didn't matter. Eric walked. His father said he needed the exercise. But his father drove his flashy sportscar, purchased with his dirty money.

"Could he have been sick?" Mrs. Cunningham asked.

Eric let out a quick expulsion of breath. "He never gets sick."

His mind churned along with his confused emotions. He flexed his fingers around the handle of the pistol once more. He could make them bring his father. His eyes scanned the frightened students and then landed on Mrs. Cunningham. With a wave of his weapon, he motioned to the phone hanging on the wall. "Call the office. Tell them I want them to bring my dad here."

She hesitated as though understanding what he planned to do. "Eric, this isn't the answer."

His eyes hardened, and he aimed the gun at her. "Do it!"

* * *

Tristan Crowther had nearly fired his weapon. He still wasn't sure what had stopped him from squeezing the trigger when the boy had lifted his gun. Perhaps it had been the look in his eyes. Oh, there had been anger, all right, but he didn't want to hurt this woman. Tristan could sense it.

The woman blinked hard against the tears swimming in her eyes and crossed the room to the phone. The boy lowered his gun fractionally, and Tristan let out a sigh of relief. They still had time.

1

Five Years Later

A HOTEL CONFERENCE ROOM FULL of students. An unstable gunman.

Gage positioned himself outside the door and peered through the opening. Even though the scene before him was a reenactment, he instinctively evaluated the situation. No outside windows, two doors. The gun, a nine-millimeter semiautomatic pistol. The owner, a white male in his late twenties.

Gage rubbed his damp palms on his gray slacks and reminded himself to breathe. The door across from him remained closed. Where were the police? Surely, that was where they would enter.

A woman at the side of the room rose from her seat. Gage recognized the calm voice before he saw her face. Mrs. Cunningham. The woman who had saved his life.

His gut clenched. He wasn't Eric anymore. He'd left that past behind. Today, he was simply an observer, not the man holding the gun. The would-be shooter waved his weapon in her direction, and Gage's heartbeat picked up speed.

"Shut up!" The gunman took aim. "Sit down, and shut up!"

She didn't sit, nor did she stop talking. "I'm not a threat to you." Her calm, soothing voice continued. "You're the one with the gun. You're in control." Steely courage resonated within the words. "No one has to get hurt."

Those words transported Gage back in time to when he had been the man holding the weapon and those words had been directed at him.

"Put the gun down," the woman continued.

A hand gripped Gage's shoulder.

Startled, he turned to see an enormous black man in full military gear carrying an assault rifle.

Using hand signals, the man motioned for Gage to trade places with him.

Gage took a step farther into the hall to leave the doorway clear.

The man spoke into his communications headset. "I've got a visual. Other classrooms are secure."

The presence of a Southern accent in the man's voice, the combat vest, the man's sheer size. Gage recognized all three traits from that night so many years ago, the night that continued to haunt his dreams.

Inside the room, the gunman's words grew louder. "Sit down, or I'll shoot!"

"Now," the military man by the door said quietly.

A single gunshot sounded.

Gage jerked back. His breath backed up in his lungs.

The military man beside him rushed into the room. Shouts echoed. Orders ensued.

Gage forced himself to look inside, to see the results of the military's presence.

The would-be shooter lay on the ground, and the soldier who had been at Gage's side a moment ago now stood over him. Another man with sandy hair knelt at the gunman's side as though to check his wound.

Gage glanced at the ventilation shaft to see the grate had been removed, the barrel of a rifle visible. He closed his eyes, remembering all too well a similar scene. He rubbed at the scar on his shoulder.

He wasn't the man on the floor today. He hadn't been the man holding the gun.

Riley, the owner of Palmetta Institute, walked into the room. Rather, she was Riley Crowther now.

"Thank you, everyone," she said.

Her entrance ended the exercise that had been far more realistic than Gage had thought possible.

One of the soldiers extended a hand and pulled the fake gunman to a stand.

"As you saw, in this scenario, our gunman wasn't here to shoot just anyone. He had a target, someone specific he wanted to harm." Riley waved at Mrs. Cunningham. "In this instance, a teacher who had a personal relationship with the gunman was able to keep him talking. That gave the emergency responders time to formulate the best way to diffuse the situation."

A discussion ensued on the risks of Mrs. Cunningham's response and how to evaluate the threat. After twenty minutes, the class was dismissed, and the students filed out.

As soon as the classroom emptied, Riley walked toward Gage. "I'm glad you could make it."

Gage shook her outstretched hand. "I'm still not quite sure what I'm doing here."

Three men approached, the two who had entered the classroom and a dark-haired man who stood about six feet tall.

"Guys, I want you to meet someone." Riley put her hand on the sandy-haired man's arm. "This is my husband, Tristan, and these are his teammates, Quinn and Seth."

"Good to meet you," Seth said, his Southern accent even more pronounced now that he wasn't preparing to attack.

Gage shook his hand and repeated the process with Riley's husband. When Gage turned his attention to the third man, Quinn, he saw the recognition in the man's dark eyes.

"It's been a long time," Quinn said.

"You know each other?" Tristan's Texan drawl slowed the words but didn't hide his confusion.

"In a manner of speaking. I rarely forget someone I've had in my scope."

"Someone in your scope? You aimed your rifle at him?" Seth looked from Quinn to Gage and back again. "Wait, you do look familiar."

"You all met Gage a few years ago when we were in North Carolina," Riley said.

Tristan's eyes widened, and Gage read the recognition and concern there. Apparently, Riley hadn't told her husband that her company had offered a job to a known criminal.

"You were the shooter," Tristan said.

Gage clenched his jaw. How did he explain that he wasn't the same person as the confused fifteen-year-old kid who had been brainwashed? Could these men understand that he had tasted what a normal life could be, that he wanted to create that for himself? Or would they always see him as a criminal who got off easy when the judge sentenced him to a mental hospital for six months instead of jail?

"I asked Gage to come in for an interview." Riley stepped forward. "I think he could be a valuable addition to our staff."

The silence that followed Riley's revelation spoke volumes.

"Riley, I'm sure your husband and his friends will want to talk you out of that idea." Gage forced himself to look at Quinn. "You were the one who shot me?"

"That's right."

"Thank you for not killing me." Gage stepped back. "Riley, you have my number." Gage started down the hall, but he made it only ten yards before another familiar figure appeared in front of him. Mrs. Cunningham. His former teacher.

* * *

Nadia Cunningham studied the man who stood before her. Had she not known Eric was coming today, she doubted she would have recognized her former student. Once an overweight teenager who had been a constant target for bullying, Eric had grown several inches and turned the baby fat into muscle. He had also lost that haunted look in his eyes. She suspected if the girls who had shunned him during high school saw him now, they would be lining up to give him their phone numbers. At least, they would if they could get past the memory of him holding a classroom full of students at gunpoint.

"Eric Rhodes. It's so good to see you."

"I go by Gage Stewart now. The name my father gave me didn't have much of a future."

"I can understand that. You aren't the same person you were back then." And he wasn't. Nadia noted the way Eric looked her in the eye, the rigid, almost military posture.

She glanced at Riley and the three SEALs. She hadn't expected any of them to recognize Gage. Noting the speculative looks the men were casting his way, she reached out and touched her former student's shoulder. "Come with me. I'll show you around."

Gage nodded. He followed her into the classroom where the last exercise had taken place. "Today's class. It was based on me, wasn't it?"

"Yes." She stopped by the podium in front of the room. "The incident at your high school was one of the successes amid a lot of failures. It was also a failure in that the administration did nothing to help you even though the signs of abuse were obvious."

"No one wants to see what isn't comfortable," Gage said.

"You're right. That's why your insight would be so valuable here."

"Like I told you on the phone, I'm not interested in reliving my high school years over and over again."

"You've already done that," Nadia said. "You talked about it in therapy, you relived it during your trial, you spent six months learning how to put it behind you."

"I put it behind me," Gage said. "Why would I want to open myself to all of those emotions again?"

"Because you can make a difference." She leaned against the table in the front row. "Riley lived through a shooting too. Her perspective of being a victim makes her company the best in the country in training educators and first responders."

"I gather she hired you because you're a teacher who stopped a shooting."

"That and because I was part of the system that failed you."

"You were the only person who tried to help me."

"We both know it wasn't enough." Her voice gentled, a reminder of when she had offered a flicker of light in his dark world. "Bringing you onto the staff gives her company the one perspective she's missing."

He looked around the room, his gaze lingering on the air conditioning vent where Quinn had been hiding earlier. "What would I be doing?"

"Riley can explain that better than I can. For now, let me give you a tour. As soon as she's done talking to her husband, we'll meet up with her."

"They don't want me here."

"I wouldn't say that," Nadia said.

"One of the things I always loved about you is that you always spoke the truth."

"Okay, you're right. They don't want you here, but Riley will make them see reason. She always does."

ABOUT THE AUTHOR

Traci Hunter Abramson was born in Arizona, where she lived until moving to Venezuela for a study-abroad program. After graduating from Brigham Young University, she worked for the Central Intelligence Agency for several years, eventually resigning in order to raise her family. She credits the CIA with giving her a wealth of ideas, as well as the skills needed to survive her children's teenage years. She currently lives in Virginia with her husband and the youngest of their five children. Traci loves to travel and enjoys coaching her local high school swim team. She has written more than thirty best-selling novels and is a seven-time Whitney Award winner, including Best Novel of the Year in 2017 and 2019.

bookbub.com/authors/traci-hunter-abramson

@traciabramson

facebook.com/tracihabramson

instagram.com/traciabramson

traciabramson.com